The
Pilot's
Girl

BOOKS BY CATHERINE HOKIN

CATHERINE HOKIN

The
Pilot's
Girl

bookouture

Published by Bookouture in 2022

An imprint of Storyfire Ltd.
Carmelite House
50 Victoria Embankment
London EC4Y 0DZ

www.bookouture.com

ISBN: 978-1-80019-703-9
eBook ISBN: 978-1-80019-702-2

For Robert,
for everything and always

PROLOGUE

The image was so vivid, Hanni could hear the child laughing.

A little boy. His hair dark like Freddy's, curling like hers. A curious boy with an eye for patterns. His pockets permanently bulging with pebbles and feathers and oddly speckled leaves. He was so perfect, so real. Hanni could see him a few feet away from where she was sitting. Crouched at the edge of Viktoriapark's tumbling waterfall, observing the way the spray danced over his head, working out the quickest pathway up through the slippery stones to the top. A child full of life and utterly fearless.

His father's son – and mine. The most beautiful boy in the world. He would be the best of the two of us wrapped up into one.

She whirled round, her eyes still blurry with sunshine and dreams. Forgetting that she had just dashed all Freddy's hopes that the two of them might have a future together. Forgetting all the *we can't*s and *we mustn't*s she had piled up between them.

'Maybe I'm wrong and it's not impossible for us – maybe—'

The sentence snapped before Hanni could finish it. As the boy in her head looked up and smiled; as his smile switched from Freddy's open grin into her father's smirk. One change of focus and the possibilities shattered.

Hanni dropped Freddy's hand. She rubbed the sun with its

tricks and false promises out of her eyes. She jumped off the bench and away from him.

'Maybe what, Hanni?'

The desperation on Freddy's face was too hard to look at. His need of her was too raw, so close to the surface another word would split its wounds open.

Hanni shook her head at him and raised her hands like a wall. Freddy kept on coming.

'What did you mean? What were you looking at?'

He was on his feet, his arms stretched out and searching. One more misstep and she would lose herself in them.

'Nothing.'

What could she say? *I saw the world that I want?* That would be the truth. But so would, *I saw the wrong smile; I saw the shadow that would break us,* and that truth was stronger.

'I saw nothing, Freddy. A trick of the light.'

She stepped back as he started to argue. She forced herself to be deaf and blind to him.

'Stop, I can't hear it. I have to go.'

'You don't, Hanni. You don't.'

But his words were lost in the splash of the water and the call of a bird, and Hanni had gathered up all the pain that had lodged tight round her heart and was gone.

CHAPTER 1

29 JUNE 1948

He was going back.

It was a strange thought. It also wasn't the right word. *Back* implied returning to a place where somebody or something was waiting or wanting him. That definitely wasn't true, but he could hardly use *home*. Back it would have to be. To Berlin, after eleven unasked-for years away. That was a strange thought too.

It wasn't supposed to have been such a long separation. There wasn't supposed to have been a separation at all. In 1937, when his father had pushed him onto the ship which would take him across the sea to a family who didn't want him any more than the one he was leaving, Aaron had expected him to turn round. To say, 'Don't worry, you can get off now, you're not really going.' Aaron had stretched over the railing, shielding his eyes against the wind and the salt-sharp spray, straining to see the lopsided slope of Elkan Müller's shoulders and the backward tilt of his hat among the crowds thronging the pier. Expecting his father to be the one coming back, asking if Aaron had finally learned his lesson. Elkan hadn't done that. Elkan hadn't been there. Aaron had waved and he had called, but he hadn't been able to catch a single glimpse of his father.

Then the gangplanks had lifted. The pier had slipped away. A slate-grey lacy-topped gap had opened up between the ship and the shore and the time for searching and hoping was done. The SS *Hamburg* had followed the fleet of tugboats which would act as its escort out of Cuxhaven Harbour and into the unimaginable expanses of the North Sea. No one had come back for Aaron.

One mistake. That was all it had taken for him to be banished at sixteen from everyone and everything that he had ever known. To become a charity case, taken in by an uncle who had sponsored Aaron's visa out of duty not love – and who never missed an opportunity to regret that.

Except what I did wasn't a mistake – it was an act of bravery my father would never have been capable of. They should have praised me for it, not panicked.

Planes were rumbling across the tarmac outside the briefing-room window. The squadron commander was reeling off a list of numbers which was intended to impress on his men the serious-ness of their mission to break the Soviet blockade currently encircling Berlin. The city's population; the amount of food that was going to be needed to feed them; the number of Soviet troops stationed in the city. Tony – because that was who he was nowa-days; that helpless boy Aaron had been long swept away – was barely listening. He was barely in the room. Unlike his fellow pilots, his head wasn't filled with starving Berliners or gun-rattling Soviets or even the drone of the planes lifting off from the Westover Air Force base and already heading out towards Germany. His head was filled with the sound of the marching feet that had made his blood pump a dozen years earlier. With his first sight of the Hitler Youth pack plastered in swastikas, marching through Mitte and looking for trouble. With the thrill that had run through him at the first shout of 'fight!'

The gang he was part of had dropped silently into place the moment the call to arms had flashed through their neighbour-hood. It was never going to be an equally matched battle. The gang knew the streets; the Nazi bully boys didn't. They had blocked off the alleyways and trapped the fascists inside a circle lined with knuckledusters and nail-studded sticks. They were eager to prove themselves and ready for trouble, although not as ready as Aaron had been.

'Rough your opponents up. Break ribs. Leave bruises and enough scars to remember us by. Send a clear message that these are our streets and there's no place for their kind in any of them.' *Don't kill* wasn't said, but it was understood.

By 1936, when Aaron had pushed his way into his local branch of the Ringvereine – the network of gangs whose connections ran like a web through central Berlin – his fellow members were more concerned with keeping themselves alive than with killing their enemies. Since Hitler had outlawed them in 1933, gangs were no longer protected by crooked policemen; they were hunted instead by the Gestapo. Berlin's gangsters had learned to move carefully in the face of that threat. Except for a handful who wouldn't, like Aaron.

Aaron hadn't heard *don't kill*. Once the first punches were thrown, he hadn't heard anything. Not his comrades' shouts at him to stop or the boy's pleas for mercy as he collapsed, blood-soaked, to the ground. Once the first punches were thrown, Aaron was all feet and fists and fury. He wasn't sorry when the boy was finally dead, or when his companions melted away, or when the sirens started screaming. He was too caught up in the rush of his own power, in the relief of an escape from the anger he lived in. But then…

They gave up on me.

He had stumbled his way home with his knuckles bleeding. He had fallen into the apartment with his clothes ripped and red. That day, he had been king of his world. That day, he had also, according to his father anyway, 'broken the last piece of your mother's heart you haven't already shattered'.

They made me into a stranger.

His parents had frozen him out of their lives. His siblings – all except his littlest brother David, who could never be persuaded that Aaron was anything less than a hero – had followed their lead. The gang members he had sworn a blood oath to had melted away, afraid of the speed of his violence and where it might lead them. His family had treated him as if he was a dangerous package that had to be shipped anywhere, at any cost, before it contaminated the rest of them. No one would see him for what he really was: a fearless fighter who had wiped out one of Hitler's evil acolytes. Who would wipe out a dozen more if he was given the chance.

Because they were too trusting and that got them killed.

The truth of that hurt as much now as it had then, and Tony still couldn't push it away.

Because they thought that being a good German would save them, that being a good German would matter more than being a Jew.

Tony had understood the stupidity of that even as a boy. He had spent every moment he could, long before he joined the gang where he met others who were as angry with the new Germany as he was, trying to protect his family. Trying to make his parents face the reality of where the speeches and the rallies were leading. He had brought home the newspapers with their filthy anti-semitic cartoons. He had catalogued each new 'Jews Forbidden' sign as it appeared in their neighbourhood. And he had repeated over and over that this wasn't the Germany that they knew anymore. That the Führer and his party had divided the world into *them* and *us* and the Müllers would never make it onto the side that mattered. For all his efforts, he might as well have been howling at the moon.

Aaron had chosen action; his parents had chosen retreat. They had enrolled their children in Jewish schools and rushed to the synagogue, as if new classrooms and more prayers would beat back the race laws. They had pretended that the bricks which smashed the windows of their small jewellery shop were thrown by silly boys, not hooligans wearing swastikas. They had chosen to believe that the increasing persecution was a temporary thing, a madness which would end as quickly as it began. That the country they loved would return to its graceful self again. They had refused to consider leaving their home and becoming anything other than the Germans they had been for generations. Their stubbornness had driven Aaron to distraction, but he couldn't make them budge.

They wouldn't leave, but they wouldn't let me stay.

He had never been able to push that truth away either.

'It's for your own good, to keep you safe.'

His father had kept saying that during the whirlwind days between what his parents insisted on calling his crime and the day earmarked for his leaving. Aaron hadn't believed him. Aaron had known that 'for your good' meant 'for ours'. That Elkan's words could be distilled down to 'we don't want you'. It had broken his heart. But it hadn't broken his love for them, then or now.

Whatever his family had done to him, they were good people, far better people than him. Tony knew what they had sacrificed: that the cost of his papers and his passage to America had drained the last of their savings. He knew that their disappointment in him ran far deeper than the Hitler-boy's death. He accepted that they had no reason to love him. But he had loved his family, every last one of them. Being sent away didn't change that. All the years apart didn't change that. What hurt most was that he had never been given the chance to prove just how deeply he felt.

'Wake up, Miller – we're moving out. Stop dreaming about the *Fräuleins* you're planning to charm and get yourself over there and do it!'

Tony joined in with the laughter which greeted the squadron commander's shout, although he didn't find it – or any jokes at his expense – amusing. Anywhere else but the briefing room and someone would have paid.

He picked up his holdall and followed the rest of his group out onto the airfield, moving slightly apart as the usual rough and tumble which accompanied the start of a new mission began. His fellow pilots were fizzing with adrenaline, pushing at each other, grabbing at rucksacks and kitbags and pretending to fling them over the waiting transport plane. Tony kept his distance and held on tight to his bag. What it contained was more precious to him than any of the supplies he would soon be ferrying into block-aded Berlin. It contained the last scrap of who he had once been.

Buried deep beneath his clothes was a photograph that had been thrust into his hands by his mother, in the last blurred moments before the front door slammed shut between them. It was a sprawling group shot. His parents, his elder sister and his brothers, and a collection of uncles and aunts and cousins. A dozen of them besides his ten-year-old self, all gathered together in their summer finery on a daisy-studded lawn, waving at the camera and laughing.

There wasn't a day that went by when Tony didn't take a moment to step out of his life and look at that picture. At the people who had once loved him, who had thought that his actions meant that he didn't love them. Who thought he had let them down.

They were wrong. They were also all dead, lost to the National Socialists' murderous bloodlust, a horror for which no one had ever been called to account.

Tony strapped himself inside the plane's cavernous interior and wedged the rucksack tightly between his knees. He didn't know what going back meant. He didn't know what it would feel like to be once again in Berlin, but he was certain of one thing: a crime had been committed and nobody had paid. One day, somehow and soon, Tony Miller was going to correct that mistake.

CHAPTER 2

They're back. They're bombing. Move.

Six weeks into the Soviet blockade of the city and the roar of the engines still jerked Hanni out of sleep ready to run. Day and night, the planes never stopped coming: whatever the hour, Berlin's skies were thick with them. Some of those hours, it was true, were easier to navigate than others. In the daylight, Hanni could see what was or, more accurately, what wasn't happening to her beleaguered city. Stepping out of her front door didn't put her in danger. The pavements didn't tremble and collapse into craters as the cargo transports passed overhead. The buildings didn't crumble and fall. The air wasn't left too thick with brick dust to take a clean breath. Outside in the sunshine, Hanni could hold herself in one piece. She could trust that it was 1948, not the last terrifying weeks of the war, and – although she might flinch from the noise above her – she didn't cower or start frantically looking for cover.

With the skies free of the black shapes that had once fallen like rain, the 'it's an airlift, not an attack' she too often muttered to herself in the dark sounded believable. Without the explosions that had once turned the ground as unsteady as water, the newspapers' promise – that the American and British pilots were bringing bread with them, not bombs – sounded like the truth, not a trick. Daylight hours were manageable. The night was a very different prospect. In the night – or in the blinking seconds between sleeping and waking when the world was a blurred and still dream-haunted thing – it was easier to believe in air raids and firestorms than allies.

Those were the seconds when Hanni shot up in bed convinced that it was April 1945 and Berlin was caught up in a very different kind of siege. Those were the seconds when her head filled up with decisions she barely had time to make. Whether to run for the attic or the cellar to escape the bombs and the shells and the Russian soldiers crashing through the streets. How much food and water she could carry into whichever space she prayed would be the safe one. And with the certainty that her mother was still alive and afraid and in need of Hanni's help. The confusion was brief perhaps, but its impact ran through to her bones.

Hanni knew from the weary faces on the streets that she wasn't the only one who regularly sprang awake in the same muddled state, re-sorting enemies into friends as dawn broke. Knowing that did not stop her heart pounding. And now that the skies were overcrowded as the number of transports flying into the city increased and planes were crashing out of the clouds as well as filling them...

She dragged herself out of bed and steeled herself against the shock of a cold-water wash. At least the Russians had decided to throw their controlling ring around the city in the summer, when the lack of coal and the consequent power shortages were less of an issue. God help them all if the blockade proved unbreakable and Berlin's road and rail and river links to the rest of the world remained cut when winter hit. Or if the Allies decided that they couldn't afford to carry on supporting Berlin with food and supplies in the way that they were currently, extravagantly, promising. Or if a new, even more terrifying, kind of war stormed its mushroom clouds across Europe and put her city on its front line the way the Soviets had threatened that it would.

One breath at a time. Giving into fear won't make any of this easier.

Hanni raced through the bathroom and into her clothes before the weight of the day became unmanageable and turned her attention to her camera bag. Checking that the lenses and the bulbs and the films that she would need were all in place was a calming ritual. Once that was done, Monday was Monday again and simpler to step into.

Frau Greber, her landlady at the Blücherstraβe boarding house where she had lived for almost two years, was already clattering round the kitchen as Hanni came down the stairs. She didn't disturb the breakfast preparations.

Her photography assignment today was to cover a press conference intended to allay public fears about the increasing number of collisions and near misses which had occurred in the first weeks of the Allied airlift of supplies into the city. It had come courtesy of *Die Neue Zeitung*, the most popular newspaper in the American sector of occupied Berlin and one of Hanni's most valuable clients. She had haunted the editor's office until he had given in and given her the job. The nest egg she was saving was currently a small one, but it was growing, and every piece of work she could grab added to the pot which would one day, she was determined, become *The Hanni Winter Photography Studio*. Focusing on the dream of that was a very good antidote to the planes and the shortages. And there was also the added bonus of American hospitality…

The press conference – or publicity stunt, as the police colleagues who provided her other main strand of employment would call it – was being held a short walk away at Tempelhof Airport, the centre of the American airlift operation. Breakfast there meant unlimited sugar-drenched doughnuts and real coffee, which was almost as welcome as the generous day rate the job paid. It would certainly be a change from the watery porridge and day-old bread which was all Frau Greber's food allocation could provide.

Which is still a lot more than some can manage.

The beggars appeared almost as soon as Hanni exited her front door. Not the crippled men the war had left destitute and condemned to the streets, but two women who approached her with their heads down and their hands out. Hanni heard stories like the one they told her a dozen times a week; it didn't make hearing them any less heartbreaking. Both women had children to feed and no connections in the black market or anywhere else to help them find supplies. Both were crushed by the hunger that had returned to stalk the blockaded city as cruelly as it had in the war's dying days. Their pinched faces suggested that, for many, starvation's miseries had never truly left.

This is medieval: the Soviets cutting off our food to starve us into submitting to their rule and to their way of life. It's barbaric.

If the women's haggard faces were any measure to go by, it was also starting to work.

Hanni had lived a comfortable life, even during the worst years of the war. She wasn't proud of that; she was horribly aware that most people hadn't. She had seen hunger in its worst forms, and the memory of the blank eyes and matchstick limbs it had brought with it still haunted her. Berlin was not yet in those desperate straits, but the fear that it soon would be ran through the streets like a poison.

Everyone living there knew that the city could not feed itself, that it drew the milk and meat and grains its two million citizens depended on from the provinces around it. That was a weakness the Soviets were well aware of. The partition of Germany in 1945 between Russia and the Western Allies had put those food-filled provinces under Soviet control and co-operation was therefore essential if everyone in Germany was going to stay fed. For Berlin, which was isolated deep within the Soviet-controlled sector of Germany, that co-operation was its lifeblood. The Soviets were well aware of that weakness too.

Two months ago – when the Soviets suddenly decided that they were done trying to accommodate their political beliefs with those who opposed them – food was the weapon they chose to fight with. It was very effective. Berlin's meagre supplies were used up in weeks. By August, the hastily organised Allied operation to lift food and coal from anywhere that could spare it and fly those desperately needed resources into the city had barely made a dent in the volumes that were required. Berlin was once again where it had been in 1945: desperate for help and dependent on a calorie allocation administered by the Americans and the British. An allocation that was – as it had also been three years earlier – far too low. That left those forced to live on it empty and tired.

Or begging.

Hanni gave the women what coins she could and wished she could take them with her to Tempelhof. They needed the plentiful food that would be available there far more than she did.

And far more than the Americans do. They must be the best fed people on earth.

Hanni hurried down the road, refusing to let herself indulge that thought. The American troops who were now stationed in Berlin might be better fed than the German civilians and better housed, and a few of them might still think that they were better people, but they were here, they were helping. There were enough divisions in the city without turning on the hand that was literally feeding it.

No one smiled as Hanni walked past them; no one said hello. Everyone was heads down, heads filled with their own problems; no one had the time or energy to be neighbourly. The citizens of Berlin were as divided as their city.

When Hanni had begun working as a crime-scene photographer with the Kreuzberg police force in 1946, Berlin might have been separated politically between the four occupying powers, but it had still operated for all intents and purposes as one place. Police officers in the British, French and American sectors had shared their resources and their knowledge with their German colleagues in the Russian-controlled boroughs. That co-operation hadn't always been official, but its existence and its value had been understood. Now there was no co-operation at all.

Berlin had split into two distinct blocks – with the Soviets controlling one side and the western Allies controlling the other – and all pretence of collaboration had vanished. Now the city shared little beyond a name and a language. One currency had become two, and organisations which had once worked together, including the police, had split their leadership and their practices and had transformed themselves into very different animals. When Hanni went into the Kreuzberg station now it was rife with rumours about the Gestapo-style tactics being employed by the police on the Soviet side, including torture and the kidnapping of anyone the East thought might be of value to them. A practice which had become an increasingly worrying occurrence.

And, to compound all that, with each closed road, with each cordoned-off bridge and barricaded river, the Soviets had flung Berlin back in time.

One blink and we could be in the last hopeless days of the war again.

It was barely nine o'clock, but the streets of Kreuzberg were busy. Not with people hurrying to work or hurrying their children to school: no one, apart from Hanni, was hurrying anywhere. Slow-moving queues snaked around the bakeries and the grocery shops designated as distribution centres for the food the Allies flew in. Or what passed as food. So many of the supplies were despatched in their dried form to maximise the cargo planes' capacity, the shops were half full of powder. Hanni had lost count of the number of times the papers had printed their favourite blockade cartoon – a stork flying a dehydrated baby into the city. Very few people found it funny anymore.

She skirted round the quiet lines, stepping carefully over the roots of trees which would soon be hacked down for firewood. The pavements, thankfully, were clear now and not choked by rubble the way they had been at the war's end, but there were still too many bomb sites that were little better than wastelands and too many untouched ruins. The post-war rebuilding programme, like so much of life in blockaded Berlin, had been put on pause for the lack of the materials it needed to move forward.

Hanni continued down Mehringdamm towards Viktoriapark and the airport complex, trying not to count the number of windows she passed which were covered with tar paper rather than with glass, or the homes which were no more than cellars. There were people gathering at the park too, although in clusters there rather than in queues. Viktoriapark's black market was a fraction of the size of the ones which had colonised Alexanderplatz and Potsdamer Platz, but it was a constant presence. Acting as a nest of criminal activity, or as a lifeline, depending on the state of the commentator's stomach.

Hanni stopped, ignoring the traders who tried to catch her eye, and nodded to the two dishevelled boys acting as market runners. They were part of a gang of misfits and lost souls who divided their time and their incomes between guarding the market sites, supplying information on their rivals to the local police forces and acting as the guardians of the city's secrets. All of the boys were known to Hanni from her photography work, although some of them had only come on to her radar since she began working with the police. They all trusted her – or her wallet – and they never moved her on when she took out her camera.

Hanni began framing the scenes in front of her, imagining them as part of one of the series of exhibitions she was already planning to hold when she finally opened her own studio. She snapped busily, focusing on the cigarette-filled suitcases and the flashing hands darting above them as a title jumped into her head: *Black Market Days: From the Bombs to the Blockade*. It would be a success, she could feel it: none of the city's galleries had tackled anything as current.

She collected a couple of dozen shots, finishing with a few pictures of the runners, dwelling as she always did on their pinched and too-old faces. Her favourite subject, Oli – who she had met on the first murder case she had worked on and who she intended to feature – was nowhere around, but the other boys made good studies.

The market began to grow busier as she worked, filling with characters each of whom merited their own exhibition. Despite the press conference which was meant to be the focus of her day, it was hard to drag herself away. Hanni's police work fascinated her, but it was the telling of everyday stories that still intrigued her the most.

Although everyday stories are not the ones I promised myself I would tell.

She stopped and forgot about her current project as the past, as it always did, came pressing. There was another exhibition needed, a far more brutal one. An exhibition that only her studio could show.

That could finish me as soon as I open it.

The market whirled on without her as she pictured the way she would set her work out: the whitewashed walls and the black-framed photographs set starkly upon them. Photographs of children who had lost any hope of life before they had begun to live it. Photographs of adults whose faces had been carved by starvation and fear down to the bone. And the other one. Her father. Glowing with health and immaculate in his uniform, his smile as bright as the silver skull set into his cap. And then the question everyone would ask overlaid itself across the images in a banner headline Hanni couldn't ignore: how on earth did you manage to take photographs as damning as these? She was no closer to finding a suitable answer for that.

'Look at me – I'm Al Capone!'

Hanni pulled herself back from the impossibility of 'because I was there'. She turned towards the boy who was whistling at her. He had stuck a too-big hat on his head and struck up a pose, one hand forming a gun and the other waving a cigar that was fatter than his wrist. Hanni pulled her camera in front of her face again, glad of the distraction of shutter speeds and light readings.

There were pictures which still had to be shown. There was a score with her father, Reiner, which still had to be settled. None of that was for today. Today, the sun was shining. Today, there was work which could bring her dreams a little closer, work which promised a dash of the glamour that had been very thin on the ground. Whatever the past continued to demand of her, Hanni couldn't pretend she didn't have a yearning for that.

Glamour.

Hanni was ashamed that she could have matched that word so thoughtlessly to her destination. Tempelhof Airport might be an outpost of American authority now, but a change of ownership could not so easily wipe away its history.

She followed the United States Air Force officer assigned to the press party through the building, nodding and smiling as he pointed out its features, acting as if she had never been inside its vast halls before.

The airport's fabric had changed. Half its once sparkling floor-to-ceiling windows were boarded up, and the marble floor which stretched through its lobby was dulled by dirty boot prints and oily splatters. Hanni didn't see any of that. She saw the halls as they had been ten years earlier, when she and her parents had been shepherded to the front of their busy lines. As the towering spaces had looked after the airport had been redesigned by Hitler's chief architect, Albert Speer, who had intended it to be the gateway to the Third Reich's new capital, Germania. In Speer's vision, Berlin was to be both renamed and refashioned into a city that would outshine the rest of the world, and Tempelhof was to be its awe-inspiring first point of welcome. He had turned the building into a soaring extravaganza, its columns inside and out topped with the eagles whose spreading wings had inspired the structure's wide curves.

And he filled it with swastikas. And a giant portrait of Hitler, which my father always stopped in front of and saluted.

Hanni had to force herself to keep smiling and to keep

walking and to not shiver at the memory of the life she had once been caught up in. To hold herself in the present and to be the Hanni Winter she was now, not the girl she had been at fifteen. The daughter of a high-ranking SS officer who had been a close friend of the Führer and his inner circle.

'What have I missed?'

She started as Matz Laube, assistant inspector with the Kreuzberg police and one of her favourite colleagues, appeared at her elbow. He had materialised at her side at the back of the party while she was still lost in who she used to be. *The truth about Hanni Winter* – the first response to his question which jumped into her head – was hardly a suitable answer.

'Nothing much. A load of facts and figures about the airlift I didn't really listen to. No one has tackled him about the plane crashes yet.'

She frowned as Matz straightened his tie and tucked in the shirt which had come loose as he hurried into the building.

'Why are you here anyway? Isn't... Freddy not you meant to be the liaison officer on this one?'

Why can't I say his name without tripping over it?

It was obvious from Matz's sideways glance at her that he was wondering the same thing.

'In theory, yes, but he was never actually coming. You know he's got no time for all this public relations stuff. And he's hardly flavour of the month with the Americans after he upset them last year, so Brack decided I should be the face of the department on this one.'

Hanni shrugged as if Freddy's presence or lack of it didn't matter to her. His absence should have been a relief – having Freddy there would only make the day more complicated. It wasn't. It was Freddy's face she had been hoping to see. If only he knew how to play the game, as Matz would call it. If only the two of them weren't...

She stopped herself from heading down a pathway that had nothing good at the end of it. Hanni had resolved to stop indulging any dreams about a future that involved Freddy since she had torn herself away from his waiting arms a year ago in Viktoriapark. He wasn't there and that, for so many reasons, was no doubt for the best.

Freddy Schlüssel was widely regarded – and not only by Matz and Hanni – as one of the best detectives in western Berlin. He had earned himself hero status in the department, and in the city, after the string of murders he had solved, with Hanni's help, the previous year. But as intuitive and brave as he was, he was also a far less biddable man than his deputy Matz. Chief Inspector Brack, the commanding officer of the Kreuzberg division, hated him, and the Americans thought he couldn't be trusted. None of that, in Hanni's opinion, was Freddy's fault. Brack was a brute who had managed to bury his dubious wartime record in the then Nazi-run police force, and he hated Freddy because Freddy was Jewish. And Freddy hadn't meant to annoy the Americans – he had simply done what he needed to do to solve a difficult case. All of that, never mind their complicated relationship, made easy-going Matz a far simpler companion. Hanni still wished it was Freddy standing beside her. Which also hadn't escaped Matz's attention.

'What is it with you two, Hanni? When we all worked together on the SS Killer case, I would have bet a month's salary on you and Freddy becoming a couple. Now you act as if you've barely met. Wasn't there something between you? Did I get that completely wrong?'

Hanni couldn't meet his eyes. There was nothing she could say. *Yes, you were wrong* was a lie; *no, you weren't wrong at all* demanded answers she couldn't give him. The spark between her and Freddy had held a heat too fierce to dampen it, but how could she admit that to Matz when they could no longer admit it to each other?

It hadn't always been like that. When Hanni and Freddy had met, in November 1946 in the ruins of a Third Reich ministerial palace in Wilhelmstraβe where Hanni had discovered the first of what would become a series of bodies, the attraction between them had been instant. They had both felt it; they had both, for a moment, acted on it. She knew that she wasn't the only one who had dreamed. That attraction was still there: in his eyes when he thought she wasn't looking at him; in hers when she was certain that he wasn't looking at her. And so were the barriers Hanni had put up and couldn't begin yet to break.

Matz didn't know that those barriers existed. He knew, as she did, that Freddy Schlüssel had once been Freddy Schlüsselberg. That he was Jewish and had lost his entire family to the killing camps. What Matz – and Freddy – didn't know was that Hanni Winter had also changed who she was in the wreckage of the war. That she had once been Hannelore Foss, the daughter of Obergruppenführer Reiner Foss, an ardent National Socialist who had helped administer Theresienstadt – the ghetto town in Bohemia where thousands of Jews had been promised a paradise and had lost their lives instead – and the Leitmeritz slave-labour camp a few miles from it. A man Hanni hated. A man who had not only survived the war by rewriting who he had been in it, but one who had thrived in the years after, despite all the blood staining his hands. Who – with a new identity as Emil Foss, not as Reiner – had made a very successful career for himself working for the education division in the British sector. And a man who had threatened to kill his daughter if she exposed him, and had already tried.

Hanni couldn't tell Matz any of that, and she definitely couldn't tell Freddy. She knew – because she had once attempted to explain the secrets of her life to someone else who had loved her – that he would hate her if she did. The thought of that stopped her breath. The pain her betrayal would cause him if the truth came out – because what else would Freddy see her silence as but betrayal – would stop her heart. Hanni had therefore let Freddy think what he had chosen to think. That she wasn't free, that she couldn't let herself love him because someone else had staked a claim on her first. It hadn't stopped him. It hadn't stopped her. They both pretended that it had.

Hanni couldn't explain a word of that to Matz. Luckily, his kind heart kicked in and she didn't have to try.

'Ignore me. It's your business, not mine. I do think Freddy's a fool for not snapping you up though, and it looks like I'm not the only one.'

Matz nodded to the officer who was waiting for them to join the rest of the party and who beamed more broadly than he needed to when he caught Hanni's eye.

'You know what Freddy's like: all tight-lipped and closed off. Maybe he needs waking up.' Matz grinned. 'Maybe it's time to make him jealous.'

Hanni had no interest whatsoever in making Freddy jealous – the last thing their relationship needed was games. And if she had chosen to go down that route, she wouldn't have picked their rather earnest guide as her partner. She – along with every other woman at Tempelhof, if the constellation of pink cheeks was anything to go by – would have given the jealousy-making role to the dazzling specimen of American gallantry that was Captain Tony Miller.

'Dear God, did they get him from central casting?'

It was hard not to laugh at Matz's jaw-dropping reaction when the captain stepped up to the microphone and his senior officer introduced him as 'the bravest and, dare I say it, most dazzling pilot in the United States Air Force'.

The welcome was rather overdone, but the description certainly suited the young pilot. The high chiselled cheekbones and the shock of black hair could have been borrowed from Montgomery Clift. He wore his battered olive-green blouson and flight-wrinkled trousers as elegantly as if he was dressed in a tuxedo. When Hanni raised her camera to take his photograph, the smile he snapped on had a professional sparkle. And the German he addressed his audience in was faultless and didn't grind to a garbled halt a few words into his greeting. It was hard to look at Captain Miller and not hear a film score.

Hanni did her best not to notice any of that. She was there to do a job and, in her book, that required her to see her subjects clearly and not be overimpressed by them. She shushed Matz, who was ruining her concentration, muttering about how unfair it was of the Americans to present Berlin's girls with such a perfect specimen of manhood when Berlin's men were in such a sorry state. She selected her lens and went to work, taking a series of shots as the captain described the new measures the airport was introducing to improve safety. It was a perfectly pitched speech. It emphasised the increased tonnage of food and supplies the planes were bringing into the city and the faster turnaround times, rather than the dangers posed by mid-air collisions and plummeting wreckage. It was all very eloquent, but Hanni doubted that the posse of girls who had thickened their lipstick and positioned themselves in front of the small stage heard a word of it.

'Talk about lambs to the slaughter. They'd lie down and hand him the knife.'

Matz's eye roll was deliberately melodramatic, but the sentiment wasn't misplaced. Hanni switched her attention away from the captain and began to photograph his fan club instead, closing the camera in on their bright eyes and breathy lips.

The medal-laden colonel who had managed to make his way through the scrum quicker than his young officer grinned as he watched her.

'He's quite the weapon, isn't he? Let's hope the Soviets take as much notice of him as Berlin's *Fräuleins* apparently do.'

Hanni threw him a smile, which clearly wasn't as warm as the one he had hoped for, and loaded a new film as Captain Miller made his way towards the press area. It took him a while to navigate his way through the handshakes, and to dodge all the slips of paper the giggling girls thrust at him. His smile never once slipped.

Hanni didn't join in the clamour of excitement that greeted his arrival. She stood back, camera in position, and shot picture after picture as the captain dealt as charmingly with the press pack as he had with his fluttering admirers. He listened carefully. He answered their questions with a steady good humour. He brushed off the hazards of flying heavily laden cargo planes into an airport surrounded by five-storey residential buildings – where the runways were so fragile they had to be relaid between landings – as 'all part of the job'. There was no doubt that the Americans had chosen their spokesman well.

And then the questions stopped and his smile was suddenly trained directly on Hanni, and it was very hard not to be dazzled by it. Or to be charmed by the way he immediately insisted that she should call him Tony.

'Your dedication to your work is flattering, miss, but surely I've used up enough of your film. Maybe we could get a shot of the ground crews instead? After all, they're the ones who do the real heavy lifting.'

Hanni lowered her camera. Tony's attention at such close quarters was almost overwhelming. His movie-star looks were just as perfect in close-up, and his dark eyes instantly filled her head up with clichés. She had never met anyone who looked so intently at her. His steady gaze locked onto hers cut everyone else out of the picture.

We call him the Ringmaster... there's no one more skilled at putting on a show.

The memory came from nowhere and made her stumble back. The Ringmaster was one of her father's nicknames from Theresienstadt, where his charm had helped hide the town's true horrors and his skill with a whip had added to them. It was a fear-filled name for a fear-inducing man and it had no place here.

'It's nothing. The wrong heels and a pothole.' She waved away Matz's steadying hand and pulled herself together. It was a shock to realise how vulnerable she was, and how easily she could turn a ready smile and a charming manner into something more sinister.

Did he notice I'd done that? Should I apologise?

There was a hint of a frown flickering across Tony's face. Hanni had no idea how to explain the undeserved comparison that had swept over her, so she adjusted her camera strap and overcompensated instead.

'Of course, yes. The ground crew. That's a great idea. But maybe you could pose with them as well? Let me get a shot of all the stars of the show together?'

Matz – who had never seen Hanni come within a mile of the way she was currently gushing – was staring at her with his eyebrows raised. Tony's face by contrast had brightened. Leaving Matz and the others behind, he led Hanni across to where a group of overalled workers were scurrying backwards and forwards between a recently landed plane and one of the airport's cavernous hangars. Packets of cigarettes – which were once again Berlin's most stable form of currency – appeared from the small bag slung over his shoulder. There were clapped backs and grins all round, especially when Tony took his turn with the heavy crates. Hanni took refuge behind her lens again, the more natural shots she was now able to take making her feel instantly better.

At the end of the hour allocated for the visit, she had a set of photographs she knew would delight *Die Neue Zeitung* and her emotions more firmly in check. When Tony turned to her again, she decided to enjoy, not mistrust, his attentions.

'They've given me a forty-eight-hour pass to stay in the city as a thanks for doing this, rather than sending me straight back to the main base at Fassberg. I've not seen anything of the city yet, although I've been flying in and out of it for weeks. We don't normally get to leave Tempelhof at all, the timings between landing and leaving are so quick, so I don't want to waste a minute of it. Will you have dinner with me tonight? Show me a little of Berlin from the ground for a change?'

Hanni's immediate reaction was to say no. Although fraternisation between German civilians and Allied soldiers was no longer forbidden, Hanni never accepted dates from the British and American men who asked her out. She rarely accepted any dates at all.

Which surely needs to change.

She was twenty-five, she should – as her landlady frequently pointed out – be working less and having more fun.

And meeting men who aren't Freddy.

It was an uncomfortable, alien thought. She had spent two years trying to manage her life so that there might be a place in it for Freddy. It hadn't worked. There were too many days when she couldn't see how it ever would.

She fiddled with her camera lens. Tony was waiting for her reply, his handsome face beaming down at her.

Frau Greber would love him. Me going out with him would give her enough gossip to warm her for weeks.

Maybe a harmless flirtation would be a good thing. Maybe it would help her heart heal a little. And maybe it would stop her seeing Reiner everywhere and assuming that all charming men were monsters.

'Okay, yes.'

Her answer sounded gauche and too blunt. Tony's face was caught somewhere between a frown and a smile, and she wondered for a moment if he was going to retract the offer.

She took a deep breath and tried again. 'I mean I would like to have dinner with you very much, yes. Thank you.'

His grin reappeared with a lightning speed Hanni couldn't help but warm to. Perhaps – if he carried on smiling at her like that – some of the uncomfortable *maybes* might stick.

CHAPTER 3

16 AUGUST 1948, EVENING

He hadn't expected everything to still be the same, but he had
expected to feel some kind of connection.

Tony knew what the air raids had done to Berlin – he had,
after all, been one of the pilots who had unleashed the terror
which destroyed it. On the bombing days themselves, the clouds
of dust had been too thick to see anything beneath the explosions,
but he had seen the photographs and the newsreels; he had been
briefed on the damage. Tony had steeled himself against the loss
of a number of the city's key landmarks. He had still presumed
that he would know his own birthplace. The reality was a shock.
The city was no longer his; he could no longer map it. He had
walked it from midnight to dawn and got lost so many times his
body was spinning.

Nothing in Berlin was where or what it should be. Street after
street had been pounded into empty spaces and left blank, or had
been renamed, their German identity vanished under a layer of
English or the Cyrillic shapes he couldn't decode. The elegant
department stores, with their domed atriums and chandeliers and
hushed chocolate-scented tearooms – where his mother had
forced him to sit in scratchy smart clothes – had disappeared.
From what Tony could see, Berlin's old shopkeepers traded now

out of gloomy rooms with gaping shelves. And Berlin's new shop-keepers laid out their wares beside blackened and pockmarked train stations or in weed-filled squares where bustling offices and restaurants had once stood. The business of commerce had become furtive and joyless, and he hated it. The city's gloss and glamour had gone, and he hated that more.

'It was bombed and then shelled very badly, especially in the last days when the fighting ran from street to street. Its heart gave out, and this blockade has stopped its restarting.'

Hanni had left her explanation there. Neither of them had acknowledged the part American planes had played in the devastation. She hadn't asked Tony directly if he had ever flown anything into the city other than bread. He wouldn't have told her the truth if she had. Very few things bothered Tony Miller's conscience, but memories of the bombing raids he had flown over Berlin in 1944 could still wake him up in a cold sweat. He hadn't wanted to take part in them – he still had some loyalties left to the city, despite what his family had suffered – but what reason could he have given for staying away? He had been too valuable a pilot to leave behind. He had been too keen to hold on to the all-American war-hero image he had cultivated to suggest that he might be better deployed elsewhere. He had climbed into his cockpit and gone where he was told, as if this raid was no different to any of the others he had made his reputation in. That had not been easily done.

Destroying Leipzig hadn't troubled him, or Hamburg. He didn't know those cities; their citizens were of no interest to him. He could dismiss the people caught under the nightmare his squadron rained down as Nazis who deserved their fate. But Berlin... in the end, that nearly undid him and nearly derailed his career. There had been a moment up in the skies when all he could see was a daisy-studded lawn and a photograph full of smiling faces and he had forgotten how to fly. His second had been the hero that day and Tony had been 'overtired', as the base doctor had brusquely put it. There had been a rest period after that, involving a psychiatrist Tony had very easily outwitted, and a secondment to a public relations and pilot-recruiting drive he had proved to be very good at.

The lapse was a short one. Tony had stuck himself back together. He let his charm – which he had already learned was as valuable a skill as a steady set of nerves – rebuild his reputation. He packaged Berlin away, telling himself that the flower-filled garden a boy called Aaron remembered playing chase in had been destroyed long before his bombs got to it. That the family he loved had died at crueller hands than his. That had helped. And when it didn't, when the anger burned too bright, there was always the other remedy.

The anger was burning now, which was hardly a surprise: he had held on to it on the flight which had brought him from America as securely as he had held on to his rucksack. And walking Berlin's confusing new contours and counting his losses had fired it up even brighter. The holes where buildings should be gnawed at him. The holes where his parents and his sister and his brothers should be. He had badly needed a remedy to soothe his fury over those empty spaces; he had wondered if the remedy might be Hanni.

Hanni had struck him at first sight as an easy enough target, particularly as she had proved herself to be remarkably trusting. She had believed his stranger-in-the-city plea as the sole reason for wanting her company. She had let him walk her home after dinner, although the streets were dark and unlit and there would be nobody to save her. It would have been the obvious thing to let the solution be Hanni, except Tony had never been a particular fan of the obvious. And he had learned enough over the evening they had spent together to treat Hanni Winter with more caution than he had initially thought she deserved.

Hanni wasn't some anonymous girl in some anonymous town. She worked for the police. She had colleagues who cared about her and a landlady who knew not only that she was going out for dinner, but who she was going with. That made Hanni a risk, and Tony was far too good at what he did to take risks.

And she liked to tell stories through her photographs, or so she had told him at dinner. Hanni didn't know it, but 'It's about how you tell the tale when it comes to pictures, exactly like it is with words' was the line which had saved her. Good stories told well – as Tony had also already learned – opened doors as smoothly as charm did. So the answer wasn't Hanni, but it had to be someone. Tony had led Hanni safely to her doorstep and then he had moved on.

It didn't need to be a girl; it didn't need to be anyone in particular. In the end, it was a boy. A nondescript, too-skinny boy wandering alone along a deserted street. Asking for a cigarette in a voice that was a little bit drunk, a little bit bleary. Too slow to wonder why Tony had moved behind him. Too slow to pull at the cord when it snaked round his neck. Limp and lifeless within seconds.

There was no blood – Tony's methods were far more efficient than they had been in the days when his fists and his feet did the work. There was calm when it was done. The anger rushed out of his body with the boy's last breath, and peace rushed in, which was the intended result. But the warm feeling didn't last. It never did. The boy was simply one more in a line of killings which had left Tony feeling hollow as quickly as it had made him feel full.

Because there's no purpose to what I've done beyond the immediate release, and I'd hoped for better than that here.

The thought struck him from nowhere. It made him pause and reflect in a way that he had never done before. It made him kneel down by the boy's body and properly look.

The boy was lying on his side, his hair draped over his face. He looked peaceful. More peaceful than Tony felt. That wasn't right and it wasn't what Tony had expected. Killing in the city he had been forced out of – from where his family had been despatched so callously to their deaths – was, he suddenly realised, supposed to be a far more satisfying affair.

Extracting some form of revenge for his losses had been a motive in his return to Berlin, but Tony hadn't spent any time dwelling on what that might mean. He had always focused on the killing itself, not on what came after it. Taking a life had been a reflex, a relieving of overheated emotions, as instinctive as scratching an itch. Now that he had carried out his first killing back on German soil, and now that nothing had changed, the realisation that it should have done consumed him. *There has to be something different* filled up his head. Something that would make the passing sense of relief become a more lasting part of him.

Tony straightened up and looked around. The street was deserted, but that didn't mean it was safe.

He moved away from the body, his movements slow and steady so as not to attract attention. There was no visible mark on him for anybody to notice. His kills were clean things. Now that he had swapped his fists for a thin cord – and carried the cord away with him – he left no trace of himself on the body and no trace of the body on him. The kills were clean things and they were quick. And quick was no longer what Tony wanted.

They are too fast. They are done and then so am I. So if I want the relief they bring me to stick...

There had to be more...

He cast around. It wasn't until his wanderings brought him to a shell of a building which he actually recognised that the word he was searching for came to him. The ruin was the Neue Synagoge on Oranienburger Straβe where his parents had taken him to services and concerts as a child. The word he wanted was *ritual*. The religion of his childhood had been filled with those: the dietary laws which ruled his mother's kitchen; the rules governing what could and couldn't be done on the Sabbath; the Torah passages he had memorised for his bar mitzvah. Rituals, according to his mother and father, gave meaning to every stage of life.

And meaning is what is missing from these deaths.

It was as if Elkan was shouting into his ear.

Once that first moment of awareness came, other ideas began tumbling. Perhaps what was needed was a more carefully chosen victim. Perhaps there had to be an act of mourning. Tony's pulse stirred, his pace quickened. He didn't have the solution yet and he didn't expect to, but he could sense one was coming.

His mind fizzed as he walked down the dark streets, caught up in a torrent of questions.

What if this was about something more than satisfying an immediate need?

What if I was to change the pattern of the killings, so that the people I take aren't randomly plucked?

What if the choice of victims mattered?

What if their deaths could...

He came to a halt as another word flew in to sit next to ritual. What if their deaths could make amends?

Tony didn't know what *amends* could mean yet any more than *ritual*, but holding it and mulling over it made walking through the new shape of Berlin a more manageable endeavour. It stopped him flinching at the ruins and the written-over street signs as he made his way back towards Tempelhof. It made him blind to the black-market pitches and the shabby men gathering around them, preparing for another money-grubbing day.

You strike me as lost, Captain Miller. You seem like a man far from home.

Tony had hated that. He had wanted to kill the psychiatrist who had dealt with him after the Berlin bombings for saying it. But he had wanted to go home, that was true. Not to find the Müllers anymore. Tony had done his research after the war's end – he knew that they were gone, on trains, to camps, into hell. So not to find the loved ones he had lost but to make his birthplace pay for all it had stolen.

This invisible, secret scurrying through Berlin wasn't how he had imagined his homecoming would be. For long enough after he had left, Tony had imagined that his return would be a heart-warming one filled with tears and embraces and his father's apologies. Then the war had come and the Nazi machine had unleashed a ferocity against Europe's Jews that not even Tony's hatred of the Party had anticipated. A ferocity which had wiped away his family but not his love for them, or his need to prove how deep that love ran.

And now I might have found a way.

By the time he got back to the airport, which was already busy with the day's planes, Tony had a new sense of purpose and the seeds of a plan. Adrenaline coursed through him. He ran towards the nearest hangar and offered himself up for the next flight, his forty-eight-hour pass forgotten.

Half an hour later, he was back in the skies, staring down at the city as the plane lifted and the engines roared.

The streets might be broken, but Tony no longer cared; he was going to make them his own again.

CHAPTER 4

17 AUGUST 1948

'The woman who found him thought he was drunk. Until she got a closer look at his face.' Freddy moved back from the body and made room for Hanni to step in with her camera. 'She wouldn't normally have approached anyone in that state, but she's got a son the same age.'

'She must have had a terrible shock.'

Freddy watched Hanni circling the boy, lifting the hair back from his face with a pencil in the same careful way he had done. She was right: Freddy doubted that the woman who had made the grisly discovery was over it yet. Frau Klemm had calmed a little by the time he had spoken to her, but, according to the desk sergeant she had flung herself at, she was hysterical when she ran into the station.

'I couldn't get any sense out of her at first. All she would say was that I had to close his eyes because he looked like he'd died of fright.'

Freddy understood why the woman had said it. It was impossible not to read fear in the boy's final expression, or to flinch at how young that fear made him look. Freddy hated that the boy's last moments were so nakedly on show. He had wanted to carry out Frau Klemm's wishes, but his training wouldn't let him. The red dots colouring the whites and the matching pinpricks of blood which ran in clusters from the boy's eyelids up to his eyebrows were evidence which he needed Hanni to capture. He waited in silence as she did that, watching as her camera travelled slowly up the body, coming to rest on the brown brand imprinted around the boy's scrawny neck and, last of all, his discoloured stare. When she looked closely at his bloodshot eyes and swallowed as hard as he had, Freddy knew again why – apart from any personal considerations – he had chosen Hanni as his crime-scene photographer. There was no place on his team for anyone who could look at a body, no matter how many times they had been called to record the details of one, and not see the person who had lived in it.

As if she could ever be so unfeeling.

From the moment they had first met, Freddy had seen the kindness in her. It was Hanni, after all, who had corrected his use of *it* to *him* when she had discovered the body of the murder victim who had become their first case. It was Hanni who had prised open the closed doors of his past and reminded him that there was still a place in the world for compassion. Who had woken up his bruised and broken heart. A lack of feeling had never been the problem with Hanni.

'There is no indication that this was a robbery.'

Freddy pulled his wandering thoughts back to the job as Matz finished searching through the boy's ragged jacket and stood up.

'No one would target him for that. He's been on hard times for a while from the look – and the smell – of him. He's got no papers; there was nothing in his pocket except a handful of coins. If he did have a wallet, I doubt there'd be much in it.'

'And it wasn't a fight either.' Hanni got slowly to her feet. 'There are no marks on him except the ones on his face and his neck. His hands are grubby, but there are no tears to his fingernails or scratches anywhere I can see. I'd say that your initial assessment will be borne out by my photographs and the pathologist – that this was a deliberate killing and the victim didn't have time to fend off the attack.' She glanced back at the body. 'That band round his neck is from a ligature, isn't it? The mark is too narrow and too even to have been manually done. Did you find whatever was used?'

Freddy shook his head as Hanni reloaded her Leica and began taking pictures of the now cordoned-off street where the body had been found. He had already done a sweep of the pavement and found nothing. Despite that, he let her continue without comment – the camera's sharp eye had found things before that none of theirs had.

'What do you think?' Matz bagged the grubby coins and handed them to one of the waiting forensic team. 'Apart from the fact that it's an odd one.'

That was exactly what Freddy thought, and he couldn't pretend that 'odd' didn't carry a certain excitement within it. The murder case the three of them had worked on the previous year had been odd and it had tested him to his limits. It had also brought him a medal and a reputation as a hero, which he pretended sat awkwardly but – for a detective as relatively new to the force as he was – was actually quite thrilling. And now here was another potentially unusual case and another chance to prove his abilities.

Freddy glanced down at the body and managed to stop himself from sharing any of those thoughts. The case was not one written coldly up in a textbook: it had a victim and, no matter how unkempt and lost the boy seemed, somebody somewhere might shortly be grieving. This wasn't the time or the place for excitement.

He nodded at Matz who had opened his notebook and was already licking his pen, ready to write down Freddy's instructions. 'Odd is a good word for it. Boys get killed more often than they should in Berlin, we all know that, but it's usually knives or fists that do the damage, not strangulation. That's a method more often used by jealous husbands, or among family members. The close contact that strangling needs makes it personal and –

from the studies I've read – there's a lot of rage tied up in doing it.'

Freddy bent down, trying to decipher what he could of the boy's last moments. Apart from the eyes, it wasn't easy. Close those and sweep his hair back over his forehead and he would look perfectly at peace, and nothing about the scene suggested his death had been a drawn-out one.

'This doesn't look rage-filled, and spouse- or jealousy-based murders are more likely to take place at home than in a dark street.'

Freddy stopped and straightened back up again, his attention caught by a note he had made in his own notebook: *Why this location?*

'Unless…' He paused again, not entirely sure that what he was thinking fit the scene he was staring at.

'Unless what?'

He could tell from her voice that Hanni was wearing that look. The one she wore when she had heard some nuance in his voice even he wasn't aware of. It was why they worked so well together.

It's why everything between us could work so well together.

He shook that thought away. It was no more the time nor the place for those longings to creep in than it was for excitement.

He kept his eyes on the boy while he answered. 'I'm not entirely sure, but it's not just the killing method that feels off. The location does too. Look where we are: Heimstraβe is less than five minutes' walk from the station – it's right on our patch. That could be a coincidence, or it could mean that the murderer is a stranger to the area and didn't know how close to the police he was, or—'

'That the area is part of the reason. That the killer was sending some kind of message.'

Hanni had run with Freddy's half-formed thought while Matz was still puzzling at it.

'Hang on, I'm not with you. What do you mean by a message,

Hanni? Do you mean the boy is linked to a case? Or to someone who works at the station?'

'I don't know. It could be either of those, I suppose.'

Hanni looked across at Freddy, who answered Matz as hesitantly as she had, not wanting to dismiss any theory when his was still so untested.

'Hanni's right – those are certainly both lines we should pursue. But what I was going to say before was a bit different. I was going to say that there are other kinds of families, where the bonds are as close. Like gangs, for example – family is often a word they use to describe themselves. This boy is a scruffy kind of kid, the street type the marketeers use as runners. If he was a gang member, and his killing was related to that, he could have been left here as a warning of... I don't know... Maybe there's a turf war about to break out. Maybe it's a sign telling us to stay out of their business.'

He stopped, suddenly feeling self-conscious and very aware that, unlike him, neither Matz nor Hanni came from a world where gangs had ever played a part. His awkwardness made him snap at Hanni far more harshly than she deserved when she frowned at his fledgling theory.

'Gangs? Are they really a threat? I mean, I know the kids from the markets hang round in packs and that there's competition between the different pitches, but a turf war and a murder being used to warn the police off? Isn't that rather dramatic?'

He rounded on her – he couldn't help himself. Her naivety was suddenly infuriating. 'Dramatic? Only someone who's lived a very comfortable life could say that. For your information, there were Ringvereine branches operating in every working-class district of Berlin before the war and they had thousands of members across the city. The battles they waged for control of the streets in the twenties and thirties mightn't have been on the scale of the ones in Chicago, but they were vicious. And the gangs owned the police at all levels...'

He pulled himself up as Hanni's lips disappeared.

'I'm sorry. That was about old wounds, not you, and it was uncalled for. There's no reason you should know anything about them. I didn't mean to lecture – or insult – you.'

Her face eased back into its familiar lines and Freddy's stomach stopped lurching. He couldn't bear to upset her. If he caused her pain, he felt it; there was nothing he could do about that. And it was also not the time to be distracted by their muddled personal situation.

He coughed and stepped back behind the professional manner that kept him able to function around her. And he pretended not to see the flash of hurt in her eyes.

'But to answer your question, yes: I do think that they might be a threat again. The Nazis banned the Ringvereine and killed off most of its leaders in prison, but the gangs didn't disappear, not from neighbourhoods like the one I grew up in anyway. They resurfaced at the end of the war with the first big wave of black markets. And now the blockade, and the problems with the Soviets, could be the perfect breeding ground for their numbers to grow. The problem is that more and more citizens are getting dragged into the fringes of the criminal world to survive. Plus, the break-up of the police across east and west lines means it's harder for us to give chase into the eastern sectors when we do have a lead.'

Matz – who had been shuffling his feet since the exchange between Hanni and Freddy started – leaped in as the discussion returned to more settled ground. 'That's true – I've seen it myself. Some of the more organised groups seem to have learned how to use the division of the city to their advantage. And they've definitely got their fingers into the supplies coming into Tempelhof. There's been a couple of bad beatings over there, although the Americans are reluctant to admit it. And one of the men who was attacked was dumped back in his own neighbourhood as good as dead.'

'Exactly. Whichever gang was responsible for that assault turned it into a warning.' Freddy looked down at the boy again.

'Which is why this could be a lot of things, but it could also be a calling card. If the new gangs are organised like the old ones were, the rewards for being a member will be huge, but the reprisals will be brutal if anyone steps out of line. And the last time, far too many of the police were in bed with them, which is something else we don't want repeating.'

He stopped. Hanni was staring at him as intently as if she was trying to read his thoughts.

'Were you in a gang?'

It was too direct a question not to answer it truthfully. He tried for a smile to soften the answer; it didn't make him feel any more comfortable.

'Yes. For a short time anyway. It didn't amount to anything much: I was still a kid, even if I swaggered around wanting to break heads. But I had friends older than me. There was one in particular, who rose high through the ranks. Who might still be...'

He couldn't finish the thought, never mind the sentence. He suddenly couldn't remember where he was.

'Freddy? Are you all right?'

It was Hanni's voice asking the question – his brain registered that. But it was another one he heard, low and urgent, turning *are you all right* from a simple question into an encouragement to keep going, into the prompt he needed not to falter or fall.

'Inspector, the pathologist is here. He needs a briefing.'

Matz's formal tone snapped Freddy out of the trance he had tumbled into and gave him a task he could deal with.

Unfortunately, Hanni wasn't about to let him so easily go. She waited until Matz and the rest of the team had moved away to deal with the body and the gathering crowd of onlookers, and then she blocked him from following.

'Who might still be what?'

He didn't want to answer her. His hold on the present wasn't steady.

'It's nothing. It's not important.'

Anyone else would have read the tight clip in his voice as irritation and stopped asking. Anyone else but Hanni: she knew him too well.

'What is it? What are you holding back?'

Walk away – you don't need this.

He was still too shaken by his memories to manage the kindness in her voice.

He looked over her shoulder, searching for Matz and a reason to hurry away. Matz was at the murder van with the now stretchered body, but the minute Freddy tried to move towards him, Hanni put herself once again in his way.

'What is it, Freddy? Are you worried that your friend might still be involved in something illegal? That's not ideal, I can see that, but isn't talking to him worth a try, if you think this killing could be gang-related? He could maybe give you a way in to them.'

'No. I can't... I don't know how to... It's not possible.'

His voice cracked. Hanni moved closer. He could smell the faint floral scent in her hair. He didn't know if his knees could hold him.

'It's before again, isn't it?'

Before. She made the word sound so simple when both of them knew it was anything but.

He shook his head, to empty it of the memories surging back from their locked places as much as to put an end to her questions. But Hanni wasn't about to be stopped.

'Don't go there on your own, Freddy. Not again.'

He had never intended to go there at all and especially not with Hanni. Not when all that his previous attempts at opening up and laying himself bare had led to was her withdrawing.

Freddy looked up, even though he didn't want to look up. Her eyes held such warmth in them; her arms were a stretch away.

What if this time was different? What if this time we could find a way through to each other?

He knew it was a mistake to try. He knew that whatever had held – and was still holding – Hanni back from revealing her own war was bigger than any feelings she might have for him. That the gap between them widened whenever she learned something new about the terrible one he had lived through.

Even as the pain of revealing it pulls me towards her.

He had a sudden memory of the two of them a year earlier in his office and the way Hanni would have rushed into his arms if Matz hadn't burst in.

She wanted to help me then, I know she did. She wanted to take some of the burden from me.

And now the past was back and it was too heavy to bear. And it was Hanni standing in front of him, and nobody knew him like Hanni. Freddy let go of as much of his fear as he could and nodded.

'Yes. It's before. But I don't know if... my friend is alive anymore. I don't see how he could be.'

He gulped at the air, but the sob still tore up through his throat.

'The last time I saw him was the day he was marched to his death out of Buchenwald.'

————

'I shouldn't have survived. I didn't want to survive.'

From Freddy's first words, Hanni knew that all that was required from her was silence. In the gap that followed the shock of *Buchenwald*, she lost track of her thoughts. All she had managed in response to that was, 'Not here.'

Hanni had led Freddy to a small café a block away, ordered coffee and steeled herself against a story she knew would be far worse than the disjointed pieces of his life he had shared with her before. She had wanted to defend herself against hearing it, to control how he told it so that she could better manage the impact. It had taken all her self-control not to deluge him with questions while they waited for the waitress to come. To remind herself that this was not about how she felt. That this was Freddy's pain, not hers. Part of her had wanted to back out of the conversation completely. Her head was spinning with *I can't do this* and *I'm not good enough to do this*. And then Freddy had looked directly at her for the first time since they had left Heimstraβe and *I can't* had changed into *I must*.

Hanni poured the coffee into their cups. She pushed the sugar across the table. She couldn't offer him an encouraging smile – doing that seemed far too shallow – but she managed a nod and it brought his words slowly back.

'I couldn't imagine living on without my family. I couldn't unsee my mother and my sister being marched away. And I couldn't forgive myself for being alive when... when...'

The word was a boulder in his mouth.

Hanni stretched her hands across the table until the tips of her fingers were touching his. He didn't notice. He didn't look at her. It was clear from his faraway stare that he wasn't in the café anymore. He was back on the terrible day in February 1943 when he had lost everything, about to take them both out of the sunlight and into the abyss. When he carried on, his voice was so quiet, she had to lean across the table to hear him.

'The silence after they were taken was... vast. The column marched away, the noise of the boots and the whips and the dogs disappeared, and it was as if I had dreamed the whole thing. I saw the soldiers emptying the building. I saw my mother carrying Renny. I saw the dogs snapping at her heels. And then they were gone and the street was just a street again. There should have been thunder and lightning and storms. There should have been some break in the world to mark their passing. There was nothing. And then I was nothing and that's how I wanted to stay.'

He fell silent. He fell away from her, and there was nothing Hanni could do but wait for him to come back.

———

Freddy hadn't got his wish to disappear, although he had lain on the rain-slicked cobbles and begged with every last scrap of his strength to die. If the yellow star on his jacket – the one which was meant to keep people away – had done its job, he would have done. Nowhere in Berlin on the twenty-seventh of February 1943 should have been safe for Jews. SS Obersturmbannführer Adolf Eichmann had issued an order to make the city's workplaces free of its Jewish workers, and the Gestapo and the SS had swarmed through the city's factories and tenements to make his demand happen. They hadn't caught Freddy: a fever which had kept him stuck to his bed and a tip-off meant that he escaped capture. His parents and his brother Leo and baby sister Renny had not been so lucky.

Freddy thought he had resisted the rescuer who found him. If anyone had asked, he would have said that he had kicked out and tried to bite the hand that was pulling him to his feet. That was the story Freddy wanted to believe, but the truth was that he hadn't fought anyone, except in his head. He hadn't had the strength.

When his anonymous guardian angel had deposited Freddy with the porter at the Jewish Hospital in Schulstraße, no one there had expected him to make it through the night. When he finally emerged from the coma that had held him prisoner for a week, the nurse standing at his bedside had told him that he had a duty to the lost to keep on living. He had turned his face to the wall and wouldn't look at her. She had come back each morning and repeated the same order until he had finally given up and turned over and agreed that he would try. It had not been an easily won battle.

Berlin's Jewish Hospital had kept Freddy alive, and it had given him a home for over a year which was safer than anywhere outside its walls could offer. As impossible as it seemed to everyone in it, the hospital was a place out of time, an almost safe haven from the storms gathering around it. The facility wasn't completely ignored: there were regular inspections by the authorities, which could go badly wrong for anyone with suspect paper-work or a poorly thought-out story. Freddy had gone back to being a patient on those days, suffering from a condition that the doctors he owed his life to had insisted made him exempt from questioning. Apart from those visits, however, the hospital had been left largely untouched. It was trying to explain the strange-ness of that which brought him back to Hanni.

––––––

'The Jewish Hospital, which was where I ended up that day, was like some kind of oasis, untouched by the persecution gripping the rest of the city. None of us understood why, although everyone had a theory. Some of the staff and patients thought it was because the Nazis – despite their best efforts – hadn't yet found a way to completely purge us all out of Berlin. There were little pockets they couldn't quite touch. The old men whose medals from the first war gave them a protected status. And the men married to non-Jewish wives who refused to renounce them and their children whose *mischling* "mixed blood" gave them a shield. The Nazis hated them, the same as they hated the rest of us, but they also hated the thought of disease spreading through the city, so maybe that's why they kept the hospital going. They had to give us some form of medical treatment while they worked out how to kill us.'

The word *kill* had almost tripped him up, but he pushed on while Hanni sat in silence and tried to keep breathing.

'Or maybe it wasn't that; maybe it was money. There were rooms on the top floor where none of us were allowed to go. Where rumour had it that there were patients whose names – Rothschild and Oppenheimer – still held enough power to keep the Nazis at bay. I don't know what the truth was. I stopped asking why quickly enough; we all did. Whatever the reason, the Jewish Hospital limped on, and I kept going with it. I didn't have any other choice. No one there would let me die or despair.

Everyone had lost somebody to the soldiers and to the "resettlements" and to the trains, but nobody spoke about death. Everyone agreed instead that families were 'away'. That families would 'return when the madness was done'.

He grimaced and shook his head when Hanni tried to make a comforting comment.

'You don't understand. The denials didn't help. We repeated those lines to each other like a charm until we were all fooled by them, and that was where I fell down. I started to believe I was invincible. And because of that stupid delusion, I went outside the hospital grounds – the exact thing I wasn't meant to do. I wish I could think of a better, more noble excuse than it was spring and the sun was shining or that I was young and I wanted some fun and a cold beer. Not that the excuses matter, she would have caught me anyway – one glimpse of her sitting in the garden opposite the hospital, all smiles and blonde hair, and I fell straight into her lap.'

Freddy stopped, rubbed his face, regrouped.

'I met Stella, or she met me, and I forgot all the lessons I'd spent nearly ten years learning. That's the worst of it. I forgot that being Jewish meant being permanently in danger. That no one struck up a conversation with a stranger without a reason and that the Gestapo's searchers came in all shapes and sizes. I knew all that in the same way that I knew how to breathe and I forgot it all in five minutes. After that… an hour's flirtation in the Schillerpark became a drink in a bar. And that… well that became a beating in the Plötzensee Prison and a freight train taking me out of Berlin. And then…'

He stopped and this time he couldn't restart, and his eyes were looking at nothing Hanni could see.

Hanni knew that Freddy had told her his story more concisely than the events of it had actually happened. What she didn't know was that concisely was the only way he could tell it. That lingering over any element of what had happened would have made him physically sick.

Hanni could sense the gaps, but she couldn't fill them. She had no idea of the horrors Freddy had skipped over – how could she? She had never encountered them as close up as he had, even in Theresienstadt. Hanni had seen dreadful things there, but she had always been a step removed from their impact. Whether she liked the truth of it or not, Hanni had been part of the ruling elite. She would never have been a searcher's prey, and she had no conception of their skills, no experience of the way they had targeted and trapped the vulnerable Jewish men and women trying to stay hidden from the Nazis.

And even if Freddy had tried to tell her the full story, he wouldn't have been able to explain how alone and helpless and terrified he had been. He wouldn't have had the words to describe the shock that had gripped him in the bar when Stella flicked her hair and the dark-coated men stood up. Or the paralysing fear which claimed him when he tried to run but every space was blocked by a chair or an outstretched arm. He couldn't have made Hanni see the moment when he had tried to talk his way out of being arrested but there was too much blood in his mouth. Or how desperately he had fought to hold his head up when they had hauled him out of the van and into the prison, until the rank animal stink of the place made him gag and the beatings, in the end, made him howl for his mother.

Hanni's heart would have broken if he had somehow managed it. If he had told her the truth about the pain and the humiliation, about how quickly he had stopped caring as the guards reduced him from a human being to a plaything. Or described the packed cattle car in which he had stood wedged against bodies as smashed open as his was as they were transported three hundred miles away from Berlin to a hillside outside the city of Weimar. To a camp with the motto *Jedem das Seine* set into its gates. *To Each What He Deserves.*

Freddy did say those last words out loud. Hanni heard them but she didn't understand the way he shivered so violently when he spoke them any more than she would have understood the full

misery of the rest. It seemed such a simple phrase, but saying it
turned his face grey. What Hanni did know was that she couldn't
leave him caught up alone in such obvious agony. So she pulled
his hands into hers and looked into his eyes and said, 'Tell me
why that hurts you so much,' and, 'Please,' until he couldn't keep
silent anymore.

'Because that motto – the *deserve* part of it – had a very particular definition in the camp. It reduced us. It turned us into crea-
tures, alien beings who didn't *deserve* any claim on humanity.
That's how the Nazis saw us; that's how we were treated. Their
disgust and their hatred was in every order they issued. It was in
the way they took our hair and our names. It was in every beating
that they revelled in and every torture method they devised.
There were so many of those that the wood round the camp
where they carried out the worst of their games – the one we
learned to call the singing forest – rang solid with screams every
night.'

He ground to a halt again. Hanni realised that the back of her
hand was wet where her tears had landed on it. This time,
however, she wouldn't let him stop.

'Go on, please, tell me the rest. I can take it.'

'No.'

He shook his head when she said it again.

'I know you think you can, Hanni, but you can't, and I won't
let you try. That place was a poison and I don't want to take you
in there. What you have to understand was that Buchenwald was
a nightmare no one was meant to survive – we were there only to
be worked to death. It's enough that you know that. And that if I
had been sent to one of the stone quarries it serviced, I wouldn't
have lasted a month. I avoided that fate, God knows how. I was
allocated instead to the sub-camp at Mittelbau-Dora, to an arma-
ments factory there. I won't pretend that wasn't brutal. We
worked fourteen-hour days on rations that wouldn't fuel an hour.
But it was the same work I had done in the factory in Berlin, and
Elias was there and he, more than anything else, was my luck.'

He paused for a moment and shook his head again, although this time it wasn't at her. 'That was another word I learned had a different meaning in the camp. We say *luck* all the time out here, we say it so casually, but in there, it was everything, no matter how flimsy its promise.'

Freddy's voice had steadied. Hanni took a gamble that luck was safer ground.

'I understand that you don't want to revisit the worst parts of what you went through, but can you explain what that means at least?'

That he didn't slip away from her again or refuse meant more to her than she could tell him.

'It was the thing in the end that counted. That kept me alive. I don't know. Maybe there were other reasons that I made it through. I was desperate to live, and I had skills that I could barter for the extra ounces of bread that kept my body ticking. But everyone was desperate to live, and plenty of us had skills. A thirst for survival and a flair for languages helped, but they did not make me special; in a concentration camp, nothing made me special. I honestly believe that what mattered was luck – and I had it. The work I was assigned to wasn't difficult or dangerous. It had a simple rhythm which prevented the kind of mistakes which could have got me beaten to death or shot. And the foreman who ran my section wasn't a heartless Kapo – a prisoner who had sought out or been burdened with an overseer's job, made brutal by the fear of losing what little privilege he had. It was Elias Baar.'

Freddy suddenly smiled as he said the name, and Hanni felt her chest loosen for the first time since they had sat down.

'Tell me about him.'

This time, Freddy didn't hold back anything at all and his head came up.

'He was a legend in the neighbourhood where I was raised. And he was the one who was amused enough by my teenage bragging to let me join the Immertrau gang. That was the local branch of the Ringvereine which he ran and whose name he'd chosen because *always faithful* was the code that he lived by. I can't tell you the joy that filled me when I saw his face again. I didn't think it was an emotion I could feel anymore. You see, Elias was family: we had sworn oaths to each other when I joined the Immertrau. My survival mattered to him and his mattered to me. Elias being there made me human again. It meant that more than my body survived.'

Freddy paused and swallowed, but he didn't fall back into silence.

'We didn't make promises – only a fool made promises in a concentration camp. There was never a suggestion that one of us should give his life to save the other, but there was a reason to give help where help could be given. There was a reason to be watchful, even though the favours we traded were, by necessity, small things and well hidden. Elias had been in Buchenwald longer, so he coached me through the medical inspections where failure meant death. He asked me if I was all right and that little bit of care helped me keep going. He reminded me to keep my head up and to run, not walk, past the guards who were looking for weakness, even when my body was screaming with hunger and every step was an agony. He said, "Look at me, not at them," and never broke eye contact. And I gave him a share of the extra bread I got from the guards in payment for the Russian lessons I persuaded them would save their lives as the Soviet armies drew near. It worked – it kept us going. We kept each other in sight and in mind until the last days. Until the Allies were so close to the camp we could hear the guns booming. And then the Mittelbau camp was closed and we were marched back to Buchenwald. And Elias…'

Freddy's words disappeared again, leaving him gasping for air as if the images had choked up his throat.

Hanni wanted to rush round the table and grab hold of him, but she didn't dare do it. She stroked the back of his hand instead and kept her voice as gentle as her touch.

'You're not there anymore, Freddy, and I'm here.'

It was enough – it broke through. He blinked and managed to push himself on to the end of that sentence and into the next.

'Elias was marched out of there again and I was too ill to leave. He left and I stayed. We were separated. We didn't get to say goodbye – there was no time and no place. There was barely time for a wave. And as for the march itself…'

Hanni wrapped her fingers round his as his story once again defeated him. 'Don't – you don't need to. I know about those.'

That much was true: death marches needed no explanation. The details of the one out of Buchenwald in April 1945 had been reported by the newspapers covering the trial of the camp's commandant and its guards which had begun two years later. Twenty-eight thousand prisoners, all of them weak and sick and suffering, had been forced on a three-hundred-kilometre walk towards the ovens at Dachau. The guards had been issued with a shoot-to-kill order for anyone who stumbled and had carried that order out without mercy, leaving thousands of corpses lining the roads. It was, as the newspapers had said, a horror story to follow a horror story and one that had been played out in plain sight. And it was remembering that which finally broke Freddy.

'But you don't, not really. The thing is, people saw it, Hanni. They saw it and they did nothing. The Nazis marched the prisoners in columns past Weimar, along roads lined with homes and shops. There were bodies lying out in the open with bullets in the back of their necks. And no one came forward to protest or to help. The war was lost and still no one stood up for us.'

His hands and cheeks were wet now; people were staring. Freddy didn't seem to care, and he couldn't stop talking, even though his rising voice was also attracting attention.

'I knew that the attack of dysentery which had kept me locked inside the barracks was as likely to kill me as the march would kill him, but that didn't matter. Elias went out of the camp without me, without anyone to ask "are you all right" and to spur on his steps. I can't tell you the guilt I still carry for that. And yet apparently nobody who saw him and all the others walk by, skeleton thin and dressed in rags, felt the same weight of it that I did. That's what I can't understand, what I've never managed to make peace with. *People* lived next to Buchenwald, *people* watched the prisoners march out. The same prisoners who had been sent into their homes to work as slaves, who had cleared up the rubble of those homes when Weimar was bombed. Were we really not *people* to them? How could anyone witness that march, how could anyone know the truth of what was being done in the camp – and how could they not know when the smell and the smoke and the noise of the place ran through everywhere round it – and do nothing? How could anyone carry that knowledge and stay silent?'

He stopped, his words winding down as if he had run out of steam, and left the question hanging between them.

Hanni knew that Freddy needed some kind of answer. She couldn't offer him one. She also knew that he needed a show of compassion, and she assumed that he expected shock and horror. She felt all those things so deeply, she burned with them. And all she could offer him was the stumbling inadequacy of: 'I am so sorry. I am so very sorry.'

She could see in the way his face tightened how meaningless her words were. She imagined that he had heard them so often – filled with exhaustion or incomprehension or embarrassment from the soldiers who had liberated the camp, from the Red Cross workers who had listened helplessly to the story of his lost family – that Freddy was numb. Hanni didn't know if he had heard them the way that she was offering them up. Heavy with honesty, heavy with an agony that drained her whole body. She doubted it mattered: they were still inadequate and she had to do better.

'You are right. No one should have stayed silent. No one can be forgiven. The people who acted like that should be punished – they must be. You deserve...'

She stumbled then, against a word whose meaning had grown

dark in the shadows of Buchenwald, and pulled her hands away as Freddy instinctively tried to pull them closer towards him.

'Better. You deserve better. And that's not me.'

She was on her feet, grabbing for her coat, the tears still pouring unchecked down her face.

'Hanni, wait.'

It was clear from the way he half rose, his hands fluttering towards her, that Freddy had no idea what to do except to try to soften the pain his revelations had so obviously caused.

'I'm the one who should be sorry. I told you too much; it wasn't fair of me. There are things that should stay in the past.'

'No.'

She had her coat on. Her camera bag was slung over her shoulder and she wouldn't stop shaking her head.

'Don't apologise to me – never apologise to me. You're not the one who has done anything wrong. You're not the one who has to put it all right.'

She wasn't making sense and she was moving too fast for Freddy to catch up with her. When he shouted out, 'Hanni, wait!' a second time, every head in the café turned, but not hers.

CHAPTER 5

24 AUGUST 1948

I'm a coward: my father was right about me all along.

August's sunshine and spotless blue sky felt like a mockery. Hanni had barely been outside in the week since she had sat in the café and broken her heart over Freddy's story. She had spent her days cloistered in the sanctuary that was her basement dark-room, trying to lose herself in the safe rhythms of developing chemicals and water baths and replaying Freddy's account of the camp and the march on an inescapable loop instead. She wanted, desperately, to make amends for his suffering. She knew that nobody, least of all her, ever could. She wanted to be good enough for him, to be the woman who could offer him a kinder future than his past had been. The possibility of that was as far away as the moon.

How could anyone carry that knowledge and stay silent?

She couldn't shake Freddy's words. They had crawled under her skin and lodged there, layering new scars onto the old. She could feel their burn when she was alone and when she sat at the dining table surrounded by her fellow lodgers and when, like now, she was supposed to be working. She was failing at that as well; she couldn't hold her concentration or properly focus her camera. Freddy's anguished plea rang louder in her ears than whatever it was the colonel or Tony was saying.

What made it worse was that Hanni had heard the same shocked sentiment about wilful ignorance before. Her father had aimed it at her – with far more venom attached – on the day in March 1945 when the Allied armies were closing in on Bohemia and Reiner had announced that he was leaving his wife and daughter to their fate.

How hard it must be to be you, Hannelore. Knowing all this and yet doing nothing.

Freddy's words had been born out of anger and pain; Reiner's had been cruel and mocking. His accusation – that the silence Hanni had kept about the cruelties she had witnessed at Theresienstadt was as deliberate and damning as the brutality he had wielded there – had haunted her ever since.

Hanni knew Reiner was wrong: that the balance of guilt between them wasn't an equal thing. That he, not she, was the one who had joined the National Socialist Party and offered his life to Hitler. Hanni had been a child when the Führer took power. She had had no idea about the brutality which was about to be unleashed on her life and her country, and she had no power to stop it. When she did learn the truth – about the world Reiner moved in and what his choices had turned hers into – she had hated them both. And she had refused to be a part of the darkness he lived in. Her father had twisted her life with the path his had taken, but he had not twisted her. Whatever he said to the contrary, Hanni knew that she had tried to fight back. That she had taken all the risks in Theresienstadt that she had been able to take and survive. She had asked questions, she had dug for the truth. She had taken photographs to document the horrors she had witnessed and the part her father had played – photographs she would have paid dearly for if he had found them then. She had intended – she had *vowed* – to tell his and the town's true story once the war was over. And it was there that her guilt had taken root: she still hadn't taken that vital last step.

Reiner had escaped his crimes and rebuilt his life. He had no intention of being uncovered, and he had proved to be a very skilled opponent when Hanni had tried to reveal who he truly was. He had threatened her, promising that he would ruin her life if she ruined his. He had promised to turn the photographs he now knew she had collected against her if she denounced him. To turn them into proof that she had viewed Theresienstadt and its helpless inmates in the same heartless way that he had – as objects put there for her entertainment.

That had been frightening – what he had done to her the previous year had been terrifying – but it hadn't been enough. Hanni had refused to back down, so Reiner had fought harder. He had sown something worse than the fear that her own life would be ruined: he had made it clear that, if she tried to bring him to justice a second time, he would hurt those she loved.

I can make people disappear with very little effort – you of all people should know that.

The promise that he had made, that he could and would destroy anyone who mattered in her life – or who tried to help her – had worked because he had proved he could do it. Hanni, as a result, had stayed silent, even though it was a silence that gnawed at her soul. She had pushed Freddy away to keep him safe, but she hadn't made public the photographs she had taken, and she hadn't denounced her father and his crimes.

Because I have been waiting for a safe moment which will never come. Or pinning my hopes on an exhibition I may never get to hold.

It wasn't enough, this waiting. Listening to the horror story that had been Freddy's war had proved that. The 'I'm sorry' she had offered him, the silences she was still hiding behind, were an insult to his pain.

Hanni loaded a fresh roll of film and tried to concentrate on the press conference she was meant to be photographing rather than her own spiralling confusion.

Tony was watching her with an intensity that suggested he had noticed her attention wandering. He didn't look particularly impressed by that. Hanni pointed the Leica at him and made a thumbs-up sign, which provided Tony and the children surrounding him with yet another pose to copy. His smile switched back on, which was a relief. She didn't need to upset Tony, not if he was going to be a source of the assignments she might need if her police work dried up. A change in her fortunes, which felt – for the first time since she had begun working for the murder team – like a distinct possibility. Whatever stage the investigation into the strangled boy's murder was at, it was progressing without her and there was nobody she could blame for that but herself. She, after all, was the one who had gone into hiding.

Hanni had worked with Freddy under difficult circumstances before and had refused to let their personal issues interfere with a job she was good at. This time, she had done everything wrong. What she should have done was what she had always done in the past: taken the crime-scene photographs into the station, stuck on her work face and got on with it. Instead of doing that, she had sent the developed films via Oli and hadn't made contact with anyone about them or the case since. She was horribly aware how cowardly and unprofessional that was.

Hanni was part of the murder team – she prided herself on that. She had always been meticulous about presenting her reports and her findings herself. She had, on her first case, played a key role in uncovering what had proved to be vital clues and in interviewing witnesses when Freddy had needed a steadier head than his. A year ago, she had played a key part in capturing a killer. Now she was no longer certain if she merited a place on Freddy's team or anywhere near him. The future that thought opened up was a bleak one, not just on a personal but a professional level. Which was why she needed to focus on the assignment she had accepted and make Tony believe she was capable of more.

There had been another cargo plane crash, a bad one. Two American C-47s had been caught in the fog which plagued too many of Germany's airports and had crashed into each other, killing the four airmen on board. The accident hadn't happened over Berlin, but the possibility of more like it, despite all the promises about improved safety, had put the city on edge. The air force had responded – as Hanni was quickly learning that it always did – with another public relations circus and had, once again, put Tony Miller at its centre. And he had, once again, requested that she spend the day with him as his personal photographer. Given the possibly fragile state of her police work, it was a job she had been happy to take.

Hanni had assumed that the assignment would be a straight-forward one, requiring a handful of newspaper-friendly snaps and quickly done with. Instead, the day's itinerary was packed and Tony seemed determined to make it last twice as long as it needed to. His constant demands that she take yet another picture which was the same static smiling shot as the last were exhausting.

The first event of the day, which was once again held at Tempelhof, was another statistic-filled celebration of the airlift's success. This time Tony hadn't hurried through the waiting crowd: he had stretched the hour allotted to the visit closer to two and had overloaded the children with candy and their mothers with charm. His attitude to his audience was also different from the first event Hanni had watched him perform at. He didn't scatter his attentions indiscriminately – he focused. He leaned in and listened. He approached people rather than waiting for them to pay homage. He wrote down names and contact details, and he demanded that Hanni capture even the smallest engagement.

Every picture had to be flattering; every pose had to be the same. By the time the two hours finally drew to a close, Hanni felt more like a machine than a human and was, in a first for her, sick of the sight of her camera.

Determined to get something with more meaning out of the day, she ducked out of the goodbyes – which involved Tony kissing all the blushing cheeks he had already kissed – and wandered over instead to where a bustling ground crew was busy ferrying unloaded crates into a hangar. Freddy's comments about gangs infiltrating the airport had pricked her interest. Hanni didn't know if what he had said about smuggling was true, or what to look for, but she snapped away anyway, collecting a catalogue of faces he might find useful, poking the lens into the hangar's darker corners.

Nobody appeared to have anything to hide, but Freddy's comments about the Ringvereine and its potentially violent resurgence had unnerved her. Oli and the other street kids acted tough and pretended nothing mattered to them, but Hanni had spent time enough watching them to know how vulnerable they really were. She could all too easily imagine them being drawn into the kind of family-style gang structure Freddy had described. And as quickly falling foul of it.

A sudden flash of the strangled boy overlaid with Oli's face stilled her fingers, and she shivered. She turned to a crew ferrying and unpacking another set of boxes, looking for anything that fell, and was too quickly scooped up and sequestered. Nothing did. Hanni began to feel foolish. If there were gang members here, she would never spot them, and Oli would never listen to her if she tried to warn him away, especially if there was good money to be made.

But I could try, and maybe Freddy could too. Maybe he could be Oli's luck the way Elias was his.

Freddy had the same soft spot for Oli that Hanni did. He had once tried to persuade the boy to swap life on the streets for a place as a cadet at the police academy. Oli had collapsed laughing at that idea. But what he hadn't denied was that his life was harder than he wanted it to be and that meant that the door to reaching him – which Hanni knew Freddy wanted to do as much as she did – was at least an inch or two open.

Helping Oli could be a first step to making some kind of amends.

Hanni knew the chance of that mattering to Freddy was

wafer-thin. That even denouncing her father, which she had once thought was the key to making a future with Freddy, would be unlikely to balance out her past in his eyes. But doing something good for Oli surely couldn't hurt, and it couldn't make Freddy hate her more when the truth finally spilled.

The press pack had begun moving away; Hanni could see Tony looking round for her. She made her way back to the convoy of jeeps, thinking about Oli and how she could persuade such a hardened little character into living a safer life. It was difficult to imagine him listening to her. And it was difficult, as they arrived at the next venue, not to keep making comparisons between the new world her hosts seemed to believe they could build for Germany's young people and the one too many of them actually inhabited.

The battered-looking dancehall in Steglitz which was the day's next stop had been taken over by a branch of the American-led German Youth Activities Programme. Hanni wandered around the fringes of the crafts and sports groups set up for them to view, only half listening to Tony's directions. It was another hollow experience. The second session of the day felt even more forced than the first, and Hanni was struggling to take the kind of happy-go-lucky photographs Tony wanted. She was sure that the unguarded images she had quickly snapped and liked best wouldn't fit that criteria. When the colonel had described the GYA's America-centred activities as the 'best way to make sure the next generation doesn't repeat their parents' mistakes', the German delegates' faces had tightened as fast as if threads had pulled through them.

The children were taking part happily enough, the girls busy with scrapbooking and the boys playing basketball, but it was hard to imagine Oli wanting anything to do with it. He would like the Coca-Cola and the Hershey Bars, but as for the rest of the life it portrayed... Hanni knew that he wouldn't understand it. The war had taken Oli's childhood and turned him old. Neither Hanni nor Freddy knew his true age or where, or how, he lived, and she doubted even Tony's charm would restore his trust in the world or the forces which ran it.

Oli would laugh at him with his easy smile and his easy words. He would make it his mission to con him and probably make a very good job of it.

Hanni lowered her camera. She might as well have taken one photograph of Tony rather than the dozens she had shot: whatever the setting, they would all look the same. There didn't appear to be any edges to him, or any of the light and the shade which made for an interesting subject. It was as if he was a character in a play, without substance unless there was an audience watching.

Hanni knew that thought was unfair – she barely knew the man after all, and he had been charming, if rather closed, company on their date – but it was proving a hard one to shake.

She got into the jeep to drive to the final stop on the itinerary with no intention of using up any more film. According to the briefing sheet, that was to be a visit to a local school where Tony was to eat a lunch made entirely out of airlifted supplies in the company of a select group of children and their – no doubt pretty – mothers. They were already running late – there was a chance that it wouldn't last long. Hanni decided to try to get through the event with as much grace as possible. She would follow Tony around and point the Leica at whatever he wanted. He didn't need to know that she wasn't planning to take any more actual shots of him. Or that she wasn't prepared to take another of these meaningless assignments shadowing him, not when there was real work to be done.

She couldn't walk away from Freddy, even if that was the right thing to do. He had, once again, trusted her. He had, once again, opened his past up to her. That was something Hanni knew he didn't do lightly. At the very least, Freddy's openness demanded that she offer him friendship while the hope of it was still there. So she would go back to the station and she would apologise for not offering him more comfort, even if she couldn't explain why she had backed away. Anything less would be cruel.

Hanni was so wrapped up in her decision – and so busy convincing herself that her motives had nothing to do with the inescapable fact that a life without Freddy in it was an unimaginable one – that she was the last one out of the jeep and she missed the introduction to the school's waiting parents and teachers.

By the time she caught up, Colonel Walker had moved on from them. He was busy shaking hands with a group of identically suited men who he introduced to the rest of the delegation as 'our colleagues from the British sector's education initiative'.

Hanni moved along the line with the others, automatically focusing the camera for the required group pictures. She barely looked at the men's faces as she selected the correct shutter speed. She had taken the first snap before she realised that her hand was trembling and the resulting image would be blurred.

It's not real. It's a trick of the light or it's my wandering thoughts conjuring him up.

She steadied her hand and refocused. And the dark-haired man standing third from the left looked straight at her again. And turned with a smile into Reiner.

Hanni forgot that she was tired of taking empty pictures. She was glad to be a machine.

The afternoon dragged endlessly on. She photographed Tony and the children in stilted combination after stilted combination. She photographed the mothers and the teachers and the tight-faced cooks as they agreed with Walker that processed meat and dried potatoes could indeed be whipped into a feast. She avoided the British delegation.

She had no intention of tangling with her father – she couldn't imagine what good could come of that. And then he cornered her on her own as she changed out her film and there was nothing Hanni could do but plaster a polite smile on her face for the sake of their hosts and wait for whatever was coming.

'Hannelore – forgive me but I cannot possibly call you *Hanni* –

isn't this a surprise? And well done for smiling as if it is a good one.'

There's nothing he can do here. There are too many witnesses.

Not that anyone was looking their way. Tony was busy acting out his latest landing at Tempelhof, arranging the children in two nose-touching rows to demonstrate how tight the approach was, and his audience was spellbound.

'He's quite the showman, isn't he? There was a time when I could have made very good use of him.'

The implication that Tony would have joined forces with a Nazi was a dreadful one and deserved a withering response, but *showman* had taken the room away. The Showman was another of the nicknames the inmates at Theresienstadt had used to describe Reiner, along with the Ringmaster. It had perfectly summed up his ability to throw a glossy veneer over misery and terror. And as soon as Hanni heard it, she realised what had been gnawing at her all day. Every step of her assignment had been stage-managed. She had been directed to take photographs which told only one story. Happy children, not war-damaged ones. The success of the airlift, not the fear and the hardship that lay underneath it. Tony the storybook hero with no human frailties. There had been no questions allowed, no looking under the surface.

That's why I thought I had conjured Reiner up: I've been walking through a day full of echoes.

And now – with Reiner standing in front of her wearing his newly adopted persona and with a fake smile stuck on her own face – it was impossible to hold herself in the present and to hold those echoes away.

'Nobody, at any point, moves away from the route, and nobody who hasn't been cleared to be there moves onto it.'

The Red Cross delegation which was on its way to inspect the town was almost upon them and nerves were strained. Everyone in the reception committee, including Hannelore and her mother, had been given a copy of Reiner's map and told to memorise the route. That wasn't a difficult task. The red line tracing the precisely defined pathway the visitors would follow through Theresienstadt covered barely a third of the complex.

'Nobody will be free to wander. The cars will move from one predetermined point to the next, pausing where you see a cross marked on the map and nowhere else. Nothing will be seen that isn't intended to be seen. No one will be spoken to who isn't intended to be spoken to. Too much work has gone into this day to tolerate any mistakes.'

Reiner stopped. He wasn't looking at Hannelore, but she could feel his stare. She knew he didn't want her there. That she was only present because her mother had to be and Talie Foss wasn't, in her husband's words, 'the right kind of wife to fit my position'. Talie was a fragile creature, her grip on the world weakened since the death of Hannelore's little sister six years earlier in 1938. Reiner couldn't trust her near the delegation without a chaperone and he couldn't admit she needed that, so Hannelore was, grudgingly, present.

'Without your camera and your attitude or, God help me, I'll put you on the next train out.'

Hannelore knew that Reiner hadn't made that threat idly, no matter how vicious its meaning was. She also knew that he no longer saw a daughter when he looked at her, that he saw instead the thorn in his side. Hannelore had been that since the Fosses arrived in Bohemia in December 1943. Since she had wandered behind a prettily curtained stage into the maze of stinking attics and despair which was the real Theresienstadt and the last scales had slipped from her eyes.

What had once been a garrison and was now a ghetto was 'home' to fifty thousand Jewish people who had been promised a paradise and had been reduced to squalor and hardship instead. Hannelore wasn't meant to have discovered the truth of that. Reiner had tried to keep her out of the place in the six months since she had. He hadn't succeeded. He had also failed to make her see Theresienstadt ever again in the way that he wanted her to. Reiner was very tired of trying. By the following June, he was very tired of her.

The deportation trains he had threatened Hannelore with – which carried the inmates of Theresienstadt not to the family camps they had been told they were going to but to the gas chambers and the ovens at Auschwitz – had increased in number as the town was 'beautified' for the Red Cross visit. Hannelore knew that he would push her onto one of those without a second thought if there was any chance he could get away with it. She was still intent on defying him.

She had pushed her camera into the bottom of her handbag. She had brought a roll of film with her, which, if it was developed, would prove that Theresienstadt wasn't the safe haven it was marketed as but a place where people died starving and in fear. That it was another link in the chain that led to the killing camps. Reiner was determined to stage-manage the visit; Hannelore was equally determined to find a way round him. Neither of them trusted the other.

Determination, however, proved not to be nearly enough.

Six hours later, as the visitors drove away wreathed in smiles, Hannelore was the one who had failed. There was barely a moment when no one was watching her. She had managed one 'I'm a photographer and I—' which was cut off with a polite 'So your father said – what a lovely hobby that must be for you' which was barely a step away from a pat on the head. After that, every time she tried to approach one of the visitors ready to whisper, 'Could I have a word?' one of the guards found a reason to whisk her away. The undeveloped film was still in her bag where it had been all day. Her photographs and the truth of Theresienstadt went completely unseen: the delegates were too dazzled to believe there could be anything dark in a town which had been laid out for them with such sparkle. Hannelore hated that they could be so naïve, but she hated her father more.

Reiner and his 'embellishments', as he called them, had remade

Theresienstadt, or at least the parts of it that were visible. Every inch of the Red Cross route had been stripped free of dirt. Pavements had been scrubbed until they gleamed. Flower beds had bloomed overnight in a riot of colours. Dusty cracked courtyards had been transformed into lawns. One of the cavernous barracks had been stripped of the filthy bunks which were normally crammed into it and was now an elegant dining hall decked out with velvet-covered chairs and stiffly pressed linens. A coffee house gleamed behind pink and white awnings. A man in an elegantly tailored blue suit greeted a line of customers outside a building advertising itself as the town's central bank. And another swept the path in a graveyard where the plots were as tidy as any grieving relative could want them to be and the headstones were perfectly polished. Hannelore's heart sank further with each carefully curated stop.

She stood beside her father as the cars halted and the visitors were kept at a carefully managed distance, waiting for a movie soundtrack to start playing. Waiting for someone to say, 'But this isn't how we were led to believe life was lived here.' Wondering why no one but her seemed to notice that the conversations outside the coffee house and the grocery store were stilted and scripted. That the children's ravenous eyes were a lifetime out of step with the tiny bites of bread they had been ordered to take in the dining hall. That the headstones in the graveyard were made from cardboard not marble, and the grass they presided over was uniformly flat.

The delegates didn't notice a thing. They delighted in the display laid out for them, their smiles as wide as the ones their hosts wore. Everything they saw was another sight to heap praise on. The graveyard which would soon revert back to concrete was a 'comfort'. The neatly laid out classrooms were 'outstanding' and the never-opened books they contained were 'a superb resource'. They moved on from the schoolhouse that had, until two days before, been a slum, hoping that the teachers who had never taught there and the pupils who had never studied there were –

as Reiner explained – enjoying their well-earned vacation. They applauded the white-gloved bakers for the softness of their loaves. They oohed and aahed at the elegance of the orchestra who serenaded them. They cheered when they reached the football field in time to witness a winning goal.

Not one of them tried to probe below the pretty surface. Not one of them tried to walk through doors they were asked not to walk through. They didn't see the old and the blind who had been locked away in the attics. They didn't see the sick and the dying lying untended in their bunks. Or the lists of the thousands who had already been deported.

Hannelore knew that the delegates had heard rumours about the abuses Theresienstadt traded in – concern over those was the reason behind the request for a visit. When they didn't see any trace of those, they didn't ask questions: they accepted the feast of misinformation Reiner laid out.

They praised the goods in the windows of the shops and the elegant lines of the café and the bank, and they didn't peer into the emptiness behind their painted fronts. They went on their way satisfied that Europe's Jews were in safe hands and that Hitler and his National Socialists 'wanted nothing but the best for them'. They never asked what that meant. And later that night, Reiner, who was full of champagne and full of himself, laughed at Hannelore's despair. *We fooled them.* It became his favourite saying. Hannelore couldn't contradict him: she could take issue with *we* but not with the rest. Reiner the stage manager had won.

And no doubt plans to keep on winning.

The sound of the children running round with their arms outstretched pretending to be aeroplanes pulled Hanni out of 1944 and back into 1948. The setting was different, but Reiner – or Emil as she needed to remember that he called himself now – was still somehow pulling the strings.

'And there you go again – I can see the wheels turning.

Scratching at what's finished with, picking over old hatreds. Why do you bother when the world has moved on?'

He was using the other tone he liked to bully her with. The one that swapped mocking amusement for *I'm bored with you now*. The one bathed in *I'm right*. Hanni hadn't bitten back over his insult to Tony, but – after listening once again to the hell men like him had put Freddy and hundreds of thousands of others through – she was in no mood to stay silent at his arrogance.

'Because it hasn't and it shouldn't. Because there were crimes committed whose pain lives on, and there are people who, no matter how many years have gone by, should still be called to account.'

She might as well have stayed silent. His sigh was endless.

'That old nonsense, really? The great denunciation that will never happen. Nobody cares – can you not understand that? Look at them if you don't believe me.' He nodded at Tony and Colonel Walker, who were surrounded by grateful faces. 'Our old enemies are desperate to be our new friends, and we are more than happy to accept them. The Soviets are the bogeymen now. People are afraid of the future these days, not of the past.'

He sounded so sure of himself it made Hanni's stomach curdle.

'And you're not afraid of either I suppose?'

Reiner shrugged her question away. 'Why would I be? You're not going to do anything about it – you don't have it in you. And as for the future... that, my dear, is still to be made and is full of possibilities.'

His casual dismissal of her stung. It was also, however, expected, and she had no intention of rising to it. What had caught Hanni's attention instead was the light in his eyes at 'possibilities'. *I have to know him inside and out so that I can beat him* had been a lesson she had already learned. For one glorious moment in the previous year, it had left her holding the winning card. She could swallow a lot of insults to get to know him a little bit more.

'Is that why you are here? The Americans are very committed

to helping Germany with their re-education programme. Are you going to leave the job you have with the British and start working for them?'

It was a gamble asking Reiner anything, especially about his plans. He had survived the war and its aftermath because he had a killer's instinct for danger. He also – as he so frequently proved – had a killer's contempt for any world view that he didn't share. When he stared across the room a second time at Tony, it wasn't with amusement but disdain.

'I said *I* could have used *him*, not the other way round. "The Americans are very committed to helping Germany." Are you really that stupid? They don't want to help. They want to destroy everything this country has been and is and to remake it in their own image. They want our children to be cut off from their culture and their history, from all that their parents and grand-parents held dear. They want to turn them into basketball-playing clones of their own gum-chewing offspring. That is not what Germany needs. That is an insult. So, no, I will not be working for them. Their vision of the future is a long way from mine.'

Hearts and minds, Hannelore. Once you have those, the cause might be sidelined, but it is never lost.

Reiner had said that to Hanni eighteen months earlier, in response to her confusion about why he had taken a position in education with the British when he had never worked in that field before. Now those words bounced into her head and made her gasp. It was the smallest reaction, but it was enough to make her father remember who he was talking to. He fixed her with a glare it was hard not to flinch from.

'And that is no more your business than what went before. We had a deal, Hannelore: you keep to your life, and I keep to mine. Do I need to remind you what happens when you forget to do that?'

He didn't – the threat brought the memory of what he was capable of – and how her life had nearly ended – all too colourfully back. But Hanni was no longer the child her father could manipulate, and she stood her ground.

'I'm not afraid of you.'

She was, but she wasn't going to let him see it. She waited for his face to darken, for another snarled threat. She should have known better; Reiner burst out laughing instead.

'Oh, Hannelore, you are priceless. I used to think you were a coward, but now I wonder if I had you wrong. Maybe I should have tried harder to persuade you onto our side: with a bit of handling, perhaps you could have been an asset, not a constant disappointment.'

He was gone before she could retaliate. Back to his colleagues, who welcomed him with claps on his shoulder and loud cries of, 'Well done, Emil, she's a pretty one,' which Hanni was meant to hear.

I hate him.

The words burst through her head so loudly she expected everyone to hear them and turn round.

I hate him.

The hatred was a tangible thing, a disease raging through her body. She rejoined the press pack feeling light-headed, picking her way across the floor as if it was rolling.

'Are you okay? If you don't mind me saying, you look a little feverish.'

Tony's voice was clouded with concern. Hanni was conscious of Reiner watching the two of them from across the room. And conscious that Reiner loathed Tony and everything he stood for, which she didn't. She glanced up at Tony. Without the too-wide smile he defaulted to in public, he looked more approachable, more human.

Exhaustion suddenly swept over her, followed by a yearning to be held and comforted that she didn't have the energy to fight.

'It's been a long day, to be honest – this visit went on far longer than I thought it would – and I haven't been sleeping. Work, and the planes…'

She tailed off. Tony's frown had deepened, and she didn't know how to read it. She was about to turn away and crawl home when he suddenly shook his head, as if he had come to a decision he hadn't expected to reach.

'Do you want to come for a drink? It's closer now to dinner than it is to lunch – why don't we go and shake off the strain a little?'

Reiner was watching them, his mouth all drawn up. Hanni was about to refuse – she had no desire for further complications. But the offer seemed genuine, and Tony's eyes seemed kind, and Hanni was very much in need of someone to be kind to her, so she slipped her arm through his and said yes.

The files were proving far more difficult to navigate her way through than they should have been. The names and dates kept jumbling and the cardboard folders were slippery – Hanni had already dropped the contents of half a dozen of them all over the floor.

Three glasses of Riesling had proved to be one glass too many, which Tony, to give him credit, had carefully avoided pointing out. He had done his best to be charming, he had even – for a little while at least – seemed to find her amusing. Hanni hadn't managed matters so well. She had made a complete fool of herself and to absolutely no purpose. The colonel had raised his eyebrows when she had left with Tony, and as for the way her date with him had ended...

Hanni banged open another set of drawers, although the task she had set out on suddenly felt beyond her. She was starting to sober up, and she wasn't enjoying the wave of embarrassment that brought with it. Leaving the school with Tony when she was meant to be accompanying him there in a professional capacity had been a mistake. And the corner bar she had pulled him into – thinking it would be quiet and homely when it was actually full of solitary drinkers and the sour smell of spilled beer – had been a mistake too.

Tony's uniform had brought him frowns and turned backs from the bitter men who made up the pub's clientele, rather than the smiles he was used to. Tony had been, understandably, unhappy with that. Reacting to his discomfort – which Hanni couldn't help but think was her fault for taking him to such a terrible place, even if he was too polite to say it – Hanni had drained her first glass of wine, and then her second, too quickly.

Tony had tried to keep up a flow of conversation, but the pauses as the drinkers glowered at him had stretched. Feeling more guilty the more she drank, Hanni had overcompensated by talking too much and laughing too loudly and then, when she had finally agreed that it might be a good time to leave...

Hanni leaned her head on the cabinet and groaned. She had totally misread the hand on her waist steering her outside and she had pounced. There wasn't a better word to describe how she had launched herself at him. The second she did it, she knew it had been an even worse mistake that the rest. Throwing herself at men wasn't the way she normally behaved. She had tried to apologise to Tony and explain that. She had blamed the wine and the strange times they were living in. Every excuse she offered sounded reasonable enough, but they didn't change what she had done.

She also couldn't tell Tony the truth; she could barely admit it to herself. That, although the wine was certainly partly to blame, as was the fact that he was almost ridiculously handsome, she had acted out of character largely because she was lonely. And because she suspected that, on some subconscious level, she had wanted to do what Matz had suggested at Tempelhof and make Freddy jealous.

Which, given that the only person who could tell Freddy what I did was me and I won't, is utterly ridiculous.

All of that explained, at least partly, her impulsive behaviour.

And none of the reasons would have mattered at all if it hadn't been for Tony's reaction.

Hanni had thought that he liked her. She was single and so she presumed – because she had still learned nothing personal about him – was he. And for a brief moment when she had leaped on him in the dingy street outside the bar and kissed him with a passion that would have graced the film set he belonged on, he had definitely kissed her back. And then he had stopped and pulled away with a speed that had almost tipped her over.

The memory of that humiliation set her groaning again. Tony had pulled back and then he had brushed himself down and suggested – either extremely politely or extremely coldly, she wasn't sure which – that it might be a good idea for her to go home. Standing now in the too brightly lit office, Hanni couldn't remember if he had offered to take her. Not that she would have heard if he had – she had bolted the moment she had realised he was holding her, literally, at arm's-length.

And now I owe him an apology too.

Hanni gave up pulling at the files; it was becoming clear that the information she wanted wouldn't be found there. Nothing was going right. The whole day had been a disaster, including her embarrassment-generated idea to use what was left of it to do something good for Oli.

When Hanni had climbed rather shakily off the bus from Steglitz at the Templeherrenstraße stop, that idea had seemed like a perfectly sound one. Rather than taking the short walk home, she had gone to the station instead, determined to dig through the old case files and find a lead for where he might be. Once she had found that, she was going to track Oli down, buy him dinner, tell him about the boy who had been murdered at Heimstraße and how bad gangs were and convince him that all she – and Freddy – wanted was to find a way to help him get off the streets.

Hanni had been convinced when she arrived at the station that her plan was a good one, although when she replayed it now, it sounded like nonsense. Unfortunately, the desk sergeant had remained his usual disinterested self and had barely looked up when she explained why she had come into work at seven o'clock on a Tuesday night. Which Hanni had assumed meant he thought that her idea was excellent. And now the files wouldn't stand still and all she wanted to do was lie down.

'What are you doing?'

It was Freddy; of course it was Freddy. He didn't have any kind of life outside work – where else would he be except in the office?

Hanni steadied herself against the cabinet and turned carefully round. 'I'm looking for Oli.'

There was something else she needed to say, something important. Hanni shook her head, which was feeling fuzzy, and then, with a rush, she remembered.

'I'm sorry. That's it. I mean I'm really sorry. I was an idiot. You poured your heart out and all I could manage was *I'm sorry*. I do seem to say that a lot, don't I? I really should have managed something better.'

She wobbled to a stop as her words ran away. Freddy didn't look as pleased with her apology as she had hoped he would be.

'Are you drunk?'

His voice was as tight as Tony's had been in the alleyway.

'No, of course I'm not...' Hanni stopped. She was slurring so much it was pointless to lie. 'Maybe. Does it matter?'

Freddy didn't move from the doorway where he had taken up position as if he was guarding it.

'Well, this is your workplace, where there are standards of behaviour to be kept. Unless that isn't important to you anymore and you're intending to make your recent absence into a more permanent one.'

That Freddy was being officious with her was a surprise. He had been cross with her in the past, and he had pulled rank once or twice, but he had never acted in such a high-handed manner before. And his assumption that she didn't want to come back to work was a shock. Hanni had presumed he would realise that she was avoiding him not the job.

'I wasn't, no. Are you?'

The question came out wrong. By the time Hanni realised how belligerent she sounded, Freddy was staring at her as if he didn't know her at all.

'How did you get in this state? Where on earth have you been?'

Professional. If I sound professional, I can pull this back.

She nodded to the camera bag which she realised she had dumped more carelessly than she should have done on the floor.

'I've been working, at Tempelhof, and at a school. I've been assigned as the official photographer for Captain Tony Miller of the United States Air Force. He's one of the airlift pilots. Their best one. And he chose me for the job.'

In the silence that followed, Hanni realised that she hadn't sounded professional. She had sounded ridiculous, like a child showing off. It was too late, however, to correct herself and to tell him the truth – that the job had been dull and Tony could be a little bit boring. Freddy's face was already drawn up into a sneer.

'That one? The one Matz said looked like he'd been recruited straight out of Hollywood. Don't tell me you're impressed by a candy-wielding pretty boy? I thought you had more sense.'

If Hanni hadn't been a step behind the conversation, she would have realised that the edge in Freddy's voice stemmed from the jealousy Matz had told her to provoke. Hanni didn't hear that. What Hanni heard was mockery, and in that she heard her father. So she did not do what the rational Hanni would have done. She didn't back down and admit that, although Tony was pleasant enough company, she wasn't as impressed by him as she sounded. She leaped to his defence instead.

'Don't say that – you don't know him. You've got a bee in your bonnet about Americans because you made them a stupid promise last year and you broke it and now they won't work with you. And Tony's not a boy, he's a man – and he's a good one. He's kind and he's interested in people. He cares about them.'

Freddy's face hardened and so did his voice. 'Well don't I stand corrected. Remind me to run after his jeep the next time he visits his fans, why don't you. Maybe he'll be *kind* and *interested* and throw me a handful of cigarettes.'

They glared at each other across the room, both of them wondering how they had ended up in such a stupid fight and neither of them knowing how to climb out of it.

He's not angry with me, he's hurt. By my behaviour tonight, by the way I left things in the café. Why didn't I see that sooner?

Reiner, where her anger had started, and Tony, where her embarrassment had bloomed, fell away. Hanni wished that she could rewind and remake the whole day and that her apology had been the genuine one Freddy deserved. She was about to explain what she could of that, but Freddy didn't give her the chance.

'Why are you looking for Oli at this time of night anyway?' He glanced at the folders littering the floor. 'What can he help you with that I can't, and why didn't you come to me if you needed him?'

Freddy sighed as he began picking up the scattered papers. Hanni misinterpreted that too. If she had thought about it for a moment – or asked him – she would have realised that his frustration was with the mess she had created in the office and not with her. Hanni's head was too muddled to do any of that. Hanni heard the sigh not the words. She heard rank-pulling and irritation, and her hackles rose up. So she didn't explain herself or apologise for anything – she slammed the drawer shut and glared at him instead.

'It's nothing to do with you – it's a personal matter.'

The moment the words popped out of her mouth, she decided they were true. The wine still flowing through her system made Hanni forget about her decision to work together with Freddy to improve Oli's life. It made her forget that a year ago, she had decided against involving the boy in her battle with her father because of the danger that could put him in, or the harm that Reiner had threatened to inflict on anyone close to her. The only thought in her head was: *Reiner is up to something so I need Oli to help me find out what that is; I need Oli to tail him.*

Freddy might as well have been invisible.

Hanni's brain whirled, slotting the steps together, making them fit the plan she had come into the station with. She didn't need an address: if she put out the word that she had a job for him to do, Oli would come. If she offered him enough money, he wouldn't need to work for anyone else. Hanni grinned, completely unaware that Freddy was frowning at her. It was the perfect solution. The task would keep Oli safely away from the gangs and, if Oli proved to be as capable as he usually was at ferreting out information, it would deliver the missing pieces she needed to finally bring Reiner down.

And then I can present the whole thing to Freddy. How I looked after Oli. How I brought my father to justice. How I couldn't tell him the truth about my past until I'd done that. He won't be able to hate me then – he'll see that I'm good.

She picked up her bag, ready to leave the office and get started, utterly convinced that nothing could go wrong. When Freddy spoke, and she heard fear catching at his voice, she couldn't understand why it was there.

'What personal thing would need Oli's involvement and not mine? Hanni, if you're putting yourself in danger again, you have to tell me. You could have been killed last time. I can't go through that again.'

He reached out for her, hesitated and then pulled back again.

Hanni stared at his hand, suddenly remembering the feel of his fingers wrapped around hers, remembering where that touch had taken her imagination in the lilac-scented air of Viktoriapark.

'What's happening, Hanni? Why are you so far away from me? I understand... No, that's not the right word: I've *accepted* that we can't be together because you won't let us be, but is this it? Are you going to shut me out of everything? Are you really going to leave the team? Are we done?'

His words came out in a tumble and now Hanni couldn't look

at him, and she didn't feel embarrassed or giddy with her own cleverness anymore – she felt ashamed. If anyone had a right to be happy it was Freddy, and yet all she had done was add more layers of confusion to his life.

The wine's sparkle fled from her system, leaving her feeling sour-mouthed and sick.

'I'm sorry.'

And there they were again, those inadequate words.

Hanni couldn't speak, she couldn't think of anything to say that wouldn't make Freddy's misery worse. She wasn't, and never would be, good enough. She pushed past him and headed for the stairs. And then her conscience kicked in. She stopped and turned back to the office, desperate to be brave, to be worthy of him.

I'll tell him everything. I'll tell him it all and I'll ask him to help me catch Reiner and then... then I'll let him get on with his life and stop pretending there's a place in it for me.

The door was still open. Hanni put her hand on it, swallowed hard and steeled herself against the fury she was about to unleash. She would have done it, but Freddy was slumped in a chair with his head in his hands, looking more lost and sick with the world than she could bear him to be, and her muddled-up head didn't have the right words.

CHAPTER 6

27 AUGUST 1948

His new approach had worked; it had changed everything. Tony had achieved a sense of peace which had lasted for longer than the moment of death.

For the last eleven years – since he had left the Nazi boy lying kicked to death in the gutter and through all the other killings which followed – the peace Tony had experienced with his victim's last breath had been a momentary thing. There had been a split second when his anger disappeared, when a white mist dissolved the red, and then... nothing. An emptiness. A pretence of feelings he clothed himself in until the cycle of anger and resolution began again. This time, he had carried a sense of well-being away with him. If he paused, if he cleared his mind, he could still feel the swirl of it warming his blood. It was an extraordinary feeling. And it could be repeated, whenever he needed it, now that he had discovered the key.

Tony straightened his tie and adjusted his blouson jacket over the waist of his trousers to smooth out the line. He didn't need a mirror to inspect his appearance; he knew exactly the impression he made on the world.

His personal adjustments done, he checked the contents of his small canvas duffel bag – where everything was also exactly as it should be – checked his surroundings and slipped out of the rubble-strewn building. There was nobody about; there had been nobody about when he entered it. Steglitz – with its mix of servicemen and working men and its unassuming streets – was an easy place to blend into, whether he was wearing his pilot's uniform or his other, less obvious, clothes. And although its buildings were in better repair than those in the city centre, the borough had not yet fully recovered from the war's devastation. There were derelict houses still standing, which were perfect staging places for his transformation. If Tony had been the kind of man who believed in gods or good omens, he would have been offering them all his thanks.

The journey back to the neat little flat he had been allocated in the American compound at Clayallee was also an easy one. Tony made his way onto Berlinickestraße, weaving through the shoppers and the soldiers, smiling at anyone who smiled at him. It was the perfect afternoon to match his mood: sunny but not too hot, bustling but not impossibly so. He continued down the busy road, nodding at the glances which came his way but not really noticing them. He was focused instead on the steps he had taken – from the formulation of his plan to this first stage of its execution – and basking in their success.

He hadn't wasted any time – that was the first important thing. As soon as he had recognised that there had to be some sort of a change, he had thrown himself into pursuing it. The answer, once he began looking, had come clearly. The solution lay not in words but in a picture.

Tony had an important ritual of his own, which he had practised from the first morning he had arrived in Berlin. He got up, showered, made coffee and then he took out the photograph of his family laughing on the lawn and reminded himself who he was and where he was from. Sometimes that reminder needed only a minute; sometimes it took his knees away and needed far longer. Whether it was one minute or twenty, however, the faces steadied him. And then he had run his ritual after the night wandering through Berlin and the photograph had made him pause. He had looked at it differently that morning. He had stopped seeing a group and had separated out the individual personalities. He had remembered their quirks, their amusements and their annoyances. They had become flesh and blood again. Real people who had died without anyone to mourn them. And in that realisation lay his answer.

As Tony had suspected when he knelt by the boy's body at Heimstraβe, the choice of victim had proved to be the solution. Every member of his family who had been taken deserved a sacrifice made in their honour. Someone who matched them in looks and age, who would leave the same hole in their family as Tony's lost ones had left in his. Who he would watch die and then he would mourn in the way he hadn't been able to do for his own dead.

It wouldn't be as easy as the way he had killed in the past – Tony knew that. It would require careful planning and careful matching and having a wealth of contacts to choose from. And that was exactly what Tony was looking for: something which involved effort, which had meaning. His mother and father, his sister and brothers, and all the rest of them who had been wiped like dust from the world, deserved no less.

And now the first one is done and the first one was perfect.

He knew that the rest would be too, and he was glad that he hadn't wavered, even when wavering was what he had so wanted to do. That would have been a mistake, and it would have been Hanni's fault. She had no idea how close, yet again, she had come.

Tony's pace slowed, the sun slipped out of view. Hanni Winter was becoming a problem. One day, although he didn't yet know when, he would have to deal with her. Except dealing with Hanni, he suddenly realised, was no longer something he was quite so eager to do. Hanni had inserted herself into his life and he wasn't sure if he was ready to dislodge her. In many ways, she had dropped into the role his wife Nancy had once played: part smokescreen, part companion, part nuisance. He had developed a formula for measuring Nancy's value: *is she useful to me or is she not?* It was the same formula he was now applying, albeit reluctantly, to Hanni.

That constant weighing-up hadn't always been an entirely comfortable process with his wife, who had also managed to get under his skin, and it wasn't entirely comfortable with Hanni. And if it hadn't been for his new approach, if he had based his decisions instead on the way their encounter on Tuesday night had unfolded...

'It's him! It's the pilot!'

Tony rearranged his face back into a smile as a small boy waved and twisted his hands into the shape of an aeroplane.

Hanni's photographs had been widely published that morning – it was likely that the boy had recognised him from those. Tony wasn't thrown in the slightest by that. His afternoon's work would never be traced back to him. He wanted to be seen; he enjoyed being seen. He had, after all, been out and about most of the day, signing copies of the newspapers which were full of his picture. That wasn't a risk; it was exactly the opposite. Nobody would remember precisely where they had seen him, or at what specific time: all they would remember was the story of his smile and his friendly manner and the attention he had given them. Tony had done exactly what he always did and what had always worked: he had made himself visible until the moment he had chosen not to be.

He hitched the strap of his bag more securely onto his shoulder – not that it was heavy to carry. There was nothing in it except the currency – the cigarettes and the chocolate – he always had with him and the clothes he had worn to kill Edda Sauerbrunn. They had also been the perfect choice, as appropriate for the role as his flying jacket was when he was being a pilot. The thin blue jacket and matching trousers hadn't merited a second glance when he walked into Edda's building. Half the men in Steglitz were dressed in a similar fashion. The outfit suggested a factory worker or a cleaner, which Tony assumed was what their original owner on the air base at Fassberg had been.

The memory of him made Tony suddenly misstep.

He didn't want to think about the workman. Killing him had been a murder done for expediency's sake, not his usual style at all, and what it had involved – the removal of the man's clothing – had been a distasteful experience. It had needed, however, to be done. Tony couldn't go unseen in Berlin dressed in his American uniform, or wearing his American-made off-duty clothes. Buying a worker's cap at the black market was one thing – plenty of servicemen picked those up as souvenirs – but buying an entire outfit would have attracted the wrong sort of attention. So the opportunity which presented itself when he had been sent on a supply run to Fassberg had been too good to miss. It had allowed the plan to which Tony was now fully committed to progress. And it was that commitment which had once again saved Hanni.

Even when her behaviour almost stacked the deck against her. What gave her the idea that she was the one in control?

It was hard for Tony not to keep coming back to Hanni, even though thoughts of her threatened his good mood. She was unpredictable and he sensed there were secrets hovering around her. None of that made her the kind of woman he wanted to be around. And yet she was also talented and useful, and very attractive. Hanni, therefore, was a problem and – although Tony was loath to admit it – she was a problem he was struggling to manage.

The kiss had taken him by surprise. It had also, for a moment, excited him. It had woken up the part of his soul that he kept deeply buried, the one which hankered after love and a regular life. The part he had, briefly, entrusted to Nancy, who had also started to take liberties he would never allow. Nancy had been useful for a time: the family farm she brought with her had provided him with a way of life once the war was done. And now Hanni was useful. Her photography skills opened every door in the city. The question he had to consider, however, was whether

– or perhaps, more accurately, when – Hanni's usefulness would run out.

'Herr Pilot, Herr Pilot: *sieh mich an!*'

Another little boy was waving at him, desperate for his attention, swooping his hands up and down in wide arcs.

Tony stopped, waiting until the pretty woman holding the child's hand made the connection between the newspaper in her bag and Tony's smile. Her flattery was exactly what he needed – it pushed his confusion away. He glanced at his watch. It had been well over an hour now and, despite his misgivings over Hanni, he still felt steady. There was no emptiness creeping in.

Because it worked; because this death had meaning.

Tony gave the boy a Hershey Bar and his mother a salute and walked on, his hand slipping into his pocket as he went. The thin nylon cord he had used for the killing – a length of suspension line clipped from a discarded parachute – was safely coiled up there where he had stowed it. His shoulders relaxed; his scattering thoughts settled. The first replacement had been made, the first atonement was done; completing the task had brought peace with it. Everything was as it should be, and that was all thanks to Edda.

Tony had collected quite a few possibilities during Tuesday's programme of events at Tempelhof and at the youth centre. He had sensed that there were matches to be found in those, but there was an order to the way he had wanted to proceed and he hadn't found the crucial first one he was looking for. And then they had arrived at the school, and standing there in the kitchen was Frau Edda Sauerbrunn.

With the right light, she could be my mother.

That had been his first thought; it had almost made him giddy. The resemblance was uncanny. Edda's hair was greying and her manner was cheerful, but she was also a fraction on the wrong side of worn out, and her eyes only sparkled when she looked at the children. Tony could picture his mother engaged in the same kind of work Edda was doing: serving food, never stopping, barely noticed, grateful for any small acts of kindness she received. When he then discovered – using a fraction of the flattery he had been prepared to employ – that Frau Sauerbrunn's age was as perfect as her face, Tony knew that his first instincts had been right.

Edda was fifty years old, exactly the same age as Elene Müller had been the last time Tony had seen her. And she was as overlooked by her family as his mother had been. Her husband was always at work, her children were never at home. Her house was full of broken pieces waiting for someone to mend them, including the stove she spent most of her day at…

'Which I am here to fix for you!'

That was all it had taken to get him through the front door. Edda was so amazed that he had remembered her, so overcome that he would turn up dressed in overalls to protect him from a messy job, with a bag full – as he told her – of tools, that there had been a tear or two. And all that was needed after that was the suggestion that he should make her a cup of tea, not the other way round, and that she should sit on the sofa instead of bustling about while he made up the tray.

By the time Edda Sauerbrunn understood what was happening to her and why – and she did understand it, because Tony explained exactly who it was she would be dying for – the noose was already around her thin neck. She hadn't struggled, or not at first. The shock had turned her helpless, exactly as Tony had planned. And when she did finally hook her hands up to her neck and start scrabbling, he pulled.

She was a slight thing. It was over in seconds. Then it was simply a matter of laying her out neatly on the sofa, where her husband or her children would find her, and performing the one act of mourning no one had ever completed for his mother. Seven minutes in the house from start to finish and the peaceful feeling – Tony checked his watch again – still with him almost two hours on.

The sun came back out again. Tony forgot all about Hanni. He arrived back at the compound feeling calmer than he had done in years. He let himself into his flat, placed his bag under the bed and collected up the photograph of his family and a bottle of cream soda. Next, he went into the sitting room and retrieved the envelope containing all the names and addresses he had so far collected and the faces he had clipped from Hanni's photographs that went with them. Only then did he open the soda bottle and take a long drink, letting the vanilla bubbles wash over his tongue.

He spread the slips of paper across the table as he drank and began pulling up the faces that went with them, sorting them into possible matches. Edda Sauerbrunn had been an excellent start. It had been, by anyone's measure, a very good day. And now it was time to move onto the next.

CHAPTER 7

28 AUGUST–6 SEPTEMBER 1948

The body was as neat as the room.

Frau Sauerbrunn was lying on her back on the faded green sofa. Her grey skirt was tucked around her knees. Her eyes were closed, her hands were crossed over her chest, her head was cushioned by a soft pillow. From where Freddy was standing, a few paces back, the dark brown band circling her throat could have been a thin necklace.

It's a laying out. It's respectful.

It was a chilling thought, not a comforting one. And it was definitely odd.

'Who found her?'

Matz was waiting for Hanni to finish photographing the tea service which had been set out on the low coffee table before he could tag them as evidence. He looked up as Freddy spoke.

'The husband, Hannes. He's next door at a neighbour's flat with the two children who still live at home – a boy of fourteen and a girl of sixteen. The eldest has moved out and works now in Hamburg.' He consulted his notebook. 'They all swore they didn't touch anything, including the body, and they all have alibis. Herr Sauerbrunn runs a small public house, the Leyden Eck, on the corner of Leydenallee and Berlinickestraße. He was there until after nine. The children were at the wasteland a few blocks away, doing whatever it is kids of their age do. A dozen friends can place them there, although it seems to have taken Herr Sauerbrunn a while to find them. They don't seem to be the kind of family who keep a close eye on each other.'

Freddy nodded at the table. 'That's laid for company. Do we know who she was with?'

Matz checked his notes again and shook his head.

'Well, whoever it was, she was happy they were here.'

Freddy waited for Hanni to step back and then he bent down to take a closer look at the rose-patterned cups and plates.

'This is what my mother would call the good service – the one people use for important visitors. And look at the way the biscuits are arranged in a fan, not tipped out or left in the tin the way you do when there's nobody to impress. This feels more like an occasion than a neighbour popping in.'

Matz frowned. 'Except the husband said she rarely had friends over and never in the evening.'

Freddy straightened up. 'Maybe so, or maybe he doesn't know his wife as well as he thinks he does. But someone was here and I think we can assume it was that someone who killed her. And from the reception she laid out, it suggests that she knew whoever did it.'

Freddy checked the brief description of the scene which he had recorded in his notebook entirely for procedure's sake: unlike Matz who was wedded to his pen, Freddy's carefully honed powers of recall rarely needed a prompt.

'There's no sign of forced entry, nothing has been stolen and there's no evidence of who she'd made the tea for. So where is he? Where has he put himself?'

Neither Hanni nor Matz offered him an answer, although they both knew what Freddy meant. Killers inserted themselves into the places where they killed. They left something, or they took something; they made their presence felt. No one seemed to have done anything to disturb the Sauerbrunns' small sitting room.

'The whole scene is too peaceful.' Freddy moved closer to the dead woman. 'Nothing appears to have been moved, and she could be sleeping, but she's been strangled, so her death was a violent one. There must have been a moment of fear, a moment where she at least tried to put up a struggle, and yet look at the room and look at her. She's been arranged for whoever found her, as if that was done with care.'

'It's deliberate, isn't it?'

Hanni refocused her lens and took a close-up of Frau Sauerbrunn's red-speckled eyelids.

Freddy nodded. 'I would say so. It looks like the way that he left her is part of the story—'

He broke off as Hanni suddenly blurted out, 'Oh God!' She was staring at the woman's face through the camera, but she was no longer clicking and her face had turned grey.

'What is it? What have you noticed?'

Freddy had seen Hanni stop abruptly like this before when a clue or an image suddenly fell into place, but he had rarely seen her shaken. He waited, his nerves tingling, while she recovered herself, although he was desperate to hurry her. The murder of the boy in the street – which they still hadn't managed to solve – had been an unusual case but not as unusual as this one. He was itching to start unravelling it.

Hanni lowered the camera but stayed bent over the body as she answered.

'What I should have seen when I first came in. I've met her before, or at least I've been in the same place as her before. She was at the school I visited at Heesestraße with the Americans. I noticed how kind she was with the children.'

'That fits with what the husband said.' Matz had his notes out again and was flicking through the closely written pages. 'She was a cook and had worked there since the end of the war.'

Freddy couldn't restrain himself any longer. He leaped in and aimed a barrage of questions straight at Hanni. 'Did you speak to

her? Did she seem upset about anything? Was she one of the
people the delegation was there to meet?'

Hanni shook her head, but she wouldn't meet his eyes and that
was what Freddy noticed most. He was about to ask her if there
was something wrong and then he remembered. That was the day
when she had been out photographing the American public relations junket, which meant the day she had been drinking with
Tony Miller. The jealousy he pretended he hadn't felt then finally
got the better of him.

'Forget it. Your attention was probably elsewhere.'

He turned pointedly away from her and spoke to Matz
instead.

'Go and interview Herr Sauerbrunn again, ask him if his wife
mentioned anything about the press event. It's probably nothing,
but mixing with a very different group of people than she was used
to – some of whom seem to be professional charmers who love the
limelight – could have brought her into contact with all sorts.'

'That wasn't fair.'

Hanni waited until Matz had left the room before she rounded
on Freddy.

He knew she was right. He didn't care. He was about to snap
back at her definition of what fair meant when the door to the
apartment flew open and a too loud and too familiar voice filled
up the hallway.

'What do we have? What progress have we made?'

The man playing to the gallery and making the room even
smaller with his presence was Freddy's boss, Chief Inspector
Brack, the last person Freddy expected – or ever wanted – to see.
His appearance at a live case was unusual, particularly at one that
Freddy was leading: the chief inspector was not known for
getting his hands dirty at crime scenes, or for being anywhere
willingly in the vicinity of Freddy.

'Chief Inspector, good evening.'

Brack ignored him.

Freddy mentally bit his lip, in preparation for listening to the list of mistakes Brack was sure to accuse him of making. Brack, however, was barely a few paces into the room when his bluster ground to a halt and his face fell.

'Is this how he left her?'

Freddy nodded. 'As if she was in a funeral parlour ready for a viewing.'

A thin slick of sweat appeared on Brack's upper lip and his normally high colour faded. It was clear that the sight of Frau Sauerbrunn's neatly positioned corpse was a shock.

If it had been anyone else reacting so visibly, Freddy would have immediately expressed sympathy or concern. Brack, however, had lost any claim on Freddy's good wishes when he had used Freddy's Jewish background to throw him off a previous case. As far as Freddy was concerned, Brack was an old Nazi in a new uniform, so he stayed silent and left the 'Is everything all right, sir?' that he should have said to Hanni.

'I wasn't as prepared as I thought I was. I knew her, or at least I know her husband.' Brack mopped at his face with a fraying handkerchief. 'We trained as police cadets together, although Hannes wasn't cut out for the force in the end. He opened a bar I occasionally visit for old times' sake. When I saw the report come in that something had happened to—' He stopped, remembered who he was talking to and turned into Brack again. 'This one doesn't get messed up, do you understand me, Schlüssel? And if you don't get it solved, it doesn't stay with you. What do you know so far?'

Freddy gave him a quick rundown of the conclusions he was starting to come to.

Brack snorted and his colour swept back.

'I don't want theories. And as for the rest of your nonsense... I don't want to be told that it looks like a family killing but it probably isn't. What on earth does that mean? And I don't need to hear that, in your opinion, the placing of the body feels deliberately respectful and neither does Hannes. There's nothing respectful about this. His wife is dead. Find me who did it.'

He stormed out, almost knocking over Matz as he went.

Freddy waved the forensics team out of the hallway and into the room and gestured Hanni and Matz to follow him into the kitchen. His skin felt bruised and overripe as if it was splitting.

'Are you okay?'

Hanni was watching him with her too-knowing eyes.

Freddy didn't answer. He was overjoyed that she hadn't walked away from the murder team, but he couldn't risk showing her that. After their last messy encounter, he was determined to remain professional, and unreachable, around her. He turned his attention on Matz instead.

'Did you find anything out from the husband?'

Matz, who had more sense than to react to the tension crackling between Hanni and Freddy, shook his head. 'Not about the American event at the school, no. She never mentioned that to him. What he did let slip, however, is that the bar isn't doing very well and that he's fallen behind on his protection payments. He was very agitated about that.'

'What do you mean by protection payments?'

Matz glanced at Hanni but waited for Freddy to nod at him to go on before he answered her.

'The money he pays to keep his premises open. He's been paying a local gang, the Libelle, to make sure there's no problems with difficult customers – which they would ensure there was if he didn't cough up – and also to make certain that his supplies of beer and wine keep on coming. Unfortunately, trade's been bad since the blockade started and he hasn't been able to make his payments for five weeks now.'

'Has he been specifically threatened?'

Matz nodded at Freddy. 'Yes. He's had a couple of warnings and he took a beating a few days ago that still shows.'

'A different kind of family.'

Freddy turned as Hanni echoed his words from the first

murder scene at Heimstraße. She was staring back at the ligature mark round the dead woman's neck.

'Do you think that's what's happened here? That Frau Sauerbrunn's death is a punishment for her husband's mistakes, a gang-related murder? Could it be linked to the boy left near the police station?'

Freddy flicked through his notebook to give himself time to think. It was an interesting idea and one that had struck him the moment he realised this was another strangulation. But there were still far more inconsistencies than connections between the two cases, and he had no intention of forcing the two murders together without more proof that they fit.

'Perhaps, but it's a stretch from a young boy murdered on a dark street to a middle-aged woman killed in her own home. I know they were both strangled and I'm no fan of coincidences, but I can't see that we're looking for the same man being the culprit – everything bar the method is too different. And as for gangs? I'm not sure. Murdering a woman is an extreme kind of punishment for a few defaulted payments.'

He stared through the open door to where the murder team were fastening a length of cotton sheeting around the remains of Frau Sauerbrunn. Brack would have his fingers all over this case and the last thing Freddy needed to do at this early stage was to rule out possibilities.

'But that could be the answer, I suppose. The blockade has changed the way a lot of things work, so maybe gangs are at the bottom of this killing, or both. Let's investigate that if we can and let's not discount anything, not yet anyway.'

Hanni was watching him. He knew that she was thinking about Elias, replaying her suggestion that he should try to find him to test out the idea that gangs were involved. And that wasn't a conversation he wanted to repeat, or certainly not with so many ears listening.

And this is Hanni and she won't make me, or not so explicitly somewhere as public as this.

She understood him. It was a relief to suddenly remember that. She proved that a second later when she raised the possibility with a simple: 'Do you think you could try that avenue?'

He offered her a shrug and a 'maybe'; Hanni found him a brief smile. It was the simplest exchange they had had in weeks.

Despite the maybe, Freddy did not immediately start searching for Elias; he waited. Whatever Hanni's thoughts on the matter, he wasn't anywhere near being ready for that.

Instead, he stuck firmly to procedure. He interviewed Frau Sauerbrunn's colleagues. He interrogated her husband until the man was more afraid of him than he was of the gang members who had threatened his business. Every avenue threw up a dead end. A week into the process and with Brack biting at his heels, Freddy knew that his personal reservations couldn't call the tune anymore, so he summoned Oli into the station and set him on the trail. He refused to consider which other parts of the past might come up with the digging.

'I need you to find someone for me. I very much doubt he's alive.'

'Good. It will be a quick job then.'

Oli scooped up the money Freddy handed him and memorised the few details Freddy could provide, including his last sighting of Elias marching out of Buchenwald. Oli didn't react to that; Oli never reacted to anything. Freddy had no more idea what went on in the boy's head than he had done when their paths had first crossed three years ago. He also had no idea of Oli's age – although he guessed it was somewhere between twelve and fifteen – or where or with who the boy lived. Oli was, as he had been in 1945, malnourished and secretive, and more often on the wrong side of the law than the right one. He also knew Berlin as intimately as if every street in the city was his own, which made him, in Freddy's eyes, more of an asset than a liability. And also made him worry about Oli far more than Oli wanted him to.

'Be careful, okay? Don't mess with these people. Whatever benefits you might think gang membership brings, the men who run them are dangerous. You pay a high price for what they offer.'

As soon as he said it, Freddy felt foolish. It was hardly a surprise when Oli laughed.

'Thanks for the warning, but I can handle myself. And I'm not looking for a boss who'll nick half my earnings or break my legs.'

'I know you can manage. But I still wish you'd choose a better…'

Freddy stopped. Oli had already switched off. He was, in his own words, comfortable enough with life on the streets and he wasn't interested in any of Freddy's ideas on how to change that. He was halfway to the door when Freddy remembered that he had something else to ask him.

'Did Hanni get in touch with you?'

The hesitation before the shrug and the 'no' was brief, but it told Freddy the true state of things as clearly as the 'Why are you asking?' which should have followed Oli's reply and didn't. He let it slide only because there was nothing else to be done: it was as pointless pushing Oli as it was pushing Hanni.

'Take care anyway.'

He wasn't sure if he was saying that for Oli's benefit or for Hanni's, not that it mattered. Oli was already gone, and neither of them would have listened.

Freddy would never know if Oli had been careful or not, but he was certainly quick.

'He survived. He's in Mitte. He gave me this and said he'll meet you here tomorrow.'

Oli shoved a piece of paper across Freddy's desk, which had a time and the name of a bar on the corner of Ackerstraße and Invalidenstraße neatly written on it in a familiar hand. He was gone before Freddy could ask any questions.

Freddy's first reaction was to sob at the wonderful impossibility that his friend was still living. Then he pulled himself together and sat staring at the note for almost an hour, trying to conjure up who Elias might be now. It was hard to bring the man from the past into the present. All Freddy could see was a hollow face wrapped up in a blanket and a column of broken prisoners swaddled in stripes. Forty thousand of them had been marched out of Buchenwald. Half of those had been murdered: shot on the road or burned to death in churches and barns or dropped dead from starvation. And Elias had somehow lived. That was a joyful thing, and yet...

What did he bring out of that place and that march with him? What has the experience made of him now?

Freddy had never discussed Buchenwald with anyone beyond the heavily edited version he had presented to Hanni. It wasn't only the description of the camp itself that he had deliberately left out of that: he hadn't told her about the physical cost of being inside it. The stomach-gnawing, brain-fogging hunger. The raging thirst that had set his body on fire in the cattle car and again after he had arrived, on the days when water was measured out in drops. Or about the way the smell of the filth and the fear, and the chimneys had filled up his mouth until it was all he could taste. Or what had frightened him the most, even more than the fists and the whips and the ever-present possibility of death – the speed with which he had ceased being a man by any definition he knew and had become instead a creature of instinct, focused on nothing except a survival whose rules changed on a whim. He never wanted Hanni, or anyone else, to know one moment of that, or to know how deeply those days still ran in him. That they were baked into his nightmares and sleepless nights, into his wary way of walking through the world. Freddy never talked about the camp; he tried never to think about the camp. Buchenwald wasn't a name he made room for anywhere in his life. But he had never forgotten it, and it had never fully let go of him.

Not thinking about Buchenwald had been a lesson Freddy had learned on the first day he had stepped through its gates. He had understood instinctively that there was nothing to be gained from wondering why he was there, that there was no purpose in looking for meaning. He knew that madness was the only thing he would find if he went walking that way. Freddy had never allowed himself to think about anything in Buchenwald bigger than the daily struggle to survive it. And then the gates had opened and the outside had come back and the struggle to live with the camp hadn't gone away – it had simply changed its shape.

Freddy had had to learn to live again, to find a place for the anger and the loss which had continued to consume him long after the world had let him back in. He wasn't certain he had fully learned that lesson yet, although he had learned a lot about pain. When the gates of Buchenwald opened, they had let in all the sorrow and the terror that the struggle for survival had held at bay. When they opened, he had walked through them burdened with a guilt for being alive when so many were not which he knew would never entirely leave him. And with the shame of knowing that better men and women than him had died; that he had been favoured for no reason he felt worthy of. All that weight sat at the core of him and he had never been able to voice an ounce of it, even to Hanni.

But now there is Elias and Elias knows too.

The hours to their meeting ticked by too slow. By Monday afternoon, Freddy was running on too little sleep and too much coffee and in danger of being too jittery to make it as far as the bar where their meeting was to be held in one piece.

It wasn't a simple journey. Mitte – which was the most central of Berlin's neighbourhoods – was located in Soviet-controlled territory. One of the main East German police stations was on Linienstraβe, fifteen minutes' walk away from where he and Elias were meeting. Once upon a time that wouldn't have mattered, but blockaded Berlin was no longer a safe city to wander through, not in the Soviet sections, and especially not for a policeman.

Walking through Mitte required concentration and care.

People who were in the wrong place disappeared – bundled into fast-moving cars before they had a chance to call out for help – or were arrested for having the wrong papers. Freddy was well aware that, if he was stopped, his documents would have him arrested and that an arrest could mean a labour camp no one would ever know he'd been sent to. Or a hostage situation which could ruin his career. But he could not summon Elias to him, so he had no choice but to go. Taking the train was the quickest route, but it was also too risky – once the lines crossed into Mitte, the carriages would fill up with Red Army soldiers. Freddy therefore put on his shabbiest clothes and pulled a hat over his face and he walked.

Despite his strained nerves, it proved to be a simple thing to keep his head down. The streets in Mitte were in far worse shape than those in the western sectors, and everyone navigated the cracked pavements, wary of the split paving stones and piles of rubble which could easily break an ankle. Freddy moved as carefully as the rest, resisting the temptation to look around him for trouble, using window reflections instead to check who was nearby. Nobody took any notice of him, but it was still a relief to enter a bar whose interior was as dark as December.

'I wasn't sure if you would come. It's not the safest place for a man in your position, unless you're certain your bosses would pay the ransom.'

Everything and nothing had changed.

Elias was fuller in the face now and his hair had grown back, but his eyes were still watchful and he was still setting tests.

Freddy resisted the overwhelming urge to throw his arms around his old friend – that would have probably resulted in a shove not a returned embrace – and slid into the seat opposite him. A Helles Bier appeared. He took a deep gulp of it and tried to sound like a man who was in control of himself.

'So you made it through. That last time I saw you, I didn't think that you would.'

Elias's half-laugh was also unchanged – it was still the same part-warning, part-deflective shield that Freddy remembered from the camp.

'Did you doubt it? I thought you'd have more faith in me. What else would I do but survive?'

He doesn't want me to dig. He's packed the past away as carefully as I have.

Freddy could sense Elias's reluctance to revisit where they had last met, but he couldn't stop himself. The need to acknowledge what had been done to them in Buchenwald was overwhelming.

'Don't, Elias. Don't throw it away and make it sound easy. Tell me the truth instead.'

Elias put down his drink and his face stiffened.

'The truth? What do you want to hear, Freddy? Another horror story? Hasn't the world had enough of those?'

When Freddy refused to answer, Elias shrugged and continued in a tone that was so flat, Freddy knew it was well practised.

'Fine. How about the number of bodies I saw on the roadside? I lost count. Or what I ate to keep going? Grass and the cotton threads off my shirt. Or better still, how I got away? In the woods, in the night, when the guards were drunk and I was beyond caring whether a bullet would find me. It was a death march, Freddy. It was well named. It doesn't need picking at.'

He stopped and then his gaze flickered away to the ghosts Freddy knew they both saw and he sighed.

'You won't settle for that, will you? You always were a policeman at heart, picking till you got the answer you wanted. If you really must know, then the truth is that it came down in the end to each step. At first, it was all about staying in the centre of the column away from the guns and offering an arm or a shoulder to the ones who were slipping. Until more days passed by than any of us had the strength for. Then everyone else faded into nothing but shapes and it was about taking one step and then taking another.'

He swallowed the last of his drink and waved his empty glass at the barman.

'I took enough steps to survive. I'm not always proud of that. I imagine you carry your share of the guilt too.'

There was no response Freddy could make to that but a nod.

When Elias spoke again, his voice had settled on a steadier level.

'And what about you? You survived too. I assume you owe your version of the miracle to the Americans who rode in and liberated you?'

Freddy copied Elias's half-laugh. He sensed that the man's capacity to allow self-pity – in either of them – was a limited one and that he would stop listening very quickly if Freddy's retelling became a maudlin one.

'I do. And I owe most of it to the one I found clutching his stomach and throwing up.'

The one was something of an understatement. Although Freddy didn't know it at the time, the man he watched losing his breakfast was General George S. Patton, Commander of the United States' Third Army, the liberators of Buchenwald. To Freddy, he was just another horror-struck soldier struggling to make sense of the nightmare he had stumbled into and not doing that with enough care. So Freddy pointed his error out to him.

'The fat one offering to show you around was a guard, not a prisoner. You should be arresting, not listening to him. If you want witnesses who speak a more honest sort of English, check out the thinner ones first.'

Patton gestured to the officer who had immediately run to his side to stay back. He straightened up and pulled a hip flask out of his pocket. Once he had taken a long drink, he wiped the top and offered it to Freddy who waved it quickly away. Even the smell of the brandy made his head whirl.

'I don't think my stomach can take it – it can barely tolerate food.'

'How long have you been in here?'

What Freddy appreciated at the time, as he told Elias, was that Patton didn't offer him sympathy or promises of revenge. He spoke to him like an equal, like a man. When Freddy replied, 'Almost a year,' Patton's response was, 'Tell me… no, show me the truth of this place.'

For the next two hours, that was what Freddy did.

Freddy didn't soften anything. He took the general and his entourage to the barracks he had crawled out of when the dysentery that had kept him in the camp until the end finally retreated. He showed them the bunks that were stacked four storeys high and barely inches apart, where one narrow lice-ridden mattress had played host to two, and sometimes three, bodies. He showed them the emaciated prisoners who were still in their beds, who had gone past help long before it arrived. He walked them through a courtyard where the corpses were piled up like bleached firewood. And then he led them to the ovens and to Barracks 66, where hundreds of silent and starving children sat and watched their rescuers through eyes that had seen far worse than any of them had learned the language to explain. Finally, when the tour was done, Freddy had looked out through the wire and over towards the town of Weimar and he said what everyone in the camp wanted to say: 'They all knew and they will all deny it.'

'Then we won't let them.'

And then Patton shook Freddy's hand, which was a natural gesture for the general and a profound shock for Freddy. It had been so long since he had been touched with anything but hatred, he couldn't help but flinch from the contact.

Patton felt that, but he held on to Freddy's hand until their grip became equal.

'And you will be there, my friend, when we bring them in; you will be the one to guide them.'

. . .

'He was as good as his word. After that, they all trooped in: the good and the bad and the indifferent.'

Freddy finished the second beer Elias had ordered for him and let him call for another.

'A thousand German citizens were marched out of the town, along the same bloodstained road that you were marched down, and forced to walk through the camp and to really see it. The torture devices, the gallows, the cremation chambers with the bones still inside them. The stacks of corpses and the ones still dying. They were spared nothing, I made sure of that.'

'Do you think it made any difference?'

The weak light in the bar had stripped Elias's face back to the hollows it had worn three years earlier. Freddy wanted to say, 'Yes, of course,' and switch the light on in his friend's eyes again. He couldn't.

'I hope so. The thought of going back to those days…' He took a swift drink. 'But I don't know. The denials, the dismissal of the atrocities as propaganda or as impossible, were quick to begin despite all the evidence. Nuremburg was toothless. And for all the talk of denazification, the old men are creeping back in where they shouldn't be. My boss is one of them.'

'Brack?' Elias sat back as Freddy nodded. 'His name keeps cropping up. I assumed that was why you sent your boy searching. If rumours are right – and I think we can believe that the rumours are right – Brack's wallet is doing very well out of Ringvereine activities. Is that what this is: am I your way in to finding out how deeply he is implicated?'

It was not the response Freddy had been expecting, although it answered his unasked question about whether Elias was still involved with the gangs.

'No. I had no idea Brack was lining his pockets, although I'm not surprised that he's on the take. But as for a way in to the Ringvereine? Yes, I would welcome a steer with that. I did come looking to see if you had kept up with your old connections, although…' Freddy shrugged to mask how much he cared. 'I do need your help, but I wish that you couldn't give it, that you hadn't followed that path again.'

Elias finished his drink and signalled for the bill.

'We all choose our own way and this one fits me as well as it's always done, if not better. Why don't we cut to the chase now, Freddy: if it's not to dig for dirt on your boss and get rid of him, why are you here? Are you looking to grow your salary too? I won't pretend I'm not surprised if that's it – no one I've asked has you pegged as crooked – but maybe once a gang member, always a member?'

Freddy wasn't sure if it was another test or an offer, but he cut it short anyway.

'Not in my case, not anymore. Like you said, we've both chosen our ways. And it's not a backhander I need but your particular knowledge of the city.'

He outlined the two murders and his suspicions about them. Elias listened without comment, but it was clear from his frown that he wasn't convinced.

'None of it sounds like gang business to me. None of our members go into houses and, although our boys will break bones and they'll pull a knife if they need to, leaving dead bodies as warnings or punishments isn't something the top levels or local leaders would condone. The old unspoken "don't kill" order still stands. And we don't need the police interest in our activities which murders bring, especially not from the Soviets, who seem to have learned most of their interrogation techniques from the Nazis. We also don't need to be doing it: the blockade, and the mess the city is in, has been a godsend for us. There's plenty of business for anyone who wants it and no one, at the moment, has an appetite for turf wars.'

He began gathering up his jacket and wallet.

'I will ask around in case anyone's gone rogue and needs

reining in. I presume you understand what my asking around means?'

Freddy stayed where he was as Elias got up. It wasn't a good plan to be seen leaving together – he imagined Elias was under some kind of surveillance.

'That I owe you. Which I expected. As long as you don't expect too much from that.'

Elias left with a smile which Freddy knew was meant to be unsettling. It worked, but he was more concerned with the information Elias might be able to provide than the possible cost of it.

And now I know something about Brack which might one day be useful too.

Freddy sat in the bar for another half hour, nursing a drink that had gone warm and flat. He wasn't sure where the meeting had left him, except for probably discounting the only theory that he had. And getting a lead on gang involvement hadn't, if he was honest, been his only motive for the meeting. He had also come wanting to share the hardest days of his life with a man who had lived through them in the same way, and yet, for all his efforts, he still felt empty. He had followed Elias's lead, skating over his last days in Buchenwald in exactly the same way Elias had skimmed over the worst of the death march. All the things he had wanted to say – 'Do you remember the raging thirst, the way we had to soak up rainwater from our shirts and suck at it? Do you remember the agony of hunger and then being so afraid that the first plate of food after liberation could kill you because your stomach had shrunk so much? Do you remember the moment when they said you were free, that no one was going to send you to a gas chamber? Did you believe them?' – had all gone unsaid.

And isn't that the truth? That more will always go unsaid and the ghosts will never settle.

It was a hard thought – and a lonely one.

.   .   .

By the time Freddy arrived back at the station, he was regretting not going straight home instead – he was far too drained for the mountain of paperwork he had been intending to tackle. And then, as he dithered on the corner, trying to persuade himself that an early start tomorrow would accomplish more than a begrudged hour today, the instincts which had got him safely through Mitte kicked back in. There was someone coming down the steps from the station who he hadn't expected to see.

Freddy slipped into a doorway which gave him a clear view.

His suspicions were right – the figure was Oli. That was unexpected but not, he reasoned, particularly strange – Freddy wasn't the only detective based in Kreuzberg who used Oli's services. What worried him wasn't the boy or what he was doing there – Oli did what Oli did and there was never any point in questioning it. What was worrying Freddy was that the person running after him, calling him back, her eyes dark smudges in her colourless face, was Hanni.

CHAPTER 8

9 SEPTEMBER 1948

'The last report estimated the crowd at over two hundred thousand already, and there's another hour to go before Reuter speaks. The mood seems reasonable so far, but – if the Soviets have infiltrated the crowd in the numbers our intelligence suspects – things could turn ugly very quickly. I know Hanni isn't going there on police business, but I think it's best that she travels with you.'

Matz hadn't left Freddy any choice, and he had virtually pushed Hanni into the back of the car when she had tried to argue with him.

Alone in a car with Freddy was not a place Hanni would have chosen to be. They had had some of their worst conversations and their most awkward silences in the back of a police Maybach, and nothing about today felt like it was going to go well. Freddy had been frowning at her since she had arrived at the station to retrieve her spare lens and she was in no mood to ask him why, or to have him tell her. Her head was full of *if onlys* and there wasn't one of those she could share with Freddy.

The list of them felt endless. If only she had accepted that she was too shaken to be around anyone and had turned down Tony's request to photograph him at the protest. If only she hadn't been so distracted by Oli's revelations that she had remembered all her equipment and not had to go to the station and let Matz take charge. If only the event she was scheduled to cover was another Tempelhof press conference she could easily duck out of. And the one from which everything else led: if only she hadn't gone searching for Reiner and had let the past go instead…

Her head was bursting. With regrets and with the realisation that, on an ordinary day, she would have been running towards the rally that was causing Matz so much anxiety, not hoping that the car taking her and Freddy to it would never make it through the packed streets.

The protest that they were heading to had been brewing for weeks. Both sides of Berlin were angry, both sides were squaring up for a fight. After ten weeks of the blockade hadn't broken the city, the Soviets had decided to flex their military muscles and the Allies were sick of it.

Soviet tanks had appeared along the borders of the Russian sector, with their noses pointing towards Wedding and the Tiergarten and the nervous West Berliners who were forced to hurry past them. Soviet military police had begun crossing into the west on an almost daily basis. A riot had broken out at Potsdamer Platz when Red Army soldiers appeared at the black market. Rubble had been thrown, shots had been fired. The Americans and the British had put up barriers. The Soviets had taken them down again. The city was on edge, and winter was close. People were starting to believe the Soviet propaganda that said they would starve when the snows came, or that another war was imminent. And Berlin's anti-Communist City Council – which was comprised entirely of Germans and mattered a great deal to the citizens who had been finally allowed to vote for it – was under a concerted attack.

Carefully orchestrated mobs had marched out of the eastern sector and stopped the council sitting all summer. The Soviets had used their veto before the blockade to prevent Ernst Reuter from taking up his elected position as the city's mayor and that veto still stood. And now the popular Reuter – who had spent two years of the war in a concentration camp and loathed the forces of the right as much as he loathed the forces of the left – had called on his supporters to say 'enough'. Which they had, in a massive and organised wave of anger which had engulfed the streets around the ruins of the Reichstag.

Nobody had seen numbers massing on this scale in Berlin since the carefully choreographed military parades in the war. Normally, Hanni would have been in the thick of such a promising photo opportunity with her camera spinning. Not today. All Hanni cared about today was what she had learned on Monday night and then lost her whole week to: that Oli had located Reiner.

Oli had been his usual efficient and uninvolved self from the start of the job to the end of it. He had needed no persuasion to take it on when Hanni had told him how generously she would pay him. He hadn't been at all interested in the cover story she had come up with to explain why she was looking for Emil Foss. He had stopped her half a dozen words into that with a dismissive, 'I don't care who he is as long as there's money.' Then he had disappeared with no word and Hanni's nerves had shredded.

Hanni was nervous not only because she had previous experience of hunting Reiner down but because she had been caught out by her father before. She knew the speed such a dangerous undertaking required so the last thing she needed to do was give Reiner enough time to realise he was under surveillance. When it came to Oli, however, worrying was all she could do. In the end, Oli had reappeared, as he always did, in his own good time, but thankfully what he had achieved was worth the nail-biting wait. He had not only managed to winkle out Reiner's home address, he had uncovered the answer to the question which had been troubling Hanni for almost two years: why her father had presented himself to the British at the end of the war as an expert on education.

'He's doing what? Tell me that again.'

Hanni had listened to everything Oli told her, but she hadn't been able to take in what he said. Oli, unfortunately, was not a boy who liked to repeat himself. He didn't answer – he left the instant his message was delivered. Which meant Hanni had had to run out of the station after him to make sure she had understood it correctly.

'I've told you: it looks like he's setting up a school. I saw a classroom through a window. I've given you the address – go and look for yourself if you don't believe me. Or pay me some more and lend me a camera and I'll go back and take pictures myself.'

Hanni had said no to that – the risk of what else Oli might uncover, and link back to her, was too great – but she couldn't leave it alone. Instead, Hanni had done what Oli had suggested and had gone to the address herself. What she had found there was a school, exactly as Oli had promised, but it was also much more.

And I wish I hadn't found it or worked out what it meant.

Of all the *if only*s, Hanni definitely couldn't tell Freddy that one. Except, as she sat as far away from him in the car as she could – illogically convinced that he might somehow sense Reiner pushing his way into the air around her – the school and what it meant was all she could think about.

The location Oli had given Hanni was for a house situated among the colony of villas which stretched out along the lake shore at Wannsee. Wannsee – an area on the south-west side of the city which was famous for its lakes – was one of Berlin's most elegant neighbourhoods. It was also as full of dark memories for Hanni as Tempelhof had been.

Once upon a time, Hanni would have been ferried to whichever home was hosting her family there in the back of a black swastika-crested Mercedes. She would have been dressed in satin and silk and sporting delicate shoes that weren't meant for walking in. This time, she had caught the train from Anhalter Bahnhof clad in sturdy ankle boots and the kind of loose trousers which hikers favoured. The change of clothes made it no easier to go back.

Anhalter had been as busy as it always was, but, by the time she arrived at the smaller suburban station, Hanni had been the only passenger left in the carriage. It was too early in the day for walkers and too late in the season for the bathers who flocked to the area in the summer months, and she had seen no one else as she headed towards the water. She had taken that for the good omen she was desperate to find.

Am Großen Wannsee itself had been deserted. Hanni had hurried down the long road which bordered the lake trying not to look at the sprawling houses where she had sipped tea with her father's colleagues. Where – in 1940 when she was seventeen – she had tasted her first glass of champagne. Now the thought that she had ever celebrated anything in the company of men like those and in a street like this left a bitter taste in her mouth not even the smoothest champagne could dissolve. In 1940, there was hardly a house along the shoreline which didn't belong to a Nazi Party grandee. The Villa Marlier at its farthest end had played host to the Wannsee Conference, where, according to rumour, the decision to wipe Europe's Jews from the world had been taken. It was a street thick with secrets Hanni assumed its current residents pretended not to know. The further along its length she had walked, the harder those secrets had pressed on her.

The villa Oli had identified as being Reiner's school was tucked back from the road behind high padlocked gates. It was impossibly picturesque, more like a castle from a fairy tale than a building that could be sheltering Nazis. Wide stone steps flanked by winged lions led up to a building which was a hotchpotch of turrets picked out in red bricks and greenish grey slate. The house was surrounded by a mini forest of trees, and an ivy-covered fountain sat between the entrance and the main gate. It looked like the kind of place where Rapunzel would let down her hair. There had, thankfully, been no sign of life. There had also been no obvious way in.

Hanni had walked past the villa on the opposite side of the street, resisting the urge to linger – she had learned long ago that, when it came to Reiner, no one being visible did not mean that no one was watching. Thankfully, one more block along, she had spotted the small lane Oli had told her led to the lakeshore and the back of the property and had slipped quickly down it. Both the houses which stood between her and her goal had gardens which bordered the shore, but there was a narrow path circling round them and no boats bobbing near or anyone sitting on the lawns who might see her hurry by.

If I find a way in and he is there...

Hanni hadn't dwelt on that thought. If she managed to get in and Reiner was there, she knew that there was little chance that she would come out again. She had carried on, hugging the hedges which kept the houses aloof until she came to the wall of leaves bordering his villa.

The hedge was high and thick but it wasn't solid. There were gaps wide enough for someone as determined as she was to squeeze through. Navigating them had taken a few tangled moments while the twigs tugged at her hair and snagged at her clothes, but she did it. The lawn she stepped onto was overgrown, the rear of the house far less tidy than its front. Hanni had crouched down and snaked her way round to the building's closest edge. There was no movement; there were no lights on. And there had been one ground-floor window which wasn't properly latched. Hanni had pushed it open, hauled herself over the sill and then she had curled into a ball and listened.

The house had stayed totally silent. Hanni had still waited until her pulse settled and her breathing steadied before she began to explore.

Once she started to move along its empty corridors, it soon

became clear that Oli had been right – the house was a school, but it was a school in waiting. The classrooms were set up with desks and chairs, but not all of them were finished: some of the black-boards were still shrouded in paint-spattered sheets; some of the walls needed a last coat of paint. It wasn't ready for its students to come yet, but when they did... Hanni had moved from one room to the next feeling increasingly sick. The pupils weren't there, but, in the rooms where the posters were hung and the textbooks were waiting, the nature of the place was all too apparent. Reiner had set up a Hitler School.

The signs had been unmistakeable. Hanni had only been in a building of that type once before – when Reiner had been invited to preside over a prize-giving and taken his family with him – but she knew from that visit how they looked and how they felt. Adolf Hitler Schools had been one of the pinnacles of the Nazi education system. They were soaked in Party ideology, designed to create the future leaders of the Thousand Year Reich. The chil-dren who attended them were blonde haired and blue eyed and 'racially pure' and they fought hard to win their places. The education they received was militarily based and grounded in the principals of National Socialism. And it was grounded more than anything in hate.

Their vision of the future is a long way from mine.

Hanni had crept from classroom to classroom, her camera clicking, her father's words from the very different school where she had last met him running through her head. Cataloguing what she saw and trying not to freeze at the horror of it. Wondering if this place was one on its own or whether Reiner's ambitions ran wide and it was only the first of many.

She had photographed the charts already pinned on the walls; she had photographed the textbooks stacked on the shelves. The posters were ones she remembered all too vividly from her own classrooms: *The German Student Fights for the Führer and the People; Portraits of True German Races; The Nuremburg Laws Explained.* The books had been published after she had finished her education.

Hanni had thumbed through a handful of those. The history texts had twisted their timelines to put Germany at the centre of the world's past and its future. The 'social arithmetic' primers required students to compare the cost of keeping a 'disabled' and a 'healthy' child alive and rewarded only one conclusion as right. The biology texts found every race except 'pure Germans' wanting. Those were difficult enough to stomach, but then Hanni had opened a copy of a picture book entitled *The Poisoned Mushroom* and two pages in she had burst into tears.

The opening illustration of a mother and a child gathering mushrooms in a sun-dappled forest was beautifully drawn but the text which came after that was sewn through with evil. 'There are poisonous bad mushrooms and there are bad people… do you know who those bad men, these poisonous mushrooms of mankind are… they are the Jews.'

On and on the message went, in a series of short stories which heaped every crime the author could think of at the feet of the world's Jewish population and in a series of illustrations which grew progressively more hideous and hook-nosed.

He's going to teach this filth to another generation. And he's going to turn another generation into 'us' and 'them'.

Hanni had taken refuge behind her lens after that discovery. Filling film after film, trying not to think about Freddy stumbling over such a hate-filled building or about the kind of families who would send their children to study at it. Each room had contained the same vitriol. Each had also had a cupboard filled with the newer textbooks the Americans were frantically printing and a collection of far more anodyne posters ready to jump into place if they were needed.

If anyone ever comes here to check, he will cover all the cruelties with a false face exactly as he did at Theresienstadt.

Reiner was in every fibre of the building – Hanni could sense it. And yet, she could not, no matter how hard she tried, find a single physical trace of him. There were no pictures of the teachers or the school's founders. There were no registers filled with staff or pupil names. The only thing Hanni managed to uncover was a list of surnames stowed away in a bottom drawer, two of which she had recognised as being from the British Education delegation who had been so impressed with her father at the Heesestraße visit. Nothing beyond their last names was noted and there was no mention of an Emil, or a Reiner, on that paper or on anything else. In the end, her churning stomach as much as the fading light had forced her to stop searching. She left the way she came in, with three rolls of film full of evidence and no proof of her father.

She had no memory of the train journey back into the city. And she still had no idea what to do with the images she had gathered, beyond the certainty that they couldn't slip through her fingers the way damning images of Reiner had in the past. That these had to be the ones she would send out into the world to stop him.

'We're here.'

Hanni jerked back into the present as Freddy spoke, with no idea of where here was.

'Are you all right? You've been locked up in yourself since we got into the car.'

She nodded without looking at him and got out before he could quiz her any closer. Here turned out to be halfway down Sommerstraße where the car had ground to a halt on the edge of the Platz der Republik.

The scale of the protest was astounding. Even the parade stage-managed by Goebbels when Hitler took power and which Hanni had witnessed as a child paled into insignificance. The Platz was a sea of people wedged elbow to elbow without a space between them, and still more were coming. The noise was overwhelming. Voices soared. Cheers in support of Reuter competed with roars of protest against the Soviets and the blockade, and all of that competed with the songs which sprang up from every corner and clashed in the middle. The mood seemed to be as even-tempered as Matz had hoped it would be, but there was a brittleness to the crowd as people pushed and shoved which made Hanni wary of diving into it, even if she could have found a way in.

The wall of backs was impossible to penetrate and impossible to see over. Hanni could barely make out the platform which had been erected in front of the broken and blackened shell of the Reichstag and from where Ernst Reuter and the other speakers would address the crowds. The building – where the German parliament had once sat – had been gutted in 1933 by a fire which Hitler had blamed on the Communist Party and the Communist Party had blamed on Hitler. It was a heavily nuanced choice of venue for an anti-Soviet rally, as Freddy clearly enjoyed pointing out. Hanni couldn't focus on that. She had been due to meet Tony outside the equally ruined Kroll Opera House and she wanted to meet him alone. She couldn't see a path through to that either.

'This is pointless. I won't be able to find Tony, and even if I do, there's no chance of him getting close to Reuter, which I assume is the photo opportunity he was hoping for – not that he's explained what he wants yet. I might as well take some crowd shots and be done with it.'

Freddy waved the driver away before the car got too hemmed in to leave and frowned at her.

'Really? You're a photographer and you want to walk away from something as historic as this with a few crowd shots? Are you sure there isn't something bothering you?'

He knows I've been using Oli.

Hanni didn't know where that thought had flown in from but it stuck.

She shook her head and was about to pretend that she had seen Tony and give Freddy the slip, but he was already ahead of her.

'Fine, if that's how you want to play it, but I think you'll be sorry to miss this. We can get round the edge if we're careful, so why don't we try? I need to walk the perimeter anyway – if there are troublemakers, that's where they'll congregate, ready to sweep in and out.'

He held out his hand and sighed when Hanni wouldn't take it.

'Don't be silly, Hanni. I don't need you disappearing into this and then Matz giving me grief. It's a safety measure: I don't mean anything by it.'

It was a reasonable point, and he sounded as if he meant it. That didn't make it any easier for her to touch him or – Hanni suspected – for him to touch her. She took hold of his fingers as lightly as she could and they began to wind their way around the fringes of the packed square, moving as one and feeling, at least on her part, hopelessly separate.

I can still pretend that I've seen Tony and then duck away.

Unfortunately, Hanni lacked Freddy's height and he was ahead of her there too.

'Oh, here we go, there he is. Matz's description of the gallant captain really was spot on. Look at him standing there in that uniform as if everyone loves it. I don't know whether to go and hail the fearless hero or arrest him for making himself so easy to spot in such a vulnerable place.'

Hanni saw Tony a second after Freddy's sneering pointed him out. He was surrounded, as usual, by grinning little boys and adoring women, and he looked, as he always did, immaculate.

He doesn't look real. All the other pilots I've seen at Tempelhof are grey with exhaustion and he's blooming. It's as if he moves round followed by make-up and lighting.

Hanni kept that thought to herself. Freddy was still working himself up – he didn't need extra fuel.

'Doesn't he understand what a target he is? And I don't mean for fluttering eyelashes. If there's a Soviet snatch squad anywhere close, they'll be all over him.'

His tone confirmed what Hanni was already afraid of: that a meeting between the two men – an encounter she hadn't wanted to happen in the first place – would not go well. She instinctively dropped Freddy's hand, but not before Tony had noticed her and that she was holding it. His expression shifted to a broad smile in seconds, but the hesitation, and the appraisal, which went before he readjusted did not escape her – or Freddy.

'I thought you two were just friends. He's glaring at me the way Natan did when I came to see you that time in the studio.'

The mention of Natan moved Hanni away from Freddy's side quicker than any irritation on Tony's part could have done. Natan Stein – the son of Ezra Stein, the man who had given Hanni her first camera and then had died at the hands of the Nazis – was the one person in Berlin other than Reiner who knew Hanni's true identity. He had loved her once and then, from the moment Hanni had told him the truth of her past, because that was what she owed him, he had hated her. His reaction was one of the reasons she had never dared tell her true story to Freddy. And it was the memory of the awful day when she had broken Natan's heart – or, more accurately, the fear of history repeating itself with Freddy – which now made her snap.

'Don't be ridiculous. You're imagining things. We're friends; we're barely even that. I'm here to do a job and, if you don't mind, I'd like to get on with it. You can go. You can tell Matz that you did your duty like he wanted and I'm fine.'

Freddy's face was as rigid as hers, but Tony was already on his way over with his beam back in place and his hand outstretched.

'I am guessing you must be Detective Inspector Schlüssel. Hanni has told me a great deal about you. It's a pleasure to finally meet up.'

Hanni had told Tony almost nothing about Freddy at all beyond his name and his job and she didn't understand why Tony would pretend otherwise. Rather than stirring anything up by asking, she decided that it was best all round to say nothing and to try and get the day done with. If Tony wanted to launch a charm offensive against Freddy, she wasn't going to stop him.

Not that Tony's efforts showed the slightest sign of working:

Freddy was already making it perfectly clear that he wasn't there to be won over. His smile and his handshake were as fleeting as Tony's attempts at friendliness had been overstated.

Hanni – who had no desire to be pushed by either of them into the role of referee – unpacked her camera and gestured to some of the children who were milling around to form into a group.

'I don't know if you wanted a picture taken with Reuter, but it won't be possible. Are you happy if I grab a few shots of you and the protesters instead?'

'Whatever you can get will be perfect.'

Tony was already in position, with his hand on the shoulder of a furiously grinning little boy. Freddy was still frowning.

'What's so important about you being here today, Captain? You do realise that there are Soviet agents in among the protesters, don't you? And that if they were to kidnap you – which they very well might try given that you are a little, shall we say, obvious – we could end up with a serious diplomatic incident?'

Tony's smile didn't falter. 'I'm sure you're over-worrying, Inspector. As to what I'm doing here, there's no great agenda on my part. I'm not here for the limelight or to make speeches. I simply wanted to show my support as an American who's proud to be helping your city. I can't see that any harm will come from that. I'm sure the Soviets have far more pressing issues than me to deal with today.'

His tone was silken, but it didn't soften Freddy. Hanni winced as his face tightened. She could see Freddy's temper beginning to fray, but she wasn't going to be pushed to take sides. Or to acknowledge that there might be a jealousy involved on Freddy's part she did not know how to deal with. She waved the camera at a couple of girls who were staring wide-eyed at Tony and made an encouraging sign for them to come over.

'Tony, perhaps you could stand—'

She didn't get halfway through the sentence before Freddy spoke over her.

'What are you collecting? The phone numbers of every woman here?'

He was staring at Tony's hand and the pieces of paper folded into it.

Tony's smile disappeared. His face changed from charming to clenched.

He looks cornered; he looks dangerous.

His reaction to Freddy's needling made no sense, but Hanni instinctively raised her camera and snapped it anyway. Not that Tony appeared to notice: his whole attention was focused on Freddy.

'Would that be a problem for you if I was, Inspector?'

His voice was no louder than it had been a moment before, but there was a jagged edge to it. Hanni saw Freddy note that in the tiny pause before he shrugged.

'I don't know. Maybe there would be for their boyfriends – or for their fathers. Not everyone is as comfortable with your countrymen as you would like us to be. Not so many years have passed since the relationship between us was a very different one.'

Hanni couldn't decide if Freddy was being hostile or offering Tony a genuine warning to take better care of himself. She doubted Tony could either, but he switched his smile back on as if he did.

'Well, that is very chivalrous of you, Inspector. I like a man who steps up to protect his countrywomen's honour. But you have no need to worry.' He glanced at the scribbled-on slips and tucked them into his pocket. 'These aren't love notes – quite the opposite. They are requests for help, for work at the base mostly. I get given them all the time, even though I make it clear that there's little I can do.'

He stopped and turned and deliberately included Hanni in the conversation.

'Besides, why would I want to collect the telephone numbers

of anyone else when the prettiest girl in Berlin is standing right here?'

It wasn't until Hanni saw Freddy's frown that she registered that Tony's prettiest girl was her. She stared at him, momentarily lost for words. She didn't want him to refer to her so intimately in front of Freddy, and she couldn't think why he would, particularly given how embarrassingly their last meeting had ended. The memory of that suddenly flooded back and made her blush.

Freddy stepped away, his hands raised in mock surrender. 'So that's how it goes. Forgive me. And I'll take it as my cue to leave.'

He was gone before Hanni could call him back. But not before he cast a glance at her which made Hanni's heart ache. She could have cursed herself for the stupidity of her reaction: the disappointment in his eyes as her cheeks flared had bitten worse than sharp words could have done.

She rounded on Tony, ready to take him to task, but it was too late to say anything. Reuter had appeared on the stage, the cheers were deafening, and Tony was back in role again, hoisting children onto his shoulders, hugging a woman waving a German flag, demanding that Hanni take pictures of every pose that he struck.

She spent the next hour following Tony around the edge of the packed square. He didn't say anything else she could take exception to – he treated her completely professionally. In the end, she decided that *prettiest girl in Berlin* had stemmed solely from his need to prove himself to Freddy and had very little to do with her. What intrigued Hanni more was the cornered look she had seen flood Tony's face. She began watching him closely, rather than aimlessly snapping. She didn't manage to take another shot as candid as the one she had stolen when Freddy had challenged him, but, now she knew that the possibility of those shots existed, her camera came back to life.

It was becoming increasingly obvious that there was more to Tony than the two-dimensional persona he preferred people to see. Although Hanni knew that the last thing she needed was more men in her life with secrets, knowing Tony had some of his own immediately made him a far more interesting subject. So she followed him and she took all the shots that he wanted with a smile on her face as pleasant as his. And when he asked her if she might like to finish the day once again with a drink, Hanni was intrigued enough to say yes. And to suggest the perfect place they should go.

CHAPTER 9

10 SEPTEMBER 1948

He had slept the whole night.

Tony blinked and stretched and checked his watch. Seven forty-five. Eight peaceful hours of uninterrupted sleep: he couldn't remember the last time he had managed that.

He got out of bed, wandered into his apartment's functional kitchen and pulled out the jar of Nescafé which would buy him a new suit if he took it to the black market. He switched on the radio as the nutty scent of the coffee filled the air. AFN Berlin – the American Forces Network – was playing its usual early-morning mix of honey-toned crooners: Perry Como, Bing Crosby, Vaughn Monroe. Tony sipped his coffee and let the music wash over him. Eight hours sleeping and, before that, a job well done. He had found peace and he had found it for even longer than last time, and that was all due to Falco Hauke. He had proved to be another well-chosen and excellent target, as perfect for the role Tony had allocated to him as Edda Sauerbrunn had been.

Tony had been prepared to spend weeks if he needed, getting his second subject right. In the end, it had taken him almost no time at all. When Tony had first seen Falco loading crates onto a pallet at Tempelhof, he had thought for a moment that he was looking at his father's twin brother. The resemblance between the middle-aged German cargo worker and Tony's last memory of Elkan had been as close as the one between Edda and Elene. The two men's ages and colouring were an obvious match, but it was more than that: the similarity in the way that they walked and shrugged and tapped their chins before speaking was almost uncanny.

Tony had stopped going through his possibilities that same night and had put his efforts instead into befriending Falco. That had proved to be as straightforward as the discovery.

Falco was in awe of the gangs who had inserted themselves through Tempelhof's supply lines and was desperate to prove that he had the right connections to be a valuable cog. All it had taken to win Falco's trust and to get Tony inside his flat was a carton of Lucky Strike cigarettes and a hint that other stocks could follow on a regular basis.

'If you can get more, bring them round to my flat any Thursday night, any time before twelve. My wife and daughters are always out then, visiting relatives until late.'

He had made the process almost insultingly easy. A warm welcome guaranteed and any Thursday on offer. And then the Reichstag protest – which was a perfect opportunity for the kind of personal appearance and adulation which Tony revelled in and which always filled him with adrenaline – was announced for a Thursday and everything had fallen into place.

Falco had almost doubled in size with delight when Tony knocked on his door. He had got out his 'best beer – the really good stuff' and acted as if they were going into business together. He had still been talking about how impressed the gang leaders would be with him when Tony slipped the cord round his throat and tightened it. The look on his face had been one of surprise more than fear.

Tony let the memory fizz through his blood. Then he refilled his coffee cup and opened the kitchen cupboard where his family photograph was safely stowed behind an unopened box of Rice Krispies. He had been too tired the previous night to finish the last part of the task. Now he needed to enter Falco's name on the back of the picture, beside Edda Sauerbrunn's, with a *V* for *Vater* inscribed next to it, and to mark a small tick above Elkan's face on the front. That done, he spent a few moments quietly looking at the image itself, at his parents who were now, finally, properly honoured. He had done well. No, he had done better than that: by any measure, his plan was working.

I should go back to the club. I should drink a toast to Falco and cele-brate his sacrifice.

And with that one simple thought, his contented mood shat-tered. He couldn't think about the club without thinking about Hanni, and he couldn't think about Hanni without thinking about Freddy Schlüssel, and he didn't want to think about either of them.

'Can we go to the base? I would so love to see a real American bar and you must have one there.'

Hanni's response to his suggestion that the two of them go for a drink had thrown Tony uncomfortably off course. Despite his reservations about the impulsive way she had kissed him, Tony had wanted to see Hanni alone again and not entirely because of the jealousy that had poured off the arrogant inspector when he had referred to her as pretty. What he had not wanted, however, was to bring Hanni anywhere near the airbase or to spend too much of the evening together. The airbase was far too close to his life, and it involved an additional journey the rest of his plans didn't need. Unfortunately, he hadn't been able to think of a reason why they couldn't go there, and Tony hadn't wanted to upset Hanni – not once he'd sensed how much she mattered to Freddy.

Tony's reasons for asking Hanni to accompany him to the protest had been guided by professional rather than personal need: the photographs she took were an essential part of his research. Tony had developed a system and it was serving him well. He collected copies of Hanni's pictures and he collected the names that were thrust at him, scribbling notes on the back which described any identifying features. And then he compared his treasure trove to his family photograph. It was a method of matching relative to victim that he was happy to carry on working with, as long as Hanni stayed manageable. Whatever else the kiss had been, it hadn't fitted his definition of manageable, but he had decided, on balance, to forgive her for that. And then she had appeared at the Reichstag with Freddy Schlüssel in tow and Tony – for no reason he could put his finger on – had scented danger.

The dislike which had sprung into life from the moment the two men met had been mutual. Tony knew exactly what Freddy had seen: an overprivileged American with no interest in Berlin except what he could take from it. As for his part, he had decided as soon as Freddy opened his mouth that the inspector was full of himself and overbearing and far too sharp-eyed. The scraps of paper Tony had collected from his well-wishers – the main point of him being at the protest, no matter what he pretended about showing support – and the way Freddy had pounced on those, was a case in point. Tony was satisfied that his explanation about helping out people who were in straitened circumstance was not only a plausible one, it had painted him in a good light. He was also aware that he had hesitated before giving it and that his anger had flared, and Freddy had pounced on that too. Pounced and filed it away. That could have been a concern – Tony didn't like anyone taking any personal interest in him – but it wasn't. Tony had also filed something interesting away about Freddy: that the inspector was quite hopelessly in love with Hanni.

That knowledge had proved to be very useful in deflecting Freddy's interest in him. Especially when Hanni had blushed like a schoolgirl when Tony had decided to imply – purely in order to test out Freddy's reactions – that their relationship had taken a more personal turn. Hanni's blush had hurt Freddy, and Tony was very happy with that. It gave him a potential weapon.

Tony had a job to do in Berlin and he had no intention of getting caught doing it. He was not, however, fool enough to imagine that getting caught could never happen. At some point, if it was ever to come to a showdown between him and the inspector, Freddy's feelings about Hanni could give Tony the upper hand. It was a weakness, and Tony thrived on weakness, so he had invited her for a drink to find out what he could about the relationship. He wasn't so sure anymore that he had done the right thing.

Tony grabbed the coffee pot and poured himself a third cup. When he had extended the invitation, it had seemed like a sensible plan. Apart from the other considerations, Hanni was the kind of pretty girl he was more than happy to be seen with. He had also, more importantly, witnessed how quickly she got drunk. He had expected it to be a very quick and simple thing to extract all the information he wanted on Freddy. Hanni's request to visit the Dahlem base had, it was true, wrong-footed him, but Tony had quickly overcome that. He had risen to the challenge instead, carrying out her wishes with a style he had been certain would wrong-foot her.

Tony had taken Hanni to the most elegant establishment on the base, the Officers' Club at Harnack House. Hanni – as he knew that she would be – had been utterly smitten with the building's red and white grandeur and the almost absurdly all-American feel of its Green Fiddler sports bar. His plan had been to buy her a very strong cocktail, get the information that he wanted and then send her back into town on the train before the evening could slide on too long. Or towards a romantic ending Tony wasn't yet sure he could fully control.

His plan had started well. He had ordered her a Manhattan – the most iconic drink he could think of – and had made sure she had a cocktail stick full of cherries. She had taken a sip and grinned. And then Hanni had played him. She was a far more controlled drinker than she had led him to believe – and she was a magnet for a crowd. Within ten minutes of the two of them entering the place, her laughter and her looks had made her the queen of the club. Men Tony had never socialised with before flocked to their table to claim his friendship, and to make Hanni's.

It had been pleasant enough, for a while, to be in her company. But then the clock had started ticking and Tony hadn't been able to turn the conversation back to Freddy or see any sign that Hanni was growing tipsy enough for him to try. The cocktail he had asked the barman to make particularly strong had made no impression on her. It appeared that Hanni preferred holding the glass's thin crystal stem and playing with its cherry-laden stick, rather than actually drinking.

In the end, the time he had to play the devoted attendant had run out and Tony had begun trying to manoeuvre the evening to a close. Just as he had been suggesting, however, that Hanni might need to think about train times, a far too familiar face – and a far too loud voice – had loomed in and stopped him.

'Tony Miller, there's a sight for sore eyes and wouldn't your wife be a better one? How is she? My Rose has been trying to contact her for months and not one letter's been answered. Where have you hidden her?'

The man with the booming voice was Alex Zielinkski, a fellow pilot from Tony's days in the Eighth Air Force. A colleague who remembered Nancy from the press junket days in New York and remembered that she and Tony had married at the end of the war. He was the last person Tony had wanted to see, especially with Hanni's too-bright eyes fixed on him.

Tony had tried to fend Zielinkski off, but he wouldn't take the hint. He was too full of what a delight Nancy was and then he was too full of knowing grins at Hanni and vulgar winks and a 'Don't worry, I won't go telling tales on you', which made Tony's palm itch.

Hanni hadn't reacted to any of it, although Tony knew she hadn't missed a single moment of the exchange. She had continued to smile. She had pronounced it a shame when Tony had explained that his marriage had failed and that he and Nancy had grown too distant to pretend that they were going to stay friends. She hadn't asked him any questions, but Tony had seen her making mental notes the way Freddy had done. It had felt uncomfortably as if there was a police presence in the room. He had been very relieved when Hanni had decided for herself that it was time to cut their date short.

Tony got up again. He was restless, the coffee and Hanni suddenly too rich for his blood. He went back to the sitting room and collected the packet of names and addresses which was a lot thicker now than it had been before his trip to the Reichstag. He was being overimaginative – he knew that. Hanni was a photographer and she worked for the police: that meant that she liked detail, not that she knew how to piece together an undertaking that was very well hidden. And his old flying colleague was a fool who had never been possessed of the brains to join together even the closest of dots. Plenty of men divorced their wives. Plenty of those wives fell out of touch. Nobody would actually go looking for Nancy. She wasn't the problem anymore. Hanni was.

Tony had kissed her again, standing on the steps of the deserted train station he had walked her back to. He hadn't intended to do that. He had intended to say goodbye and pretend to leave and then catch the next train back into town himself and deal with Falco, but the air was silent and the moon was full and he hadn't been able to resist pulling her into his arms. This time Hanni was the one who had pulled away first and was immediately gone. Tony was left standing on the platform, wondering what had just happened.

The kiss had almost cost him the rest of the night. That he had wanted her so strongly had unnerved him. There had been a brief moment when he had felt vulnerable. When the confusion she had stirred up had almost overwhelmed him. Then he had woken up and anger had struck him so hard his head had started spinning for very different reasons. If he hadn't already made a plan of the order he was following and he hadn't already selected his target, he would have run after her. His target would have turned into Hanni. And yet, once again, somehow, he had stuck firm to his course and held back.

Maybe it's time to stop doing that. Maybe I don't need her camera anymore, not with the way the whole city now welcomes me in.

Tony picked up the photograph and began scanning the women captured in it – his sister and his aunts who he hadn't yet found a match for. Hanni had unsettled him, and that wasn't a state of mind he was prepared to endure. Perhaps it was finally the moment to stop delaying the inevitable and deal with her.

He took his time with the picture, poring over the women's hairstyles and the tilt of their heads, squinting at the shape of their eyes; searching for a resemblance. He couldn't find it. There was a set of lips that looked very much like Hanni's, but then he remembered her scent and her softness and the feel of her kiss, and the lips turned too thin and too pale to be hers.

Tony put the photograph down; he made himself stop looking. There was no need to hurry, to go hunting for resemblances that didn't exist. There would be a time for Hanni, he was certain of that. Its moment simply hadn't come.

CHAPTER 10

3–10 NOVEMBER 1948

Four bodies. How can there be four bodies? And how can it be the same man when the victims are so different?

Freddy rubbed his aching eyes, put the crime-scene photographs down and went back to the profiles of the men and women who had been killed. He had already been through them a dozen times, but now he read them again, searching for the clues he had to have missed. There was still nothing there beyond a list of people who had died in their homes for no obvious reason. Edda Sauerbrunn, fifty-one; school cook. Falco Hauke, fifty-four; airport worker. Matilda Scheibel, known as Matty, twenty years old; trainee teacher. Linus Spahn, eighteen…

He gave up and put the notes down too. He was exhausted with obsessing over details that refused to tell him a thing. All four had been killed in their own living rooms. All four had been found by family members who would never get over the shock of it. All four of the murders were tragedies. It was Linus's age, however, that kept hitting Freddy the hardest. There was nothing against his name in the column marked 'occupation' – and how could there be? Who was anybody at eighteen? The boy had barely started living.

He was the same age as Leo, who never got a chance to start living either.

The faces in front of Freddy began to swim and swap over. Edda and Falco could have been his own parents; Linus could have been his younger brother. Their religions were different, but their backgrounds and their ages were almost a match.

Or the ages they were when I last saw them.

Freddy gripped the arms of his chair as Rosa and Jakub and Leo started to push against the place deep inside him where they were supposed to stay buried.

Thank God there hasn't been a little girl like Renny among the bodies or I would be finished.

He forced himself to focus on the faces of the victims again, reminding himself who had actually died. He couldn't let his own lost ones come, not here. He had to have one space where he was safe from them, where his thinking stayed clear. Unfortunately, keeping them away was getting harder to do. Alone in his room, in the long waking hours of the night, he couldn't control his memories anymore; he couldn't hold them back. And if there was anyone responsible for their return, it was Elias. Freddy knew that wasn't fair, but Freddy didn't care about fair. What he cared about was having someone else to blame but himself for his carefully constructed walls collapsing.

In the immediate aftermath of the war, Freddy had walked everywhere side by side with his ghosts. There had been days when they were more real than the people actually surrounding him. In the end, that had almost derailed him, so – with a lot of time and a lot of pain and a lot of practice – Freddy had learned to control the mess the war had made of his life and to lock his family away as deeply as he had done with Buchenwald. He didn't talk about them; he tried not to think about them. He had been doing remarkably well with that – apart from the pieces of the past he had spilled out to Hanni. His repeated meetings with Elias, however, had stirred up his phantoms again, and they were vivid.

Freddy, not that he had told anyone, had stayed in touch with Elias after their first meeting. He had contacted him after each murder, trying to establish whether his theory about gang involvement carried any weight. He had thought it might actually be true in the case of Falco Hauke, who worked at Tempelhof and was known to try and court its criminal edges. The theory crashed, however, with Matty Scheibel. Freddy couldn't believe that she had any links to the Ringvereine and neither could Elias.

'We rarely kill men and we don't kill women – I told you that with the cook. And we wouldn't kill a respectable young one like her; she would never cross our path. And as for strangling...' Elias had shrugged at that as if it was unthinkable. 'Sorry, Freddy, but I've asked around like I promised I would and the answer is always the same: if there's an overlap between these murders, or that boy on the street, and a gang member, then it's a coincidence, not a motive, and it's not something I can help you with.'

Freddy knew he was right. He also knew that he should have cut off contact with Elias at that point – Elias hadn't yet called in his debt, although Freddy knew that one day he would, and that was an uncomfortable axe to have hanging over him. The thought that he might be moving even fractionally into the same crooked corner of the world as the one Brack lived in made his skin crawl. Cutting contact with Elias, however, was easier said than done. After the first couple of transactional meetings were over, the two men – with the help of a bottle of schnapps – had found a way to stop talking about who ran the city and to begin actually talking.

The first bridge they had crossed was the one which led back to the camp. They came at that carefully. Neither of them tried to make sense of the time they had spent there – they were both too realistic to believe that could be done. Neither of them wanted to dwell on the detail of its horrors. What they did manage to share were the fears that continued to grip their nightmares and the lack of trust the experience had left them both labouring under. Elias admitted that he couldn't stop searching faces, looking for the guards who had beaten him and shot his companions on the death march. That he still plotted the revenge he would take if he ever found one of them. Freddy told Elias about the SS killer he had encountered the previous year who he hadn't been sure he wanted to convict. Both men grew a little lighter as their secrets unfolded.

That done, they crossed into the harder territory that was family and the fates of those who hadn't survived. Facing those – allowing themselves to acknowledge the reality of the trains and the ovens whose images wove through their dreams – had led to long silences and back to the schnapps. There was at least a sense of pain equally shared and equally felt.

Until Elias won.

Freddy hated himself for that thought every time that it hit him, but he couldn't stop thinking it.

'They didn't all die; they aren't all gone from me.'

A handful of words but every one of them bursting with a joy Freddy could only dream about.

Elias had struck the impossible seam. He had discovered that two of his cousins who had been given up for dead weren't lost after all but had finally found their exhausted way home from the Russian camps they had been imprisoned in. Freddy had cheered for Elias when he broke that news. Then he had gone home and howled like a child for himself.

Freddy had searched for his family, the same as everyone who was still standing at the end of the war had searched – for as long as he could fool himself that there was a chance that they were on their way back to him. He had haunted the train stations and the missing-persons boards which were crammed with peeling and fading photographs and lined every platform. He had haunted the offices of the overstretched and exhausted Red Cross. The workers there had done what he had asked them to do and given him the hope he needed to keep him alive. That was all they had managed. And then the hope had become worse than accepting the truth.

After a year of chasing after women whose feather-trimmed

hats reminded him of his mother, of being laughed at by teenage boys he desperately needed to be his brother. After a year of not even finding dead ends, Freddy had made himself stop pushing. But now, if Elias's dead could come back to life...

He shook himself back into the present. This was not his time. There were other families in more immediate pain than he was and they were the ones who deserved his attention.

Not that I've got anything to offer them.

Freddy closed the folders and turned the profile pictures over so that he no longer had to look at their accusing faces. He had spent every hour in the office and he still couldn't help them. He had no more to give the grieving relatives than the Red Cross workers had scraped up for him. And no matter how many different ways he came at it, nothing about the case made sense. None of the four victims were connected to each other in any way, except for the manner of their deaths and the laying out of their bodies. There was no pattern by age or by sex or profession or by any other measure that Freddy could think of to profile them, and there was always a pattern. Logic said that with such disparate victims, it couldn't be the same man.

And yet logic says that it has to be.

He looked out through the open door of his office to the larger room it led on to. It was too quiet. His team looked as grey as he felt. None of them were eating properly; none of them were sleeping. Never mind the demands of the case, they were all held hostage by the divisions the Allies and the Soviets had torn through Berlin and ground down by the physical effects of the blockade. If another loudmouth in a bar told Freddy that he had learned to sleep through the airlift and had no problems with the reduced food allowances, Freddy would punch him. Or drag him into the station to spend a day doing the kind of concentrated, detail-heavy work which nights interrupted by droning airplanes and days spent fighting grumbling stomachs had made twice as hard as it should be.

Five months of the blockade had reduced Berlin to a noise.

And to a permanently nagging hunger that soured even the gentlest temper. The Americans and the British could boast all they liked about the success of the airlift – as far as Freddy could see neither side ever missed an opportunity to do that. The rise in the volume of supplies being flown in did not change the fact that the stand-off still hadn't been broken.

The city was landlocked, cut adrift from the world. Nothing worked as it should. Berlin's citizens went to bed and were jolted out of their sleep by the relentless hum of the planes more often than most of them had the energy to count anymore. They crawled out of bed in the cold in the same shivering way they had crawled into it, and they got dressed and then undressed again by candlelight. They ate dried vegetables and dry bread measured out in grammes. They lived with queues and the black market and constant forays out of the city on the hamstering trips they thought they had left behind with the war. They lived with the constant struggle to find food which was fresh and which wouldn't cost them their savings, or their conscience. And now that winter had arrived and the power cuts had really started to bite...

The house where Freddy lived, like all the buildings in Berlin, only received electricity for two hours a day. The time that supply arrived changed every week and bore no relation to normal human habits. Since last Friday, Freddy and the rest of the lodgers he shared his home with had been setting their alarm clocks for one o'clock in the morning. From then until three they raced around completing all the tasks that needed power or light. The week before that, the two-hour service had started at midnight. Everyone still had to get up at six o'clock to squeeze a day's work in between shopping for food and searching for fuel. And if someone somehow exceeded the neighbourhood's quota, all the power could disappear for two weeks. The only thing that never switched off was the planes. The city was closing down, turning inwards, shutting its doors.

Except for the killer. Every door still opens for him.

Freddy leaned back and stretched. His back and shoulders were cramped from too many hours spent hunched over his desk, trying to make sense of the clueless puzzle the killer had left them. Seconds later, he was glad that he had shifted position: if Brack's aim had been a fraction to the left, Freddy would have been sporting a black eye.

'Have you seen this?'

The newspaper came flying across Freddy's desk at the same instant the door slammed open. Flinging papers was Brack's preferred method of pointing out when he was less than happy with their headlines and with Freddy. As was shouting abuse heavily punctuated with 'idiot'.

'Have you seen this? They've given him a name – *The Berlin Strangler.* It's not very imaginative but it does the job, which is more than you seem to be doing. Why haven't you issued a statement that makes us at least look like we've got a handle on this?'

Freddy understood the man's frustration with the case, he was drowning under it too, but nobody tested Freddy's patience like Brack did. Every time his boss spoke to him, Freddy knew that the word 'useless' was a moment away from Brack's lips. It hardly inspired confidence. And while losing his temper in return would have brought Freddy a great deal of pleasure, he knew that it would have delighted Brack more. It would have given him the reason he was looking for to boot Freddy off the case and that wasn't a pressure Freddy's struggling team needed. So he took a deep breath instead and counted to ten, staring at the article while he thought of a suitable reply with which to downplay it.

'It's not great for the department, I know that, but this is standard fare. And it's also jumping to conclusions which I'd rather not comment on. The papers think it's the same killer and so do I, but we're a long way off establishing that, and they can scream as loud as they like for a description, but we can't give them one. That's why I haven't issued a statement and why I think, with respect, that we shouldn't. Anything we put out – beyond a request for anyone with information or suspicions to come forward – won't help. Worse, the wrong statement will give the story of a murderer roaming the streets – and the panic the papers are trying to whip up – more oxygen.'

Brack's florid face turned from its usual red to a blotchy shade of purple before Freddy finished his last sentence. 'It's always *can't* and *shouldn't* and *rather not* with you. Well, you don't get to decide. Put out an instruction to the whole city that no one is to open their doors to strangers. Put the onus on them to stop inviting trouble in and buy us some breathing space. It's basic policing, Inspector Schlüssel. You should try it sometime.'

'But that's the thing: it's not a stranger. How can it be?'

Freddy spoke without thinking and instantly regretted it.

'What the hell do you mean?'

Brack's nostrils were flaring – even his eyes looked red. Freddy could see the danger in continuing with an explanation whose details he wasn't yet happy with. Unfortunately, now that he had started, he also couldn't see how to stop. Besides, the contradictions choking up the case were obvious to him: they should have been crystal clear to a man as supposedly experienced in police work as Brack. He managed somehow not to point that out.

'I mean I don't think that *stranger* is the right message. If you look at the evidence, it all points to the opposite. None of the homes showed any sign of a break-in or a struggle. Each crime scene has contained teacups or beer bottles or some indication of shared hospitality. Whoever the killer is, the evidence indicates that he was welcomed in by his victims. That has to mean that, on some level, he was known to them.'

Freddy gave Brack a moment to respond, but the man merely glowered, so he carried on, not knowing how deep a hole he was digging for himself and too determined to make his case now to care.

'The problem is that we can't find a single connection linking the four people who have died. They don't share a school or a workplace or a friendship group, never mind all the differences between them in age and sex. None of them – unless they keep everything including basic home repairs secret from their families – had arranged for a workman to visit. And none of the killings are gang-related – I've checked.' He stumbled a little over *gang* but Brack didn't appear to notice. 'God knows who this man is who can walk into so many homes without a flicker, Chief Inspector, but the one thing I'd stake my career on is that he isn't a stranger.'

Stake my career on angered Brack as much as *stranger* had angered Freddy. He cursed and tried to pick holes in Freddy's reasoning, but – as it became obvious that it was impossible to destroy Freddy's reading of the situation with so much evidence to support him – his arguments quickly ran out of steam.

He can't fight me on this because I'm right.

Freddy's stomach unclenched as soon as he realised that, and his confidence surged back. He stopped listening to the tirade and sat in silence as Brack roared and everyone in the main office pretended not to listen, as they had pretended not to listen so many times before.

In the end, however – even though he was in the wrong – Brack was the winner. Freddy finally ran out of patience with the idiocy of, 'We need to do something and a stranger warning is something,' which became Brack's only argument and agreed to do as he was told and issue the warning. It was galling but it at least got Brack out of his office, although he bawled out the whole team as well as Freddy as he left for good measure.

The team. They needed his support right now as much as the victims' families did, and Freddy needed them at full speed.

He crossed over to the doorway. The men were flagging. Heads were drooping, shoulders were slumped. They were behaving as if the case was too big for them, which meant that it soon would be.

He glanced at the clock. Eleven forty-five. Time to play the good boss before he had to turn back into the bad one. He strode out of his office, clapping his hands so enthusiastically he made them all jump.

'Right, everyone, you've been working too hard and it's time for a break. Pens down, heads up. I'm taking you all out to lunch.'

The room instantly warmed; the mood instantly lifted. Freddy scurried round the desks, hurrying everyone into their coats, nodding when Matz asked if he should telephone and include Hanni. The meal would be a financial stretch his wallet did not need, but the goodwill the gesture gained would, hopefully, be worth it. He was, after all, going to present them when they returned with a very stiff bill for their beer.

———

Every piece of evidence from every one of the four crime scenes, every witness statement and every family interview, was to be re-examined. And that included every inch of every one of the dozens of photographs now spread out across Hanni's desk. Just looking at the size of the pile exhausted her. The only good thing that she could see was that Freddy had excluded the boy found strangled at Heimstraße from the case because the death had happened in the street not in his home. As for the rest of the men sitting staring at their own equally overfull case files...

Freddy had wrong-footed himself with the surprise lunch he had sprung on the team – not that he seemed to have noticed. It had been a welcome gesture, but then he had followed it too quickly with the order to go over old ground again, an exercise which all the detectives hated because it pointed out that they had no workable leads. Now they felt cheated as well as demoralised and their gears had ground from slow-paced to snail. Freddy did not seem to have noticed that either, which was odd, given how little he normally missed.

He's not himself. He looks haunted again.

Freddy had barely played any part in the lunch beyond paying for it. Now that they were back at the station, he kept staring into space, holding a report in front of his face as if to mask his splintered concentration.

He's as distracted by echoes as I am.

Hanni didn't know what was causing Freddy's lack of focus and – given the frosty atmosphere which had existed between them since Freddy's encounter with Tony – she wasn't going to ask. She guessed, based on her experience of him, that his lost parents and siblings were somewhere at its root.

She wanted to go to him. She wanted to tell him that worrying over family was why she couldn't concentrate on her work either. She couldn't begin to imagine how that conversation would unfold. 'My father – the Nazi you don't know about and the reason I won't let you love me – has started a school to teach another generation of little boys to love Hitler and to hate the Jews' didn't sound like a promising opener. 'Are you missing your mother?' was far too crass. And, try as she might, she knew that she wouldn't be able to focus on Freddy's father when her head was too full of her own.

'It's open. There are kids inside. They don't get brought in in the mornings or taken out again at night, so maybe they live there. And the cars that do turn up move too quick through the gates for me to see who's in them. But I did see your man Foss. He was standing at the front door, shaking hands with men as fancy as he was.'

Despite all her instincts about keeping him out of danger, Hanni had been so desperate for more information, she had sent Oli back to Wannsee. He had been far quicker this time, and he had delivered his second report in the same way he had delivered the first: with his hand out and with no interest in answering questions.

Hanni had managed to establish that by *fancy* Oli had meant smart suits, not the uniforms her whirling imagination had put Reiner's cronies in. She had also managed to squeeze out of him that he had seen Reiner only once in the three days he had been watching the building and that he had no idea how many children were enrolled there, although he had a feeling that the number didn't include any girls. When Oli had then offered – for a considerably higher sum – to go back and try to break into the villa, Hanni had told him that the matter was done. Oli was good, but his cunning was no match for Reiner's, and she wasn't going to send him unprotected into the lion's den. She was going to bring it crashing down instead.

Hanni was exhausted and unable to focus on the photographs she was meant to be re-examining because she had been up all night. Not because of the planes or because of the one o'clock power switch-on. She had been wrapped in a coat and a blanket and sat at her table in the candlelight because she had been assembling her ammunition. A packet of photographs from the Wannsee villa and a carefully worded letter, all gathered together in an envelope marked private and addressed to Tony's boss, Colonel Walker.

That had been her second decision – to send the documents to the Americans and not to the British. The first had been to stop waiting for the right moment to move against Reiner and to seize the one which had fallen into her grasp.

Hanni had no illusions about the task that was facing her. That an ex-SS officer could found an Adolf Hitler School in post-war Berlin and had potentially used Allied education resources to do it would be a huge scandal if the news broke. Hanni doubted anyone would thank her for uncovering it. She could imagine the British receiving the documents and racing to sweep the whole thing away. She could imagine the Americans doing the same, but there was at least a chance if she sent them there that conversations would be needed between the two administrations, that something would leak out to a wider audience who would demand action. And Colonel Walker was a name that she knew, so Colonel Walker was the recipient she had chosen.

It had not been an easy letter to write. Hanni had kept it brief. She had included the location of the school and an outline of what she believed its purpose to be. She had suggested that more men than the ones whose names she had uncovered were involved; that the rot could run through the whole British education department. She had mentioned – because she had to point the finger at him somehow – that she had also seen the initials EF recorded in an accounting ledger but her film had run out by the time she discovered that information. She hadn't included her own name. She hadn't elaborated on the initials or explained who EF might be. Her father was too clever a man to get caught by a lie, and he certainly wouldn't confess. The best thing Hanni could hope for was guilt by association, an irony whose parallels with her own life wasn't lost on her. It hadn't been easy, but it was finished, and once the sending was done then...

Hanni wasn't sure what would happen then, although she knew the waiting game would be a dangerous one. She would have to scour the newspapers for mention of the school – or for the incident, or the unpleasantness, or whatever they chose to call it if the scandal was skirted around – which would allow her to approach the authorities and tell Reiner's true story. If that failed, if the newspapers remained in the dark or were prohibited from publishing the story, she would have to rely on gossip leaking from the Americans instead. None of that would be risk-free or straightforward, but waiting for news wouldn't be her main challenge. The biggest danger came in keeping herself, and everyone whose lives the digging had touched, safe while the moment of truth was coming. Particularly Oli. Keeping him out of harm's way and avoiding any kind of trail that could loop back from the revelations to him was as important to Hanni as closing the school.

Which will happen. Which will lead to arrests.

Hanni had told herself that all night, every time her pen faltered. Even if it was held behind closed doors, there would be an investigation and then there would have to be charges. And then – when EF was identified and Emil Foss was finally behind bars and couldn't hurt anyone – that was when Hanni was going to complete the last act. She was going to take the whole of his life

– everything he had done as Reiner, everything he had done as Emil – to whichever Allied power had charge of him, and she was going to bring the whole man down. Whatever the cost might be to herself.

Hanni knew what would happen as soon as she stepped forward, even if she hadn't fully accepted it. That no matter how carefully she pleaded her own case, there would be a reckoning. That her own life would be pulled into the spotlight and called to account along with her father's. As long as everyone around her who she cared about remained unharmed, Hanni was finally ready for that. The discovery of the school, and the knowledge that Reiner's warped beliefs would remain as integral to his future as they had been to his past, had forced her hand. It was time to be brave. To stop living her life in the shadows Reiner's life had cast and to manage whatever judgement revealing both their true identities would bring. Hanni hoped that the verdict on her would, in the end, not be a harsh one. She knew that would be out of her hands.

Especially with him.

She glanced up at Freddy again. She had decided long ago that he would be the next person after the authorities to know her whole story. That she would go to him as soon as she had told the truth to the Americans, or to the British, or to whoever it was who decided to prosecute Reiner. All that she could hope was that Freddy would listen.

But Natan listened and look how badly that went.

Hanni pushed that memory away – there was nothing to be gained by poking at it. She had decided her path in the last days of the war, and now she was firmly on it. She also had more pressing worries about what was wrong with Freddy now than with what might go wrong in the future. He was staring at the ceiling again, his face drawn and ill. He looked beaten, the way he always did after a battle with Brack. He looked like he needed a success.

Hanni turned her attention back to the photographs, although she had stared at them so often she had no faith she would see anything new. It didn't matter. There was a lot Freddy needed that she couldn't do for him, but at least she could try to help him with the case. She separated the images out again into shots of the bodies and shots of the rooms they had been found in. There was nothing new of note in the second set. She picked up the first bunch, sorting them first by age and then by sex and seeing nothing there either.

What about common marks?

It was an interesting idea and one she hadn't yet tried. She began rearranging the pictures. She looked more closely than she had previously done at the band left by the ligature to see if its thickness varied. At the speckles coating their closed eyelids to see if the pattern changed. At their folded hands and neatly placed heads. The photographs began to look fresh again. There was a clue there, waiting for her to find it – she could sense it in the way the hairs stiffened on her arms.

Hanni blocked the office out and spread the pictures over her desk, including the ones where she had carefully folded down jackets and cardigans to better capture the strangulation scar. Something was niggling; something was whispering that there was another common thread.

She looked again. She twisted the pictures forward and back, angling them up to the light. She closed her eyes, took a breath, opened them and looked again. It was still there. On all of them, fixed in place like a brand. When she shouted out, 'Freddy, you have to come and see this,' the whole team jumped as one to their feet.

———

'I know what it is. I haven't a clue what it means in this context though.'

Freddy stepped back from the corkboard where Hanni's photographs were now pinned so that everyone could get a clear view of them.

'It looks like someone is following a Jewish mourning ritual, known as keriah. When it's used properly – which it hasn't been here – it's a way of allowing mourners to give vent to their grief. Or, to put it more simply, people in pain tear their clothes to show that they are suffering.'

Freddy pointed at the pictures to illustrate what he meant as he continued his slightly halting explanation.

'There is a pattern to this practice which our killer is clearly aware of. The tear is made on the clothes covering the upper part of the body and on the inner garments. So, for men, the tear could be made to the tie or sweater or shirt. For women, on the neck of a dress or blouse or cardigan. The cut – or the tear, or combination of the two – has to be purposeful; it mustn't look like accidental damage. For that reason, it's never done on a seam and it's always made vertically, travelling down the fabric for at least three inches.'

He stopped and stared at the images, all of which showed the pattern of deliberate damage he was talking about, and shook his head.

'I can explain that to you, but what I don't understand here is that – never mind that none of the victims are Jewish – it's the clothes of the dead which have been marked and it should be the clothes worn by the mourners. None of what's been done here fits with the correct rituals.'

He gave the team, whose frowns confirmed that they had never heard of the practice, a few moments to digest what he had said. It was Matz who broke the silence first.

'Does it mean anything that the cuts we can see here are on different sides of the bodies?'

Freddy was relieved to have a question he could actually answer.

'In the normal way of things, yes it does: it shows the degree of the relationship. For most relatives who are being mourned, the tear is made on the right-hand side. For parents, it's always done on the left and over the heart.'

Hanni leaned forward. 'Which is exactly where the rips have been placed on Edda and Falco.'

There was always a moment in an investigation when the incident room tightened as if a jolt had run through it. That was the moment teams waited for, the one which said: it isn't hopeless – there is something here. Freddy could feel it now. He could see the spark of it brightening everyone's faces.

He turned back to the photographs, focusing in on the detail both Matz and Hanni had noticed. 'That's well spotted, thank you. So if I was to follow that through, and if we were all to imagine for a moment that what's happening here is a version of the mourning ritual that I've outlined and that the placing follows convention and is deliberate, does it mean that the killer is identifying Edda and Falco as parents?'

He gave the room, and himself, a moment to take that idea in.

'Could it also suggest, by the same logic, that the younger ones are perceived in some way as children? Maybe cousins, or a brother and a sister?'

Everybody carried on staring at the photographs, but nobody answered him. Freddy couldn't blame them for stalling. He wanted to run with the theory – he would be glad at this stage to run with any theory – and he could feel how desperate the team was for anything to leap on. The problem was that, if there was some symbolism here, he couldn't yet see what its meaning was. He decided not to pretend that he could.

'I don't know if anything I've said fits what's been done to these bodies, although my instincts tell me I am on the right path. All we can be certain of is that every victim's clothing has been marked and that the marks appear to follow some of the rituals associated with the Jewish faith, but not in any conventional way. I don't know yet what that tells us, although I'm certain there is a message for us to decode. It's not the most straightforward theory I've ever floated to you and it is, unfortunately, all that I've currently got. So if someone else has an idea what the marks could mean, I think now would be a good time to share it.'

He waited, but everyone was still looking at him blankly – except Hanni, who wasn't making eye contact with him at all.

'All right, let's leave that for a moment then, let it mull. Did anyone find anything else?'

There was a pause and then Matz spoke up.

'Yes, sorry, boss. This photograph stuff pushed it out of my head. There's a fingerprint unaccounted for.' He nodded at one of the men sitting in the row behind him. 'Häusster found it logged against one of the coffee cups found in Matty Scheibel's apartment. There isn't a match to anyone we know who regularly visited her.' He glanced down at the notebook he was never without. 'She was a quiet girl by all accounts. Not many people in and out of her place; not the type to bring home a stranger. We've got it running through checks.'

He stopped. When no one else volunteered anything, Freddy thanked him and Häusster, although the discovery of a stray fingerprint wasn't as helpful as he made it out to be for the sake of morale. All Berlin's police records before 1945 had been destroyed in the war's bombing raids when the Red Fort, the old police headquarters in Alexanderplatz which the Gestapo had taken over, was obliterated. The checks Matz had alluded to rarely pulled up a match nowadays, unless the person the print belonged to was a regular and recent offender. Nothing they had uncovered about Fräulein Scheibel suggested she mixed with anyone who could be labelled as that. Freddy, however, forced a smile onto his face. It wasn't a breakthrough, but it could be – as the cuts in the clothing could be – a start, and a start was all that was needed.

This time when he asked the team to 'get combing again – there could be more clues hiding' they went to do it with a far quicker step. The only person who lingered was Hanni.

'I didn't want to bring this up in front of everyone; I could see we were all getting stuck and these rituals – if that's what they are – are complicated things. But I can't believe that the way the clothing has been torn isn't intentional and important. So...' She paused as if she was testing out what she was about to say. 'I know you said that the rips are on the wrong clothes; that they should be made on the ones worn by the mourners, not on the ones worn by the dead. But here's the thing... What if the killer isn't just killing but mourning as well?'

The moment she said it, Freddy could hear the logic in her idea. That did not mean, however, that he could jump immediately on it.

'So are you saying that he's grieving for the people he's killed or for their families?'

Hanni shook her head. 'That seems like a stretch. Why would you feel sad for your victims or the ones you've caused pain to? But what if he's using these deaths to mourn his own relatives, in a way that couldn't be done when they died?'

That was also a stretch, but Freddy had worked on a case with Hanni before which had stretched his thinking and he was more than ready to take that risk again.

'Okay, let me try to follow that line through. Would the implication be then that Edda and Falco are meant to be the killer's parents? That Matty and Linus are his sister and brother? That he wanted to kill his own family and he couldn't do that, so he's picking on substitutes?'

He stopped. Something about that didn't sound right: the crime scenes had been too gently left to suggest a killer who hated his own relatives enough to murder them. There was usually far more frenzy in an attack like that. He started to backtrack.

'Hold on, I think I'm losing myself here. And why the use of keriah? We've already established that none of the victims were Jewish, and if the killer is, then he's got the rituals wrong. And if he isn't Jewish either, then why do it? Or if he is, why do it wrong? I want to go with this, Hanni, I really want to find an answer, but if we're not careful, we're going to start spinning past any theory the team – or Brack – will buy into.'

Her sigh could have been his. 'I know, it's really hard to

unpick. But maybe it's the angle we're looking at, for the victims and the tearing, that's wrong. What if he does understand the practice and he's adapting it?'

Hanni got up and repinned the photographs on the corkboard so that the ones of Edda and Falco were next to each other.

'I agree with a lot of the points you just made. The crime scenes don't imply hatred – they imply love, or at least respect, for the people who died, which is why they're so hard to read. So what if the victims symbolise something, or someone, else? What if, in the killer's head, they are, as you said, meant to be his own family, but not because he wanted to kill them. What if they're the people who he, like thousands of others, couldn't properly mourn when they died?'

Freddy stared from her to the images. With the photographs lined up the way she had put them, it was impossible to argue that the cuts were a coincidence or were in any way random, and it was impossible not to follow her logic.

'In other words, you're suggesting that the use of keriah is intended. That it could imply, in some way we can't see yet, that he's mourning his own losses from the war. That maybe he's a survivor of the Nazis' brutality and the rest of his family weren't.'

Hanni shrugged, a gesture Freddy recognised. It didn't mean that she was uncertain of herself or her ideas. It meant that she was offering Freddy a way out of them. Her next words confirmed that.

'Perhaps. I don't know. None of this is my area. It's only a thought.'

Except that nothing with Hanni was only a thought, and the last time she had come up with a theory that seemed wildly off course, she had been right.

Freddy stared at the rest of the team who were buried back in their folders, wondering what their practical brains might make of her thinking.

The idea sounded in so many ways far-fetched, and yet hadn't he done something similar himself? Hadn't he swapped the faces of the dead in the photographs for the faces of his own murdered family? What if that was what the killer was doing? There was at least a pattern to be found in considering that theory: the victims were all different, but they had all been chosen for some purpose, and they had all been treated post-death with more delicacy than he had seen in any murder before.

And they were all left for their families to find and to grieve for. They weren't hidden or disposed of in some way that meant they couldn't be found. There was no doubt left about the way that their lives ended.

The killer had spared the families that bottomless hole. They would never have to wonder, or torture themselves, over exactly what had happened. He had killed, but he hadn't left the relatives in the limbo that Freddy was still stuck in. For a brief moment, Freddy wondered if there was a kindness in that, and then he pulled himself together. There wasn't – it was still murder, and the rationale he and Hanni were trying to pull together was still a very strange one.

'So let me get this straight: are we saying that our four victims could be – in the killer's mind – his dead parents? His dead siblings?'

When Hanni answered, she kept her voice as neutral as Freddy had kept his.

'Perhaps. Perhaps everything he does comes from grief and is an act of remembrance: the murders themselves, the domestic settings, the cuts on the clothes, the care with the bodies. We're seeing Edda and Falco, Matty and Linus, but the faces he sees when he's with them could be very different ones.'

She was talking about replacements, or atonements, or sacrifices. They were words that were guaranteed to make Freddy shiver and yet, on some primal level, he understood the impetus behind them. No one had performed the rituals of mourning for Rosa and Jakub, or for Leo and Renny. No one had spoken over their bodies or been allowed to weep at the moment of their death. That was a gap in the order of things Freddy had never known how to fill. What if the killer had found a way to do it?

'Can that really be it?'

He turned away from the photographs whose faces kept muddling with ones he did not want to see. There was sense to be found in the scenario they were building, even if it was more twisted than any killer he had ever seen. But sense alone wasn't enough.

'You know that Brack would throw me off the case in a heart-beat if I went to him with a solution like this. He wouldn't under-stand or accept it. And besides, it still doesn't solve our other problem: none of our victims are in any way connected and yet, whoever this man is, they all welcomed him into their homes.'

'A stranger who isn't a stranger. Someone they think that they know but they don't.'

Hanni's eyes were as bright as if a light had snapped on. Freddy suddenly felt it too: the shiver of a clue they could more easily work with. *Stranger* was the word he hadn't been able to get past: it hadn't occurred to him until that moment that it could be another word with more than one meaning.

'You mean someone in the public eye, don't you? Like a politi-cian who's always in the newspapers. Or a film star or a singer. Someone who feels accessible, even though they're not?'

Hanni nodded. 'Yes. Haven't we all done it? Thought we know people we don't because they are always creeping into our lives? We discuss articles we've read in magazines or interviews we've heard on the radio all the time, as though we're an expert on some star or some speech maker who we've never actually met. We criticise their opinions the way we do with members of our own family. We hear a throwaway comment about a favourite restau-rant or holiday spot and assume we know their tastes when, in fact, we know nothing about them at all.'

Freddy stared at her.

When we are like this – working in tandem, trusting each other – we make the best team.

He momentarily forgot the case and the incident room and slipped into the intimacy with her that his heart so often ached for.

'So what are you saying, Hanni? That I should be combing the streets looking for Gary Cooper?'

Her sudden smile made his hungry heart leap.

'Very funny. I think someone would have noticed by now if Gary Cooper was wandering around Wedding carrying a noose. But there are plenty of other people in the papers who readers admire or get crushes on. Look at the effect...'

She stumbled and her voice trailed away into, 'Well, you know what I mean.'

'You were going to say Tony, weren't you?'

The moment Freddy said Tony's name, he wished that he hadn't. Hanni's face closed. The warmer mood which had sprung up between them disappeared. And yet he kept pushing. And once he started, he couldn't stop.

'Well, that's an interesting thought. And you're right: look at all the women who throw themselves at him and at all the men who act as if his *hero* status will rub off on them if they hold on to his hand long enough. I think you've got something there – I doubt there's a door in the city that would stay locked if Tony Miller knocked on it.'

He couldn't control the sneer in his voice; he suddenly didn't want to.

'And when did the killings begin? Before the Americans came or after? Maybe we should start looking at flight patterns; maybe you've hit on—'

'Stop it.'

Hanni's face was white, her fists clenched. She looked as if she wanted to slap him.

'Stop it. You're being ridiculous. You sound stupid and bitter and—'

She bit down on the word, but Freddy heard it anyway. And hated it because it was true.

'What? Jealous? Of that preening idiot? Are you serious? You're the one who's being ridiculous, or very full of yourself, now.'

His words were too harsh; his voice was too loud. Heads were turning and Hanni's eyes were no longer soft – they were furious.

'I'm sorry, Hanni. Really I am. That was totally uncalled for.'

It was a genuine apology, but it wasn't one that she had any interest in hearing. Hanni waved it away with a sharp flick of her hand and stalked out.

Freddy wanted nothing more than to run after her and keep saying sorry until he made her accept that he meant it. If it hadn't been for the raised eyebrows and the muttering from the rest of the team, he might have done exactly that. Instead, he let his pride win.

He turned his back on the room and pretended to be focusing all his attention on the corkboard and the photographs. The pretence didn't help. All he could see was Hanni's shocked face and her anger. And all he could hear, no matter how hard he tried to convince himself that it wasn't important, was *when did the killings begin?*

CHAPTER 11

21 DECEMBER 1948

He'd had to steel himself for this one. The first night he had gone out to do it, he had failed and come home without a tick to add to his list. The second time, he had stumbled again and taken the woman he had chosen as his Aunt Bettina's twin instead.

It's not because I'm weak; it's because children are different: children are not meant to die.

Tony fervently believed that. The Nazis hadn't – they had shown no more compassion to the children that they had murdered than the adults, sometimes less if the horror stories about drowned newborns and toddlers thrown alive into ovens were to be believed. That was what got him through the task in the end – knowing that his hesitation proved that, although he was a killer, he was better than them.

Tony knew what the Nazis had done to children: they were not the kind of details that, once learned, anyone could forget. He had listened in disbelief to the numbers of the dead being announced in hushed tones on the radio stations which carried reports from the Nuremburg trials. Over a million youngsters – and the clerks tasked with the terrible job nowhere near finished counting – murdered because they had been born Jewish or Romani or some other race or religion that didn't matter to the future as much as being 'pure Aryan' did. Or because they were not up to National Socialist physical and mental standards.

Tony had read the accounts of the T4 programme, the murder of the disabled by gas or by starvation or by lethal injection. He had also read the reports from Auschwitz and Josef Mengele's twin-obsessed laboratory there. About the experiments to alter eye colour; about the surgeries to test a small body's capacity to navigate unrelieved pain; about the dirty needles which were stuck into tiny arms and legs in order to fill them with disease. He had read about everything the Nazis had done; the reports were like a drug to him. Tony knew just how cruelly the Nazis had treated the youngsters they had branded as 'other'. They had shown those children as much contempt as they had shown the adults who had tried to protect them. His reluctance to take a barely begun life came out of the horror of the too many who had already been lost.

But the job still had to be done.

It had, thankfully, been one of his quickest. The child hadn't suffered, and he looked angelic in death. Tony settled the boy's head as gently as he could onto the cushion he had placed in the crook of the sofa and folded the little hands across a jumper that was too thin to withstand the bitter cold currently gripping the city. Then he paused and closed his own eyes and reordered his thinking.

Not 'the boy': that doesn't honour either of them. This is for David.

As hard as it had been to carry out, this death mattered too much to have gone undone. This one was for the younger of his two brothers. The child who had come unexpectedly, as his mother had delicately put it, who had been her miracle. The child who had loved his big brother Aaron no matter what he did. David deserved his atonement as much as Tony's parents and his other siblings and his aunt had deserved theirs. Perhaps more so: if love was a thing to be measured, David had shown Tony the most.

If I had been there, I would have saved him. I would have made it my mission to save him.

He shook himself. That kind of thinking had to go too. Now was not the time to be focusing on failure. Now was the time to be remembering his baby brother as he had last seen him. Eight years old, as scruffy haired and scabby kneed as a cartoon boy in a newspaper strip. Gazing up at the teenager Tony used to be as if he was golden and refusing to listen to a single word which would tarnish that tightly held image.

The best of us all and never allowed to grow up and know it.

That was a good eulogy. David's short life could not bear the weight of a longer one and neither could Tony. He opened his eyes, laid his hand on 'David's' forehead and repeated the words aloud. Then he made the rip at the neck of the child's shirt that he wished he could make in his own clothing. It was hard to keep the ritual secret and to mourn unseen, but at least he was mourning. He had gone long enough without the comfort of that.

That done, Tony straightened up and carefully checked the room. There was nothing of him in it. Not that anyone would have noticed anything untoward in the place. It was as much of a mess as the child's mother.

'I'm in Der Nussbaum most nights – I sing there. It's a friendly place and the beer is cheap. You should come in and find me.'

She had thought she was being seductive, but Tony was disgusted by her. What kind of a woman admitted that she was singing in a bar and never at home in the same breath as she had confided in him that she had a young son? It was little surprise that the child's face had lit up when Tony knocked on the door armed with a bag full of candy and a *Captain America* comic. It was probably the most attention the poor scrap had been shown in years.

Tony swept the half-eaten bag of Tootsie Rolls and the picture book back into his rucksack and let himself out of the apartment. There was nobody around to see him leave; there had been nobody around when he entered. From the dilapidated state of the building, he imagined more of its residents spent their evenings in Der Nussbaum than in their own flats.

He was tired, but it was the good kind of tired, the one that follows a job well done. He could mark six faces on the photograph now with a tick. He had stood in mourning for six of his family. His heart felt less bruised; his shoulders felt lighter. He was ready to speed up his programme.

If they knew, they might finally be proud.

He stepped out onto a street whose paving stones had been as broken looking when he walked down them as the war-damaged houses which lined it. Something was different about it; something was better. He stopped and looked properly around.

There had been a snowfall while he was inside. It had settled in deep mounds, covering the litter and the potholes, leaving the cracked sidewalks sparkling and new. Tony smiled at the sky as the flakes started tumbling again. Leaving them cleansed, that was the word. As cleansed and as peaceful as him.

CHAPTER 12

23–25 DECEMBER 1948

The journalists had been kept waiting too long; the mood had grown restless: Freddy could hear the muttering before he came into the room.

Six murders: how am I supposed to admit the impossibility of six murders and then admit I can't solve them?

He slid into his seat, struggling to meet anyone's eyes. He knew what they expected; he knew he couldn't deliver it. He knew the mood would turn ugly when that became clear. Ugly was the only mood Berlin seemed to know.

It wasn't only the reporters who were looking for blood: six months into a blockade which showed no signs of collapsing and the city was a volcano ready to blow. It wasn't hard to understand why. Daily life for most citizens was a complicated and exhausting thing. People's confidence, that the Allies would stay, that the blockade would be broken, had evaporated.

Berlin was nervous and the Soviets knew it. Their propaganda initiatives had heated up. The *People's Radio* broadcasts – which came out of the East but were heard on all sides of the city – were filled with promises of plentiful food and the very best housing for anyone willing to relocate their lives to the Soviet sector. The East's newspapers were filled with reports about the 'demoralised' British and the 'worn-out' Americans who were ready to ship out and leave Berlin to its fate. The constant chipping at morale had unsettled so many people, the Allies had retaliated with overextravagant promises of their own. There were weeks when Berlin seemed like nothing more than a stage for a shouting match. And now a killer who nobody could see and nobody could find and everyone was terrified of had been thrown into the mix.

The city needs a hero and I haven't stepped up.

Whatever fury against his failures was coming, no one could be angrier with Freddy than he was with himself.

He cleared his throat, conscious of Brack's rigid bulk beside him, fully aware that the chief inspector would not step in to save him if he drowned. And then he began the speech he knew would get shouted down faster than he could finish it.

'Thank you for coming. I do not, I am sorry to say, have favourable news. It is my unpleasant duty instead to have to announce that the killer who has already struck five times across the city has struck again. Two days ago, on the twenty-first of December, the body of Jochen Stahl aged eight—'

He didn't get any further than that; he hadn't expected to. A child's murder was always the one that tipped the scales. The room broke into a roar of indignation that Freddy let come.

'Six deaths? How can you still have no clue who the killer is?'

'Are you still saying it's all the same man?'

'Are you still telling us to be wary of strangers?'

That, at least, was a question he needed. Freddy raised a hand the instant he heard it, and the room – to his relief – fell silent. An eight-year-old boy had let someone into his home and he had paid for that with his life. Freddy had already stopped believing in strangers – now he needed the rest of the city to stop believing in them too.

'No. I am not. All of our victims, including Jochen Stahl, welcomed their murderer in. The term *stranger*, or at least in the way that we have been using it to date, does not fit that scenario.'

Brack shifted and coughed. Freddy carried on without looking at him.

'This is an unusual case. And so, perhaps, is the theory that I want to now share with you.'

He waited for that to sink in before he resumed, keeping his voice as measured and steady as he hoped the press reaction would be.

'It is my increasing belief that the man we are looking for has a degree of familiarity, of the type that could open any door in the city to him. Someone, perhaps, with a public face. Someone who everyone believes that they know. In other words, someone who is a stranger and who also is not.'

He stopped. There wasn't a sound, but there were plenty of the bemused frowns Freddy knew would be etched deep into Brack's face. He couldn't be thrown by that. His only concern was that the journalists listening to him would take away and report a new kind of warning.

'Leave here and print what you like about our slow progress – it's a frustration I share. Be as angry as I am that we don't yet have a suspect. But help us as well.'

No one was muttering now; every face was turned towards his.

'I don't know who the killer is, but you might. You may have taken his picture. You may have written articles about him. He may have appeared on your radio shows.'

There was a brief – overconfident – moment when, 'He could be someone you think of as a hero; he might even be an American,' almost leaped out of Freddy's mouth. He managed, just, to stop himself from saying it and from wrecking his career.

'Give it some thought. Come to me if anyone – no matter who – has given you reason to be suspicious. More than that, get the message out to your audiences that this man – this murderer – is not who they think he is. However you phrase it, make this much clear: the killer is charming and clever, so be on your guard and don't be the next one to get taken in.'

There was nothing else he wanted to add – or to answer. He had sounded as authoritative as he possibly could, and the reputation he carried had to count for something.

Although not, apparently, with Brack, who barely waited for the room to clear before he snarled, 'What the hell was that meant to be?'

Freddy heard the menace. He stared at the briefing paper spread out in front of him while he debated how much of his suspicions he could share, and more particularly at the notes he had scribbled across the margin earlier that morning. How many times had he written and circled the letter T? He scooped the document into his pocket before Brack noticed.

'I asked you a question, Schlüssel. I asked you what you thought you were doing.'

The chief inspector was on his feet, towering over Freddy's slighter frame with his fists curled.

'Are you planning to pull in every politician and celebrity in the city for questioning, or do you have someone in the frame for this?'

Brack's stance was meant to be intimidating. It didn't work. It also didn't inspire confidences that Freddy knew Brack would use as evidence that he was losing his grip.

He stood up as slowly as he dared and looked Brack squarely in the eye.

'No, I don't. What I do have is a hunch about the type of man we're dealing with. What I was trying to do was my job. I haven't caught the killer yet, as you keep pointing out, but I can do the next best thing: I can do everything in my power to keep Berlin's citizens out of harm's way. Isn't that the least that should be expected of us?'

He was gone before Brack could work out how much of what he had just said was an insult.

. . .

Freddy trudged through the deepening snow, his hat pulled down, his chin lost in the folds of his tightly wrapped scarf. He had made himself as shapeless and invisible beneath his thick layers as he could, although that no longer seemed as important as it had when he had set out earlier that morning. There was no one to worry over or to avoid eye contact with. The streets of Mitte were as empty of people and, more importantly, of soldiers as they had been when he had first ventured into the Soviet sector.

Maybe there's an amnesty for strangers on Christmas Day. Maybe that's their gift to us.

He had barely remembered when he woke up that it was Christmas and he hadn't given any thought to how the Soviets celebrated the holiday. Now that he was inside their territory, he hoped it had involved distributing enough vodka to the army to keep them good-tempered – or asleep.

Before the day itself had arrived, Freddy had also given no thought to what a blockaded Christmas might mean. He knew – from the friends' homes he had once visited – what the customs for the season were. When he was a child and feeling excluded from all the fun, he had envied his friends those. The trees laden with tinsel and glass baubles; the advent calendars with their enticing little windows; the roast goose and slabs of marzipan-scented stollen. He had begged Rosa to celebrate Christmas once – it had been one of the very few times when she had got genuinely angry with him.

It was impossible to tell if any of those treats were waiting inside the silent houses he was currently passing. If his landlady's attempts to be festive were any measure of the times, he doubted it. She had tried her best, but the pine tree she had dragged into the living room that morning was straggly and crooked and the chicken she had spent a small fortune on for Christmas dinner was woefully anaemic.

It was those preparations which had driven Freddy out of the house. She had invited him and the other lodgers with nowhere else to go to join her family at the rather hopefully named feast she was planning. Freddy had declined. Her attempt to recreate and share the season's normal traditions was a kind one, but those traditions weren't his and they couldn't be, even if he wasn't ready to admit that he no longer had any left of his own. Freddy had lost his family and he had lost his faith. There were no more rituals to mark the celebrations that once marked the turning points of the year. Hannukah's candle lighting and the matzoh and bitter herbs of Passover had disappeared from his life along with the Friday night Shabbat dinner. All Freddy had now was empty spaces and a longing for someone to belong to which worsened with every holiday, no matter whose religion those fell from.

And a reputation across the city which is only just holding.

Most of the reports from the press conference had not dealt kindly with him. There had been a number of unsubtle hints about young detectives who weren't doing well under pressure and the need for older, less fanciful heads. Brack had left copies of those all over the office. The one comfort, however, was that the majority of the papers had also told the story which Freddy had hoped would be told: that not even the safest stranger was truly safe and that the only defence against the Berlin Strangler was a firmly shut door. The superintendent, although he had not fully understood Freddy's reasoning, was prepared to cut him a little slack for that. Freddy knew that the slack wouldn't last; that another dead child and no suspect could end his career. It was a prospect which had stopped him from sleeping properly for the last two nights. That and the extent of his jealousy, which had almost run away with him at the briefing and undone all his hard work.

The thought of what would have happened if he had announced Tony Miller as a key suspect had woken Freddy up before dawn in a cold sweat. Brack would have fired him on the spot, and it was not as if he had a shred of evidence to back up the allegation. He might loathe Tony. He might wish Hanni had never met him. But none of that made the American a murderer.

The snow had started to fall again. Not in the soft powdery drifts which made the world sparkle but in sheets of wet sleet that worked their way inside collars and cuffs and soaked through even the most snuggly wrapped clothing. Freddy pulled his scarf tighter, although the wool had grown unpleasantly damp, and wished he hadn't deliberately chosen a route that was so far from the subway.

Or left the house at all.

There had been no place for him at his lodging house, and the thought of returning to the station and wading back through evidence which wouldn't talk to him was too miserable. Freddy missed his family with an ache that cut through him and there was no point in pretending he didn't. He had decided, therefore, to retrace his past's footsteps and to see if – as had happened to Elias – any new ones had been laid. It had proved to be as point-less and dispiriting an exercise as all the others he had made.

Since the war's end, Freddy had revisited every place on his personal map of the city, and some that were new to him, trying to find any mark left by his family. After he had given up on the Red Cross, he had haunted the Mariendorf Displacement Camp in Schöneberg, visiting it until long after most of the survivors who passed through its gates had moved on. He had also returned more than once to Mitte and to both their old flat in Ritterstraβe and the tenement building the Schlüsselbergs had been reallocated to in Bachstraβe after their first home was seized. One was a wasteland. One had been rebuilt with homes that had wiped away all traces of the ones which had stood there before. The new occupants were pleasant enough, but no one remem-bered the Schlüsselberg family or wanted to discuss the fate of lost Jews. The only site Freddy hadn't gone back to was the Jewish Hospital which had sheltered him. Or at least not until today.

Today, Freddy had convinced himself that the Jewish Hospital was exactly where someone who was ill or confused, who had been lost for years, would go when they finally found their way back to Berlin. He had ignored the voice in his head repeating, 'It's not what Elias's cousins did. They arrived at a station and went straight to the Red Cross, like the posters tell returners to do.' Instead of listening to that, he had walked the nine kilometres from his lodging in Methfesselstraße – which had felt more like twenty as he grappled with the drifting snow and the hazardous ice – persuading himself that Christmas would bring a miracle. Persuading himself that, if not a mother or a sister, there would at least be a letter or a record waiting for him there. Or a kind-hearted person who knew which part of the Nazi war machine had claimed the best parts of his life.

Freddy had arrived at the hospital entrance in Schulstraße more fearful of the past than he had expected to be, looking over his shoulder for a swing of blonde hair or a dark overcoat. He had conquered that. He had found a way past the janitor shivering in his hut. He had managed to hold on to his hopes as far as the pockmarked front door before they failed him. The hospital was all broken buildings and exhausted staff who were too worried about the hospital's uncertain future to care about its past. He had stayed for an hour until he got under too many feet and he had left before whatever holiday truce had allowed him inside lost its patience, with nothing learned from the journey except that he was a fool.

That had been an hour ago, or so Freddy assumed – it was too cold to uncover his wrist and look at his watch.

His pace had slowed on the return leg of the journey, and the lack of anything to eat or drink since the previous night had turned his brain fuzzy. Which meant that he didn't see the man who was as preoccupied and as tightly swaddled against the weather as he was until they met in a collision which made them both bounce.

Freddy's first reaction was to laugh: the impact of their padded bodies had been, as he pointed out, completely absurd. His second – when the other man didn't share his amusement –

was to reach for the gun he wasn't meant to be carrying, in case the overcoat he had crashed into concealed a Soviet soldier. His third was disbelief: the man pulling his hat down and trying to hurry away was the double of Tony Miller.

'Okay. Now I really am missing my breakfast and seeing things. Unless you have a twin in the United States Air Force, that is.'

He could have dismissed it as a coincidence. If the man hadn't been so keen to ignore him and scurry past, Freddy would probably have managed to accept that explanation. But the instinct he relied on was telling him to block the path and the man's getaway, so he did. There was a brief pause and then the man tipped back his hat and revealed himself.

'No, you're right, it's me. I'm out of my area, you've got me, but give me a break and don't shoot.'

Freddy had to hand it to him – it was a slick recovery, even if Tony's taut smile and narrowed eyes were in sharp contrast to the mock cower he immediately dropped into.

Freddy glanced round, the empty street suddenly feeling not safe but exposed. Whatever Tony's reason for being in Mitte, it could not be a good one. Freddy immediately slipped into policeman mode.

'What the hell are you doing in the Russian sector? If you get caught over here, you could put more lives than your own in danger. Didn't I make it clear at the protest that you're a target?'

'And you're not? Wouldn't an inspector from the west be as good a prize as me?'

The playful stance was gone; the mocking tone had grown edges. Tony's hand had strayed to his pocket. Freddy noted that – it was usually the sign of someone reaching for a weapon – but he was more thrown by the man's voice.

He doesn't sound like an American.

Hanni had mentioned Tony's fluency with German, but Freddy had addressed him in English the last time they had met and had never heard him speak the language before. His Berlin accent was faultless – there wasn't a hint of a transatlantic twang.

Everything about this is wrong, and he's not going to back down if I continue to challenge him.

Freddy took a step away and let Tony feel as if he had the encounter's advantage. He smiled, raised his hands in a deliberate imitation of Tony's pretended surrender and dropped his voice as if he was sharing a confidence.

'And now you're the one who's got me. You're right: neither of us is where we're meant to be and both of us are courting trouble, but I won't tell if you won't. I don't know what your excuse is, but as for me...' Freddy shrugged and decided to share something personal to see if he could win something personal back. 'I'm blaming my transgression on Christmas: I don't celebrate the holiday, but it gave me a hankering for family, which sent me out here.'

'You don't celebrate it? Why not?'

Tony's response was not the one Freddy had expected – he had presumed Tony would make some bland comment about holidays being hard when you're away from home or launch straight into an excuse for his own wanderings. The reply he actually gave was a more interesting one than that, so Freddy decided to follow it.

'Because I'm Jewish.'

Tony's face didn't so much lighten as shed a dozen years. His frown disappeared. His hand came out of his pocket. It was a startling shift from man to boy which revealed someone far more human than the façade Freddy had previously encountered.

'I didn't know that.'

He's trying to forge a connection.

It was an odd thought and an uncomfortable one given how much Freddy had already decided he disliked the man. It convinced him, however, that – if he wanted to fully understand who he was dealing with – he needed to pick up whatever this attempt at friendliness was and turn the jousting into a proper conversation.

He nodded, as if 'I didn't know that' implied something more.

'Being without them is one of the things that makes today difficult, even if the holiday isn't mine. When I said I had a hankering for family, I don't mean I was visiting them, or at least not in a physical sense. My parents and my siblings were murdered by the Nazis.'

And now the face staring at him turned from young to raw.

'Then what are you doing over here? If there's no one to find, I mean. Is this where you...'

Tony paused. Freddy waited and let him find the right words.

'Did you live here with them before?'

Before. It was the same word Hanni used. The one that recognised that there had been a time then and there was a time now and that the war ran like a crack between those two states. The one that recognised the depth of the suffering.

Tony's face was no longer polished; it was naked. It was hard not to see that and answer him from the heart.

'Yes. And I came here looking for... echoes, I suppose.'

Freddy kept his eyes fixed firmly on Tony's face as he continued, noting the curiosity there and the flashes of what looked, oddly, like pain.

'There's nothing of our home left, but there's a hospital over here which sheltered a number of Jewish people – including me – who were forced into hiding when things got... really bad. It was a safe place then and I got it into my head, stupidly I know, that my family might have made their way back to Berlin. That they, or at least some word of them, might be there now. They weren't, of course, and no one could help. It was another dead end in a long line of them. I could try to pretend that I'm used to those, but I'm not.'

Tony, once again, seemed to latch on to only part of what Freddy was saying. His expression shifted again.

'You're Jewish and your family were murdered and yet you

work for the police? How could you do that when there was no difference between them and the Party?'

It was a challenge. His voice was all spikes.

Why on earth does it matter to him?

Freddy kept his answer as straightforward as he could, while his brain tried to play catch-up.

'Because I believe in justice. Because without a decent police force the alternative is vigilantes or mob rule. Or the kind of tyrant taking power that I never want to live under again.'

Tony stared at him, his mouth drawn into a tight line. His hand was back in his pocket. Freddy could sense a threat. He was certain that his answer had angered the American. He was also certain that he was missing something, and that he needed to walk away and figure out what that something was.

'That's my reason for straying into the wrong sector, but you still haven't said what you're doing here. I presume it's not for the same family-centred reasons as me.'

It was a throwaway comment; Freddy had said it with a smile. It acted on Tony like a splash of ice water. His face lost its edges and became bland again; his body expanded. He turned back into Captain Tony Miller.

'Well, that would be quite a story and not one someone as American as I am can claim. No, Inspector, my reasons are far more mundane. It's the usual thing: souvenir hunting. I heard about a black market operating near Große Hamburger Straße which deals in Soviet military objects. I fancied picking up a few pieces, and today seemed like it would be a quiet one to carry out that kind of business.'

He was lying; Freddy would have bet his badge on that – he had passed that way already and Große Hamburger Straße was as deserted as the rest of the sector. He didn't point that out: an empty street in the wrong sector of the city was not the place for a challenge.

'Then I should let you go, before it gets dark and the market packs up, or the soldiers reappear.' He stepped to the side so that

Tony could continue past him. 'And I assume that I don't have to tell you again to take care.'

The smooth face was back in place, accompanied by a cheery wave and an invitation to go for a beer Freddy knew Tony had less intention of honouring than he had.

Freddy turned away and let Tony go, even though all his instincts said follow him. He headed back down the street towards Kreuzberg, no longer aware of the weather, his mind whirling. It wasn't only the purity of Tony's German accent, although that was remarkable. It wasn't only the lies about what he was doing in Mitte or the menace Freddy had felt in their initial exchanges. Something else was niggling at Freddy about the new sides he had seen of the man.

He was back at the empty police station with his coat off, ready to bury himself in a mountain of paperwork when he finally realised what it was.

He knows suffering. He knows it in the same life-changing, world-ripping way that I do: it was engraved on his face when I told him what had happened to my family.

And as the first stone dropped, the second and the third fell swiftly into place.

Tony had said *Party* the way someone who had lived under the Nazis would. And he had flinched when Freddy had talked about vigilantes and mob rule. Freddy didn't yet know what any of that meant, but he was starting to guess, and he could sense guilt and a potentially twisted story brewing. And a man very different to the apple-pie American Tony chose to present to the world.

If he was Jewish, if he had relatives over here who were murdered, why not say so? It's common enough.

Freddy's dislike, and his mistrust, of Tony hadn't been jealousy, or not entirely. It had been a hunch, born from experience and instinct. Something about Tony was badly off-key.

Freddy got up and bundled himself back into his layers. His brain was pushing him towards conclusions he wasn't yet ready to make. What was needed was proper police work: he needed to pull everything Tony appeared to be – and everything Freddy was beginning to suspect that he might be – to pieces. The captain, however, was no fool and he had layers of protection around him. Which meant Freddy needed someone equally as good at slipping in and out of the shadows. He had to go back out into the cold and find Oli.

CHAPTER 13

4 FEBRUARY 1949

Oli was dead. No, Oli had been murdered.

No matter how many times she heard them repeated, Hanni couldn't catch hold of the words.

He had been found on a building site two weeks ago, positioned in exactly the same way as the first boy they had found at Heimstraβe had been. Lying on his side, his eyes open, a brown mark running in a neat circle round his neck. Oli's was the first crime scene where Hanni had been sick. It was the first one where Freddy had cried. Now the team was bandying round terms like *copycat* and *coincidence* – even though those were words which Freddy believed made investigators lazy and whose use he normally banned – and they were looking for two killers. One who went into homes in search of his victims and one who left young boys dead on the street.

And that one, the one who killed Oli, was surely hired this time by my father.

Nothing had happened in the weeks since Hanni had posted the evidence to Colonel Walker. There hadn't been a breath of scandal about a Nazi school being discovered in Wannsee anywhere in the press and there hadn't been a snatch of gossip around the airbase or the bars either. If it hadn't been for Oli's murder, Hanni might have believed that the school was still open and flourishing, but the coincidence was too much. If the villa had been discovered, if Reiner's dreams of winning hearts and minds had been destroyed, he would have wanted the person who uncovered his scheme to pay. And that person was surely Oli. Hanni was convinced that Reiner was responsible for his death. Which meant that she was responsible for his death. The guilt and the shame in that was overwhelming. It was a weight in her stomach, a dry rasp in her throat.

As soon as the murder van had driven its too-small cargo away, Hanni had run from the scene and headed straight for Wannsee. Everything there was as she had feared it would be. The house was deserted. The gates were padlocked; the lower windows were boarded up. Whether the press knew about its discovery yet or not, the Hitler School had surely been found.

Hanni had stood on the corner staring up at the shuttered windows, imagining her father looking out and spying the small figure pressed into the hedge, wishing she could turn back time and play everything far more carefully. Wishing she hadn't put Oli in her father's sights, without any warning of how dangerous Reiner could be. Or believed him when he told her that he was the king of surveillance because believing that had suited her needs. She had been blinded by thoughts of revenge, and she had ignored what she should have never lost sight of: that Oli wasn't the king of anything – he was a child. It had taken all Hanni's strength not to curl up and sob at her stupidity.

She had been so caught up in herself that, when a man leaned over the wall of the adjoining property and addressed her, all Hanni had been able to manage was a stumbling, 'Do you know why the school is closed up?'

The man had looked her up and down before taking out a packet of cigarettes. He hadn't offered Hanni one.

'No. And I didn't know it was a school, so you're steps ahead of me. It was the police who came and closed it. Well, I'm saying it was the police, but who knows with the way this city is going.

Whoever they were, they were wearing dark coats, they told me not to ask questions and they emptied the place. They built a bonfire on the back lawn which smoked the rest of us out – you can still smell it if you go down by the lake. That was weeks ago and no one's been here since. Why do you want to know?'

Hanni hadn't been able to tell if his manner was belligerent because he didn't like strangers or if that was simply his way. She had known that she didn't trust him, so she had ignored his question and kept her own brief.

'Do you know what happened to the staff? To the teachers and the people who owned it? Or to the children who came here?'

The gardener had shrugged. 'They were a private lot; they didn't notice people like me. And as for the children? If this was a school like you said it was, it must have been one for the rich. Why would anyone go bothering about them? They always end up on their feet.'

He had still been grumbling about his lot in life when Hanni walked away. She couldn't face questioning him anymore; she'd had to keep moving. The school might have been discovered, but that didn't necessarily mean that Reiner had been discovered too.

She had gone from Wannsee to the second address Oli had given her, which was an hour's walk away in Nikolassee. It hadn't taken long to find her father's home among the elegant mansions there. It was another turreted villa, on another grand street. And it was also padlocked and deserted and the owner – some 'bigwig who worked for the British and kept himself to himself' according to an old lady walking an equally slow-moving dog – was long gone.

Oli was dead and Reiner had vanished and Hanni was in limbo. She had no idea if her father was under arrest or if he had escaped. Or, if the latter was the case, what he was planning to unleash next or how she could stop him if he kept slipping away. And she was so angry, she burned with it. Oli was dead and now it was Reiner's turn to pay.

She had gone straight back from Nikolassee to the police

station and locked herself into an office with a telephone line. Nobody had asked what she was doing; everybody had been knocked into silence by the brutality of Oli's death.

Hanni's first call had been to Reiner's workplace, the British Control Commission at Fehrbelliner Platz. She had asked to be put through to Emil Foss; she gave her own name. She no longer cared that making contact with her father was dangerous; that accusing him of ordering Oli's murder would be more dangerous still. One hint of his guilt was all that she needed to go straight to Freddy. She would take him Reiner's story and she would take him her own and she could be hanged for it all as far as she cared as long as the truth got some justice for Oli. There was, however, no Emil Foss to accuse. There never had been according to the clipped official her call was put through to. When Hanni mentioned the other names she had gathered at the school, he had ended the call.

Hanni was too furious to be put off by that. Instead, she had picked up the phone again and dialled the number Colonel Walker had given her to use after her first assignment with Tony. She was more circumspect this time: she hadn't given his secretary her own name. She did not have time for the explanations revealing herself would involve. She had pretended to be a journalist instead, on the trail of a rumour that could turn into a scandal. One mention of a school run by a group of ex – or not so ex – Nazis which the American command apparently knew about but hadn't made public and the officious woman had put her straight through.

Walker hadn't recognised her voice – Hanni had thickened her accent to make sure that he didn't – but he had been very certain in the answers he gave her. Her rumour was 'complete nonsense'. Her sources were 'troublemakers'. A school of that type in Berlin was 'a total impossibility'. Hanni had listened to a response that felt scripted and she had been the one who ended the call. Whatever the truth was, it had been carefully buried. Whoever had been involved had been spirited away. Or had escaped before they were caught.

Hanni had tried to believe in justice. She had tried to believe that any cover-up had been for public consumption only. That, behind closed doors, there had been an investigation and wide-sweeping arrests and that the non-existent Emil had been thrown into a jail cell to rot. She had tried, but she couldn't. And she was angry with herself beyond measure for where her naivety had led. While she had been waiting for justice, there had been a warning, a tip-off. With Reiner's extensive web of informants, Hanni knew she should have counted on that. She should have known that Oli would have been discovered; that Reiner's instincts were always on the alert. Not that the details mattered. However he had done it, the outcome was the same: Hanni had played her hand wrong, Oli had paid for that with his life. The only thing she wasn't sure of was whether Reiner had traced a line back from Oli to her.

Alone now in the office, unable to push Oli's broken body out of her head, Hanni began to hope that he had. She knew her father. She knew that, if he thought she'd had a hand in engineering the school's demise, Reiner would, eventually, come into the open and go on the attack. And then she would fight back and finish him.

———

Oli was dead. No, Oli had been murdered.

And his blood is on my hands.

Freddy hadn't shared that admission with anyone in the station, but he couldn't hide the truth from himself. He had sent the boy into the Soviet sector to check whether Tony really had made black-market contacts there. Before that, he had sent him searching for Elias and tangled him up in the affairs of God knows how many gangs – men who held life cheap no matter what Elias had said about codes of behaviour. He had put Oli into danger time and time again, and now Oli was dead. Who was responsible for that tragedy if not him?

Elias.

If gangs were involved, then Elias was involved, or so Freddy had persuaded himself, if only to stop himself breaking under the full weight of the blame.

'Was this your doing? Did you have Oli killed? He was a kid; he never hurt anyone. I swear to God, if you don't own up or you don't find his killer, I'll have you for this. I'll drag in every last one of your members and beat them black and blue until I get to the truth.'

Freddy had no memory of making the journey to the bar in Mitte. He hadn't thought out what he was going to say. He half ran, half fell down the steps into the dark room and he yelled. Within seconds, one of his arms was in a twist up behind his back and there was something cold pressed under his throat. Freddy didn't care. He didn't stop yelling. He only survived because Elias stepped forward out of the gloom and nodded to his minders to step back.

'You need to calm yourself. Or I'll forget that we're friends and hand you over to my men.'

If Elias had matched Freddy's fury, Freddy would have stayed fighting. It was the man's quiet certainty that calmed him.

'That's better. I am sorry that the boy is dead, but that is how boys who play with fire frequently end up. I did not order his murder. I doubt anyone in the organisation did. Why would we? However, as a courtesy to the friendship you seem to have lost sight of, I will ask some questions, see what I can find out. But mark this, Freddy: if even one of my men ends up paying for your informant's death, you will regret it. And you never, under any circumstances, come onto my patch and threaten me like that again. You won't walk away unscathed if you do.'

Elias had had Freddy marched out of the bar after that and out of Mitte. If any of the Soviets patrolling the neighbourhood noticed, they kept well away. There had been one message from him in the fortnight since then, a curt note which could be distilled down to 'it was no one of ours' that Freddy immediately burned.

Freddy knew that Elias had deserved better treatment and that it was on him to mend the bridges he had so foolishly destroyed. His priority, however, was Oli. Or – as Brack had put it, without any interest in the personal cost of the boy's death to his subordinate – his priority was 'to catch the plague of killers you've managed to unleash'.

In the first days of the investigation, Freddy had allowed the word coincidence to fly around the office. As the crimes continued, he had also been persuaded to go along with the theory that there could be two separate killers. One who was responsible for Oli and the first strangled boy and one who was responsible for the home-based attacks, and that one of them was copying the other. A coincidence could be possible given the two separate locational patterns. As was a copycat, if Oli's murderer was trying to throw Freddy off the scent. There was a logic to both ideas. Logic, however, did not make either scenario feel right.

Freddy knew that copycat killers were a very rare breed, whatever the newspapers might think. He also couldn't find a single incident of two stranglers operating at the same time in the same city, and he couldn't find any record of a strangler who had killed multiple victims in one place outside a crime novel. Or find the link between all of the murders that a nagging thought kept whispering was there.

It was late when Freddy finally got up from his desk. He had virtually lived at the station in the two weeks since Oli's body had been found. Now he was exhausted, his stomach had passed from grumbling to groaning and he was badly in need of air which wasn't stale with coffee and sweat.

Apart from a light glowing in one of the interview rooms on the other side of the corridor, there was no one around when he came out of his office. Freddy was glad: he was done picking over and over the case. Halfway down the stairs, however, he met the desk sergeant on his laboured way up.

'Excellent, that's saved me a trip. Can you give this little lot to Fräulein Winter? According to the book, she hasn't signed out for the night.'

Before Freddy could argue, the sergeant thrust a paper-wrapped bouquet of roses into his arms and disappeared down the stairs again, moving much faster than he had moved coming up.

Freddy's heart plummeted as he stared at the flowers. They were velvet soft, and the thick crimson petals were heady with scent. They were the kind of blooms which were far too expensive for his pocket, and their quality was rare in the shops in Berlin, especially in the winter months. Which meant, or so Freddy assumed, that the sender was Tony. He had no desire to deliver them, but neither could he pretend that they hadn't arrived.

He turned reluctantly around, resisting the temptation to drag the bouquet across the dusty concrete, and headed back to the second floor. If Hanni hadn't left, she was presumably the one making use of the interview room to catch up on work.

He knocked and pushed the door open, already saying goodbye as he shoved the flowers towards her desk. And then he stopped and looked at her properly. The desk was covered in crime-scene photos of Oli and her face was covered in tears.

'Why are you still going through them, Hanni? It won't help: there's no more clues to be found.'

She didn't answer. She wiped her eyes and gathered up the pictures, and then she noticed the flowers.

'What are you doing with those?'

'Sarge asked me to bring them up because he was too lazy.'

Freddy dropped the bunch on the table and a card fell out. The moment Hanni read her name on the envelope, she shoved it away. Freddy couldn't help but notice that her hand was trembling and that she showed no pleasure at receiving the roses. He also couldn't leave that alone.

'I presumed they were from Tony.'

To his surprise, Hanni shook her head.

'He wouldn't send flowers here; I'm not sure he would send flowers at all. Things between us aren't really like that...'

She trailed off. It was clear that she wasn't going to volunteer any more information about her relationship with Tony. Or show him the card and reveal who had actually sent the bouquet, and Freddy had too much pride to ask. It was also equally clear that she wasn't as thrilled by their arrival as their sender had surely intended her to be. Freddy looked down so Hanni couldn't see how much that mattered.

She doesn't sound as if she's in love with the American. Or in love with whoever these came from.

The sudden rush of relief made him sit down, and then it made him open up in the way he only ever opened up with her.

'I think it's my fault Oli died and I can't live with myself.'

Hanni looked at him blankly, but at least she didn't tell him to stop.

'I kept putting Oli in danger. I sent him after the gangs when I was looking for Elias, and then I sent him into the Soviet sector to check up on—'

He stopped. He didn't know how to bring Tony back into the conversation without them slipping – as they too often did when the captain's name was mentioned – into awkwardness or anger. When he looked up at Hanni and she was already frowning, he presumed anger was where they were heading, so he finished the sentence with 'Tony' anyway.

To his surprise, she didn't get angry. She didn't react at all. She seemed, if anything, to have grown stiller.

Freddy swallowed and carried on.

'I met him on Christmas Day in Mitte and nothing about the meeting was right.'

He explained as succinctly as he could about the black-market cover story and his suspicions that Tony's past, and perhaps his present, were not as straightforward as the American would have the world think.

'I know I got... upset last time we talked about him. And I made a fuss about flight patterns when I've no grounds to believe he's involved in the... in anything. But now? I don't know what I'm saying exactly, except that too much about him doesn't add up. So I sent Oli after the black-market contacts Miller claimed that he had, and I asked Oli to do a bit of shadowing, to see what he could pick up. I think that sent him into all the wrong places.'

The way that Hanni was looking at him was unnerving. Her eyes were dark and lifeless; Freddy wasn't certain how much she had heard. And then she spoke and he realised her eyes weren't lifeless. They were filled with despair.

'Involved in the murders. That was what you were going to say, wasn't it? Is that what you think? That Tony has something to do with them? And with Oli's death too?'

Freddy stared at her, momentarily lost for words. He hadn't been intending to say anything about Tony's involvement with the stranglings – he was operating off hunches and wasn't at all sure of his ground – and he hadn't been thinking about any connection between the pilot and Oli's killer at all. But now that Hanni had mentioned the two things together, all he could see was the band round Oli's neck.

'I don't know what I'm thinking.'

He paused: Hanni, after all, knew Tony Miller far better than he did.

'That was an odd thing to ask, Hanni. Do you think Tony could have anything to do with all these deaths? Do you think he's someone who's capable of killing?'

Hanni didn't shake her head or nod or shrug. She was so still it was unnatural.

'I don't know. I've never considered anything as extreme as that before; I've had no reason to. I do know that he's capable of anger, but we've both seen that. And that he's secretive and he doesn't like anyone prying into his life.'

She stopped. She looked as if she was working through a list she had only now started to piece together.

'At the protest when he was watching you, and then when he and I went to the base for a drink, I saw a different side of him. Something came up that night about his ex-wife – who he had never mentioned to me before; he had never mentioned anything personal to me before. Another pilot questioned her whereabouts and Tony didn't like that at all. I don't know if that means anything. But he does have a public face I'm not sure I trust.'

She took a deep breath and her voice faltered. 'And I suppose, if you really want to go there, he does fit the profile we discussed and you outlined at the press conference. The stranger who isn't a stranger.'

She stopped and frowned and rubbed a hand over her forehead as if to settle the thoughts that were gathering there.

Freddy held his tongue, resisting the urge to leap in and add his own ideas to the ones that were so evidently troubling her.

'I don't think I actually know Tony Miller at all. But you're right: something about him doesn't add up. And if you asked me if he has something to hide...' Hanni paused momentarily, her shoulders slackening as she let out a long breath. 'Well then I'd have to say yes, even if I don't have any proof of that, beyond a few photos where he isn't smiling. And maybe... maybe that something is big enough to kill for, if Oli somehow found out what it was.'

The room thickened as Edda and Falco and all the cut-short lives they couldn't yet find a killer for crowded in. There were so many questions Freddy wanted to ask, but – for a moment at least, before all the implications of what they had both said needed to be dealt with – there was only one that mattered.

'I thought that you liked him?'

Hanni shrugged. The gesture looked helpless.

'I did. Or at least I thought I did. It would be closer to the truth to say that I don't know what to make of him. Sometimes I think that he likes me and that he wants to be with me, and sometimes I think I get in his way.'

She trailed off as Freddy reddened and then she recovered herself.

'I do agree with you though: Tony Miller is not the straight-forward man he presents to the world.'

They were in tandem again, even if the ground they were treading on felt like a dangerous thing. That knowledge gave Freddy the confidence to continue.

'I agree that he's not straightforward. And, as odd as this sounds, I'm not even sure that he's an American, or not through and through. Surely an American wouldn't say *Party* the way that he does, or speak such impeccable German with such a localised accent, or know loss in the brutal way so specific to this war that I'd swear Miller does. I'm starting to think – even though it sounds ridiculous to say it given the image he's so carefully culti-vated – that he may originally be from Germany, possibly even from Berlin, and not from America at all.'

Hanni didn't argue or answer. She slumped in her chair as if she was drained.

Her hand was still lying on the table next to the card. Freddy desperately wanted to reach out and take it, to anchor himself in her touch. He stuffed his hands in his pockets instead. Oli's death had left Hanni fragile, and he wasn't used to seeing her in that state. He couldn't tell if she would welcome or shrink from his efforts to comfort or be close to her.

He cleared his throat and attempted to shift the mood back to safer professional shores instead.

'We're agreed at least that something's not right here, and I can't let that go. It would be wrong, given all that's happened. But as for how we move forward from here...'

She looked so exhausted, part of Freddy wanted to stop. It was the policeman part of him which made him press on.

'We could look into him, Hanni. I think that we should. Just the two of us for the moment: it's too risky, too unthought out, to involve anyone else. I don't know how easy it would be, but maybe we could start by trying to establish his movements; we could see if and where he and the victims overlap.'

He paused. There was a logic to everything he was saying, but there was also – if he looked through Brack or his team's or the city's eyes – what felt like madness in actually doing it. Which meant he could only try if Hanni was with him.

'Could we, Hanni? Could we think the unthinkable? Could we act on it?'

Hanni held his gaze for a moment. He could sense her running Tony through her mind, pulling all the strands of him together. It was a huge relief when she nodded. And then she glanced down at the photographs again and her face crumpled. Her grief was so vivid, Freddy could hardly bear to look at it. He fixed his gaze on the roses instead and then he remembered that there was another question niggling at him.

'That night you were in the office, you said you were looking for Oli, that there was something you needed him for that was personal. And then I saw you, in September, running down the station steps after him, looking worried. Was he doing a job for you as well as for me?'

In his need to find something to talk about other than Tony, he had put the question too bluntly. Hanni shrank into herself and didn't seem to be able to find him an answer.

'Forget it – it doesn't matter. It's none of my business.'

There were echoes in the room Freddy suddenly didn't want to be present. Oli, filling them both with guilt. A sender for the flowers who he needed to stay in the past. *It's my fight, and I can't let myself love anyone until it's done.* Words Hanni had spoken almost two years ago, about some other man whose relationship to her he had never understood or got anywhere close to the bottom of.

Hanni, however, did not seem to have heard him. She finally answered his question in a voice that was frighteningly flat.

'Yes, he was. I wanted to give him work to keep him safe, or that's what I convinced myself anyway. I may well have done the complete opposite. That's the thing here, Freddy. Oli's blood may not be on your hands at all – it may very well be on mine.'

He was on his feet, ready to hold her, ready to do anything to wipe away the agony flooding her face, not caring and not needing to know what she thought she had done.

'Don't. If you touch me, I'll fall to pieces and I can't let myself do that.'

It was Viktoriapark again.

It was every time they had got close enough to break through the wall she had built so high between them again.

It was *I can't* and *don't*, and he – as he always seemed to be – was powerless.

Freddy's arms dropped back to his sides.

Hanni picked up the card, left the flowers where they were, and the pattern they were both trapped in played itself out in the same painful way.

Freddy was alone with his empty arms aching, and Hanni had pushed him away and was gone.

CHAPTER 14

26 FEBRUARY 1949

The apartment was too small. He needed the sky.

Tony dropped into a chair and pulled off his tie. The block-ade-beating publicity circus had claimed most of his days since the start of the year and he was sick of it. He hadn't been born to make speeches and shake hands. He needed to fly. He missed the thrill of take-off, the challenge of piloting his plane through fog and narrow landings. He missed the engines' roar.

Engines had been Tony's first obsession. When he had finally arrived in Pittsburgh in 1937 – wearing a name that had been remodelled by a lazy immigration official on Ellis Island but felt more suited to his new life – he had refused to take up the school place that was waiting for him. He had gone to work in his uncle's car factory instead. He had loved the work. He had loved the smooth touch and the hot smell of the metal, the intricacy of the engineering process. He had spent two years learning every aspect of the assembly line until he could strip an engine down and rebuild it with his eyes shut. Then, in July 1939 – in the week of his eighteenth birthday and the day after his citizenship papers arrived – he walked out of his uncle's house and he never went back.

He didn't have a plan except to get away from another family who didn't care about him. His parents, whose letters to him were far less frequent than the ones he sent them, had refused to let him return home and had promised to join him in America as soon as they could. Nothing in the newspapers about Hitler's stranglehold on Germany suggested that there was any real possibility of that, and Tony's uncle had pleaded a poverty he couldn't claim to have when Tony asked him to sponsor a second set of visas. Tony hated his uncle for refusing. Once 'no' had been said, he couldn't stay in his house and keep his hands off the man's jowly neck any longer. So he left.

The first train out of Penn Station had been going to Seattle, so Tony went to Seattle. The first company he interviewed for was Boeing, so Tony went to work for Boeing. He found his next obsession there. By the summer of 1941, he was no longer building engines, he was delivering planes. By the following year, he had won his wings in the United States Army Air Force and was on his way to war with the country that had got rid of him. There had been no mother or father present to witness his passing-out ceremony – there had been no word of them for two years – but there were plenty of giggling girls delighted to hang on the arm of a dashing and apparently tragically orphaned young pilot.

One of the girls Tony met through the Savannah Airbase he was assigned to in Georgia survived dating him, one of them didn't. He left two bodies behind him at the California training centre he had been based at before that: an older woman and a middle-aged man. As for Seattle...

Tony had lived there for over two years; he found it difficult to recall all the lives he had ended during that time. Not that anyone else would have been able to map them out either. Tony had always been too careful for that. He had got into fights in Pittsburgh, and there were girlfriends he had frightened there, but he had never been foolish enough to kill so close to his home.

He had forced himself to live with his anger instead and, when he couldn't do that anymore, he had left. After that... he was more careful still.

He lived in places that sprawled or had satellite towns or, like airbases, had rapidly changing populations. No one he took had a family or ties. No one he took was easily connected to the others – or to him. He never established a pattern of age or sex that could get him caught. Who his victims were didn't matter. He sought them out when he needed to find peace and then they died, and some of them were found, and nothing ever came of that either. There was no one to demand an investigation. There was no one to remember their names except for the detectives who were forced to file the murders they couldn't crack as unsolved. Not one of the names from his past ever came back to bother him. Except for Nancy's.

Tony was so tired of hearing about her.

Nancy had been his attempt at a normal life. He had met her in 1944 in New York, and she had stayed in touch with him. When he found himself demobbed two years later, she had been waiting. He had followed her to her family farm in Texas and pretended to be a cowboy until he couldn't bear that life anymore. Then he had moved to the Plains, with Nancy tagging along behind him, to take to the air again and spray crops until he couldn't bear that life anymore either and the blockade had forced the Air Force to once again start looking for pilots.

Nancy was part of his past, a failure and a mistake. Tony had no desire to be reminded of Nancy, but Alex Zielinkski – the fool Hanni had flirted with in the Green Fiddler Bar – wouldn't stop trying to make him remember.

Maybe I should put Zielinski's name onto a new list.

It was tempting; the idea of a second list. Tony's programme had moved on quickly since the child's death. Nine of his family were now accounted for, which meant only three more atonements were needed, and one of those would be dealt with tonight.

That was excellent progress, but it didn't mean he had to stop doing what he did if the urge took him. Zielinski could be part of his next set of tasks – one of the names to be put on a new list filled with nuisances. Although, as annoying as he was, Zielinski's name wouldn't be the one at the top. That honour would go to Hanni.

Tony got up and poured himself a shot of bourbon, which he sipped as he packed up his duffel bag.

He was very tired of Hanni. She wasn't grateful and she wasn't useful, and absence, in her case, hadn't made the heart grow fonder. She hadn't taken any of his calls in almost a month, and she hadn't sent him a single word of explanation. Tony wasn't happy about that. He also suspected that she had taken pictures of him that would do him no favours if they were circulated. He had seen her watching him, raising her camera when she thought he was off guard; setting up shots designed to make him uncomfortable. Tony didn't want her judgement, and he didn't want eyes as observant as Hanni's scrutinising him. He also had no desire to waste any more time debating whether he could risk entering into a relationship with her, no matter how much he had been tempted. It was finally time to deal with the problem that Hanni – as they all eventually did – had become. And then it would be time to deal with Freddy.

Tony picked up the bourbon bottle and poured a second, smaller measure. Enough to wash away the sour taste which collected in his mouth when he thought about the inspector, not enough to threaten the coming night's task. Hanni was a disappointment, but Freddy Schlüssel was dangerous. Tony had recognised that fact at the Reichstag and he had felt it again in Mitte. If it hadn't been for Freddy suddenly revealing himself to be Jewish, the man wouldn't have survived Christmas Day.

What if I had opened up the way that he did? What if I had told him some of the truth about me? Perhaps that would have softened his hostility.

It wasn't a new thought. It had first occurred to him when the two men had walked into and then squared up to each other on Sophienstraße. When Freddy had explained his family's fate at the hands of the Nazis – and taken Tony completely by surprise – Tony had momentarily considered doing the same. The possibility of unburdening himself had suddenly seemed like an attractive one.

He had allowed himself to imagine shaking Freddy's hand and saying, 'They took my people too.' He had allowed himself to imagine admitting that he was also in Mitte retracing his past. That he had been heading towards Große Hamburger Straße not to visit a black market but to stand in the place where his school had once been. That he had planned to go to Linienstraße after that and look for the site where his father's jewellery shop had once stood. To see if – as Freddy had put it – there were still echoes.

He had almost opened up his life for the first time since he had left Berlin twelve years earlier, but then common sense had stepped in. Freddy might be Jewish, but he was also – perhaps more so – a policeman. He would listen, he would probably sympathise, but he would also take the information away and burrow into it. Freddy wouldn't turn away from Tony's life – he would look closer in.

The way he was doing when he sent the boy to follow me.

Tony folded his blue workman's jacket into the duffel bag and picked up the nylon ligature. He'd had that with him in his pocket at Mitte. He had been tempted to wrap it round Freddy's neck when he'd first bumped into him. He would have done it if he hadn't been so certain that Freddy would have fought back and attracted attention. He coiled it up carefully now and packed it away, imagining the rattle of the inspector's last breath. Freddy wouldn't be so lucky a second time. Freddy was the worst of them all: Freddy had forced him to kill a child.

Tony had disliked Freddy from the moment they met. Then – after the press conference, whose *beware the stranger you know* message Tony was certain had been aimed on some level at him, and their subsequent meeting in Mitte – he had grown wary of the inspector. Now he hated him. For putting the boy on his trail. Oli, that was it: that was the name the child had finally surrendered. For making Oli a problem with only one possible solution.

It had taken Tony a while to realise that he had a shadow dogging his footsteps. The boy was good. He blended in. Tony had noticed him once or twice, but he had been in a pack then, one of the street kids who constantly crowded around him. He hadn't paid Oli any particular notice. It wasn't until he popped up twice in the Russian sector that Tony began to grow suspicious.

Tony had never dismissed Freddy's warnings about the dangers of roaming around Mitte or Friedrichshain, or any of the other Russian-controlled neighbourhoods, although he had pretended to. He knew how dangerous those areas were and that him getting caught in one could cause an international incident.

Tony was willing to take the risk because there was something he could get in the Soviet sector which he couldn't get anywhere else: a gun. That wasn't his preferred choice of weapon. Tony was a proficient marksman, but he had never enjoyed shooting the way so many of the men who had trained with him did. He wasn't about to change his main method of killing, but since Tony had met Freddy, the idea of owning a gun had consumed him. If he'd had one of those in his pocket on Christmas Day rather than the noose, the inspector might have paid very quickly for stopping him. A gun therefore felt like a good insurance policy.

Tony had been as careful buying the weapon as he was doing everything else. He crossed into Mitte three times before he made the actual purchase. And it was as he was on his way back the third time that he realised he was being followed.

Tony didn't like remembering that day, but there were times he couldn't avoid it. It hadn't proved difficult in the end to duck down an alleyway and grab the boy. The child was quick, but he wasn't as invincible as his scurrying around the darker sides of Berlin had led him to think. But what he had proved to be was remarkably tight-lipped.

'Why are you following me?' had been answered with, 'I'm not.'

'Who told you to do it?' had been answered with, 'Nobody.'

Even when Tony had showed him both the ligature and the gun – and proved the danger he was in – Oli had kept insisting he was innocent.

What Oli hadn't counted on was that Tony was a patient man and he had more tricks up his sleeve than the broken bones the boy had clearly been expecting.

'Did Schlüssel send you?' was greeted with a shrug and a blank face, but Oli wasn't so clever when Tony asked, 'So was it Hanni then?'

It was the look that spread over the boy's face which gave him away. Not about who had sent him but about where his heart lay. After that, all it had taken was: 'Tell me why you've been tracking me or I'll make you watch while she dies.'

Oli had spilled Freddy's name at once, followed by a heartfelt, 'He knows that you're a bad man,' which had revealed how young the boy behind the bravado really was. Killing him had been horrible, almost as horrible as killing the child who had died for his brother David. Oli, however, had seen the nylon cord and Oli was nobody's fool, so Oli had to die. Which was Freddy's fault. So Freddy would be the second name on Tony's new list.

And maybe I'll make him do what I threatened the boy with and watch her die first.

That thought was as warming as the bourbon.

Tony picked up his bag and left the apartment. Hanni and Freddy could wait, although their time was coming. His work was going well – once tonight's task was done he would be close to the end of it. Then the follow-up project could begin.

That was a cheering, warming thought.

Tony stopped on the doorstep for a moment and looked up. The night sky was velvety, the moon was soft, its glow spilling out and blurring the base's hard edges. He stared at the stars, picking out their constellations and patterns, imagining his plane dancing between them. It was soothing, in the way that the skies he loved were always soothing.

He shouldered his bag and moved away from the apartment complex and into the darkness with a lighter step. Perhaps he couldn't fly as much as he longed to, but the future felt suddenly brighter.

CHAPTER 15

25–28 MARCH 1949

'I'll put myself forward for the press conference circuit again. I've neglected it since Oli died, which hasn't helped us. And I'll ask to be Tony's photographer, if he'll have me. I know you don't like the thought of it, but if this investigation is going to go anywhere, we need to get close inside his circle, and there's no one who can do that but me.'

Freddy hadn't been comfortable with Hanni's suggestion at all: he was afraid that associating with Tony could put her in danger. Hanni suspected that he was right, but she couldn't see that they had any alternative. The only thing she was confident of was that her brief infatuation with Tony had vanished – if she was honest with herself, it had never really started. Whatever Tony was, he wasn't Freddy, and no amount of trying to pretend that didn't matter had stuck. And now Tony was potentially...

Hanni still didn't know the answer to that, but she trusted her own instincts and she trusted Freddy's, and she knew that, whatever they discovered about Tony, it wouldn't be good.

Not that they had made any progress. Their attempts to dig into Tony's life had been, by necessity, careful ones, and they had ground – along with everything else about the case – almost instantly to a halt.

Hanni had lost nearly the entire month of February to her shock over Oli and her fear and frustration over Reiner. As the case stalled for a lack of new leads, she had avoided the police station and the American press office and had focused on the freelance newspaper assignments which were far less taxing. Unfortunately that meant that she'd had no access to Tempelhof, and the cargo-handlers she had photographed there had very little interest in talking to Freddy. When they, reluctantly, did, they had no knowledge whatsoever of Tony's flight plans. It had proved impossible to tie down Tony's movements, except for the days on which he had been wheeled out as the Air Force's star turn, and neither she nor Freddy had, as yet, come up with an alternative angle for that, or for any other aspect of the case.

The investigation was stalling, but the strangler wasn't. Despite Freddy's warning, more doors had opened, more murders had been committed. The number of victims whose deaths matched Edda Sauerbrunn's had now risen to ten. It was an impossible number. *Ten* sent shock waves crashing through the station. *Ten* – when it was printed by the papers in letters large enough to fill half a page – crackled horror through the streets. And *ten* had added years onto Freddy.

None of the details had changed as the numbers grew: all the victims had been strangled in their own homes; all of them were unconnected beyond the manner of their deaths; all the crime scenes were calm ones. The Kreuzberg investigation team was worn out and the press were hysterical. The only thing Freddy no longer feared was being dropped from the case – no other detective in Berlin, at any level, would touch it.

'Cracking the case of the Berlin Strangler has turned into the textbook definition of a poisoned chalice: whoever manages to solve it will become the city's hero, but no one has any faith anymore that it can be solved. All any detective hears when the subject comes up is the sound of his career crashing. Which is what mine will probably do, especially if Brack finds out who we've started to suspect. He'll have my guts if he gets one breath of that.'

Freddy had confided that to Hanni one evening when the rest of the team had gone home and the second floor was deserted. They had been kneeling in a cleared space, as they had been for too many nights, surrounded by photographs, trying to tie the ones where Tony was lost in a sea of laughing faces to the ones where the faces were dead. They couldn't do it and they couldn't give up. The only good thing – although neither of them had acknowledged it – was that working together and sharing a secret together had brought the two of them closer again. There were unspoken rules: the newly revived bond was strictly controlled and it was strictly related to professional matters. Freddy hadn't asked why Hanni believed that Oli's death was her doing; Hanni hadn't volunteered an explanation. They handled each other as if their bones were brittle, but the coldness had gone and the closeness was back. Whatever else she was sorry for, Hanni was deeply grateful for that.

The impact of Oli's murder had continued to ripple through both their lives. Freddy had turned inward. Hanni was battling sleepless nights in which she lay awake picking over how little she had done to make the boy's life better, despite all her good intentions. Knowing that Oli had held her – and the rest of the world – at arm's-length didn't help. And what she also now knew – and what conversely should have made her sleep easier – was that the cause of his killing wasn't Reiner. The note which had accompanied the roses, in its gaps, if not in its words, had spelled that out.

Hanni had known from the instant that she saw the bouquet clutched in Freddy's hand who the flowers had been sent by. It wasn't the first of its type she had seen. Hanni had received a similar bunch from her father before: a stack of overblown and over-perfumed crimson blooms with silken edelweiss sprigs wound round their stems. The note that came with the first bunch hadn't brought news that she wanted and neither had the second. It proved what she had feared: that Reiner wasn't lying forgotten in some Allied jail charged with reviving old hatreds, that he was instead as free to carry on brewing his poison as he had always been. And – if he was to be believed, which Hanni had long ago learned that he should be – his school might be gone, but his dream for winning the loyalty and the minds of a new generation was nowhere near dead at all.

My dear girl,

Here we are again: a change in fortunes – although this time in mine rather than yours – heralded by a bouquet. Perhaps it will become a family tradition.

I have to confess, I do not know how deep your hand was in this affair, or if it was in it at all. Perhaps you have, once again, surprised me. I will do my best when I can to find out.

Suffice to say, I am no longer in Berlin and I have no plans to return there, not until there is a great change in the city. An enterprise I was connected with has come to an end. Luckily, that was merely one link in a long chain, and my fortunes, and my plans, continue to prosper.

That may mean something to you; it may not. I feel that the probability points to the former, but that is not my current concern. I am not done, my dear; you should know that – hearts and minds remain very much for winning. And although I am not near your side in person anymore, there are people watching you. Do not ever forget that. Wherever I am, Hannelore, there will always be people watching you.

He was the usual ten steps ahead of her.

The message in the note was as cryptic as the one contained in the edelweiss – the flower favoured by the National Socialists – which he had twined around the stems of the roses. It was also unsigned and unaddressed and untraceable.

That her father was free from any public association with the Wannsee school and gone from the city was, Hanni knew, both a blessing and a curse for her. It left her free of any immediate threat from him but also without the evidence she needed to bring him to justice. The only vague consolation that she could find in his message was that Reiner wasn't the one who had ordered Oli's death. If he had, mention of that and of her part in the boy's downfall would, no matter how obliquely, have been threaded through his words. That absence absolved Hanni from guilt over Oli, but it also tipped the balance of its burden towards Freddy.

Hanni didn't want that for him. She didn't want anything but good things for him.

So I have to help him solve the case by doing what I can to find out the truth about Tony.

Which would have been all very well except that, whenever she called the base and asked to speak to him, Tony wasn't there.

The guard at the American base proved to be as young and persuadable as the one who had turned a blind eye to her at Theresienstadt, although at least this time Hanni knew it wasn't him she was putting in danger. It took her little more than a bright smile and, 'Please, I so want to surprise him,' to get access to the Dahlem compound and to Tony's address. She walked away along the perimeter road knowing that the guard was watching her, presuming he was calculating what her cheapest price would be. She didn't care. She had got into the base's accommodation area; she had confirmed Tony was present.

And I have surprise on my side which might catch me something.

Tony was certainly surprised when he opened the door. It was also clear – in the moment before his face reassembled itself into his customary affable mask – that he wasn't at all happy to see her.

'I know, I know. I shouldn't have turned up without warning, and the gate-guard shouldn't have let me in without warning you either, but please don't put the blame on him. I wouldn't take no for an answer, although I swear that he tried. The thing is, though, I've been trying to call you and I couldn't get through and

I really wanted to apologise for being so hard to reach when you tried to offer me more work. So here I am to apologise!'

She kept up the babble without pausing for breath until Tony had no choice but to step aside and invite her in.

'You must have thought me dreadfully rude, but the caseload at the station has been overwhelming and then there was a family issue, and you know how impossible they can be.'

Hanni chattered on about nothing while Tony ushered her into a small sitting room, and she noted how spartan that was.

'Anyway, my time is much freer now and that's why I'm here. If you need my services as a photographer again, I'd be delighted to step back up and get snapping.'

She came to a stop with a grin which demanded a smile in return. Tony returned it reluctantly, but he did return it. Hanni chalked that up as a success.

'Well, goodness me, that was quite some arrival. I never had Hanni Winter pegged as a whirlwind before.'

Tony had recovered himself very quickly, which Hanni had expected him to do. Now she had to make sure he didn't take charge of their meeting. She kept talking so that he didn't get a chance to, prattling enthusiastically about 'how wonderful it must be to have a place of your own' as he waved her to a cushion-less sofa and perched himself on the edge of a chair. As Hanni settled herself in with another flurry of compliments, she noticed him take a surreptitious glance at his watch.

'I'm sorry. I've been thoughtless and I've caught you at a bad time. Do you have another press conference to go to? They do seem to be sending you out on the stage quite a lot.'

Tony shook his head, but he kept his sleeve pushed back.

'I don't have a press conference, no. I'm actually flying, for the first time in too many weeks. I'm about to go on a supply run to Fassberg. I'm going to be away until Tuesday at least.'

The change that came over Tony's face as he said 'flying' was remarkable. It brightened with a delight Hanni knew – because she had seen so much in him that wasn't – was genuine. She forced herself not to jump too eagerly onto that. Or on the fact that he was about to leave his apartment empty. There were opportunities there – even if she hadn't worked out what they were yet – and a man who was normally completely closed off had opened two chinks into his world. Hanni wasn't about to get clumsy and fumble either of those. She smiled and switched to a less breathy tone than the one she had been confusing him with.

'You're glad about that, aren't you? About flying again? You've missed it.'

It was as if another man had entered the room. Tony's smile was no longer a reflex – it was a broad grin and his eyes were genuinely sparkling.

'More than I can tell you. I know that the Air Force needs me here, that morale-boosting is vital, but being kept out of the sky has been torture.'

'Tell me how it feels.'

Hanni leaned forward so that she was close enough to touch him but deliberately didn't. 'I've never flown but I'd love to. If you have time, it would be wonderful to hear what it's really like up there.'

She broke off and coughed. 'I don't suppose you have any tea, do you? My throat is so dry from the walk here.' She smiled again as Tony nodded. 'And please don't stop talking while you make it. Tell me being up in the heavens is as wonderful as I've always imagined it to be.'

Her interest worked. Tony left the kitchen door open, and once he began talking, he couldn't stop. He described the feel of the controls and the power they contained as if he was holding them. He told her how magical it had been the first time he broke through the clouds. He brought her a teacup with the teabag and the spoon left in it the way she had asked him to do and carried on waxing lyrical about the beauty of the skies with more enthusiasm than she thought he was capable of. And he didn't drink the coffee he had made for himself, and he didn't notice that she hadn't touched her tea. What Tony also omitted to do was look at his watch. He made no mention of leaving at all until the clock in the hall suddenly chimed the hour and he jumped up in a panic.

'I have to go. If I don't, I'll miss the slot and God knows when I'll swing another chance past the colonel.'

Hanni mimicked his flustered jump to his feet and was immediately all concern.

'Oh my goodness – well of course you must go. We can pick up the photography stuff when you get back. Why don't you grab your things and I'll tidy up in here.'

She waved him into the bedroom, keeping up a blur of movement while she collected the cups. It took less than a minute to wrap the teaspoon in tissue and drop it into her bag. When Tony re-emerged with his flying jacket on and clutching his holdall, she was waiting for him at the front door, wearing her coat and her most purposeful expression.

'I enjoyed that, talking to you.'

He moved towards her. For a moment, Hanni thought he was going to kiss her. To her relief, he reached across her instead and plucked a key from the dish on the shelf beside the door.

There's a second one.

Hanni didn't move. She hadn't had any kind of a plan for what she would do when she had arrived today; she hadn't had time to work out what Tony being away from his apartment might offer her. Now she had a teaspoon which he had touched stowed away in her bag and the possibility of sneaking back into the flat without him. All she had to do was distract his attention again.

'Do you have everything?' She nodded at the duffel bag he was holding. 'I can never leave the house on a trip unless I've checked my luggage twice.'

Tony frowned – the thought that he could forget anything important had obviously never occurred to him – but he looked down at his bag exactly as Hanni needed him to do. It was a split-second glance, but a split second was all that it took to flick out her hand and sweep the second key from the bowl into her pocket.

'Silly me, of course you have – you're a professional at this after all. Shall we go?'

She managed not to cheer when he closed the door firmly behind them and led her away.

'Captain Miller isn't on the base tonight.'

'I know. Which is why I'm here to see Captain Jones.'

The name she had chosen was a generic one. The kiss she planted on the guard's cheek stopped any more questions. Five minutes later, Hanni was letting herself into Tony's apartment. And then, once she was inside, the adrenaline that had got her that far drained instantly away. Hanni had to lean against the door until her heart stopped hammering.

I should have told Freddy that I was coming here.

It was a sensible thought; it would have been a sensible thing to do. Except that Freddy would have stopped her, which was why she had spent the last forty-eight hours avoiding him.

She had barely slept since she'd left Tony's apartment on Saturday. It had been a struggle not to race back to the compound on the Sunday and to wait instead until Monday when there would, hopefully, be fewer people around.

Hanni had passed most of Sunday in the Tiergarten, wandering around the lake and lingering in the café, doing whatever she could to fill up the hours and keep away from Kreuzberg in case Freddy took it into his head to come looking for her. She had spent the Monday hiding in her darkroom and avoiding the station, certain that he would drag the secret of her visit – and her intended return – out of her the moment that they started speaking. She knew he would have been furious at both. And now that didn't matter anymore because it was Monday evening and she was in Tony's empty apartment and what Freddy didn't know wouldn't hurt him.

It was too cold to stay in the hallway and, frayed nerves or not, Hanni didn't have time to waste – for all she knew, Tony's plans could have changed and there was no excuse that would explain her presence in his flat. She shook out her tight shoulders, dropped her bag and began moving methodically through the rooms, sliding open drawers, easing open cupboards. Noting exactly how and where the contents were placed before she moved anything. Stopping every few minutes to listen for any sign of movement on the road outside. Grabbing the key without Tony noticing had been an unexpected piece of luck and Hanni wasn't the type of person who put a lot of faith in luck.

The apartment wasn't a welcoming place. It wasn't just the sitting room which was spartan – the rest of the flat was as soulless. There were no mementos to give it a personality; there were no personal touches to give it a heart. There were also no secrets to find.

Hanni paced from cupboard to cupboard feeling increasingly dispirited, trying to convince herself that one more sweep would reveal something more damning than the teaspoon was likely to be. That had seemed like such a find when she took it and then, in the calmer light of day, she had realised how tenuous a piece of evidence it actually was. Even if the forensics lab could lift a fingerprint from the metal and match that to the one found at Matty Scheibel's flat – and that was a big if – and they could then use the print to establish a link between the girl and Tony, he would talk his way out of it. The odds were that it would never even get as far as him: Brack or the Americans would shoot its implications down first. The teaspoon was a tease – it wasn't enough.

Hanni began another circuit, telling herself that this one would work. She pushed her fingers beneath the drawers and into the furthest corners of the highest shelves. She searched through his belts, looking for one whose width matched the ligature mark left on the victims. Finally, she did what she hadn't wanted to do – because putting everything perfectly back into them would be a difficult challenge – and emptied his incredibly neat kitchen cupboards.

Most of the brands they contained were American and unfamiliar. On any other day, she would have been distracted by that and tempted to start tasting. Today was not that day. Hanni worked through the shelves one at a time, her heart sinking when she opened a particularly well-stocked one. She unloaded that slowly, mapping its contents. She was still focused on transferring the products she had removed so that they stood on the counter in a mirror image of the shelves when the photograph tumbled out from the back.

It had been hidden, which meant it was important, which also meant that she couldn't remove it from the flat or damage it in any way. Hanni picked the image up with her fingernails and took it through to the sitting room where the light was brightest. She sat down and made sure that her hands were dry and steady. Then she took a deep breath and she looked at it.

It was a garden scene. A lively rather than a formal shot with bodies leaning in haphazardly towards each other and heads closely pressed. Hanni guessed from the resemblances that ran across the cast of a chin and the angle of eyes and noses that most of the people in it were related. The snap also appeared to have been taken by one of the subjects: there was a slight blurring to the figure furthest to the left which suggested the use of a self-timer. It was a charming picture of a happy family on a sunny day. When it was taken, it would have been an innocent one. It wasn't that anymore. Not only had it been deliberately hidden rather than left out on display, there were small tick marks floating above ten of the smiling faces.

Hanni refused to let herself react to that – there would be time enough for emotions later. She took her camera out of her bag and carefully photographed the front of the image. Then she turned it over and photographed the neat writing which covered the back and listed the victims' names. She took a dozen more shots of the faces, closing in on those which looked familiar, whose twins she had already catalogued under far nastier circumstances. Then she carried the picture as carefully back into the kitchen as she had carried it out, returned it to the cupboard where she had found it and slid the packets and the tins back into place.

We have him. This isn't a tease. This is proof.

Hanni pushed her camera into the bottom of her bag, changed the coat she was wearing for the second one she had rolled up and brought with her, and scraped her hair under a hat. She tried not to rush. She tried to move as methodically as she had when she had searched through the flat, in case the excitement bubbling through her led to a mistake. She replaced the key in the dish and slipped out, offering a silent prayer of thanks to the inventor of self-locking doors. Then she waited until she was sure a new guard had taken up position at the gate before she exited the compound.

We have him.

Halfway down the road, Hanni stopped, wrapped her arms round her body and let the laugh come.

We have him.

There was nothing else in her head. There had been nothing else in her head since she had found the photograph. And then the wind whipped up and nipped at her ankles and another thought crept in.

We have him. Now how in God's name do we get him?

CHAPTER 16

29 MARCH–5 APRIL 1949

Comes the Hour, Comes the Man: The Hero Helping to Feed a City

Try Killing on Our Streets and We'll Be Here Waiting

Freddy stared at the two images lined up side by side on his desk. One was rendered in colour and printed on a glossy magazine cover, the other was black and white and poorly laid out on cheap, flimsy paper. He assumed it was Brack who had left them both there.

With absolutely no clue as to how closely linked they are.

There was no note. Freddy assumed that the display was intended as an insult, a clumsily executed reflection on the job he was – or in Brack's eyes was not – doing. It was a change at least from being yelled at.

The most eye-catching of the two was the one gracing the front of *Time* magazine. That featured Tony in full hero mode. Its composition was, in Freddy's eyes, as much of a cliché as the accompanying headline; he could imagine Hanni laughing if she saw it. The captain had been pictured in his flying costume, standing fists on hips in front of one plane, while another circled the clouds above him as if it was waiting for his permission to land. Tony's body was facing the camera; his gaze, however, was trained into the distance. His expression was as thoughtful as if he was contemplating not only the intricacies of the blockade but exactly how he was about to single-handedly resolve it. He was all square shoulders and square jaw, a vision of strength and control and command. Freddy was surprised Brack hadn't scrawled *spot the differences between him and you* across the cover in red pen. That image was ridiculous; the second one was disturbing.

Freddy flipped the magazine over and turned his attention onto the poster with its stark type and far grainier photograph. In contrast to Tony's heroic stance, these men had their hats pulled down and their faces averted. Their intent – which was written not in a furrowed brow and a world-beating uniform but in the hammers and clubs they were holding – was as easy to decipher as Tony's unspoken claim to be saving Berlin. Anyone seeing it, including the killer who its message was aimed at, would know exactly who was defending the city.

Freddy put the poster back down and rubbed at his temple where a headache was threatening. According to the address of the beer hall where volunteers to the cause were being invited to gather, this particular example had come from Wedding. Freddy had already seen its twin plastered across Kreuzberg and Neukölln, and he imagined replicas could be found all across the city. Ten dead bodies, ten homes turned into murder scenes and no suspect in sight had hardened Berlin and unleashed packs of vigilantes onto the streets who were determined to do the police's job for them and hunt down the strangler. Their efforts were already making themselves felt. Two men who had, separately, wandered into the wrong neighbourhood had ended up in hospital badly beaten. One had lost an eye. Freddy knew it was merely a matter of time before somebody – an innocent some-body – was so badly hurt that they died. He would blame himself for that and so, quite rightly in his opinion, would everyone else.

Freddy had tried to calm the city through official channels and he had failed: Brack had refused to do anything to rein in the vigilantes or condemn the beatings. When Freddy had then – far more humbly this time – approached Elias instead for help, Elias had sent him away with a stinging, 'If you don't like other people doing your job then do it better yourself.' There was nowhere else for Freddy to turn after that.

I have brought mob rule back to Berlin.

It was a sickening thought that Freddy didn't know how to counter. He also had no idea how to point the finger of suspicion at Tony.

After the debacle of trying to map Tony's movements, he and Hanni had spent days poring over Hanni's publicity photographs, trying to find a match for any of the faces Freddy had scrutinised at the funerals. Their efforts had come to nothing. The next job would be to revisit each of the victim's families, making sure to ask very carefully worded questions. Re-opening those wounds was not a task Freddy relished. The one visit he had already managed to make, to Jochen Stahl's mother, had not gone well. She had remembered meeting Tony in the days before tragedy had struck but, when Freddy tried to dig into her somewhat hazy recollections, she had nothing to offer except praise. Tony had sent her a personal letter of condolence which she had clutched to her chest as if it was an icon. That had made Freddy feel sick. The gesture was either very caring or, if Tony really was guilty, it was frighteningly manipulative. The thought that he might encounter similar letters and reactions at the other victims' homes was a slap in the face he wasn't yet ready for.

He threw the magazine and the poster into the bin and dragged himself up from his desk. Matz was hovering, waiting to call the team together for the morning briefing. Freddy had nothing to say that he hadn't already said. There was nothing in his head beyond a bunch of clichés about continuing courage and darkest hours which could have been borrowed from Winston Churchill. He doubted those sentiments would endear him to anyone. He emerged from his office anyway and he slapped on a smile. Nobody bothered to return it.

'Are we ready then?'

He had absolutely no idea what he was going to say next. When the door burst open and Hanni flew in, her hair escaping from its pins and her face flushed, he could have cheered. At least nobody now was staring at him.

'Inspector, could I have a word with you before the meeting starts?'

'You're okay then?'

That wasn't as bad as the 'Where the hell have you been? I've been worrying myself sick about you' which had almost tumbled out of his mouth, but his intensity still made heads swivel. He waved her quickly into his office and shut the door when Matz tried to join them. Her urgency suggested that Hanni had found something. Whatever it was, no matter how small, sharing that with the men would be far preferable to giving them another empty pep talk.

'Where were you yesterday? I checked and there wasn't a press briefing.' Freddy stared at Hanni's suddenly flushed face and the penny dropped. 'You went to see him, didn't you? And you've been avoiding me since the weekend because you knew I would stop you from going.'

'Yes and yes and none of it matters. Or it won't when you see what I've brought you.'

Hanni talked him through everything she had done with a speed which wouldn't allow him to be horrified. Then she dropped a small bundle of photographs onto his desk.

'I finished developing them this morning which is why I'm late in.'

She sat down and stayed silent as Freddy fanned the pictures out and went carefully through them. It was a while before he could accept what he was seeing.

'Is that one there Tony?'

Freddy pointed to a boy at the centre of the scene, sitting on the ground with his head on the knee of a smiling woman who shared his dark hair and strong features.

Hanni nodded. 'I think so. You can see the resemblance even though he's much younger and, if this was taken in the late twenties or early thirties the way the clothing suggests, he would fit the age frame.'

'So the woman he's leaning against is presumably his mother.' Freddy paused and lifted the image back up to the light. 'And she could also easily be Edda Sauerbrunn.'

Hanni nodded at that too. Freddy sat quietly for a moment, letting himself absorb the link he had just made. Then he picked up the shot Hanni had taken of the back of the photograph and read out some of what was written there.

'This list. It surely proves what we thought all along: he's been finding lookalikes for his family. The *M* after Edda must stand for *Mutter,* the *V* next to Falco for *Vater.*' Freddy picked up the garden scene again and checked the grouping. 'The similarities between them are uncanny. And if we follow the logic he seems to be using, the two letter *B*s must be *Bruder* and the *S* is for *Schwester.*'

Freddy carried on matching up the letters for cousins and uncles and aunts with the men and women the camera had captured.

'It's an extended family – it has to be, and he's killed like-for-like.'

Freddy knew without sending for them that the photographs of the other victims would be as closely matched to the garden shot as Edda and Falco: their faces were engraved on his memory. He also knew that he should be feeling elated – he was holding the solution to one of the worst murder sprees the city had ever seen in his hands. All he could feel was a bone-aching sadness, for the people, in the picture and in his city, who were gone.

Hanni waited, giving him the moment he needed to collect himself, and then she leaned forward and picked up the original group shot.

'Ten bodies so far and ten ticks. I'm pretty certain that this was taken with a self-timer by someone in the photo, which means that there were twelve people there that day. That's twelve not including Tony. I think we can guess that they all died in the war. And I think, given the way he's used ticks and initials, that he's planning to take a life for every life taken from him.'

You're Jewish and your family were murdered.

Tony's words from Mitte floated back into Freddy's head, swiftly followed by, *And the same terrible thing happened to his.* He sat back. Tony was as much of a vigilante as the men he had inspired to go hunting for him. And, like them, his task wasn't finished.

'So if there are twelve family members and we're right that he's the killer, then there are still two more murders to come.'

He looked up at Hanni. All their hunches had led them in the right direction. It was still a dead end.

'And there's nothing we can do to bring him in, so how are we going to stop those from happening? There's nothing on this picture beyond a vague resemblance to tie Tony to it. I'm assuming that Miller isn't his family name, that he's changed it, but there's no clue recorded here which can help us with that. There's no quirk in the handwriting we could try to match up or any personal inscription. There's nothing but where you said you found it, which was somewhere you weren't meant to be. It won't fly with Brack. It won't fly with anyone.'

Hanni's sigh sounded as if she had drawn it up from her feet.

'I know. When the photo fell out of the cupboard where he'd hidden it, all I could think was: *We have him.* Then I came away and all I could think was: *But what now?* It's as though we've everything and nothing to celebrate: we have our killer, and we don't.'

Exhaustion swept over her face. Freddy saw the depth of it and pulled himself quickly together.

'No, come on: we can't let ourselves be so bleak. This is good, Hanni. This is really good. All right so we can't prove the link, or not yet, and we can't use this to pull him in and accuse him, but it's the start of an actual case. We'll get him, I know it. If there's one piece of evidence, there has to be more.'

His brighter tone snapped her out of the darker mood she had almost fallen into.

'But there is – I should have told you that first. I brought back a teaspoon from the flat that will have his prints on it. I sent that to the lab this morning to see if they could extract anything good and find a match with the print retrieved from Matty Scheibel's flat.'

She needed his enthusiasm, so Freddy rose to the challenge.

'That's fantastic, Hanni. That's another building block.'

He didn't say the obvious – that there was nothing but her word about where she had found the teaspoon to link it to Tony and that meant it wasn't evidence at all. They both needed at least the pretence of a win. He stared at her, wishing he could pat her on the back or shake her hand the way he would have done if it was Matz standing before him and feeling awkward even at the thought. Touching Hanni, even on the tips of her fingers, could never be an idle thing.

'You have done an amazing job, never mind a dangerous one. Thank you.'

The pride colouring her face made Freddy feel ten feet taller.

'We can box him in with this. We can carry on trying to gather evidence – finding out what we can about the people in the photograph and how Tony is linked to them, revisiting the families, keeping a close watch on whatever he does. We can try to force him into making a mistake. This is it, Hanni: this is progress.'

The smile on her face turned his excitement real. The glow in it danced through him.

Freddy got back to his feet. Matz was still lurking outside his office; the team was still waiting. The photograph had to remain a secret, but he could mention the potential for a fingerprint match in the broadest of terms in the briefing. He could push some confidence back through his men.

As he got up so did Hanni. She reached over the desk to gather up the pictures at the same moment that he did and her fingers accidentally brushed across his. Her skin against his crackled.

'What would I do without you?'

The words came from nowhere. He couldn't dismiss them as an overblown professional compliment: his tone was too caressing.

Hanni froze. Then she turned and looked up at him and there was a light in her eye he had been waiting to see there for months.

If I looped her fingers through mine, if I kissed her, she wouldn't push me away.

The certainty was overwhelming. Freddy stepped the short distance towards her, his hand reaching out to her cheek.

'Matz is watching.'

It wasn't a no, which meant it could be a *wait*. She hadn't jumped back from him. When he blinked and made himself reach for the door rather than for her, her smile was a gentle one and the light was still there.

Maybe he's gone, whoever he was. Maybe the flowers were a farewell present. Maybe there is another chance for us.

It was a lot of maybes to balance, but there hadn't been anything close to maybes before.

Freddy opened the door and let Hanni go through it. Then he followed her out into the main office with his head up and his shoulders back, ready to lead a meeting in which he finally had something to say and as confident as any hero on a magazine cover.

———

Being back in the skies had put a spring in his step Tony thought he had lost.

He had piloted both the flights to Fassberg and back with – as his admiring crew put it – an exceptional level of skill, even when one of the landings was suddenly threatened by a dreadful turn in the weather. His crew had cheered him onto the base. The pilots at Fassberg, who had heard his reputation for bravery and had now seen it in action, applauded him. Tony had returned to Tempelhof clutching the copy of *Time* he had been presented with in the bar and feeling every inch the star the magazine had called him.

His triumph turned out to be a short-won thing. As soon as Tony stepped through his front door, the exhilaration brought on by the engine's thrust and two perfectly executed landings evaporated. The dish he was about to drop his key in was out of its carefully positioned place on the shelf.

Someone has been here.

Tony dropped his bag and crouched in the hallway, sniffing at the air. The flat was empty now but somebody had been in it. He could sense poking fingers.

He moved slowly into the sitting room and then moved as carefully around the rest of the apartment, checking for other signs of disturbance. Nothing had significantly changed; too many things were ever so slightly different. His shirts lay flattened in the bureau drawer as if they had been too conscientiously pressed down. His belts weren't as tightly coiled as when he had left them. The thin layer of dust which had collected on the unused top shelf of the wardrobe had been disturbed and had drifted down onto the shoulders of his coat hangers.

Someone has searched through the whole flat.

He knew exactly who had gone snooping.

Tony went into the kitchen, his fists flexing, swallowing at the anger pushing up through his throat. He was furious with her, but he was also furious with himself. He should have taken his spare key with him. And – as he suddenly realised with a shock – he shouldn't have left anything for her to find. The realisation of what Hanni could have discovered brought him up with a jolt. He had remembered to take the envelope which contained the details of his potential targets with him to Fassberg, but he had forgotten to pack the photograph.

Which was her fault.

He picked that thought over, along with the sudden certainty that Hanni's ridiculous chatter and bustle had been deliberate. That she had not only arrived at his apartment unannounced because she had been trying to pry into his life, but she had also intended all along to distract him. He grabbed the back of a chair to steady himself. He wanted to put his fist through the wall.

I need to be calm. I need to be as methodical as she will have been.

He couldn't check the kitchen as carefully as she would have done if his blood was up, which meant that he couldn't unleash his anger. Or not yet.

He went to the sink first.

One of the teaspoons was missing.

Tony poured a glass of water and sipped it slowly as he worked through what that meant. A missing spoon was significant. It suggested that Hanni suspected him of something. Given that the whole city was obsessed with the same crime, it didn't take a lot of wit to work out what. Its theft, however, was no proof that Hanni had come back to the flat when he was away. She could have taken it on the Saturday afternoon and decided that was enough evidence. The moved clothes and the dust fall could be his imagination; he could have knocked the bowl containing his spare key out of position himself.

Tony let each uncertainty run through his head as he turned to the cupboard where his secret was stowed. He didn't believe that any of the excuses were true. And as soon as he opened the cupboard door, he knew she had been ferreting.

The packets and jars had been put back in the correct places but they had not been replaced with his meticulous attention to detail. Labels had shifted a fraction round from the front where they were meant to be facing. The spacing between the cans and the boxes was uneven.

Tony slowly emptied out the lower shelf, imagining Hanni doing the same and trying to remember where everything fitted. When he moved the box of Rice Krispies, he was momentarily surprised to find that the photograph was still there, until he realised that, whatever else Hanni was, she wasn't a fool. She wouldn't have taken the picture away and made herself obvious – she would have brought her camera with her instead.

He took the photo out and held it up to the light. There was a tiny impression in the top corner which he guessed was where a fingernail had pressed into it.

She knows. She – and Schlüssel, who she no doubt ran straight to from here – will have worked out what it means.

He left the picture on the counter, returned to the sitting room and sat down on the sofa.

Hanni knew what he had done. She would live long enough to regret that. Tony's stomach started to twist. He had almost made himself vulnerable to her again. He thought he had conquered that. He had managed to dismiss Hanni as a nuisance. He had been ready to deal with her, and then she had taken him in again, with her interest in flying and her interest in him. When she had widened her eyes and hung on his words, that interest had seemed genuine. He had been flattered by it, fooled by it. Hanni would live to regret doing that too.

Tony shifted on the sofa, his skin smarting as he realised how near he had come to disaster. There had been a moment on Saturday, and afterwards when he lay in his bunk at the base and thought about her, when he had seriously considered letting Hanni live. No, there had been more than one moment.

Hanni had got into his head. She had been there when he had lifted the first plane out of Tempelhof and when he had brought it safely down again through a blanket of fog which had wiped away the airbase. He had pictured her both times, watching him, admiring him. When he was alone in Fassberg, he had imagined telling her about the speed with which the clouds had thickened and the skies had gone dark and how sharply the threat of crashing had tested his flying skills. He had imagined her eyes sparkling as she listened. Nancy had been scared of planes and then she had been bored by them, but Hanni had genuinely seemed to care. There had been something very attractive in that, something he had thought – for a moment at least – he might take a risk on.

Whatever the people of Berlin believed, the blockade was crawling towards an end, or towards the promise of one. The Soviets had begun to accept that they couldn't break the city. That the ten thousand tons of supplies coming in now on a daily basis was a force to be reckoned with and that, when it came to the Berliners taking sides, the Allies were the clear winners. Negotiation was no longer an impossible word.

As a consequence of the rumours swirling round the Allied command posts, some of the pilots had begun to talk about life *after*. And, away from Berlin and its demands, Tony had begun to wonder what after might look like for him. He had, in fact, gone beyond idle speculation: he had done what he had promised himself he would never do again after the debacle of Nancy. He had let himself imagine building a future with someone. He had let himself imagine not being lonely; not being angry. He had wondered about the possibility of love. And it was that wondering – that hope of finding someone who shared his greatest passion – which Hanni had drilled her way into.

Which was a nonsense. She tricked me. She could have destroyed me.

He got slowly to his feet again, his limbs heavy with the depth of her betrayal. Hanni had snatched away all the joy he had rediscovered in flying. That was a reason to hate her. She had snatched away his idea that he could live a normal life. That was another. The list of reasons to hate Hanni was growing.

Tony went back into the kitchen, made a jug of coffee, opened and heated up a can of chicken soup.

Instead of letting the rage melt into his bloodstream where he would have to act on it, he let himself breathe through it, the way he had learned to do in Pittsburgh. There was no need to hurry; there was no need for him to be the one who suffered. His plan had got him a very long way. Now his plan had to change, but there could be strength in that.

Tony finished eating and washed up his dishes, and then he

picked up the photograph again. There were two people – an aunt and an uncle – left on it to honour and there were two people who deserved to die. Hanni who had made a fool of him and Freddy who he was sure she had done it for.

He left the photograph where it was. He went back to the sitting room, poured a shot of bourbon, lit a cigarette.

Tony no longer cared about Zielinski. There would be no second list anymore and there would be no more looking for the faces who most resembled his loved ones. There was no need: there would still be two deaths, and two deaths would do. After that, he would forget about new projects in Berlin. He would request a transfer, go back to America and start over somewhere new, safe in the knowledge that his long-ago promise to honour his family, to demonstrate his love for them, had been kept.

He took a drink, he savoured the cigarette and he let himself enjoy what was to come.

That the next person to die at his hands would be Hanni.

CHAPTER 17

16 APRIL 1949 – AFTERNOON

Spring is in the air.

Hanni had heard that phrase repeated more times than she could count, but it had never meant very much to her beyond a pleasant greeting. This Easter, however, 'spring is in the air' had become a physical thing and she couldn't stop sniffing it. The bakery round the corner from her lodging house smelled like a bakery again and everyone outside it was smiling.

Hanni had slipped out before breakfast to pick up the extra rolls of film she needed with no intention of lingering. Her days were packed full with the investigation. Carrying out the interviews with the victims' families that Freddy couldn't share out with anyone else on the team. Poring over the photographs she had taken at the press conferences, trying to find faces that might match up with the two members of Tony's family who were still unaccounted for. She had no time to notice anything but work and especially not queues which were a permanent fixture. This morning, however, was different. Not only was everyone in them smiling, they were gossiping together and laughing. And the scents which poured out of the small shop when the door opened were too delicious even for Hanni to ignore.

She joined the slowly moving line, dodging around the children plastering themselves across the bakery window. When she finally caught sight of the display set out there, she almost did the same thing. The piles of confectionary were as wonderful as the lemon and almond scents had promised they would be. Loaf after loaf of *Osterbrot* filled the wooden boards, their rich dough plaited and wound into wreaths and decorated with bright yellow paper chicks and fat pink paper rabbits. And in the centre of those was a sight no one who had lived with shortages for so long had expected to see: a circle of *Osterlamm* cakes, the holiday sponges shaped into plump little lambs and covered in drifts of powdered sugar.

Hanni licked her lips as the memory of their buttery taste filled her mouth. She was as excited as the rest of the queue at the thought of such luxury. But she did not believe that their appearance heralded the end of the blockade, or not in the way the rest of the chattering crowd pressing round her clearly did.

This isn't a coincidence, although it's a much more subtle approach than another statistic-filled press release.

The extravagantly stocked bakery was a propaganda exercise, Hanni was certain of that. She imagined that the scene, and the delighted reaction which had greeted the display in Kreuzberg, would be replicated all over the American-controlled sector. 'This must mean that the Russians are beaten' ran round her like an echo – so loudly in some cases that Hanni couldn't help but wonder if the shoppers had been paid to proclaim it. It was hard, however, to be cynical when the brimming shop was bringing so much pleasure.

Ten months earlier when the blockade had been announced, there had been no pleasure in the streets at all. People had panicked. They had descended on the shops like locusts, buying up anything edible their wallets could stretch to. The bakeries and the grocers had been emptied in hours. A few weeks after that – when the break on the city's supply lines started to bite and the airlift had barely started – the size of a wallet no longer mattered. There had been nothing left in the shops to buy. *Submit to the Russians or starve* had stopped being a vague threat best left for politicians to deal with and had become an everyday anxiety. Faces had grown pinched, shoulders had gone down; parents had begun to fear for their children.

And yet here we are, still standing. Surrounded by headlines that suggest that the blockade is over and the battle for Berlin's heart is won.

Food Stocks at Triple What They Were a Year Ago

The Miracle of Flight: Four-Minute Turnaround for Planes at Tempelhof

Daily Tonnage Breaks All Records: 13,000 delivered in Twenty-Four Hours!

Whatever else was based more on optimism than reality, the last two claims were certainly true. Hanni – who had managed to not only get herself back onto the list of approved photographers but had once again been specifically assigned to Tony – had already been sent the briefing sheet detailing those successes. Whether the first headline was as accurate as the others was debatable, but that also didn't matter. What was important was that everyone in the queue was holding a newspaper filled with good news and everyone holding that was thrilled with the Americans. A success that the second treat on offer would surely turn into a triumph.

Hold on to Your Hats, Here Comes the Easter Parade!

Join us at the Tiergarten on Saturday, 16 April from noon till late for a family celebration... Cheer the latest record-smashing efforts of your brave American pilots... Bring the kids for Easter egg hunts and carousel rides and a guaranteed feast for all!

The Easter Parade. Colonel Walker had come up with that

name, although his festivities were intended to celebrate the convoys of planes sweeping into the city, not a stream of flower-covered hats. Hanni had no need to join the crowds cooing over the posters advertising it. She had already been invited to photograph Tony's starring role at the event and had been briefed on the details. She also didn't want to look at the photograph that went with the invitation. That was an earlier shot she had taken of Tony, standing square on to the camera in his favourite pose and flinging his flight cap in the air. The shopgirls had stuck one on the window and they – and apparently every other woman who passed by it – kept pointing and swooning at it. Hanni kept her head turned firmly away. The sight of his smiling face made her feel sick.

It wasn't comfortable feeling so out of step. From the giggles and the grins, the announcement or the picture – or both – had certainly worked their magic on everyone else. If the shoppers in the bakery were a representative sample, the whole of Kreuzberg was planning to be at the party. Hanni was hardly surprised. From the mutterings in the station all week about cancelled leave – because almost every police officer in Kreuzberg and the surrounding boroughs had been pulled in to help with security – the Americans were expecting numbers which made their guarantee of a feast dependent on a parade of cooks, never mind pilots.

'It won't be as open as it sounds. Look at the way they've used *your* and *family* in the rhetoric. This isn't a free-for-all – it's about "good Germans" thanking the Americans for keeping them fed and the Americans thanking "good Germans" for letting them do it. It's a show. Nobody will be allowed in without careful checking. And you can forget about any Soviets getting inside, even if they are the real audience for the event.'

Brack had given Freddy a public dressing-down for being a cynic and had put him in charge of security out of spite. Everyone else knew that Freddy was right. There were dozens of places where the Americans could have held their blockade-busting party, but they had chosen to do it in the Tiergarten, in sight of the Brandenburg Gate and the Soviet soldiers who patrolled that area. It was yet another move in the propaganda war endlessly circling the city.

Although Hanni had to be present at the event, she wasn't looking forward to it: it would be the first time she had seen Tony since she had searched through his flat. That was a deeply unsettling thought, even if both she and Freddy refused to admit it. Hanni had promised Freddy that she wasn't worried about coming into close quarters with Tony again. Freddy had promised her that he wasn't worried by that either. Both of them were lying. Both of them were now firmly convinced that Tony was the killer. They were not, however – despite all the efforts they had made and the long hours that they were still working – one step closer to proving that. Which meant that there was nowhere Freddy could take their suspicions where there was any chance that they would be believed.

Without flight plans, and given how many engagements he often attended on the same day, it had proved impossible to determine exactly where Tony had been at the time of each killing. The forensics lab had found a fingerprint on the teaspoon, but it was too smudged to make a match. Freddy had taken a copy of the photograph Hanni had discovered to the Red Cross to see if anyone recognised, or had received any enquiries about, the family in it. He had drawn a blank. And they hadn't been able to catch Tony out. Despite there being ten ticks not twelve marked on the picture, murder number eleven and murder number twelve still hadn't taken place.

It had been over two weeks since Hanni had found the photograph. It had been over six weeks since the last strangled body was found. That was as much of a factor in the lighter mood on the streets as the better-stocked shops and the easing up in the power cuts allowed by the better weather.

The newspapers were beginning to speculate that the killer had stopped, or had moved on. That the threat of neighbourhood vigilantes had driven him away. The gossip in the cafés and pubs, and in the Kreuzberg police station, suggested that much of the city had begun to believe that conclusion was true. Only Freddy and Hanni thought differently, and only Hanni wanted to act decisively to stop Tony before the next killing spree started.

'Which it will. It doesn't make any sense for him to have abandoned his mission when he's so close. He's waiting for something, and we've a duty to tell what we know before he finds whatever that something is and starts up again.'

'No we don't.'

As the days since she had found the photograph went by, Hanni had continued to try to persuade Freddy to take what they suspected about Tony to Brack or to the Americans. And each time she tried, Freddy refused.

'I want to stop him. I want him to pay for every one of his crimes. But we don't have the proof – we won't be believed. He'll be protected, or warned and he'll get away. I won't have that on my conscience, so you have to trust my way of doing this. The Easter Parade celebrations are the key: he's going to be speaking, he's been given a starring role. If we look at the few patterns we've managed to map out, this is exactly the kind of attention he seems to feed off. He'll carry out the next murder on Saturday night – I can feel it.'

Freddy's approach made sense; it also set off a dozen alarm bells Hanni couldn't ignore.

'You're going to risk trying to catch him in the act, aren't you? You're going to play that card again, never mind the mess it got us into the last time.'

'What choice do I have? How else are we going to bring him in?'

Hanni hadn't known how to answer that and Freddy's 'I've learned my lesson, I know what I'm doing' hadn't reassured her in the slightest.

. . .

Spring was in the air at the Tiergarten too, which was a comfort to everyone in Berlin who loved its green spaces.

The war had snatched the heart out of the city's most popular park. During the conflict, vast stretches of it had been dug over for vegetable plots or plundered for firewood. In the immediate aftermath of their victory, the Allies had plundered it too. They had removed the statues of long-ago emperors and military heroes which had lined its main thoroughfares since the turn of the century in order to teach Berlin exactly who was in charge. Not every citizen had cared about the memorials or had even known who the marble figures were, but they all resented the way their country's history was removed so forcefully from them. Since then, the park had become sad and neglected, a wasteland, not a treasure. Now it was finally in the process of returning to life.

A massive replanting programme had begun as soon as the last winter frosts of the year had faded. A quarter of a million young trees, and more mature ones, had beaten the blockade and been flown in to Berlin from all over Germany. By April, the Tiergarten's newly wooded spaces weren't anyone's idea yet of a forest, but they were flourishing. There were areas of shade again. There were places for couples in love to slip away into.

Or for people with secrets to hide.

Hanni turned her back on the trees circling the edge of the area where the Easter Parade celebrations had been set up. The afternoon had enough challenges without her adding imaginary ones to it. Reiner might be stalking her dreams – she hadn't been able to shake the threat that he was, as he had promised, still watching her – but he was hardly the type of man to lurk behind tree trunks. And Tony was too highly visible a presence to disappear out of sight – or not in daylight anyway.

Although with so much going on here, perhaps he could manage it.

The Americans had run all the checks on the attendees Freddy had predicted that they would. The festival area was still crowded, and there was so much going on, it was hard to keep track of anyone.

Hanni had filled up two rolls of film with background material. She had photographed the bustling trestle tables and the brightly painted carousel which had been swarming with children since the first set of families had been ushered in through the gates. She had snapped the stage draped with star-spangled bunting where the victory speeches would be held, and the lanterns strung through the trees ready for lighting at sunset. And so many pictures of the people. Not only the merrymakers all dressed in their Sunday best, but also the pilots who had been trotted out on display equally as scrubbed up and shiny. There were so many of them running round in their smartest uniforms, it was as if the Air Force had sent one for each child.

The young pilots were unfailingly enthusiastic. They had opened the festivities by organising an Easter egg hunt and had helped the children with the search for marshmallow kisses and marzipan eggs. Now they were handing out wooden airplanes and organising flying competitions, leaving the parents free to help themselves to apple juice and glasses of *Radler* – the thirst-quenching mix of beer and lemon soda which made its yearly appearance in Berlin with the first sign of the sun – and cheer on their offspring.

Hanni knew she could sell the photographs she had taken of those lively scenes to all the city's newspapers, including the ones in the East whose captions would bristle with outrage about American pilots buying favour. And that she would get an even higher price for the photographs of the uninvited guests: the Soviet tanks pressed round the Brandenburg Gate and the Soviet troops on heavily armed manoeuvres. Not that any of the partygoers were focused on them. They were concentrating instead, as they were constantly being exhorted to do, on the entertainment and on the food.

The battalions of cooks had been as busy as the pilots. They had also clearly been under German instruction and in possession of ingredients that would have made them into millionaires on the black market. There were endless platters of cheese and sausage and sauerkraut. There was the promise of tureens filled with lamb stew and mashed potatoes and green beans to follow the speeches. And there were cakes, extravagant Easter cakes of the type Hanni hadn't seen since she had licked their sticky sweetness from her fingers at family parties before the war. *Blutennusskranz*, a hazelnut and walnut confection baked in a ring, and *Oster Kirschtorte*, a layered sponge filled with cherries and slathered in thickly whipped cream. The tables they were displayed on were three deep with admirers, but Hanni found herself unable to approach them. The luxury they promised – combined with the music from the carousel and the lantern-filled branches – reminded her too strongly of very different days.

When I was young enough to believe that my father was a decent man and I had no idea how the world worked – or how dark it could be.

She moved away from the cake table and hid behind her camera, the only reliable way for her to focus on the present and keep the past at bay. She took another shot of the drinkers celebrating at the trestle tables and another of a chocolate-smeared child. Then she made the mistake of training her lens on Freddy.

He was so on edge she could almost hear his nerves jangling and his plan to stop Tony falling apart. She could see the list of problems running through his head: *the crowds are too big and too busy; there are too many children darting about; using a gun here would be insanity.* Hanni was aware, because he had told her, that Freddy had come armed, even though he wasn't supposed to be carrying a weapon. Brack had banned any of his officers from carrying a gun at an event so filled with families, whether the Soviets would be looking to cause trouble at it or not. Hanni had thought that was very good advice. Freddy hadn't, and he had brought a second gun for her, although she had refused to take it.

And, if anything goes wrong, he won't be able to use his, and there's no way that the two of us alone can keep track of Tony, not when it gets dark anyway.

That – and the lines etching Freddy's face – decided her. She could see Tony assembling a group of children and looking around for her. Tony would have to wait. Hanni stuffed her camera away again and headed over to Freddy, who was standing next to the *Radler* tent and doing a very good impression of being the spectre at the feast.

'We need a better strategy.' She waved a hand at him as his face tightened even further. 'I'm not trying to start an argument. I know you want to stalk him, to see who, if anyone, he's following and catch him out before he strikes. Fine, do that. But I need you to do a couple of other things as well.'

He was still frowning, but he nodded at her to go on. Hanni took a deep breath and then began talking very quickly so that Freddy wouldn't be able to find a space to butt in and contradict her. She knew he wouldn't like anything she was about to say.

'I want you to tell Matz everything we suspect about Tony. No, don't argue, don't say anything: listen to me first. Matz will believe you – he always believes you and he's always loyal, you know that. More importantly, he will be an excellent other set of eyes, which we badly need. And when you've done that, I want you to go and speak to Colonel Walker and to ask him to take a meeting with you on Monday. Make up a reason; it doesn't matter what – if tonight goes the way that you want it to, you won't need it anyway. If you do both of those things, then I won't go to Brack. If you don't, then I will.'

'You wouldn't dare.'

Freddy's body was so taut, Hanni thought he was about to explode. And his eyes were full of betrayal. She stood her ground anyway; she had no other choice.

'I would, and, whatever you think, I would be doing it for you. There's another life at stake here, Freddy, maybe two: you know that as well as I do. Perhaps you'll catch Tony tonight, perhaps you'll be able to stop him. Or perhaps you won't. Maybe he's not going to kill anyone from here at all. All we know for sure is that he will murder again and we can't let that happen. Not when there's a good chance he'll slip away from us.'

Freddy glanced round at the swelling crowds and enough doubt flickered across his face to let Hanni press on.

'You told me that you'd learned your lesson from the last time we followed this catch-him-in-the-act strategy with a killer. I believe you. I also know that you wouldn't be trying to trap Tony in the same way if you had any other leads. So if I can trust you, then can't you trust me? I don't want to go to Brack, so don't make me have to. Ask Matz for help and set up a meeting with Walker. Cover all our bases. I don't want to betray you, Freddy, I swear I don't, but I won't stand back again and let another person die.'

Freddy didn't answer her straight away. He watched the women giggling over the cakes, insisting that they couldn't possibly eat anything so rich and then sneaking a slice. He watched the children racing around the tables with their toy planes stretched up into the sky. Hanni knew what he was doing: he was imagining them laid out in their homes with dark brown rings stretched round their necks. She waited while he properly considered how much was at stake. When he finally looked at her and sighed in agreement, not in frustration, her shoulders unknotted.

'Okay, you win. I'll speak to Matz and I'll get his help now, and I'll speak to the colonel about Monday. Will that do?'

He waited for her to say yes, but she wasn't quite done with him.

'And if you can't catch Tony tonight but you're certain that he's chosen a target. If you have any reason to suspect that he's going after them but there's nothing that you can do, you'll go to Brack yourself? At once?'

The pause between her question and the answer she needed went on too long, so Hanni did what she hadn't done in a very long time. She reached out for his hand.

'It's for you, as much as for whoever Tony might pick. You

can't take the blame for any more deaths, Freddy – you'll break. It's your soul that's at stake here as well.'

The moment she said the words out loud rather than worrying over the truth of them in silence, they sounded over-dramatic. The clasp of his fingers in hers felt overly intimate. Hanni tried to untangle them, but he stopped her. She tried to damp down what she had said with, 'I'm being silly, ignore me,' but he stopped her doing that too. He didn't give either of them a moment to think. He twisted her fingers tighter through his and then he pulled her towards him and kissed her.

The kiss didn't last long, barely a handful of seconds. Freddy didn't try to explain it. All he said was, 'I'll do what you want, I promise.' Then he dropped hold of her hand and headed towards the gate where Matz was on duty. And left Hanni stuck fast to the spot like one of the park's new trees, with her lips and her heart burning.

CHAPTER 18

16 APRIL 1949 – EVENING

There were hundreds of people surrounding him, but he only wanted one of them to be there. Freddy threaded his way through the packed tables and the couples who had started rather clumsily to dance and headed towards the gate where Matz was checking a group of latecomers' papers. His limbs were as shivery as if he had been struck by the flu. He couldn't stop smiling. They had been on the brink of another fight, another pulling away from each other, and then Hanni had taken hold of his hand. It had been the simplest gesture, the smallest movement, and it had changed everything. He could still feel the press of her fingers. He could still feel the warmth of their kiss. His mouth had met hers for barely a moment and yet that moment had consumed him. And now he needed the day to be done and everyone else to be gone so that he could have her to himself and kiss her again.

And not talk. Especially not about the past where all our problems seem to begin. Neither of us needs that kind of conversation again.

It was the thought of *conversations* which brought him immediately back down to earth. He didn't want to rehash old misunderstandings with Hanni and he didn't want to talk to Matz or Colonel Walker either. But he had promised her that he would –

after that kiss, he would have promised her the moon – so there was no going back on it now.

Freddy leaned against the temporary fence which had been erected around the festival area, waiting for Matz to wave in a family and also – because he was far too kind-hearted to refuse their pleadings – a pair of scruffy street urchins who definitely wouldn't fit anyone's definition of good Germans. The boys' narrow faces and bony limbs suggested that it had been a long time since they had eaten a decent meal. And their shrugged *we don't care* attitude to whether Matz would let them in or not suggested that they would never admit it.

They could be Oli's little brothers, all bravado on the surface and hollow beneath.

And with that thought, the kiss and its magic were gone.

Freddy sagged against the fence so heavily the thin metal rattled in protest. Whatever he might say to the team in public, he no longer believed that Oli's death was a coincidence or the work of a copycat killer. Tony had murdered Oli, and probably the boy they had found in Heimstraβe, as well as the ten other victims. Too many murders had slipped past him and – as Hanni had correctly pointed out – he couldn't bear the burden of more. Which meant he needed to swallow his pride.

'Leave that for now, Matz.'

He straightened himself up as Matz turned away from the gate and the pleas of another ragged and paperless boy.

'Are you all right, sir? You don't look too good.'

It wasn't an idle query. Matz's voice was full of the compassion Freddy knew would one day make his assistant a better detective than him.

He wasn't all right at all, but he nodded anyway.

'I'm fine. But there's something I have to tell you which I should probably have shared weeks ago.'

He began to describe the conclusion he and Hanni had come to about Tony as succinctly as he could. Matz listened in silence.

And then Matz did what Hanni had promised Freddy he would do: he believed it.

'I'm not going to lie, I wasn't expecting that. But we both said from the start that there was something fake about Miller. He's always felt made-up, as if he was following a template of what the perfect American hero should be. And he's a cold fish – I've never liked the way he looks at Hanni, as if he can't decide whether she's useful to him or not.'

It wasn't until Matz made that observation that Freddy remembered what Hanni had said about never being sure whether Tony wanted to be with her or whether she got in his way.

'Hanni said something like that too. And now I think about it, when he looked at her that day at the protest, I had the weirdest feeling that he was assessing her value.'

He stared at Matz, his brain suddenly whirring. 'What if I've played this all wrong? What if Hanni is in more danger from him than I thought? Maybe I should find her and tell her that she shouldn't be here at all.'

'Good luck with that. She'll chew your ear off and tell you she's more than capable of looking after herself, which—'

Matz didn't get a chance to finish that thought – someone was shouting his name from the far side of the stage where a scuffle appeared to be starting.

'I'd better go and see what that is. There's been reports that the Soviets are using the treeline as cover to get in, and we don't need any trouble with them. Or I don't, unless I want to find myself back on desk duties.'

He called a junior officer over to take charge of the gate and turned back to Freddy. 'What do you want me to do about our mutual friend?'

Freddy glanced around – everyone's attention was focused elsewhere. He drew the spare gun he had brought with him out of his inside coat pocket and pushed it into Matz's hand.

'Keep eyes on him, the same as Hanni and I have been doing. If he moves away from the main area or seems to be tracking some-body, follow him, but signal to me first if you do. And don't use this or Brack will do worse to you than put you on desk duties. It's for protection, or for a deterrent if you need it. Threaten him if you have to, but don't fire. Are you clear about that?'

Matz hesitated for a moment and then he nodded and hid the gun away.

'Let's hope a deterrent works – this isn't the place for bullets.'

He headed off to where the scuffle had all too quickly descended into a fight, his hand stretched flat against the weapon in his pocket, the rest of his manner calm. Freddy watched him go, uncomfortably aware that he had been so wrapped up in his own problems, he had neglected Matz's talents.

I'll put that right. I'll let him take the lead on more cases and I'll make sure he gets the recognition he deserves when this one comes through.

Deciding to also trust Matz's instincts about the way Hanni would react if he started to fuss, Freddy began scanning the crowds again for Colonel Walker, feeling more confident about snaring Tony than he had done an hour ago. The first difficult conversation had gone well: Matz had come through as Matz always did. Freddy had a feeling that the second one was going to be a lot tougher.

———

There were hundreds of people surrounding him, but he only wanted one of them to be there.

No, that wasn't true. He wanted two of them, but he couldn't put himself at the level of risk that taking them both at the same time would require.

Tony watched the crowd from the deliberately visible position he had taken up at the side of the carousel. He had been watching the packed festival area all afternoon. Now that the sun was starting to sink and dusk and drink had begun to release inhibitions, it wasn't an edifying sight. The happy family atmosphere was slowly crumbling. The children were overtired and over-stuffed with sweets, and too many of them were crying and should have been in their beds long ago. Their parents, who were sleepy with too much stew and too much cake or had been topping up their beer with a far stronger tipple, were intent on ignoring them. A number of the men, and one or two of the women, had grown belligerent and rowdy. There had been at least one fight behind the stage between groups of neighbours who were too drunk to recognise each other and which all of the participants blamed on troublemaking Soviets. The event was threatening to turn ugly, and as for the behaviour during his speech...

Tony had been very unhappy with the day's programme as soon as he realised that he wasn't the highlight of it. He had presumed that he would be the only pilot present – he was, after all, the one featured on the poster and he had never had to share a stage with his fellow flyers before. This time, however, he was barely the star, he was merely the last on a far too long bill of speakers. By the time Tony's turn came, a barrage of shiny-faced boys in smartly pressed uniforms had already addressed the crowd, shouting statistics and bragging about their exploits. Insisting that 'I'm just a regular American but today I'm also a Berliner!' with too much enthusiasm and too little care for their audience. The claim had worn dangerously thin.

Tony had walked up to the microphone uncomfortably aware that the Germans who had been forced to sit through the speeches before they could eat were tired of applauding all the victories they had been told to be grateful for. The reception he received proved him right: he was greeted by a tide of comments of a kind which had never been thrown at him before. Someone – to great gales of laughter – had called him a 'pretty boy'. Buoyed up by the reaction to that, someone else had asked if he was only there because Hollywood charged too much for 'the real Mont-gomery Clift'. No one cared when he described the dangerous landings he had endured to keep them all fed. No one called him a hero. Instead, there had been demands for a vote of thanks for the German ground crews who, according to the man yelling across Tony's first words, had built the runways and did the real work. Tony had acknowledged that; he had given the toast and he had led the applause which followed it. He hadn't enjoyed doing it – or sharing any aspect of the spotlight – one little bit.

And she wouldn't stop taking pictures. Not even when she could see I was being humiliated and turned into a joke. She loved it.

He was definitely finished with Hanni.

'You've given me less money than him. It's the same for us all or we're not doing it.'

Tony pulled himself back to the task in hand. He didn't believe the child – he knew the three boys staring at his wallet would sell each other out in a heartbeat – but he dropped another coin into the grubby hand anyway and did another quick sweep of the crowd. The singing was growing louder, if not more tuneful; the makeshift dance floor was packed. It was impossible to clearly pick out a face. He couldn't have designed the chaos better himself.

Tony had been aware since the day's festivities started that he was an object of scrutiny. He could hardly miss it. Freddy and Hanni, and the third one Freddy had dragged in – a gangly individual who looked as if he should still be in the classroom and had fallen for even the flimsiest sob stories at the gate – might as well have had signs saying *we can see you* fixed on their heads. Their surveillance methods were hopeless. They had spent most of the afternoon and the early evening standing out in the open and staring straight at him. Since the third one joined in, they had also begun circling him, presumably waiting to see if he was getting ready to pounce. It was insulting: they clearly had no sense of how meticulous his preparations were. It was also dangerous. It was clear to Tony that, no matter how unsubtle their methods were, Freddy and his little band were moving in for their own kill.

And getting closer to me and mine than they should.

Tony had seen Freddy talking to Colonel Walker. He hadn't
been able to hear what was being said and it was obvious from
the colonel's frown when Freddy approached him that the
conversation wasn't one of his choosing. Tony had taken very
little comfort in that. Walker had listened and, whatever it was
that Freddy wanted, he had nodded and agreed. That had made
Tony's pulse race and not in a pleasant way. He had far preferred
what he had seen earlier: Freddy in the act of kissing Hanni.

The kiss had been a fleeting, blink-and-miss-it moment, but it
had happened, and Hanni's face had glowed when it was done.
That had made Tony's pulse race far more happily. It had proved
to him what he had long suspected: that hurting one of the pair
would badly damage the other.

*He will fall apart when I remove her and the threat to me will be
gone.*

He would still kill Freddy anyway.

There were three of them watching one of him. On paper, that
sounded like very poor odds. But this wasn't a paper exercise and
that wasn't a statistic which worried Tony. He wasn't a gambler
but he was a master at sleight of hand: three people might as well
have been none if all of them were looking the wrong way.

He gave the boys another coin each for good measure and sent
them back down to the main festival arena. The street children
were frighteningly easy to manipulate: most of them were so
desperate for food or for money or for the slightest bit of attention, they would do whatever they were asked without question.
Very few of them were as bright as he sensed Freddy's little friend
Oli might have been.

Tony gave the spoiled children on the carousel another wave
as the three invisible ones sloped off to follow their instructions.
One walked towards Matz, one walked towards Freddy, one
walked towards the night's prize. Tony continued to stand where
he was and smile until all the boys were in place and all the heads
which should have been trained on him were turned away. Then

he slipped into the darkness where no lanterns had been strung and he did the only thing left for him to do. He waited.

———

'Miss, miss. I can't find my brother. My parents said we could stay on for a bit on our own, but I think he might have gone home without me. Or he might have got lost. The last time I saw him was by the carousel. Can you help me? It's getting dark and I'm scared.'

Hanni stared at the boy who had suddenly materialised at her side and was now tugging none too gently at her sleeve. His lip was wobbling and he was very young. Her first instinct was to drop to her knees and reach out to him. Her second instinct stopped her: there was something not right with the child. His jacket was threadbare and grubby, and his face was unhealthily pale. That could have simply been a sign that he came – as too many of Berlin's children did – from a family enduring impossibly hard circumstances. Hanni didn't want to judge him for that, but it was his eyes, not the state of his clothes, that stopped her from bending down and offering him comfort. There was a bleakness in their expression which made a mockery of his trembling mouth. He didn't look like a child who would be concerned by the dark – he looked like a boy who would thrive in it. That was the shadow which made Hanni uneasy. Which stopped her from asking 'What can I do?'

She pulled her coat away from his clutching fingers instead and glanced around for Matz. He was in an open space near the main gate where she could easily spot him, but he was also crouched down and talking to a child and she couldn't get his attention.

'Miss, can you help me?'

The voice was wheedling and desperate, but Hanni wouldn't let herself listen.

Don't let anything distract you.

Freddy had been very clear about that and now Matz was distracted and by a child as well. Hanni's instincts were telling her this was wrong, even as her brain was telling her not to worry – that Matz had the kind of manner that children were drawn to and this was nothing more than a coincidence.

She turned in the other direction and began looking for Freddy. He was at the front of the stage where he had spent the last few hours, but he was also turned away from her and speaking to someone, although this time she couldn't see who.

'Miss? Did you hear me? What should I do?'

The boy was staring up at her, his shoulders hunched, his skinny body shivering. He looked so utterly desperate, Hanni finally crouched down the way that he wanted her to. Any other response would have felt inhuman. Whatever Freddy had said – and clearly wasn't following himself – it was hard to stay suspicious at such a sorry sight.

'Forgive me. Yes, of course I'll help you if I can.' Now that she was at his level and taking him seriously, the boy's eyes warmed up. 'Tell me your brother's name so we can try and find him. And tell me yours too.'

He answered her clearly – his voice was loud enough to be heard even in the midst of the singing and the music. The name he gave her bounced straight away again.

Hanni stood up and stepped back, her hands outstretched as if to push him away, although she wasn't aware she was doing that.

'I'm sorry, I don't think I heard you right. What did you say you were called?'

His pinched little face was a picture of innocence.

'Odi. I said my name was Odi. It's short for Odis, but nobody except my mother uses that.'

Hanni was certain he hadn't said Odi at all, but before she could recover herself and challenge him, a thin hand crept into hers.

'Please, miss. What if he's gone into the trees and the Russians have got him? What if they take him to one of their camps? My mother will never forgive me.'

He began to move towards the carousel, tugging at Hanni to follow, his lip trembling again.

He didn't say Oli; he can't have said Oli.

But Oli was what Hanni had heard and the name had thrown her off balance. She forgot about not being distracted or that she shouldn't go anywhere, even as far as the carousel, without alerting Freddy. The boy's expression was too frantic to ignore and he kept repeating *please* in a whine that she couldn't shut out. Her head was spinning with thoughts of Oli's last moments. What if he had said please in the same helpless way? What if he had begged for his own life the way this boy was begging her to help save his brother's? How could she fail him? How could she forgive herself if her hesitation cost another child his life?

She stopped looking where she was going and stumbled. Odi pulled harder.

'This is where I last saw him.'

He pointed to the line of trees which stood a short distance from the garishly painted horses and shrieking children.

'He jumped off before me when the ride stopped. I think he ran into there.'

Hanni knew that the reforested area was too newly planted to be as dense as it looked. That the setting sun had filled the spaces where the branches didn't yet reach with thickening shadows. She still didn't want to go into it.

'I think we should stay here and ask some of the pilots to come and help search with us. They would be quicker than me.'

But the boy wasn't listening and his grip was a strong one. Before Hanni realised how fast they were moving, they were over the treeline and under a canopy of leaves which was surprisingly dense. She tripped as a mess of roots which were far older than the newer plantings caught at her feet. The light from the lanterns and the carousel dimmed. The shouts of the drinkers and dancers faded into a whisper.

'We really shouldn't go any further. We should stay here and shout for your brother to come. What did you say his name was?'

But the boy hadn't and he didn't.

It took Hanni a moment to understand that her hand was empty. That she was alone.

She spun round, flinching as a branch brushed over her face. Logically, she knew that she was barely feet away from hundreds of people. That all she had to do was take a few steps and this would be revealed as a very unfunny joke or as an attempt at a robbery. Except that her camera bag was still on her shoulder and her purse was still in her coat pocket and the boy who should be robbing her was gone.

Her heart started jumping. She spun around again and realised that she had confused herself, that she didn't know which way was out and which way was further in.

Which doesn't matter because the trees can't possibly stretch very far. Whatever way I go, I'll get out again quick enough.

She took a step in the direction she hoped was the right one. She didn't get a chance to take another.

A hand clamped round her mouth. A hard piece of metal thrust itself into her back. And a too familiar voice whispered, 'Hello.'

———

'How did it go with Colonel Walker?'

Freddy broke away from the group of men he was refusing to allow anywhere near the stage area and made a face the colonel would not have wanted to see.

'About as well as I expected it to. It seems Brack was right and that my reputation with the Americans for not being trustworthy has spread from the army across to the air force.' He shook his head as Matz immediately sprang to his defence. 'It doesn't matter. I didn't care what they thought of me last year and I don't care what they think of me now. The main thing is that I got what

I wanted – Walker's agreed to meet on Monday to review today's security arrangements, which is what I told him was the issue. That should keep Hanni happy and hopefully we'll have our man caught by then and the Americans will have to listen to me, not the other way round.' He stopped and frowned. 'Talking about Hanni, do you know where she is?'

Matz nodded. 'Yes, she's over by the main catering tent, covering that section like we agreed.'

And then he looked in the direction he was pointing and the frown spread from Freddy's face to his.

'Or she was the last time I checked.'

Freddy waved away the group of drunks who were close enough to overhear their conversation.

'When was that? Exactly when, Matz, not a guess.'

'Not long ago. Ten minutes, twelve at the most.' He fumbled in his pocket and stopped again as Freddy glared. 'Sorry, force of habit. There's nothing in my notebook anyway. I've been trying to do what you said and not rely on it.' He saw Freddy's mouth tighten and caught himself. 'Sorry. It can't be any longer than twelve. I had just checked my watch when the kid came over and she was definitely in place then. What? What is it?'

All Freddy's senses were firing – it was hard not to shout.

'Which kid, Matz? What did he want?'

Matz pulled his notebook out this time, as if the mere act of holding it would sharpen his memory. Freddy could feel him rooting through the last half hour, his brain trying to sort the details his pen normally took care of.

'It was a boy, one of the street kids I let in because they looked hungry and there was so much food here. He seemed genuinely distressed… He said his friend couldn't get in and nobody but me could sort that out. I tried to shake him off, but he was very persistent. So I followed him to the gate and—'

'There was nobody there?'

Matz nodded.

'And then the boy vanished too?'

Matz nodded again and then jumped as Freddy let fly a volley of curses.

'I shouldn't have gone, I know. You said not to get distracted and—'

Freddy cut across him. 'We got tricked. You and me both. You were busy at the gate at the same time I was behind the stage, where another supposedly distressed kid sent me to break up a fight which had vanished by the time I got to it. And then I got mixed up with a load of idiots looking for trouble who I swear someone had stirred up.'

'It could be a coincidence.'

Matz stopped that line of thought as Freddy flinched at the word and then his jaw fell.

'Oh God. Never mind Hanni, where's Tony? Can you see him anywhere either?'

Freddy blanched. If Hanni was gone, Tony should have been his next thought. No, Tony should have been the first person whose visibility he checked on. Or refused to stop watching in the first place, no matter how clever the boy was.

I was right. It was her he was after. I should have trusted my own instincts and not listened to Matz.

There was no point in saying it. Matz was already on his toes, craning over the crowd, his face clammy with the same cold sweat that had just engulfed Freddy.

'He's been standing beside the carousel since he came off the stage.'

'And now he's not.'

Matz shook his head. 'No, he's not.'

And then he asked the questions which were now whirling in a sickening wave through Freddy's head.

'What if Miller knew we were on to him and he's the one playing us? What if the boys were his doing and there was another who he sent to Hanni? If she's not here and he's not...' He broke off and swallowed. 'We need to look for Hanni.'

'We don't just need to look.' Freddy's face had aged twenty

years. 'If he's got her, we need to find her, Matz. We need to find her while we still can.'

———

'Keep walking. Don't scream when I take my hand away. Don't try to fight or to run. One mistake and I'll shoot you.'

He's going to shoot me whatever I do, leaped into Hanni's head, immediately followed by, *Not if I don't let him.*

Tony was behind her, his face and his body out of sight. The barrel of what was unmistakeably a gun was jammed into her back. He was holding her so tight, his steps felt like hers. Hanni yelped as his hand moved from her mouth to her arm and twisted it.

'I told you not to scream.'

He was pushing her forward, deeper into the shadows. Every time she lost her footing on the tangled undergrowth, he wrenched harder.

'Someone will come.'

She kept her voice to a whisper and was afraid a whisper would be too loud. Tony tightened his grip on her arm, but he didn't break step.

'Who? Freddy? Good, let him. I'll deal with you both at the same time if I have to. Speed things up.'

Freddy was in his sights too; Freddy would be the next one he killed. If Tony had said that to scare her even more than he already had. the threat had the opposite effect. Whatever else happened, Hanni was not going to let Freddy die, which meant that she couldn't die either. She was afraid – only a fool could be in the position she was in and not be afraid – and she was in danger, but she had been put in that position before and she had survived. She knew that, but Tony didn't.

'He'll stop you. He's got a gun too.'

Tony laughed. His breath fell damp and warm on her neck. Hanni could feel his skin on hers where the sleeve of her coat had fallen back. She could smell him: coffee and nicotine and the mix of musk and lime that was his cologne. He was all around her, filling her nose and her mouth; it was hard not to be sick when she breathed in. She shuddered; she couldn't hold that back. That made Tony laugh even more.

'What's the matter, Hanni? I thought you liked being nice and up close with me. That was the impression you gave outside the bar. And you certainly got under my skin at the flat.'

He knew she had been there. He must know she had seen the photograph. The danger she was in started to swell.

'You worked it out, didn't you?' His voice was a whisper now. 'Clever girl. And I assume you've shown the copies you made of my picture to your equally clever boyfriend. But you haven't told anyone else, have you? There's three of you after me, but not the rest of the force or your brute of a boss, or mine. I'm still Tony the hero to them. My guess is that you've kept your suspicions a secret because they'd make you sound mad. So maybe not quite so clever after all.'

There was no point in trying to break away – his hold on her was too strong. There was no point in insisting anymore that she would be rescued. There was no counter-threat or promise of better terms if he surrendered that she could offer.

But every minute I'm alive buys me another minute.

Hanni licked her dry lips and decided to try calling his bluff.

'Yes, you're right – I've worked it out and Freddy knows too. But what I don't understand is why you've taken me. There were twelve people in the photograph, there are ten people dead and there was only one woman left who you hadn't marked with a tick. I'm half her age; I look nothing like her. With all the effort you've put into finding the matches you've found for the rest of what I assume is your family – and how cleverly you did that – why change the system now? Don't you want to complete the job in the same careful way that you started it?'

It was a gamble, challenging him. Letting him think that she had some insight into his mind. But Hanni had nothing left to do but gamble and, if she was certain of anything about Tony, it was that the sure-fire way to snare him was with flattery.

'So you understood that? About the importance of the matching?'

It had worked. He had slowed down and the gun was no longer jammed so painfully into her spine. Hanni forced herself not to react. It wasn't enough of a slackening to let her escape, but it was a moment of respite she could work with.

'Not at first. We couldn't find any pattern at first. We couldn't come up with a profile of the killer. It wasn't until we saw the photograph and paired that up with the victims that the similarities emerged. It was quite astonishing, how you achieved such perfect matches. It must have taken a lot of work to get it right.'

'Don't, Hanni. You'll make a fool of yourself.'

This time, his mouth was on the soft lobe of her ear and she couldn't hold back the revolted shiver that ran through her. This time, Tony didn't laugh – he kept on talking.

'Here's the thing that you need to remember: I've fallen for your flattery before and I won't fall for it again. I don't care whether you thought my work was clever, or cruel, or crazy. Your opinion doesn't matter to me at all.'

It hadn't worked. He wasn't flattered. He was playing with her. Whatever she tried – whether she screamed or begged or somehow managed to twist round and fight him – she wasn't going to walk away from the trap he had put her in. Hanni could feel a sob pressing up through her throat. She swallowed it down, but Tony still heard it.

'That's better. I don't want your compliments. I want you crying; I want you afraid. I want you to suffer the terrible kind of death my family suffered. I want you to know that it's coming and that it won't be peaceful. It won't be quick. You won't be surrounded by the kind words of your loved ones. Your death will be lonely and it will be painful, and the people you leave behind will know that and they will suffer for it too.'

For a moment, Hanni could feel Reiner beside her, as if Tony knew who she really was. As if he could smell the camps and the gas and the ovens on her and was making her pay. She almost asked him how he had discovered her secret, and then she realised that he hadn't. That he wouldn't have cared if he had. That she was nothing more to Tony than a body, playing a role in the fantasy of revenge he had created. That all he needed from her was her death. Tears filled her eyes, but she blinked hard, refusing to shed them: she wouldn't give him the added pleasure of sliding into self-pity. If she was going to die, she was going to die as herself, not as the helpless victim he wanted her to be.

'Why shooting?'

He hadn't expected the question. It made him slow his pace again.

'You've strangled everyone else, including Oli, because that was you as well, wasn't it? So why shoot me?'

Tony shifted the gun a little higher, running the barrel slowly up the length of her backbone.

He wants me to know why I'm dying.

Hanni could sense the story bubbling in him in the same way that he had sensed her tears. She suddenly knew, as strongly as if she had witnessed his previous murders, that there were two stages to the killing and that the explanation came first. And that there was a difference here: she didn't have a noose round her neck; she had a voice.

'Tell me the reason why. If I'm going to die, you owe me that much.'

He didn't answer as quickly as she had asked him. The pause was long enough for Hanni to think she had lost, that he had worked out she was trying to distract him and buy herself time. It was hard not to gasp with relief when he eventually spoke.

'Because you found me out, so therefore you can't live.'

He didn't appear to have noticed that their pace had slowed again.

'But I'm going to use you first.'

His voice had deepened – it was thick with the promise of a

story he was proud of and eager to tell. Hanni knew that the grounds to base it on were flimsy, but he wasn't focused on the moment of her death anymore and there was a faint promise of hope in that.

'This gun that you can feel in your back is a Russian one; the bullets inside it are Russian bullets. Do you know why that matters?'

Hanni didn't have a clue so she didn't need to try to make her answer sound genuine. 'No, I don't, but I want to.'

Tony's voice settled into a storyteller's rhythm.

'It's actually very straightforward. Like I said, I'm going to use you – to whip up an incident that will make everyone forget about the Berlin Strangler and divert any attention from me. We're almost on the edge of Soviet territory; another few minutes and we'll be inside it. And that's where I'm going to shoot you and leave you, mortally wounded and bleeding to death. Then I'm going to double back and find the search party you're so sure is coming and play the hero they expect me to be. "I heard a scream; I heard gunfire." Once I say that, what more will they need? They'll follow where I point and your body will be lying there waiting on Soviet soil – with any luck, there will be a Soviet soldier already kneeling by your side and covered in your blood. Can you imagine the chaos that will break out then?'

When Hanni answered yes – because she could picture it all too vividly – his laugh and the 'so describe it' which followed made her stomach heave. She had no choice but to do as he said. She didn't bother to whisper anymore; he didn't seem to notice.

'The Soviets will be blamed. The papers will explode with it. A police photographer snatched from an event she was covering for the Americans. A woman brutally murdered. The headlines will scream for blood and 1945 and all the atrocities that the Russian army inflicted on Berlin then will blaze back through the press. God knows how far it could escalate. Perhaps there will be no more talk of ending the blockade. Instead, two sides more suited to a fight than a compromise will push each other back to the brink.'

The delight in Tony's voice was as sickening as the smell of him. 'That was a very good summary of my plan. Which is perfect, don't you think?'

It was anything but; it was terrifying.

Hanni didn't bother to reply – she let Tony carry on talking while her mind scrambled for a way to escape.

'The outrage will fuel the whole city. When they see the pictures of your broken body and read the outpourings of hatred about the animal who killed you, no one will care about the strangler anymore. But just to be sure, in a few days, another body will be found. In the American sector this time. A Soviet soldier with a noose in his pocket and a photograph in his backpack covered in little red ticks. The case will be completely wrapped up. The Soviets will be in the frame again, which will be an interesting sideshow, and every vigilante in the city will be claiming the credit. Like I said: it's perfect.'

He was holding her so close to him, his grip on her bare skin felt like a caress. Hanni managed not to cry out or to shiver as Tony carried on, although she wanted to howl.

'You made me change my plan, Hanni, which I wasn't at all happy about. But you also made me come up with a better one. Now I get away, with my reputation intact and my record unblemished. What a win. I might not even need to kill Freddy, although I shall. Perhaps I should be thanking you not—'

He broke off. His body tensed. He had heard it in the same moment as Hanni. A rustling which could be the sound of an animal passing or – please God – could be a foot stepping cautiously over a tree root or an arm brushing away a tumble of leaves.

Hanni held her breath, waiting for a shout, expecting Tony to shoot. And then another sound came, louder this time, sudden. A fallen branch or a pile of twigs snapping with a crack that ricocheted through the silent night air.

Everything happened too fast for thinking about.

Tony flinched at the noise, stumbled and lost hold of her arm. The gun dropped from her back. Hanni threw herself forward, hit the ground face down and half-rolled, half-crawled, burrowing beneath the thin carpet of leaves she couldn't imagine would cover her. Her cheek tore against a stone, her shoulder smashed into a tangle of roots, but she kept moving with no idea where Tony was, fully expecting to crash into his feet and his gun.

'Stop!'

The shout tore through the trees. Hanni froze and curled up tighter, but it wasn't Tony.

'I told you to stop!'

It wasn't Freddy either. It was Matz. Who was without a weapon or an ounce of Tony's cunning.

Hanni scrambled to her feet and hurtled back towards the voice, yelling as loud as she could.

'He's got a gun! Get down – he's got a gun!'

The noise that followed her cry was too loud to be the snap of a branch. The flash of light which turned the tree trunks silver was too bright to be a lantern or a carousel. Hanni dropped to her knees as a flock of birds screeched into the sky and the forest shivered.

'He's got a gun.'

She didn't know if she shouted or whispered that; her ears were ringing and her words were muffled.

'He's got a gun.'

Nobody answered. There was nothing around her but silence.

———

'You have to come away now, sweetheart. There's nothing to be done.'

He kept saying it, in a voice made thick and clumsy with tears, but Hanni couldn't move. Her hands were sticky with blood; her dress was stiff with it. She knew Matz was dead – she had held his hand as the life drained out of him – but knowing it and believing it were two different things. As for feeling it... She would rather lie down now and never stir again from the wood than suffer the pain that was coming.

'It was my fault.'

She was aware from Freddy's sob and his 'Please, Hanni, no, not again' that she must have already said that. She couldn't remember speaking before. She couldn't stop speaking now.

'I did it all wrong. I didn't do what you said. I let myself get distracted. I was suspicious of the boy; I knew that I shouldn't have followed him, that I should have alerted you or shouted for...'

She looked down at Matz's body and couldn't say his name.

'Hanni, listen to me.'

Freddy had dropped to his knees beside her. His hand was under her chin, turning her head towards him. His eyes were sunken and red-rimmed. His voice kept cracking.

'We were all played, sweetheart, all three of us. Miller must have known we were on to him – he must have guessed you'd been in the flat. The business with the boys was him. He sent one to distract me too, and another to distract Matz. And then he snatched you, which must have been his plan from the start. If this is anyone's fault, it's mine. I underestimated him. I let you go back to him.'

The pain and the guilt poured from him, as deeply felt as hers.

Hanni fumbled over her words as the world started spinning.

'The boy who spoke to me, he said he was called Oli.'

'Oh dear God. I could kill him for that, never mind for the rest of it.'

Her head was on Freddy's shoulder; his arms were her anchors.

'That was a trick too, wasn't it? To make sure that I followed.'

She felt Freddy nod, but he didn't speak, not until her breathing had calmed. Then he moved her very slowly away from him and looked into her eyes.

'I'm sorry, Hanni, but I have to ask. Did Miller tell you anything? Before... before he did this, before he ran?'

Hanni's head was empty; her mouth was too dry to shape her scattered thoughts. She knew there were answers he needed to hear, but she was exhausted. She wanted to crawl away, to find a tree and curl under it. To fall asleep and to wake up with Matz's death no more than a nightmare, the stuff of an enchanted forest and a twisted fairy tale. She wanted to run away from the world. Except there was Oli and there was Matz and ten other once-loved people lying dead and they needed her to carry on. She straightened up slowly, unsure of her body.

'He confirmed what we already knew, about the photograph and the way that he did the matching.'

Freddy had hold of her arm; he was helping her onto her feet. There were others present – Hanni could see their dark shapes beyond the ring made by the lanterns Freddy had sent for after he'd found her. Two of them were holding a stretcher; one was holding a sheet. They were waiting to take Matz away, to set up yet another crime scene. Hanni wanted to yell at them to go away and not touch him, but Freddy was talking again, trying to fix her in place.

'There was nothing else? No family name, no background. Nothing about his past?'

His voice was gentle but it was insistent.

Hanni shook her head. 'No, none of that. He had a plan and that was all he was interested in. He was going to kill me, and then he was going to kill you, and he was going to get away with that and the rest.'

'How on earth did he think he was going to do that?'

Hanni told Freddy the details of how Tony had intended to frame the Soviets as briefly as she could and then it was her turn to hold him as he cursed and kicked at the ground.

'He can't escape – I won't let him. I'll take this to Brack and then I'll take it to Walker. I'll launch a manhunt like this city has never seen.'

'I'm coming with you.'

She wouldn't listen to his protests about the bruises she was covered with or the shock she was in.

'I'll get those looked at, but I'm coming. I was the one who heard what Tony said. I owe it to Matz to tell it.'

Freddy sighed, but he knew better than to argue. He nodded and waved at one of the men still observing a respectful distance.

'There's a doctor here who will look you over. If he clears you, you can come.'

He slipped his hand under her elbow and tried to move her away from the body.

'Please, Hanni, let the team do their job. They're grieving the same way that we are.'

The truth of that was written across the shocked faces now coming towards them. Hanni knew that this was a death whose ripples would stretch out over many lives. That knowledge – of how loved Matz had been and how much he would be missed – made his dying no easier to bear.

She let Freddy put his arm round her shoulder; she leaned in close to his side. As they began to walk, she wasn't entirely sure who was holding who steady. And then Freddy suddenly stopped.

'What have you got there, in your hand? Is it something forensics need to see?'

Hanni looked down. The object she was clutching was as bloodstained as she was. It wasn't until Freddy groaned that she realised what it was.

'It's his notebook. It was on the ground. It must have fallen out of his coat when he…'

She stared at the battered book, she stared at Freddy and then the world slipped away and in roared the pain.

CHAPTER 19

17 APRIL 1949

'Tell me the whole thing, from start to finish. And begin with who killed him.'

Brack's voice was unnaturally quiet. Hanni hated the way his stillness controlled the room: he was far easier to ignore when he shouted. The chief inspector had not, however, raised his voice once. Not when he learned of Matz's death, or when he arrived at the morgue to view Matz's body. Not when the exhausted team reassembled at the station first thing on Sunday morning, or when he ordered Freddy and Hanni into his office. Everyone had expected to be bellowed at and the silence had unnerved them.

The team was floundering, blindsided by grief, confused by their boss, and neither Freddy nor Hanni could help them. They couldn't answer a single question – about what had happened in the woods, about why Hanni was covered in bruises, about the rumours that the killer had been a Soviet spy – until they had lain the truth before Brack. It had been a relief when he finally summoned them both in. And then Freddy started talking and nothing felt like a relief at all.

'It was the American pilot, Captain Tony Miller.'

They waited for the shouts and the cursing. Brack stared at them, his mouth open. Beyond a strangled 'You've got to be kidding me', he seemed incapable of speech. Freddy wasn't a great deal better – his opening line was as lifeless as if he had memorised it.

'It took us a long time to piece the whole picture together and there's a lot of the detail still missing.'

His attempt at an explanation was unbearable to watch and to listen to. Freddy's eyes were lost inside dark pouches; his voice was robotic, thick with fatigue. Hanni knew that the last thing he wanted to be doing was recounting the events of Saturday night. Barely a dozen hours had passed since they had knelt by Matz's dead body. Both of them were still bathed in grief, incapable of accepting that someone so full of life could be so suddenly gone. What they needed to do was mourn. Not at a funeral neither of them could bear the thought of. Not with silence or with tears but by getting out onto the streets and searching for Tony. Which Brack wouldn't let them do until he had picked the whole case clean.

Hanni leaned forward and caught Brack's eye, trying not to wince as spikes of pain stabbed through her. There wasn't an inch of her body that didn't feel jarred. Her arms and legs were covered in blooms of purple and blue and laced with a fine web of red-inked scratches. She pushed her battered hands under her knees as Brack stared at them. The very least she could do was try to help Freddy get through the ordeal.

'I was part of this too, Chief Inspector. Perhaps I could explain some of what happened?'

The look Brack turned on her was withering.

'I'm sure you could *explain* it all, Fräulein Winter. I am sure you could put the whole debacle in a much better light. But I want to hear it from the inspector, without you reshaping his actions the way you did so skilfully last year. You are in here for no other reason than to stop you talking out there, so sit back and be quiet.'

His disdain was humiliating, but Freddy resumed talking before she could argue or defend herself. He managed to speed up, although his voice stayed empty. He led Brack through each step of their attempt at an investigation, from their first suspicions to Hanni's discovery of the photograph, as concisely as he could. And he managed better than Hanni could have done not to stumble when Brack snarled and snorted. None of it was easy to sit through: it was impossible not to hear all the moments where Brack could explode.

Freddy finished with the scene at the Tiergarten, with Matz dead and Tony vanished. With the American officers all gone by the time Freddy emerged from the wood, in case the trouble they knew was brewing had been started by the Soviets.

'I didn't order a search then. Our men were devastated by what had happened and this will need a level of co-operation from the Americans I knew I couldn't start pushing for last night. Miller has fled, I'm pretty certain of that, but the city is blockaded and he can't have got far. I judged that it would be better to brief you and start the search for him today than run at it haphazardly last night.'

Brack swore at *I judged.* When Freddy finally stopped, the chief inspector stared over their heads for what felt like an eternity and then he finally asked the question Hanni had been dreading. The menace running through 'So tell me now why I was kept so utterly in the dark' crept like mould through the room.

'Because I didn't think you would believe me, given the way everyone in Berlin sees Miller as a hero. It took me long enough to accept that he could be the strangler and, before last night, the proof we had that he was dangerous was flimsy at best.'

It was a brave answer, but it didn't help Freddy. Brack's shoulders were so rigid, the sinews in his neck sprang out like whips.

'But you told Matz Laube, didn't you? And he, presumably, believed you. And then he followed orders from you which I hadn't sanctioned. And he got himself killed for his pains.'

The *ands* fell like hammer blows. Freddy's face tightened. It was the only visible sign of the misery Hanni knew he was filled with.

'For which I take full blame. I thought I had the situation at the Tiergarten under control. I thought I could bring the captain in. I made an error of judgement.'

The disgust which spread across Brack's face was chilling. Hanni didn't know how Freddy could sit under its threat and not recoil.

'But you didn't bring him in, did you? If this tale you have brought me is true, what you actually did was let a very dangerous man escape. It was a disastrous call, Inspector. None of this plan to catch Miller at the festival was thought through or under control. Isn't the truth, in fact, that this whole enterprise was about your ego? And now that ego has cost us one of our most promising detectives. Not the best day's work, was it? And what do you propose to do now? Are you going to tell this same story to the Americans and expect them to rush to your aid? Or are you going to run round Berlin by yourself, waving a gun, and treating me to yet more *errors of judgement?*'

It was an unfair and unkind speech. To his credit – and to Hanni's relief – Freddy stayed perfectly calm, even when Brack's response to his answer was another snort and another curse.

'No, sir, I am not. And yes, now that you are in the picture, I do plan to tell Miller's immediate superior, Colonel Walker, the full extent of what we suspect Miller has done, including last night's killing of a German police officer. I want to request his assistance in launching a manhunt. I hope I have your backing for that.'

'Do you indeed?'

Brack shook his head in the slow way Hanni knew was intended to belittle Freddy.

'You know, don't you, that they won't listen to you? That they will cut you off the moment you start throwing out accusations. And then they will close ranks round their man and we won't be able to deliver justice for anyone. That, Inspector, will be a public relations disaster, and it will be your badge gone not mine. So, no, I won't be giving you my backing, or anything else.'

He's hanging him out to dry. It's not right.

Hanni opened her mouth to protest, but Freddy stepped in first.

'I am sorry about that. I think that you're probably right. I doubt that they will want to listen – or help. The thing is, I don't care. If they turn me away, I'll go back. And I will go back again and again until I make them take me seriously and co-operate. Isn't a little personal humiliation the very least Matz's memory deserves?'

The cold fury in Freddy's voice turned Brack's face puce.

'Who the hell do you think—'

Freddy didn't give him a chance to finish the sentence.

'There's something else, Chief Inspector. You see, I'm not going empty-handed to the Americans – I have something to barter with. They – as I'm sure you well know – have been having serious problems at Tempelhof. The gang infiltration there is out of control. They're skimming goods out of every shipment that comes in and rerouting what they steal onto the black market and it's the Air Force's reputation that is suffering. It's a bad situation for them. It could lead to a turf war between the gangs who are greedy to get in on the action, which would be equally as bad for the city. But I have an idea which could bring the piracy and its problems under control.'

The balance in the room had shifted on the word *gang*, in the slight pause which Freddy left before he said it. A pause which struck Hanni as oddly theatrical but had worked on Brack as effectively as if Freddy had leaped up and whipped out a gun. The chief inspector jerked forward. His eyes narrowed; his body pulled itself into a square.

'Interfering with what goes on at the airport is not a path I would go down if I were you, Schlüssel. That's not a plan I'd advise.'

Freddy shrugged. It was the smallest movement, but the message it carried was the loudest sound in the room. The balance shifted again and Brack was suddenly holding none of the power.

'Why? What's wrong with it? I'm proposing to offer the Americans protection from the racketeering which has infested their operations. All I want in return is their help to avenge Matz's murder and to catch the man who has kept this city living in fear for months. Where's the fault in that? Surely no one would put gang, or personal, interests before making Berlin a safer place, or bringing a murderer to justice?'

'Dear God, you are a pompous fool.' Brack's bellow and his bluster was back. 'The Americans will never trust you, not again, no matter what you offer them. And if you start interfering in gang matters, you'll make enemies who will destroy you quicker than losing the strangler will.' He laughed suddenly, but it was a mirthless, hate-filled sound. 'Good. If I can finally be rid of you, then good. Go to Walker – you have my blessing. Try to make friends where you haven't any. It's your mess, Inspector; it's your funeral.'

Freddy got to his feet and nodded to Hanni to follow him. When he reached the door, he turned before he ushered her through it.

'There is a mess, Chief Inspector, but it's not mine. I'm not the one looking the other way and lining my pockets. My hands in this business are clean. All the corruption, all the rot, everything that needs to be scourged from the force and replaced by the kind of man Matz Laube was belongs to men like you. It's Matz's funeral we're facing. That's heartbreaking. But if there's any justice in the world, it will be yours too. I'll bury my friend and then I'll bury your career. And that won't be heartbreaking at all.'

Freddy stayed steady until he was out of Brack's office and into a corridor where there was no one except Hanni to see the fight drain out of him. He crumpled. She caught him. They stood entwined, arms round each other, heads pressed close until Freddy's breath calmed and Hanni found enough of her own to speak.

'What was that about? Why do you want to make an even

bigger enemy out of Brack? And what have you got that will persuade Walker to help bring Tony in rather than sweeping the whole disaster away out of sight?'

His lips brushed her hair as he straightened. 'A gambling chip which could be worth nothing. You're right – I don't want to make a bigger enemy of Brack, but what choice do I have? He was never going to get on board with this. And I don't doubt that the Americans will do as you say and try to sweep the whole case away. If they do, Brack will side with them for the sake of their support in the future, in case he runs for promotion or for political office. But the thing is, he's been taking backhanders from the gangs – that's what I was getting at in there. One word of that to the superintendent and he's finished – in the police, in politics, everywhere. And now he knows that I'm onto him, that I can ruin him, he surely won't dare to get in my way. As for Walker...' Freddy rubbed his eyes. 'I don't know if he'll listen or help, but I have to try to win him over somehow.'

It was clear that he was exhausted, that he was losing track of what exactly he was trying to say. Hanni reached up and brushed the hair from his eyes and let her hand cradle his cheek. His head lolled as if he could fall asleep standing there.

'You're not making sense, Freddy. What is the gambling chip? How are you going to win Walker over?'

'Through a debt that I need to repay, a loyalty I maybe shouldn't try to claim again. It's Elias, Hanni. I think he could be the one to fix this. And I need you to come with me to see him. I'm not steady enough after last night to do it alone.'

Elias.

Hanni didn't know what to say. She didn't know that Freddy had found him or where that had led to, and she didn't know whether Elias – never mind the history he and Freddy shared – was someone she was ready to face. She said none of that. Saying that she wouldn't go or voicing any of her confusion wouldn't help Freddy now. She nodded. Her reward was the relief which immediately flooded his face.

'And when this is done, Hanni, we have to—'

'No.'

Now she could find the word she had instinctively wanted to say seconds earlier.

'No.' She shook her head. 'Not talk, Freddy. Don't say talk. All we have to do when this is over is what too many others can't do anymore. We have to live.'

There were doors opening and closing, footsteps coming. She reached up and grazed her lips against his and then she dropped his hands and followed him to the stairwell that led out of the station.

All we have to do is live.

They were brave words. It was what her heart longed for; it was what his eyes told her that he longed for too. If she refused to get stuck in the past and she added *And we can do it because Reiner is gone* to them, they might almost begin to sound real.

The past, however, had very long arms.

Hanni sat in the back of an unmarked police car as it sped them through the grey streets of Mitte trying to hold on once again to the year she was in. The sight of so many Soviet troops formed up in columns or lounging on corners was a shock. She had to fight not to shrink away from the window when the car slowed and they glanced in. Not to slip underneath the memories of breaking glass and the screams of the women being dragged from attics and cellars less fortified than hers. It was hard too not to step back inside the Tiergarten's trees and to feel Tony's breath on her neck as he outlined his plan to kill her and frame a Soviet soldier. To know how easily that plan could have worked. She couldn't stop seeing danger. By the time they arrived at the bar where Freddy said Elias held court, *we have to live* sounded like the naïve kind of nonsense a child would have uttered.

'Everyone will act like they're going to hurt us, but they won't. Or not you anyway – I may have some ground to make up.'

Freddy's deliberately light tone as he led her down a short flight of steps into a room from which daylight had fled was not reassuring. The low rumble which spread around the bar as he steered her towards a table at the back did not sound like a welcome. Neither did the 'You've got some nerve coming back here' more than one of the scarred drinkers muttered and which Freddy hissed at her to ignore.

'I'm not here for trouble, and I'm sorry for how things went between us before.'

Elias did not get up. He did not take the hand Freddy offered him. But he did wave at the ring of glowering men who had immediately appeared behind him to stand back. That settled Hanni's pulse a little.

'Have you brought her to keep the peace?'

Elias swept his eyes over Hanni. He did not return her weak attempt at a smile.

'Will she need to?'

A silence fell between the two men which Hanni sensed was multilayered and which she couldn't read. She watched them weighing each other up, testing how much strength was left in their bond. And then Elias finally held out his hand and said 'sit' and Freddy's face loosened.

There was a flurry of drinks and clean glasses and a more comfortable chair for Hanni than the stool she had been about to sit down on. When all that was done, Elias turned his attention to her. His gaze was too direct to be comfortable.

'You're a photographer, I understand? Freddy says you do excellent work. And were you as stripped of family as we were by the war?'

She knew it was a test and she didn't know how to answer it, beyond a stumbled, 'Yes, but not in the same way.'

'Leave her be, Elias. She's private about her past and we've all been through enough to respect that. And although I'm glad to be doing it, introducing Hanni to you is not why I'm here. I need your help again, but this time I've something to offer you in return.'

Freddy outlined the truth about Tony, which Elias listened to without any comment except for, 'And your boy Oli was his doing?' Freddy answered that with a nod and an apology, which Elias waved to a stop three words in.

'That's why I've come to you again: Miller can't get away with Oli's death or any of the others. We need to catch him, and if he's gone into hiding – which is what I suspect – I'm going to need people out there who can comb through the streets better than any policeman.'

As soon as Freddy explained what he needed, Elias turned to the ring of minders around him. They answered as one when he asked, 'Can you do it?' Then he turned back to Freddy and his question was just as concise.

'And what do I get in return?'

'Control over the security of the supply chain at Tempelhof.'

For the first time since Freddy and Hanni had entered the bar, the hostility that had greeted them cooled.

Hanni listened as the two men traded backwards and forwards. Neither deferred to the other, both laid out their cases in the same stripped-down way. Although it disturbed her to do it, it wasn't difficult to picture them in Buchenwald, swapping the favours that would keep them alive for another day, making every decision and every moment count. Living a life a chasm away from hers. And all the time they talked, Elias kept glancing at her. He didn't say anything, however, until Freddy excused himself to go to the bathroom.

'How private is private?'

Hanni picked up her glass and took a sip of wine which was rougher than she was used to. Whatever she said was a minefield – all she could do was play for time.

'What has Freddy said?'

Elias shrugged. 'That there is someone in your past keeping the two of you apart. That worries me. That he loves you, which –

given how vulnerable he is beneath his capable surface – worries me more. I trade in secrets, Fräulein Winter, but I don't like them and I don't like the people who keep them. Especially when they do it well.'

'What's going on?'

Freddy was back, staring from one to the other. Hanni couldn't look at him, not after what Elias had said about love.

Elias was the first to smile.

'Nothing, although I think I may have told the young lady more about your feelings for her than you might have done.'

Freddy's protests and Elias's mock defence of himself brought the meeting to a close in a far warmer way than it had started. Elias led them to the door himself and then – as Freddy slipped out to make sure that the car was safe and ready – he gripped Hanni's elbow.

'Don't hurt him. You have a heaviness hanging round you that I don't like – that disturbs me. He is family to me and I am family to him – don't get on the wrong side of that.'

He shook his head as Hanni flustered into a denial.

'I don't want your story – that is for him. Whether you tell it is between you and your conscience.'

He leaned in closer as Freddy appeared at the top of the steps and beckoned her up.

'I'm not threatening you. Like I said, I trade in secrets, but I don't trade in threats. I am simply hoping that you will do the right thing by a man who, for good and for ill, I think of as my brother.'

He dropped his hand and let Hanni go blinking back into a daylight which had been made far sharper by the hour she had spent in the dark bar.

'What did he say to you, about us?'

Freddy looked suddenly too young and too hopeful to be asking the question. Hanni didn't have the reserves left to properly answer it.

'It was nothing – teasing. Big brother stuff.'

He liked that – his face glowed. He began running through the agreement he had made with Elias and how he was going to sell that to Walker in return for his co-operation.

'We'll get Miller, Hanni. We'll prove how dangerous he is and we'll unmask him. Tony Miller, or whoever he turns out to be, won't get away with what he's done. Nobody can hide their secrets or their crimes forever.'

Hanni nodded and she agreed, but all she could see was Elias looking at her as if she was the dangerous one, and all she could think was, *So why do I think that I will?*

'You moved your appointment, Inspector.'

Colonel Walker glanced at Hanni's purpling cheek and the patchwork of scratches which appeared as she took off her gloves.

'And is it the same problem with security that is still troubling you?'

Freddy settled himself into his chair. Hanni was aware enough of his patterns in these situations to know that he would take his time and take the lead, and that she would be infuriated by his slowness.

'Not exactly. Security is the issue, yes, although not with the Soviets the way I alluded to on Saturday, despite what you might think happened at the Tiergarten that evening. What I actually wanted to talk to you about was Tempelhof.'

'Tempelhof? What's that got to do with me? Or you? I'm too busy to have my time wasted, Inspector, and I'm not here to act as your liaison with other departments.'

The colonel looked ready to terminate the meeting. Freddy wasn't about to give him the chance.

'I'm not here to waste your time, sir. I'm also aware that the airport is not part of your command. But Tempelhof is everyone's problem, and I think we could help each other if you just hear me out. Berlin has turned into a hock shop in the last twelve months.

Anyone with the right – or perhaps I should say the wrong – connections can make, in the words of one of your own newspapers, a "fast buck" here. And Tempelhof is the centre of the problem – it's acting as a direct supply line into the black market. That is not a good situation for the city. I imagine it's a PR nightmare for the Air Force. And I think I can help sort it out.'

Walker's deepening frown indicated that he was more than aware of the problems spinning out from the airport and not at all pleased to be reminded of them. He did, however, sit back and listen as Freddy outlined the proposal that he had agreed with Elias: that the Air Force should employ Elias's men at Tempelhof and pay them to act as its policemen. And he didn't immediately dismiss it.

'It's an interesting idea, and it's about as conventional as anything else that goes on in this city. And I'm not saying that it wouldn't work, but here's the thing: I'm not the right person to green-light it, and I don't understand why you're the one bringing it to me. I thought you were a murder detective, not the man in charge of curbing illegal trading, which I imagine is as thankless a task as hunting down an invisible strangler. Why do I feel that I'm being... let's not say bought perhaps but softened up?'

Freddy's shrug suggested that he had been caught out and that he wasn't concerned.

'Because you are. Elias Baar is a key figure in Berlin's gang structure and a deal with him will keep the airport under control and the streets quieter than they're threatening to be. And I don't imagine it will do your reputation much harm when you spin the idea and sell it the way I'm sure you can do. But, no, you're right: Tempelhof is not the main reason we're here. And if I am softening you up it's because what I have to say won't be easy to hear and I wanted to prove my value.'

Walker grimaced. 'You mean you want me to believe that, whatever I might have heard to the contrary, you can be trusted.'

It was a dance – one man moving forward, offering a concession, inviting the other one in – and Hanni had no time for its meandering pace. They had been carrying a secret for weeks, a secret that had got Matz killed. Elias was right: nothing good came of hiding the truth – something she, more than anyone, was all too aware of. So before Freddy could start sidling round the houses again, she jumped in.

'Tony Miller is not who you think he is. He tried to kill me on Saturday night, and he shot and killed a police inspector. And this invisible strangler that you mentioned? That's him too. He is a murderer and he is dangerous. He's also on the run and needs stopping before he kills again. Which he will.'

Walker recoiled as if she'd hit him. He tried to speak and didn't appear to be able to find his tongue. Freddy turned to Hanni with a glare which could have stripped paint, but he at least didn't try to undercut what she had said.

'That was perhaps a more abrupt explanation than I had intended to open with, but it's the truth. All the evidence indicates that Miller is the killer who's been terrorising the city. We believe that he has German roots and that he's here in Berlin to avenge his family who were murdered by the Nazis during the war. He also killed Matz Laube – and tried to kill Fräulein Winter – because he knew he was about to be captured by us. And now he has escaped and we need your help to find him and to bring him to justice.'

Freddy had raced through the charges against Tony in case Walker shouted him down. He could have taken far longer: the colonel was staring at him as if he was speaking in Greek.

'That is preposterous. Captain Miller is a hero. He's loved by everyone in Berlin.'

'Which is how he's got away with murdering its citizens for so long.'

Hanni jumped in as quickly as Freddy had done, outlining their 'stranger who isn't a stranger' theory and describing the photograph she had discovered in Tony's apartment, while the colonel shredded his pad.

'I don't believe you. I think that this is a tale fabricated by a bunch of communists to discredit American personnel, or it's the revenge of a spurned woman. Whatever it is, it's a disgrace, and I want you to leave.'

'Call him in.' Freddy's request cut through Walker's rising indignation. 'If Miller is innocent, he'll be in his living quarters able to disprove everything we've said. So call him in and let's give him a chance to have his say.'

Walker would clearly have preferred to throw them both physically out of the room, but he picked up his handset instead and dialled his secretary, instructing her to summon Miller to his office at once.

'You had better be prepared to apologise profusely when the captain arrives or the next call I make will be to end your career.'

Freddy didn't reply. The silence stretched. When the telephone rang a few moments later, all three of them jumped.

The message he received was a short one. Walker's expression was far less commanding when he put the phone down.

'He's not there, is he? And nobody knows where he is?'

The colonel didn't look at Hanni as he answered her, and he didn't seem to be able to meet Freddy's eyes either. 'No, he is not. And, before you ask, neither is he flying or away with an agreed leave of absence. But none of those things mean that he's capable of committing such appalling crimes.'

The shake in his voice turned the last statement into a question.

Freddy leaned forward. 'His belongings are gone too, aren't they, except maybe for his uniform? He came back last night, after he killed my officer, and he collected his things and now he's on the run, exactly as I said he was. And you have a duty to help us find him.'

And then Walker's head came back up and his voice was all steel again.

'No I do not, Inspector. My only duty is to the American Air Force and its reputation, and I will defend that at all costs.

Captain Miller will be found and, if there are charges to answer, he will answer them to us. And now I think we are done.'

His reaction wasn't a surprise – dismissing them without agreeing to help was exactly what both Hanni and Freddy had feared he would do. But Hanni had spent the morning running over the past and she was ready for him.

'No, we're not. You see, what you're suggesting is a cover-up and there have already been enough of those.'

She sensed Freddy turn towards her again, but she kept her eyes firmly on Walker. He had grown very still.

'I meet a lot of journalists in my line of work, Colonel, and there's been an interesting story doing the rounds for a while now. About a school in Wannsee that was there one minute and gone the next. A dreadful kind of place with a frightening agenda whose existence was, or so it seems, also the subject of a cover-up. But you know all about that, don't you?'

'Leave us.'

'What?' Freddy whipped round to face Walker as he realised the order was aimed at him. 'Why? What's going on?'

'Wait outside please, Freddy. This won't take long, but you have to trust me to deal with it.'

He started to protest, but Hanni shook her head.

She didn't look at him as he slammed out. She kept looking at Walker. She had a feeling that if she took her eyes off him, he would vanish as neatly as Tony had done. And she couldn't let him take any control over what was coming. Hanni held the silence until Walker shifted in his seat and opened his mouth to manage her, and then she went on the attack.

'You knew about the Hitler School. You had the names of the men – the one-time Nazi officers – who set it up. You had photographs. And yet no one has been prosecuted or even called to account. How do you think Ernst Reuter would react if he knew about that, or the Soviets?'

She immediately understood why Walker held the rank of colonel and why the blockade's press and PR machine had been put into his hands. He didn't try to deny it or ask how she knew or what her involvement had been. He evaluated the danger and took the quickest way out.

'What do you want?'

Hanni swallowed hard. She had to stay focused: if she grabbed too greedily at his implied offer, she could lose the key part of it.

'Firstly, your agreement to give Inspector Schlüssel whatever men and resources he asks for to assist with the manhunt. Secondly, your word that you will hand Miller over to face German justice if you catch him first.'

'And if I don't agree to both of those things, you will go to the press about the school?'

Hanni nodded. 'Which I will also do if you break our agreement and don't give the victims' families the chance to get the justice they deserve.'

Walker sighed. Hanni doubted that he would stick to his word about the second condition, but the first was good enough for now.

'Fine. Bring Schlüssel back in and I'll see he gets whatever he needs.'

She gave him a moment to let him feel as if he had dealt with her efficiently and then she shook her head.

'Not yet. There's something else I want. I want to know what happened to the Nazis who were involved in setting that place up. Or at least to one of them – the man who calls himself Emil Foss. I want to know where he is.'

Walker had been making a note on his pad. He looked up at her as if he wasn't entirely sure what she had said.

'Why do you want to know about him?'

It was the first time – other than with Natan Stein – that Hanni had ever been asked to describe her connection with her father. It was not the first time she had considered what she would say.

'Because his name is not Emil but Reiner. He is a war criminal, a high-ranking member of the SS, and he did terrible harm to my family.'

It was short and it was as close to the truth as Hanni could make it. It was also all she was prepared to give him, whatever came next.

And then Walker replied and his reaction was not the interrogation into her allegation and her background she had expected.

'And again, Fräulein: why? Why does where this man is now or what he is doing matter? I'm sorry that your family was harmed, but the war is done and war criminals – no matter how evil they were, or are – are not at the top of anyone's list anymore.'

'But they should be!'

Hanni could no longer hold the measured tone she had been clinging to, not in the face of such a callous reply.

'People here have suffered beyond anything you can imagine. The agonies that were inflicted are still felt. The losses do not get any easier. The horror of the way millions of men and women and children were murdered does not fade. None of that has ended with the war; none of that is *done*. So why should the men who created the hatred, whose life's work was the hatred, walk away with no consequences?'

'They shouldn't.'

There was no steel in Walker's voice now. There was nothing callous in his manner. There was nothing but a weary acceptance of the world, which Hanni couldn't bear.

'But they will. The world is desperate to move on, Fräulein Winter, even if you're not. In a month or so, the blockade will be over. After that, West Germany will declare itself a federal republic, a separate country from the East, and Germany will be split in two for good. No one will care about anything then but the future and the new kind of military threat that the future brings with it. The year 1949 will be declared a kind of Year Zero, a resetting, a new starting point. Nobody will be searching for Nazis then.'

'But I have photographs that prove who he was!'

Walker shrugged. 'You have – if I understand the implications of your knowledge on this matter correctly – photographs of empty classrooms, which it would be easier to believe date from the war than from now. And if you have others, I imagine they could be as easily discredited. I'm not saying it's fair – please don't think that. But I am saying it's the way the world will go.'

Hanni couldn't look at him anymore – her soul was in pieces.

'But what if forgetting is impossible? What if some of us have to keep searching? What if we cannot get close to a reset until the old sins have been paid?'

Walker didn't answer. He got up and crossed to a filing cabinet and pulled out a folder.

'Here. If it matters so much, take this.'

He handed her a sheet with two names printed on it which Hanni recognised from the school ledger, alongside addresses of a town in Bavaria and another close to the Black Forest.

'These were two of the ringleaders. They were tipped off and they got away, but British Intelligence located them as far as the places listed here. There are eyes on them there for now, but that's all and it won't be for long. And as for your Emil, or Reiner...' He dug out another piece of paper. 'His connection with the school couldn't be proved, despite the warning that he could be involved, which I assume you sent to my office along with the photographs.'

He shook his head as Hanni started to speak. 'Don't tell me how you got them – it's better that I don't know. The same as I don't need to be told what you're going to do with the information I will deny you were ever given here.'

He handed her the file entry marked Foss and a blank sheet of paper. Hanni scribbled down what she needed, staring at the few words she had recorded about her father as if she was willing them to speak.

'He's in the Harz Mountains.'

Walker nodded. 'Apparently. And there are eyes on him too. But if he keeps a clean slate, that will end soon enough.'

Hanni folded her notes away, her heart pounding so loudly her ears rang with its beat. Reiner really was gone. He was hundreds of kilometres away, surely too far away to reach the web of informers he had boasted about having in Berlin, too far away to be watching.

'You could leave it now, Hanni.'

It was the first time Walker had ever used her first name. It made him sound gentler than the uniform and the rows of medal ribbons suggested he could be.

'He would be a fool to come back, and you would be a fool to go chasing him. Whatever he did, whatever hold he had over you, could end and you could walk away. You have choices, Hanni. You don't have to let the past rule the rest of your life.'

It sounded so simple the way that he said it. And his voice was far kinder than the ones shouting the exact opposite in her head: Natan's; Elias's; her own.

Hanni stayed silent when the colonel called Freddy back and promised the help he had asked for. She told Freddy no more than the barest bones of the school story when he asked her and said no more than she had threatened a scandal if Walker didn't co-operate.

When Freddy called her remarkable as they climbed into the car, she smiled. When he suggested, 'We should go somewhere quiet and raise a glass together for Matz,' she agreed. And when he kissed her on a rain-spattered pavement outside her boarding house, she kissed him back as if she had never had a moment's doubt about what he could be to her.

And she chose to switch off the voices.

CHAPTER 20

10 MAY 1949

Now you see me, now you don't.

Every time Tony spotted a newspaper stand crammed with copies of his photograph, he had to fight an urge to grin. He was everywhere and he was nowhere and – despite everything that he had done to hurt it – he was still the city's darling.

Hero Captain Goes Missing

He hadn't been revealed; the implication was that the Soviets had snatched him. He had not been turned into a monster. His disappearance had instead become part of the city's propaganda war and the search the papers were appealing for help with was a carefully worded thing.

Tony assumed that the cloak of secrecy which had been thrown over his crimes was Colonel Walker's doing and that the headline – which was certainly a far more palatable one than the more honest *Hero Captain Revealed as Killer* would have been – had been ordered with an eye to the Air Force's reputation. It also suggested that, whatever the colonel knew or intended, he wasn't about to start screaming about murderers and manhunts and dancing to Freddy Schlüssel's more vengeful tune.

Tony's image was strewn across Berlin and not only as the man he was now. The photograph of the 'tragically lost family someone must know' which included him as a child was as thick on the racks as the one of his smiling face staring up at the skies. Not that he was worried by that. Whatever conclusions the police had clearly come to, no one had publicly connected the two.

The story around the family shot was also a deliberately fuzzy one: an unnamed relative searching for loved ones lost in the war and desperate for anyone who could come forward with clues. There was no hint of a link to the Berlin Strangler whose activities had fed the papers' love of horror for months and who was now barely mentioned. The photograph was far too small for the tick marks to show. The name Müller wasn't included. Tony was there – and was not.

None of that was a surprise to him. What Tony understood – and his trackers apparently didn't – was how easy it was not to be found if not being found mattered and how easy it was to become invisible in a city, especially when that city was as disjointed as Berlin. Tony had learned the value of anonymity a long time ago in Seattle and he had put that lesson into good use ever since.

If anyone had ever asked him to describe his real self, Tony would have given a very simple answer: whatever else he was, he was clever. And by clever he meant quick to pivot and always prepared and never ever complacent. He took pride in being those things. He wasn't about to be anything else.

Tony had enjoyed an excellent run in Berlin. He was angry that the run had ended before his task had, but that hadn't derailed him. Being caught out was not the same as being caught, and Tony had no intention of being caught. He had planned his disappearance on the basis that he wouldn't be. That need to disappear had, it was true, come rather sooner than he had expected it to, but the timing made no difference to how he had approached it.

Tony had estimated that he could lie low for two months, possibly three, before his carefully saved money ran out and his lack of papers or a regular job aroused suspicions. He had assumed that there would be some kind of search, but he hadn't expected it to find him. Berlin's sectors were strictly defined: no one police force or Allied power could keep track across all of them. It was also the same as every other busy place he had lived in: nobody looked properly at anyone else.

When Tony had been a hero, his admirers had seen his good looks and his uniform and his hands filled with cigarettes and candy. Now that he was nobody, all anyone saw was a beard and a battered coat and a man as down on his luck as a dozen others they ignored every day. His German was impeccable; his accent had been born in the city. The unscrupulous landladies who rented him a tatty room by the night didn't care who or what he was as long as he paid their extortionate rates. Two to three months of a shadowy life was bearable. It was long enough to work out a plan and not long enough to get lost in. In the end, it was also more than double the time that he needed.

The blockade was over; the battle for Berlin's soul was done. The airlift had gone from strength to strength and the less official supply lines feeding the city had flourished. The Soviets had come back to the negotiating table and an agreement had been reached. At midnight on the twelfth of May, the barricades would lift and Berlin would be free. Trains and trucks and boats would flow in and out, their goods and their passengers unchecked, and Tony intended to be happily ensconced on one of those newly available routes. And then…

Then he would leave Germany by the quickest means he could. After that, the world was his to explore. France probably, Britain definitely. New countries, new cities, another reinvention. An easy enough thing to accomplish when so many people whose lives had been displaced were still on the move across Europe and names and birthplaces were fluid things, too often forgotten or gladly remade. When there were so many possibilities waiting. All of that change was still to come, and Tony was ready to embrace it, but before that…

He slipped into a run-down bar where the customers determinedly ignored everything except their drinks and ordered himself a small beer.

Before that, there were the celebrations which had been announced to mark the blockade's ending. A night of packed streets and truck drivers who would be greeted as the city's new heroes. Who would be feted the way the British and American pilots had been, who would be happy to carry grateful passengers with them on their return journeys. And before that…

Before that, there would be another murder.

Hanni or Freddy, one or the other, which amounted to both. Tony hadn't decided which one to take; he wouldn't decide until he saw what opportunities the night provided – whoever he killed, the other's life would be ruined.

He sipped his beer and checked the noose which – now that he was also the prey – he kept permanently in his pocket. Celebrations had always worked well for him: guards came down, crowds swallowed people up; one quickly and quietly done kill would go unnoticed.

Tony assumed that by now Hanni and Freddy had some sense of how he operated, that they would expect him to be there, finishing the job their interfering had stopped him from completing. The nub of failure in that was something else the two of them would pay for.

He waved at the barman, counted out the coins he could afford to be a little more generous with and ordered another beer. Two nights to wait, two lives to end and then a quiet slipping away to freedom. Clever really wasn't a strong enough word.

CHAPTER 21

12 MAY 1949

'His real name is Aaron Müller. He is German by birth, from Berlin, and the police in' – Freddy glanced down at his notes – 'Weatherford, Texas have just discovered his wife's body.'

'Is there anyone close to him he hasn't tried to kill?'

It was a fair question, and the clamour that followed it was far easier to deal with than the shocked silence which had gripped the incident room a few moments earlier when Freddy had revealed the Berlin Strangler's name. He let the anger run – it was, he knew, mostly for Matz – and then he called the men back to order. There was too much to manage to let emotions run out of control, for his own sake as much as his team. He waited while copies of the two reports which contained the latest information he had collated on Tony were distributed, and then he directed them to the shortest one first.

'As you will see detailed in here, it appears that Nancy Miller was last seen alive in March 1947. No one reported her missing or expressed any concerns over her welfare until September of last year when another pilot flying the blockade route began asking questions about her whereabouts. Before that, Miller seems to have told enough people – including her family, who he had moved her away from – enough conflicting stories to confuse the trail. The Captain Zielinski referenced here – whose wife was apparently a friend of Mrs Miller's before she married and was concerned at the lack of contact – kept digging and getting nowhere and, according to his testimony, Tony Miller wasn't one bit happy with that. Based on that – plus our allegations – his superior, Colonel Walker, requested a search of Miller's last known private address in the States. Mrs Miller's body was found in a grave on the property. That in turn has led to a re-examination of a number of unsolved murders in the places where Miller previously lived. It would appear that covers a lot of locations.'

Freddy gave the room a moment or two to digest that information and then he turned to the second, longer, report which included the photograph Hanni had uncovered.

'Despite all your hard work, the search for Miller has not turned up anything of value yet. The family photograph on the other hand – which was circulated across Germany as well as in Berlin – has had some success. I received a phone call from Hamburg yesterday, from a man who identified himself as a distant cousin of the Müllers. This Herr Heitmann confirmed that they were, as we suspected, Jewish and that everyone in the picture – apart from the boy at its centre – is listed as having been murdered during the war in one of the camps.'

He stopped and swallowed before the shake in his voice betrayed him. He needed to remain professional, to not make this personal, but the sudden urge to read out the list of names of the victims and to offer them the respect of a prayer for the dead was overwhelming. Freddy knew that doing either of those things would defeat him, but he couldn't move on.

'Excuse me, Inspector, but did this cousin also confirm that the boy in question is Tony?'

The question was – as Freddy assumed Hanni had intended it to be – a lifeline. It reminded him of who he was now and what was expected of him.

He nodded briefly in her direction and recovered his voice.

'Yes, he did. Luckily, his local library carries *Time* magazine. I asked him to compare the image of the boy with the image on that and, when he called me back, he said the resemblance – to the garden shot and also to photos he had seen of the father, Elkan Müller, as a young man – was unmistakeable.'

'So how did Miller stay alive when the rest of them didn't?'

'Did he escape from a camp?'

'Did the family know what an animal he was?'

The questions began pouring, re-establishing the steady back and forth of a briefing that Freddy could work with. He was promising to answer everything that he could when Brack slipped in through the doors at the back of the room.

'From what Herr Heitmann remembered – and he was quick to say that he didn't know the whole story – Miller was shipped off to an uncle in America in 1937 or '38, after "some trouble", as he put it, with a Nazi patrol. If that trouble was bad enough for Miller's family to secure him a passage out of Germany when those were increasingly difficult for Jews to get, then whatever the incident was, it must have been very serious. I would hazard a guess that it was Miller's first kill, but I couldn't push Heitmann any further on what exactly had happened. As far as he's concerned, he hasn't just rediscovered a missing relative, he's now cousin to a national hero. He'll find out the truth of that soon enough, but it wasn't my job to tell him.'

There was a pause and then an indignant voice sprang up.

'So we know his backstory and we know he's a killer, but what happens now? We've had men on the streets – ours and the Americans – looking for Miller since Easter Sunday and there's not been as much as a sighting. Are we supposed to keep looking or do we assume that he's disappeared for good?'

Freddy kept an eye on Brack – who was leaning against the closed door and had not, yet, made his presence felt – as he answered.

'We want justice for the dead, don't we? That means we keep looking. Miller is still in Berlin – I'd put money on it. Not only is it pretty hard to get out of here, but according to the photograph, there are two family members, a male and a female, who are still, for want of a better word, unavenged.' He glanced over at Hanni. 'Miller killed Matz and perhaps, now that the net is tightening around him, Matz's death will stand for the male relative still unaccounted for. And Miller also tried to kill Hanni but he failed. If we follow his pattern, that should mean that there's one murder, a woman, still to be done. So...'

He looked at Brack for some show of support, but the chief inspector's face remained impassive.

'As you all know, the blockade lifts tonight and the main celebrations will be held at midnight at City Hall. If Miller is true to form, an event on that scale will bring him out into the open. That's when I think he'll kill again, and after that, when the city is no longer locked down, is when I think he will really disappear. Which means we have a very small window to catch him in.'

'And a very dangerous place to be doing it.'

Heads swivelled as Brack stalked to the front of the room and gestured to Freddy to move out of the way.

'Easter Saturday was a disaster. Tonight will not be; tonight runs my way. There will be no guns carried. If anyone says otherwise, ignore them. The area will be crowded; emotions will be running high. The story of the blockade's ending is not going to be about trigger-happy policemen and a riot.'

He paused and fixed his stare on the youngest detective on the front row who immediately cowered.

'That's my first order. The second is as simple: if the inspector is right in his assessment and Miller does appear, you pull him out discreetly. No one shouts. No one makes a scene or lets him make one. No one, under pain of dismissal, uses the word strangler or murderer. I don't want a lynching any more than I want a riot. And one last thing: if the American security forces who will also be in the crowd – and not necessarily in uniform – get to Miller before you do, there is no arguing over who has the most right to hold him. We have an agreement that they will hand him over to us. Whatever anyone else in this room thinks about that, I trust it.'

Brack paused again and this time he turned and looked directly at Freddy. 'This is not about egos or medals or newspaper headlines. This is about keeping our citizens safe. Do you all understand me?'

There was a forest of nodding and a room full of 'yes, sir's. Brack gave the team the benefit of another hard glare and then he swept out, leaving Freddy red-faced and fuming behind him.

'Don't let him get under your skin. He's trying to rattle you into making a mistake. Don't give him the satisfaction.'

Hanni's advice was sensible, but Freddy snorted it away. Brack was already so far under his skin it was smarting.

'I don't trust him, any more than I trust Walker. I think he'll let the Americans extract Miller themselves tonight and that will be the last we see of him. Brack will collude in a cover-up and – as long as the strangler doesn't strike again – nobody but the victims' families will care that there'll never be an answer to who took their loved ones.'

And no one will ever pay for doing it, which is worse.

He didn't need to say that, not to Hanni anyway.

'Then don't let him.'

Freddy had been about to try and do what he had failed to do on Easter Saturday: to pull rank and tell Hanni that she couldn't be at City Hall. To insist that, this time, it was too dangerous to put herself back in Tony's path. And then he took a proper look at her clenched fists and her jutting chin and all he could hear was Matz warning him not to attempt it. He pushed the impulse to keep her safe down, although it was a struggle. There was more determination shining from Hanni's eyes than Freddy had seen in the rest of the team for weeks. He needed that certainty near him. The way her next words made his spirits leap proved it.

'I mean it, Freddy. We can't let Brack, or Walker, run this. I know there'll be hundreds, probably thousands there tonight and that looking for a man in a crowd that size who's determined not to be found – and pinning our hopes on finding him – is madness. I don't care. We were the ones who solved this and now we have to be the ones who end it. Tony Miller is not the American's and he's not Brack's. He's ours.'

He could have kissed her. Brack's belittling and his unsubtle attacks disappeared. Hanni had cut to the heart of the matter, the way that she always did. Miller was theirs and Miller was going to get caught. Freddy had never felt more ready for a fight.

Freddy lost sight of his men within the first five minutes of arriving at Rudolph-Wilde-Platz. The once-grand building in Schöneberg which now served as West Berlin's city hall still bore heavy scars from the war and most of its central bell tower remained ruined. Nobody tonight cared about that. The square flanking it was packed, bodies pressed shoulder to shoulder, hip to hip. Five faces in any direction and the features blurred as their owners erupted in cheers and twisted from side to side, straining to catch the first glimpse of the fruit- and vegetable-laden trucks the afternoon's broadcasts had promised were already making their way to Berlin.

Freddy twisted round with them, although it was his team he was straining to see, not the convoys. He couldn't make anyone familiar out. He had no way of knowing whether his officers had taken up the surveillance positions which had looked like the most logical ones before anyone realised what an impossible scrum they were facing. He had no way of knowing which of the men wearing uniformly dark coats were normal citizens and which were plain-clothes American servicemen. Or which were the Soviet agents who were rumoured to have infiltrated the crowds. And he could only hope that the bangs and the squeals which constantly punctuated the cheers were caused by Berlin's beloved fireworks and weren't a cover for anything more sinister. The night had barely started and it had already exhausted him.

And the celebrations – as Brack had pointed out – were no place for the fight he was suddenly less sure about winning.

'You were right – madness is the word for this. We'll never find him.'

Freddy had to shout to make sure Hanni could hear him. He was determined not to lose sight of her this time. Or contact. He had already checked a dozen times that the hand he was holding grimly on to was hers.

'We will if he wants us to.'

Freddy came to an abrupt stop and was loudly sworn at by the bodies who instantly ploughed into him.

'What do you mean?'

Hanni fought to stand still and stay close to him as the swirl of the crowd threatened to separate their fingers and sweep her away.

'Think about it, Freddy. If Tony is looking to kill someone tonight, doesn't it make sense that the target would be me or you? We've ruined his plans; we've got in his way. He could very easily be stalking the both of us. I couldn't say that earlier or Brack would have ordered us to stay away, but don't you think it makes sense?'

It did. It was exactly why Freddy hadn't wanted Hanni at the celebrations in the first place. Caught now in the middle of such an impossible sea of people, he wished he had gritted his teeth and ordered her not to come.

'Then why are we sticking together and acting like sitting ducks? He's already tried to murder you and I don't want him trying again. I need to find you an escort. You have to go...'

But his words whirled away in another volley of fireworks and in the sharp crack of the rattles half the crowd had apparently brought to count down the hour with. Voices swelled in a roar around him, shouting out the seconds until the blockade ended, a time span which had already shortened from twelve to nine. Bodies surged as if they were melded together. And then Hanni's hand slipped from his and Freddy was left clutching panic-stricken at air.

'Six, five, four…'

The count had turned into a chant worthy of a football terrace. It swallowed his cries for her; it swallowed everything. *Two* and *three* soared. *One* disappeared beneath a roar loud enough to have drowned out a squadron of Tempelhof's planes. Someone grabbed Freddy and twirled him around. Someone else caught hold of his elbows and kissed him. Bottles appeared; the air grew sticky with toasts and spills. Freddy pushed through what was turning into a victory party, shouting Hanni's name until his voice cracked, but she was out of his sight and his reach.

Freddy turned, tried to double back to where he had last held her, tried to force another pathway to open. He caught sight of two of his men, their heads thrown back, cheering and laughing, their duties clearly forgotten. He thought he saw Brack standing on the city hall's steps, stretched his arms up to wave and signal 'get more men in here' and lost his footing the moment he tried.

Another wave of excitement ran through the crowd as someone with too much beer inside him and too much imagination announced that he could hear a truck arriving and Freddy was spun round again.

His throat was raw from shouting. He had lost all sense of time. His arms and shoulders ached from all the hands that had grasped and pummelled them. Hanni was gone. Tony could be ten paces away and Freddy wouldn't have known.

Or, please God, Tony could be somewhere else entirely.

Freddy latched on to the thought to keep away the blind panic at Hanni's disappearance that was threatening to paralyse him. Tony didn't have to be here. He could be at any of the train stations which would be as packed as the Platz, ready to jump on board the first one that pulled out again. Or at one of the newly lifted road barriers. And if he was, if Tony had never come, he was surely as good as gone from Berlin. Out of Freddy's jurisdiction and free from blame but at least far away from Hanni.

Wherever he is, he's not here.

Perhaps it was a false hope born out of wanting nothing so much as Hanni to be safe. Whatever it was, Freddy didn't care. It was as if a light had flashed through the packed crowds and burned away all the certainties he had come with. Tony was too clever for this. Tonight was the first night he could safely escape. Surely he would be too focused on that to bother about settling scores, or so publicly? If completing his task still mattered to him, he could kill anywhere; he could kill anyone as long as it got the job done. Why would he risk being seen at such a huge gathering? Half the men had lost their hats; strangers were throwing their arms around each other. If Tony was here, someone would snatch away whatever disguise he had chosen. Someone would loop him into an embrace and would remember the headlines and his smiling face. Someone would shout out, 'He's here – our missing hero is found.' Tony's reappearance on the night that the blockade he had battled against crumbled would become the stuff of folklore.

No, Tony was too clever to get sucked into that.

'We've got it wrong!'

Freddy swung round, shouting the words again and again in every direction, desperate to make himself heard.

'We need to throw a cordon around the main train stations. We need to make sure that all the trucks leaving the city are searched. Can anyone from the Kreuzberg division hear me? Hanni, are you there?'

And then, from nowhere, she was. He could see her – or he could see the sleeve of a green checked coat raised in the air a dozen paces in front of him and a tumble of hair whose curls could surely be nobody's but hers.

'Hanni!'

The girl – who, bizarrely, seemed to be flying over the crowd's heads – turned and then swooped away again. It was a split-second sighting but that was all Freddy needed for hope to rush through him. He started to call out again. He got halfway through her name, but then there was a sudden pressure from behind him that he couldn't ignore. The press of a body against his that was too close, too still. A second or two slipped by. Freddy waited for a hand to land on his shoulder, for the invitation to 'celebrate and drink with us' that would refuse to take a no in reply. There was nothing but a slowly drawn-out breath that landed damp on his ear.

His brain whispered, 'Duck down, turn round.' His body was too slow to obey.

A shape that was narrow and dark and gone the instant he saw it flashed over his face and snaked round his neck. There was a tightening. A tug that prised him onto his toes, hands flailing at the air. He tried to call out, but his throat had closed. He tried to reach out for a hand or a sleeve, but his balance had shifted and his fingers could do nothing but hopelessly wave. No one could hear him; no one could see. And a split second later, neither could he.

CHAPTER 22

13 MAY 1949

She had almost had him and now he was gone.

The events of the previous night were so vivid, it was hard to accept that she wasn't still living them. The crowds had torn them apart, swallowing Freddy, engulfing her. Hanni remembered spinning, being pulled this way and that, fighting to disentangle herself from the clapping and the cheering and stand her ground. She had no idea how long that had taken: once the roar of the countdown was done, time had turned elastic.

'If we do get split up, make for the steps. You will be safe and visible there.'

Hanni had tried to act on Freddy's advice, but it wasn't easy: the linked arms she had to wriggle through were as tangled a barrier as the hedge bordering the Wannsee school. She had pushed on anyway; she had made herself as small as she could. She had carried on calling Freddy's name, ignoring the idiots who offered to be him. She had carried on looking for Tony. By the time she had caught the edge of a cry which surely contained *Hanni*, her senses were screaming.

Hanni had swivelled towards the voice the second that she heard her name – that moment of stopping and straining her ears to the air was crystal-clear in her memory. She had stretched onto her toes, pushing and shoving to get a better view. It had been an impossible task: there had been nothing to see except broad backs and blurred faces.

'Lift me up.'

The man whose sleeve she had tugged had burst out laughing and obliged.

'Spin me around. I need to see the whole square.'

A circle had opened as he hoisted her into the sky, the watchers pointing and applauding as if she was performing a circus trick. Hanni had ignored them and focused instead on keeping her balance and praying that the hands circling her waist wouldn't lose their tight grip. She had swung through another arc, another dizzying swoop, and suddenly there he was: Freddy, barely a dozen paces away. She had cried out his name ten times louder that time, but it had still whirled unheard away. She had cried it louder again as Freddy had staggered and slipped sideways and there, standing all too solidly behind him, was Tony.

'Put me down!'

Time had stopped after that, but Hanni hadn't. She had been running before her feet touched the ground. She had still been too late. A dozen paces away was still half a dozen too-solid men, half a dozen dancing women. She had pushed and kicked and fought her way through, spitting back at the curses she met with. She had yelled, 'Tony is here, Tony has got Freddy,' until she thought that her lungs would shatter. No one had reacted – or no one except him.

There had been a second, Hanni was certain of it, when Tony's eyes had met hers. When he had stared directly at her. When he had nodded with a cold delight she would see in her dreams for years. And then Tony was gone. By the time Hanni got to Freddy, he was crumpled on the ground, his white face a scar in the dark, and the crowd had filled in the spaces. And now they wanted her, yet again, to relive those terrible moments.

'Are you all right, Fräulein Winter? Do you need a glass of

water? I appreciate that it hasn't been easy to go through all this again.'

Hanni shook her head and glanced over at Freddy who was sitting in a silence she knew wasn't the fault of his bruised throat.

Superintendent Herwig referred back to his notes and continued.

'As I was saying, the Americans – although we were not aware of this at the time – had put a security detail on both you and Inspector Schlüssel because they believed that you were Miller's most likely targets. Which was perhaps something that we should have done too.' He paused and looked at Brack, who didn't reply. 'Well, that's not for now. They, thankfully, were in position behind the inspector when Miller appeared with his noose. Their quick thinking saved his life and also apprehended our fugitive, without any of the disturbance being witnessed. It was, as I am sure we can all agree, an excellent result.'

'What happens now?'

Freddy's voice carried a harsh rasp it hurt Hanni to hear.

'They caught Miller. I'm assuming they extracted him safely from the crowd. That was yesterday, but he's not here at the station. So what comes next: when will they hand him over?'

Herwig closed his folder and assumed the type of smile and careful tone which heralds the wrong news.

'That is what I brought you both in to explain. As well, of course, as expressing my gratitude for your diligent efforts in solving the case and for your lucky escape, Inspector. I am aware of the deal that was struck with the Americans – a deal, I must say, that I should have been appraised of before last night. I understand why you struck it, and I cannot fault your motives. But it is not, I am afraid, going to be a practical one to put into effect. Other considerations – as I am sure you will understand, given the delicate political state of the city – must come first.'

The pause which followed went on too long. Hanni couldn't bear it – she couldn't stop herself filling it.

'No! No, that's not fair. Walker gave us his word.'

She waited for Freddy to jump in and support her. He was staring out of the window and biting his lip, and he wouldn't meet her eye. She had no choice but to storm on.

'I'm sorry, Superintendent, but Colonel Walker promised that Tony would face German justice. He promised that there wouldn't be a cover-up, except a cover-up is exactly what you're suggesting is happening here.'

Herwig's face switched from sympathetic to blank. 'That is not a term you will utter outside this room, Fräulein Winter. As for Colonel Walker, he has returned to America this morning and no longer holds any jurisdiction over this case. And as for Miller – his fate will rest in military hands. There is no "cover-up". What there is, however, is a perfectly proper respect for the chain of command and the needs of future co-operation. We have agreed to drop our request that Miller is handed over to us. The chief inspector signed off on that decision yesterday, and I see no reason to discuss it any further.'

Brack had undercut them, just as Freddy had predicted he would. Herwig's next words – which blocked Hanni's anguished, 'How on earth could you do that?' – confirmed it.

'What you perhaps fail to understand, my dear, is that, while the blockade may have ended, Germany, whether we like it or not, remains an occupied country. The Allied armies will be here as long as the Soviets are here, and we need to work effectively with them. Chief Inspector Brack has done some excellent work to suppress the gangs who have infiltrated Tempelhof and to improve security there. That has gone a long way to cementing our relationship with the Americans. Our discretion over this matter with Miller will go a long way to sweetening it.'

Freddy's hands were balled into fists, the knuckles as white as his face had been when Hanni had thought he was dead. And his voice was no longer rasping.

'And what about the boy, Oli? He had friends; he is missed. Or the families of the ten people killed in their homes? Do you think they will learn to call the murders *this matter*? And what about

Matz Laube's mother? Do you think *this matter* will help her mourn more easily for her son? Do you have a plan for *sweetening* them too?'

Herwig frowned. 'I appreciate that you have a personal stake in this, Inspector, but that is not a helpful attitude. I am also a policeman and I am sorry, believe me, that the families will never know the truth or have a culprit to blame or a trial to find answers at. I hope that, eventually, time will provide the healing we all ask of it and that the rest of the city will also be able to move on from the fear everyone has endured. The strangler is caught; there will be no more killings. It's not perfect, I won't pretend that it is, but it is over.'

Freddy shook his head. Hanni knew it was the word *over* he objected to. The superintendent did not know Freddy well enough to understand that.

'Don't be disheartened. Your work will not go unrecognised and neither will Fräulein Winter's. I am sure that we can find you both a pay rise. And Miller will pay for his crimes. He will be charged with his wife's murder and no doubt with others. He will go to the chair.' Herwig got to his feet. 'I hope you can take some satisfaction in that, but now you must excuse me – this is one of those days with too many demands on my time.'

Brack stood up as Herwig left the room. Hanni and Freddy deliberately didn't.

'He'll let you have that snub; he'll pretend to himself that you're frustrated and you earned it. He won't give you any more rope. The case is closed, so don't go looking for ways to play the hero. And don't get in the way of the deal I've done with the Ringvereine that cuts your friend out.'

Brack smiled the easy smile of a man who was certain he had won as he reached for the door.

'Or do both those things and get sacked and make my life easier.'

Hanni waited until Brack was gone before she erupted.

'You're not going to settle for this, are you? A pay rise and silence?'

Freddy's eyes were flint; his face was set in sharp lines.

'Are you serious? Do you think I'm as easy to pay off as Brack? If he gets his way, that's ten families who will never know the truth. Who will never understand how or why their loved ones came to die. There's no peace in that. Do you honestly think that's what I want for them?'

'No, of course not.'

Hanni took a breath to slow down an anger which was with secrets and with lies but wasn't with Freddy.

'I know what you live with; I know how much answers matter, even if they can't change what happened. So why don't we do what we both want to do? Ignore Brack and tell the families the truth and be damned for it if we have to? I have contacts on the papers and the radio; so do you. We could pull them in, unless—'

She stopped. She could see in Freddy's eyes that there was no unless. He didn't care about the consequences and she wouldn't insult him by saying it.

'A press conference then – tomorrow morning?'

Freddy nodded. 'Tomorrow morning.'

The sigh that followed was thick with frustration and longing.

'Maybe it will do more than help the families find peace. Maybe there will be such an outcry the Americans will be forced to hand Miller over to us and justice will get properly done.'

Hanni managed a smile, although not one that lasted. It was a nice thought. But they both knew that – whatever else happened as a result of their honesty – Tony Miller was already long gone.

CHAPTER 23

14 MAY 1949

The press conference wasn't held at the station but in the hall of a local school where there was a stronger chance of keeping Brack in the dark until it was over.

They had both rehearsed their parts very carefully but, when Hanni stood up to play hers, she wasn't certain that her voice would hold. She was afraid. Not of what she and Freddy were about to do. Not of the possible consequences. It wasn't calling a press conference that had been a disastrous mistake.

'We need to go into the station separately, and you'd better go home first. Your career will never survive the gossip otherwise.'

Freddy had grinned and kissed her as he guided her down the dark stairs and out of his lodging house. He had pretended his advice was a joke. Hanni knew that it wasn't. The male detectives gave little thought to their own crumpled suits, but they would notice quickly enough if she appeared a second day in exactly the same outfit. There would be nudges and winks and unfunny comments about clothing shortages. Or she would be subjected to the sort of over-interested scrutiny that the post-boy had treated her to that morning, when he had met her on the pavement and wondered if it was a late night or an early morning that had saved him a trip to her landlady's front door.

Hanni hadn't bothered to answer him. Her head had been too full of Freddy; her body had been too new with Freddy. The night she had spent in his bed had been unexpected and so long dreamed of, she was barely aware of the world.

'I thought I had lost you, I thought you were going to die.'

The words she had bottled up in the station had bubbled over as soon as they left and had dissolved all the walls she had constructed between them. The sight of Freddy lying on the ground with a thin cord circling his neck had stopped her heart. His cough and his joy as he came back to life and saw her kneeling beside him had restarted it. If he hadn't been forced to go to hospital and then to the station to make a statement, she would have been in his arms that night. So Hanni had no interest in a post-boy's brash comments. And she had no time to check through what he had brought. Not until she had repaired her hair and changed her clothes and stopped grinning like a fool into the mirror. She didn't take any notice of the post until she was almost out of the door. Then an overly bright photograph emblazoned on a postcard had caught her eye and she had forgotten how to walk or to breathe.

'Are you ready? I can do the whole thing if you've changed your mind.'

Hanni took hold of herself and shook her head and followed Freddy to a small platform set out with a table and two chairs. The hall was packed with journalists who were still speculating as to why they were there. Neither of them sat down straight away. They had already agreed that Freddy wouldn't bother with a long explanation in case Brack had got wind of their plans. He began speaking without asking for quiet, knowing that the hall would settle itself soon enough.

'I have a statement that I wish to make. I will not be taking questions after it. Before I begin, Fräulein Winter is going to remind us why we are here today.'

He sat then, leaving Hanni standing alone.

She didn't take the piece of paper she had intended to read from out of her bag. She didn't trust her hands not to tremble, and the next moments could not be about her. Besides, she had memorised every word she planned to say. She looked out over the frowning faces and she began.

'Edda Sauerbrunn. Fifty. Wife to Hannes, mother to Vincent, Kay and Caspar. A hard worker, a good woman. Falco Hauke. Fifty-four. Husband to Silke, father to Petra and Cathrin. A hard worker, a good man. Matilda Scheibel, known as Matty…'

Three names in and the room was in silence. Five names in and every head was bowed.

Hanni's voice grew stronger, louder. By the time she finished the list, the hall was heavy with grief.

Freddy waited until she took her seat and then he got to his feet.

'Every one of those people was loved. Every one of them was murdered. It is our duty today to remember and honour them, and it is my job to tell you the name of the man who the city has christened The Berlin Strangler. The man who ended their lives.'

Every head snapped back up.

'The killer of all ten, plus Assistant Inspector Matz Laube and a young boy named Oli who some of you might know, and perhaps more that we suspect but have not been able to prove, was Tony Miller, a captain in the American Air Force. If that name is familiar, it is because he is the pilot known across the city as the hero of the Berlin blockade.'

The words hung in the air, suspended like the planes Tony had once piloted. And then they landed and the room exploded. Freddy let the roar run for a moment or two and then he held up his hand.

'This was a difficult case to solve, but we' – he nodded to Hanni – 'solved it. It has also proved to be an impossible case to prosecute because politics has got in the way. Captain Miller has been removed from Berlin and has been returned to America. He will face trial there for a number of murders. He will likely be executed. But he will not answer for the crimes he has committed here or face the families in our city who he has wronged, and I am sorrier than I can say about that.'

They had agreed that those words would be their last ones. Freddy waited for Hanni to get up and then they walked off the platform together as the questions of how and why surged in a tidal wave of fury around them. The only answer they would give was, 'Ask Inspector Brack.'

The bar was one of the newer ones which had opened in Kreuzberg since the Americans had arrived. Its bright walls and equally bright music was very different to the dark traditional kind, and very few of the local police frequented it, which was, Hanni assumed, the reason Freddy had chosen it. Whatever his mood after his summons to the station, she doubted his reaction would need a public gaze. And she most certainly did not need witnesses, not if she did what she had come to do and ended up breaking his heart.

In the end, he was far more buoyant than Hanni had expected him to be.

'I got a dressing-down I never want repeated, plus a demotion to assistant inspector and I'm off the murder squad for a year or until I've re-earned everyone's trust. Brack will be on my case forever, and I doubt I'll be let near an American again, but it could have been a lot worse. I could have been out of the force for good and I really didn't want that – whatever, to quote the superintendent, the "complete disregard for orders which should have destroyed my career" suggested. I think the lifeline was down to some of the families – by the time I got in front of him, they had lobbied my case.'

Hanni tried to find him a smile, but her mouth wouldn't move.

Freddy realised she hadn't said anything and frowned.

'They won't drop you, if that's what you're worrying about. I told Herwig it was all my doing and that I persuaded you to speak up at the conference.'

Hanni stiffened. She didn't care what he had said to Herwig, but she needed an excuse for a fight.

'I didn't ask you to do that. I don't even know if I want to carry on working with the police. Maybe I'll launch my own studio the way that I've always wanted to, or join another one, or stage an exhibition. Whatever I decide, I certainly don't need saving.'

Freddy's face fell. 'I know that. I wasn't trying to do that. It was my clumsy way of saying thank you for your support. I couldn't have got through today without you, and I didn't see why you had to suffer just because I needed to give the families an ending.'

Hanni put down the wine she had been drinking too quickly. If she had been a different kind of girl, she would have cried. An *ending*. He had had so many of those and now she was about to inflict another one. *We're done. There can't be a second time. It was a mistake. I don't love you like I said I did.* All of it had to be said. All of it was lies. Some of it at least had to be made to sound true, for his sake if not hers.

Hanni shivered as all the things she shouldn't have done swarmed into the room. Hidden the truth of her past. Switched off the voices telling her that she could have no future with Freddy. Lied to herself, lied to him. Fallen in love and acted on it.

The last mistake was the worst. She should have stayed living as she had done for the last three years, accepting all that she felt for Freddy but never acknowledging it. Except now she had and the words and the feelings were out in the world where they shouldn't be. In the middle of the night – when there was nothing but darkness and stillness and them – she had let Freddy say, 'I love you,' and she had let herself say it back. It had been a moment outside time, a moment of pure beauty. It had shattered in the second it had taken to turn over a postcard.

Far away and always near.

One line. No signature. Her name and address but no greeting. Five words on one side and on the other a photograph of the Harz Mountains sparkling with sunshine and snow. One line and Hanni was made into Hannelore again. I love you, not enough. I love you, the pathway to danger. And now she had to be brave. She hadn't made good her past. She hadn't destroyed her father. She couldn't destroy Freddy by living the lie that came with being only his Hanni.

She straightened her shoulders and looked into his eyes. 'Freddy, I'm sorry but there's—'

'No, Hanni. Don't. No sorry, no words, or not the ones that I think might be coming.'

He was too quick for her; his fear was too much for her. When he seized hold of her hands and wrapped them in his, she couldn't, this time, push him away.

'Whoever he was, whatever he did, let it go.'

It was an echo of Walker's advice. Hanni couldn't let herself hear it, not when she wanted to hear it so much.

'You don't understand. I'm not what you think I am. I'm a coward, Freddy, and you don't deserve that. I have to be honest with you...'

'No, no, you don't. And if you do, I won't listen.'

His grip on her fingers was tight enough to break through to the bones. And all she could think was, *Don't let go.*

'I love you, Hanni.'

She had never seen his face so naked or his eyes so on fire.

'And I know you love me. Whatever's been holding you back, does it matter anymore? After what we were to each other last night, isn't that us now? For good? Isn't that what you want?'

It was what she wanted more than she could say.

She wanted Walker's promise that the past could be forgotten to be true. She wanted Reiner's postcard to be the last shot that he ever fired at her. She wanted to always be Hanni and to never again be Hannelore; to be a girl as reborn as Germany would soon be. What she wanted was impossible and Hanni didn't want to hear impossible anymore. What she wanted was to say, 'Yes, this is me and you now, for always, for good,' with her whole heart.

So she gave herself up to hope and she did.

A LETTER FROM CATHERINE

Dear reader,

I want to say a huge thank you for choosing to read *The Pilot's Girl*. If you did enjoy it, and want to keep up to date with all my latest releases, just sign up at the following link. Your email address will never be shared and you can unsubscribe at any time.

www.bookouture.com/catherine-hokin

Dates are so important to history – they are often the first thing we learn; they are the way we organise our view of the past. What has struck me more and more as I have studied and written about the events of World War Two is how misleading the end date of 1945 actually is. When I was younger, I naively imagined 1945 as a chessboard with all the pieces returned to their starting points and the map of Europe once again looking as it did in 1939. That is, of course, very far from the truth. The shadows of the conflict stretched on, in some cases for decades. Not just in terms of the personal cost – the lives lost and broken – but also in the chaos caused by displaced people, destroyed cities and political leaders who were still pursuing aggression rather than peace.

That is very much the background to this second book about Hanni and Freddy. Berlin was barely recovering when the 1948 Soviet blockade began, and to be plunged back into shortages and the fear of another war looming must have been a frightening experience. It will also be the backdrop to the third part of their story which will turn their world upside down again. As they are both learning, no matter how hard you try, you can't always run fast enough to shake off the past…

I hope you loved *The Pilot's Girl*, and if you did I would be very grateful if you could write a review. I'd love to hear what you think, and it makes such a difference helping new readers to discover one of my books for the first time.

I love hearing from my readers – you can get in touch on my Facebook page, through Twitter, Goodreads or my website.

Thanks,

Catherine Hokin

www.catherinehokin.com
goodreads.com/author/show/14552554.Catherine_Hokin

facebook.com/Cathokin
twitter.com/cathokin

ACKNOWLEDGEMENTS

My key characters may not be real people, but the times I have immersed them in were. Because of that, this novel, along with all the others I have written, owes a lot to all the non-fiction and academic historical writers whose work I have drawn on, as well as the often heartbreaking diaries and memoirs I have read.

I cannot list every source I've used, and many overlap with my previous novels, but there are some which I would like to specifically cite here. For post-war life in Berlin in the 1940s: *Living With Defeat* by Philippe Burrin; *Black Market, Cold War* by Paul Steege; *Policing the Cold War* by Philip Jenkins. For specifics of the blockade: *The Blockade Breakers* by Helena P. Schrader and *Daring Young Men* by Richard Reeves. For serial killers: *Whoever Fights Monsters* by Robert Ressler. For gangs: *The German Underworld and the Ringvereine* by A. Hartmann and Klaus von Lampe, and *The Criminal Underworld in Weimar and Nazi Berlin* by Christian Goeschel. For education: *The Nazi Conscience* by Claudia Koonz and *Education in Nazi Germany* by Ian R. James. For Theresienstadt: *Hitler's Gift to the Jews* by Norbert Troller. All are well worth a read by anyone interested in the history behind the book.

I owe thanks to so many people and I hope they know how much they are valued – this isn't a copy and paste from one book to the next even if many of the names are familiar! To my editor Tina Betts for her ongoing support. To Emily Vega Gowers, my insightful and delightful editor, who has, in this book as she always does, made my words far better than they were when they started. To the Bookouture marketing team, especially Sarah: you are wizards. To my son and daughter, Daniel and Claire, who are unfailing in their love and support, and to everyone in the writing community who continues to cheer on every success. It hasn't always been easy to meet in person lately but the get-togethers have been much-needed ones. And last, but never least, to my husband Robert who has now given up pretending that he can remember all the plots and who I could not write a word without. Much love to you all.

Printed in Great Britain
by Amazon